RUDY WIEBE's novels, stories and essays
include *Peace Shall Destroy Many,*
The Blue Mountains of China,
The Scorched-Wood People, Playing Dead:
A Contemplation Concerning the Arctic,
and *The Temptations of Big Bear*
("There are books that change the
shape of a literature. Think of
The Stone Angel, The Temptations of Big Bear,
Lives of Girls and Women, [and]
The English Patient."—*Books in Canada*).
A new selection of Rudy Wiebe's short stories
will be available in Vintage in 1995.
He lives in Edmonton.

A
DISCOVERY
OF
STRANGERS

A
DISCOVERY
OF
STRANGERS

a novel by Rudy Wiebe

QUALITY PAPERBACK BOOK CLUB
New York

QUALITY PAPERBACK BOOK CLUB, NEW YORK, 1995

Canadian Cataloguing in Publication Data

Wiebe, Rudy, 1934 –
    A discovery of strangers

ISBN 0-394-28119-5

1. Indians of North America - First contact with Europeans - Fiction.
2. Franklin, John, Sir, 1786 – 1847 - Fiction.
3. Arctic regions - Discovery and exploration - British - Fiction.
4. Northwest Passage - Fiction.
I. Title.

PS8545.I38D57 1995   C813'.54   C94-932384-5
PR9199.3.W54D57 1995

Detail from a painting by Toni Onley, Untitled, 1958
From the collection of Jessica and Percy Waxer
Cover and text design: Sharon Foster Design

Printed and bound in Canada

Strangely I heard a stranger say,
I am with you.

— RAINER MARIA RILKE

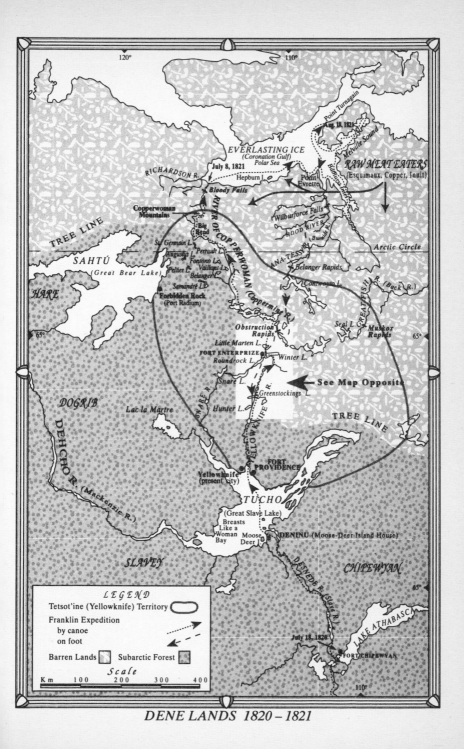

120°   110°

Point Turnagain
Aug. 18, 1821

Melville Sound

EVERLASTING ICE
(Coronation Gulf)
Polar Sea

RICHARDSON R.   July 8, 1821

Hepburn I.

Bloody Falls   Point
Everett

RAW MEAT EATERS
(Esquimaux, Copper, Inuit)

Copperwoman
Mountains

Big
Bend   Wilberforce Falls

HOOD RIVER   Arctic Circle

TREE LINE   St. Germain L.   Perrault L.   ANA-TESSY

SAHTÚ   Augustus L.   Fontano L.   Belanger Rapids

(Great Bear Lake)   Peltier L.   Vaillant L.   R. (Back R.)

Belanger L.   Contwoyto L.

HARE   Samandré L.

Forbidden Rock   Seal L.   Muskox
(Port Radium)   Rapids

65°   Obstruction   65°
Rapids

Little Marten L.

FORT ENTERPRIZE   Winter L.
Roundrock L.

See Map Opposite

Snare L.

Greenstockings L.

DOGRIB   Lac la Martre   Hunter L.

TREE LINE

DEHCHO R. (Mackenzie R.)   Yellowknife
(present city)   FORT
PROVIDENCE

TÚCHO
(Great Slave Lake)
Breasts
Like a   Moose
Woman   Deer I.   DENINU (Moose-Deer Island House)
Bay

SLAVEY   CHIPEWYAN

65°

DESNEDE R. (Slave R.)

LAKE ATHABASCA

LEGEND
Tetsot'ine (Yellowknife) Territory
Franklin Expedition
by canoe
on foot   July 18, 1820
Barren Lands   Subarctic Forest   FORT CHIPEWYAN

Scale
Km   100   200   300   400   110°

DENE LANDS 1820–1821

Prefatory Note

*The dated selections between chapters are quoted
(some with minor rearrangements) from the journals kept by
Robert Hood (1797–1821) and John Richardson (1787–1865)
during the first Franklin overland expedition (1819–1822)
to the Arctic coast of what is today Canada.*

A DISCOVERY OF STRANGERS

I

THE ANIMALS IN THIS COUNTRY

The land is so long, and the people travelling in it so few, the curious animals barely notice them from one lifetime to the next. The human beings whose name is Tetsot'ine live here with great care, their feet travelling year after year those paths where the animals can easily avoid them if they want to, or follow, or circle back ahead to watch them with little danger. Therefore, when the first one or two Whites appeared in this country, an animal would have had to search for four lifetimes to find them being paddled about, or walking, or bent and staggering, somewhere on the inexorable land.

About that time some of the animals did begin to hear strange noises, bits of shriek and hammer above the wavering roar of rapids or the steady flagellation of wind. These were strangers, so different, so blatantly loud the caribou themselves could not help hearing them long before they needed to be smelled, and some animals drifted around to see what made the trees in one place scream and smash that way, the rocks clang. They noticed creatures that looked like humans standing motionless here and there, abruptly pointing and shrieking, pounding! pounding! scuttling about all day and sometimes at night as well, when tendrils of bush along the river might spring up suddenly into terrifying flame. And the animals understood then that such brutal hiss and clangour must bring on a winter even colder than usual.

And shortly after, when wind hammered the snow hard as folded rock under the thickest trees, and growing ice choked the rapids into silence, they knew that of course they had been right. Then an erratic cracking open, or a tree splitting, could be heard so far it seemed they were alert to every sound happening anywhere in the world, and the racket these strange human beings made in one place mattered nothing at all. The animals simply moved away into their necessary silence, travelling where they pleased, as they always had inside that clenched fist of the long darkness, their powerful feathered, furred bodies as light as flecks of ice sifting over snow, as light and quick as breathing.

But throughout the dark weight of midwinter, with moss and lichens always harder to smell and paw from under the crusted snow, all the caribou knew that the sun would certainly return again. And eventually it did; its rim grew slowly day by day up out of darkness into red brilliance, until finally the cows and calves recognized themselves together as they always were, in the whole giant ball of it shimmering through ice fog, round and complete again on the distant edge of the sky. The cows lay in their hollows of snow on a drifted lake, their calves from the previous spring sheltered against their backs out of the wind.

Their blunt, furry noses lifted from the angles of their folded legs, their nostrils opened to the burning air: it was sharp as ice, gentle with all the smells they recognized, arctic and safe. Lying safe, alert in this instant of rest, they were reassured that when that blazing sun stands three times its height over the glazed levels of this lake, they will feel the restlessness of their young grow heavier within them. And then they will move again into their continual travel.

Gradually at first, then more steadily, like driftwood discovering a momentary current, hesitating into daily eddies of moss or crusted erratics but leaning more certainly down into motion along this contorted river, or this lakeshore; easily avoiding the noisy, devastated esker between Roundrock and Winter lakes and their connecting tributary streams. Seeking steadily north. From every direction more and more of them will drift together, thousands and tens of thousands drawn together by the lengthening light into the worn paths of their necessary journey, an immense dark river of life flowing north to the ocean, to the calving grounds where they know themselves to have been born.

The caribou cow with three tines on each of her antlers lay curled, bedded and at momentary rest with her calf in the lee of her body. She had once been a woman; in fact, she has already been born a woman twice. But she has never liked that very much, and each time she is born that way she lives human only until her dreams are strong enough to call her innumerable caribou family, and they come for her. One morning people will awaken, and their child is gone. They search everywhere to find her, and finally notice the two pointed tracks that come to their lodge in the hard travelling snow, and the three tracks that leave. Then the Tetsot'ine — Those Who Know Something a Little — understand what has happened.

"We have lost another good child to the caribou," they begin to wail. "She will never play and make a fire with us, or dance, or sew clothes and bear strong children, or comfort us when we are hungry and sick. No-o-o-o, oh no, no. We will never see that good child again."

And they will, of course, be right. If the three-tined cow with her calf alive beside her had had a name, it would have been ʾElyáske. All the animals knew this, but they didn't think about that.

The silver wolf who lived with the caribou had never been anything but a wolf, and he would have defied any animal, and that included the seven members of his pack, to know his name. However, sometimes when the strands of their twilight howl strayed alone and united again over the long evening hills, or his voice deepened into that longer warning other males could only hear and avoid, the silver wolf remembered himself as Naʾácho roaming alone, a presence of untouchable enigma between the eskers and the ocean, an apparition so gigantic that people are like mosquitoes to him, trifles to swat and eat whatever tasty parts he deigns to tear out of them. But Naʾácho lives best in memory; he cannot see very well, nor hear, and he hunts alone mostly by smell, so the silver wolf liked being what he is now better, though he was only a little longer than a human sleeping, or possibly collapsed in the snow. He liked the skill and nerve of having to be precisely careful. He could run so swiftly that the opening moss was far too slow to swallow him, he could see an eyelid flicker and hear a caribou calf's heart beat steady and unaware in the shelter of its mother, the folds of rocks now hid him silent as breath. And he could still smell anything he sniffed after, drawing winter air like bloody slivers into his deliberating nose. Above all, he liked the female wolf who hunted beside him.

It was that female, white as a numinous drift, who turned left to lie in wait when the silver male led their hunting pack out of the brush above the falls and onto Lastfire Lake. She had played with him below the falls all afternoon, stretching languidly near him, urinating to give him something to sniff and claw over with snow, stiff-legged, and bumping into him and dancing away and bumping until they licked each other's laughing faces, rolling over and under each other, their teeth gleaming like icicles. All afternoon the other six wolves lay easily about on the snow and watched them play, especially the heavy brown male who occasionally seemed to be a little too close, and the silver wolf would whirl on him, forcing him to creep back, crouch and fawn, even to roll over on his back with paws helpless in the air, pleading open-mouthed, throat vulnerable, like any puppy. When the white wolf finally permitted the silver male to mount her, the brown wolf sank down with his long, sharp head along his paws, watching them intensely.

And for a time the two alpha wolves were joined together, were one great doubled animal whose every hair bristled red in the level blazing light; whose twin heads pointed in opposite directions, aimed still and alert towards whatever might materialize or threaten them from anywhere within the completed circle of the world.

In the sinking light the caribou cow uncovered their afternoon food along a tilted esker, between erratics and the last dwarves of the treeline. Her yearling calf crowded down into the craters she dug, so tightly against her that sometimes he tore away from her teeth and lips the crusted lichen she unerringly smelled under the snow. As he had done all winter, his body filling out powerfully into the length of his legs, into his muscled endurance. He was a thick, solid warmth now, holding tight against her, and sometimes he thrust his head up between her hind legs, nosing for the comfort of her teats, but she bumped him away. The sunlight against the hillside was threaded occasionally with a whiff of warmth, and as the light burned lower behind the southern hills they slipped into the communal drift of cows and calves all about them, down the deep trails in snow onto the ice of Lastfire Lake. They felt the thick ice boom and crack, splitting in black branches away before them as the air grew colder. The undulating limit of horizon all around them, the hump and hollow of island and hill and lake and the long eskers, and the southern sky burning from crimson to thick red down into the slow, sheltering twilight.

They heard the wolves then begin to call and answer in their evening howl — there where the water slipped from under the ice, and smashed down into the steaming falls that thickened the willows and birch and spruce and shattered rocks and stones with perpetual ice. The wolves were always with them, around them everywhere like air, wherever they folded their legs and eased themselves into an instant of rest; that wolfsong had haunted them since they'd slept curled in their mothers' bellies, and when they jolted into air, and awoke, it lay weeping over them and remained still their eternal ruminating lullaby.

The cow had bedded at the edge of the herd which spread through its labyrinthine tracks upon the lake. Her square and triangular teeth ground the swallowed lichen rhythmically into cud as she waited. The day was closing, but it was not complete, not yet. She had only to wait while those interlacing howls sang, shivered through her and faded against the dying light, and rose again. She understood their every shift and whisper, the high yowls of the younger wolves, the deeper call of those huge mouths lifted open somewhere below the horizon, closing and opening upwards into a sky of blazing teeth. She lay replete, her mouth and stomach gurgling, while the heat of her blood beat as one with the unborn calf she carried soft and safely hidden, beat to the edges of her body, to the tips of her hoofs, in the cold that cradled her. She watched the bright bowl of sky tighten over her, the lethal edge of its darkness seeping upwards. Her thick tongue, powerful and sweet, licked into one opened nostril and then the other. There was still only the smell of themselves, strong as a vision of the immense renewed herd they will soon be, spread like grey moss over tundra in the constant light of coming summer. She waited.

And saw movement flicker where the edge of mist slid into the rumble of water. Instantly she stopped chewing, lunged to her feet, staring hard to be certain, for the air in her flared nostrils remained clean and without warning. Her yearling and the others lying nearby scrambled up at her motion, and so they all together recognized the silent wolves at the same moment: seven of them fanning out, coming on, the huge silver male they knew so well at the centre, very nearly invisible between the grey hills and the lake just before the rising of the moon.

The cows now standing with their yearling calves watched, heads poised and alert, all knowing the exact distance they would need. A few urinated nervously, some cocked one hind leg to the side, the position of alarm, and a ripple of others

rising swiftly flowed around the curve in which they lay bedded. Breath snored here and there, the cold, rigid air, still
treacherously clean, so confident in all their powerful chests.
But the seven wolves were coming on faster now, the widening
fan of them loping over the hard drifts, and then in one sudden
simultaneous motion, they charged.

Instantly the caribou along the edge nearest the charge exploded into flying snow. And their flight spread like a quick
river bursting thick and strong into the herd, and there was
really no more danger than the continual community of apprehension that was their entire life; they knew they could outrun
any wolf, the tight, hot closeness of their boned bodies beginning to stretch every intricacy of muscle into familiar speed, all
their perfect hoofs reaching, gripping and hurling their bodies
away over snow or swept ice, barely touching in their immense
communal vision of safety for ever awaiting them over the
deepest waters of lakes, always there at the spooned tips of their
united, infallible hoofs.

In that burst of dark animals like land flooding over the
frozen lake, the silver wolf ran closest to the three-tined cow.
Her calf was well ahead of her, running as strongly as she, and
they were running as they had so often run all their lives, it was
their only and continuing life and there was no particular danger for one or for the other. Until, from the sidelong treachery
of a drift, the white wolf lying there in wait, charged them.

For that moment of angle she was faster than any caribou,
even as they all whirled aside as if the lake had opened beneath
them and ripped wide their flowing forest of bodies, and still it
would seem they remained that one essential lunge beyond
danger. The calf turned a trifle slowly, turned a hesitation too

wide, and in that beat of burst apprehension the cow's concentration staggered and the silver wolf was directly behind her, her powerful hind leg stretched far back in the power-thrust of her bend towards the open lake, and he lunged for that tendon and the granite edge of her great shovel-hoof flashed up against his counter-rhythm, touched him, just barely touched him like the flicker of lightning from a storm already past, and he missed the one grip he needed all his life, the one grip he had never missed before, and his lower jaw cracked.

The small rift between calf and herd was all that mattered to the white wolf. She shifted her charge slightly, straight across the curve of the calf strained now beyond breathing for the fleeing herd, and on that line for one instant only she ran alongside him, stride upon stride, her jaws companionably gaping wide with his, and in that last second of speed they snapped into his nose, a flurry of wolf and caribou skidding, smashing over in the snow. Desperately the calf lunged to his feet, his nose-blood bursting over the wolf as he heaved her here, there, body spastic with terror, heaved her, heaved! but her teeth were clamped immovably, and then the brown male arrived and leaped up. With one gigantic bite to the base of the skull, he crushed the calf's neck.

Swiftly the other wolves arrived and circled the kill, their tongues lolling between the daggers of their teeth, panting clouds into air dripping silver under the livid moon. The caribou ran on, then gradually they slowed to a walk, and finally panted into great scraggly islands on the deepest northern reach of the lake. They were very tired now. It seemed the length and depth of the lake they had run was multiplied into their exhausted fear, here where moonlight was beginning to lift the great hump of Dogrib Rock up over the last edge of trees, the solitary erratics waiting along the skyline like relentless totems to guide them in their travel north into the open tundra, fifty or sixty or seventy running days north, into the constant light of their calving grounds, travelling, travelling....

The white wolf tore the calf's throat open, and with her eyes washed by spraying blood dug in, through, to the sweet tongue. The silver male charged up, growling, and as always the others fell back before him; he sprang to the calf's belly and the six wolves, circling, waited for him to rip it open and devour the liver as was his right. But he merely growled again, deeper. And then, when they looked at him in mild surprise, they noticed a split of red seeping along his long jaw. Though he had not yet touched the bloody head, his mouth was already full of blood.

The three-tined cow did not search for the calf for which she had once, necessarily, submitted to a conjunction with a momentary bull, and then borne and birthed and nurtured and guarded perpetually for ten months; which had lain so long in the lee of her body and so often run with her in the desperate, totally terrified strength of the hunted. For those ten months it had reached into the deepest call of her every bone, blood, muscle; now she knew that if it was not beside her soon, it never would be again.

She eased herself down, front and back, into her hollow of welcome snow. With each moment she knew her name, if she had one, was becoming Dámbé ?Elchánile; but when her travel in her present direction ended it might very well be ?Elyáske again. At least for a time. And if she and her newborn calf, then, survive the coming intermittent blizzards, and mosquitoes, and hordes of botflies, and swift river crossings, and wide summer lakes and storms, and the invidious treachery of a stone splitting a running hoof — as she has for this moment survived the wolves again — she knows one of them may once again be reborn a child, and in that less fleeting incarnation gradually grow once more into this dream of being what she is now, resting, sleeping the profound safety, as deep as it is fleeting, of all continually hunted animals. Alive on the sheltering ice.

The silver wolf may live into and perhaps even through the perpetual light of summer; and when tundra light again shortens towards winter darkness he may well discover the helpless trail of the few Whites he has ignored until now. It may be he will follow them, and find them where they collapse one after the other, and gradually creep close; may gouge and gnaw and tear from each whatever he can before their corpses harden into impossiblity for the rotting lower half of his jaw, which the brown male did not rip away when he supplanted him.

A tattered rack of once-great bones, the silver wolf will recognize his death in that straggle of frozen meat briefly marking the tundra, emaciated meat of no interest to his powerful offspring. For they will be travelling somewhere with caribou, nowhere near him then, and he will not be thinking of them. Nor will the other animals who follow and feed quite fearlessly about him: the white and silver and red arctic foxes, or migrating gulls, or mice, or golden eagles, or lemmings or ground squirrels, or even the grizzly and vicious wolverine whom he must avoid by crawling away as he can. Or the great ravens, flying the stark black message of their perfect bodies over the unrelenting land.

MIDSHIPMAN ROBERT HOOD

Tuesday July 18th 1820   Fort Chipewyan

Despite the discouraging situation, though not hopeless, we were determined on pushing forwards. Till today we were fully occupied in assembling provisions. The gentlemen of the trading posts contributed what was in their power to assist us, and our voyageurs, if not contented, were silent, for they saw that solicitation could not add to our store; an uncommon exertion of thought for Canadians.

Mr. Franklin proposed that the Expedition proceed northward to Fort Providence and the Yellowknife Indians with all speed and that, besides the four English officers, it consist of three canoes and twenty Canadians, including two half-breed interpreters. Three of our four English sailors were deterred from coming with us by the dread of famine and fatigue which they said we were doomed to encounter. Only John Hepburn remained with us as servant, consigned alone to the society of foreigners, whose language he could not speak; his constancy absolved his country from the disgrace attached to it by the others.

2

INTO A
NORTHERN BLINDNESS
OF NAMES

The lake they named after her, later, was no more than an in-finitesimal detail in their grand attempt to rename the entire country. It is, however, questionable whether the English naval officers ever actually saw Greenstockings Lake. In their first coming, going north, they were portaged around it by the Canadian voyageurs who had already carried them all those months of labour from Hudson Bay, and when those who were still alive appeared again out of the north fifteen months later, they were quite incapable of seeing anything at all. Except perhaps their own frozen feet blundering along the track the Tetsot'ine hunters tramped down in front of them.

"I laughed to myself when I first saw their boss, Thick English," Greenstockings' father, Keskarrah, said much later, his relentless memory circling once more around that first and then that second moment of unforgettable English arrivals. "When he explained to us that it was for our benefit they had come to find what was in our land, I should have laughed again. Louder."

It may be that when the naval officers returned at last from their "discovery excursion" to the northern ice, trying so desperately to leave a second time, they did notice the snowshoes they had been given, which had been tied onto their feet to hold them safely upon the driven snow. Certainly they must sometimes have been aware of the muscled Yellowknife (as they named the Tetsot'ine) arms that supported them, kept them from collapsing on the wind-ridged surface of the (to them) nameless lake.

Green stockings...Greenstockings. And the deeply bitter irony of Robert Hood no longer being there. Who knew her best. No longer dragging his bent body like a question mark across ice and tundra after them.

By that time there were, of course, no voyageurs left to carry the English anywhere. But a lake under their feet would have been at least a more or less level bit of that unending snow that lay between them and Yellowknife food in a land their numbers on squared paper had not yet discovered to be twenty-six times the size of England, though they were beginning to suspect such a horror. The Ghost River, as white with ice in winter as with rapids in summer, was frozen more or less solid, but it led the wrong way, west. Nevertheless, the Yellowknife River they had first travelled and named lay somewhere south, and they knew it must offer a track past the Indians, back to the small but certain White safety of Fort Providence; though they also knew they must heave their bodies — what was left of them — somehow — around or over the river's devastating rapids. They had once, o so long, an eternity of fifteen months ago, seen each eddy and rock vista from the picturesque, foaming immediacy of a Canadian canoe, but now, to their emaciated eyes in the November glare of noon, even the most memorable, seductive rapid was unrecognizable under these lurking gurgles, these chuckles of thick, slipping swiftness, this ice like smashed teeth.

"The lake and river ice thundered cold at them the whole year they were carried to us." Keskarrah gestured to the passing wind. "Again and again. How much more did These English have to be told?"

It seemed they had heard only their own telling, as told to themselves. And the names they had vied, with such gentlemanly camaraderie, to give each interlaced lake and rapid that mosquito-driven summer, were lost in their staggering memories, all quite lost, with their lost, starving notebooks. Boudelkell and The Rat and Crookedfoot lakes somewhere flowed into Greenstockings Lake, itself a strip of water so narrow it might have been drawn into rock by the edge of a casual hand. Those three lakes were also named much later, after the Yellowknife hunters they were leaning on, who had walked north four days dragging two sleds of dried meat and fat and one of furs when all These English were already more or less dead. Only three of them needed meat by then, in their ruined shelter of logs and mud — the three who had not tried to kill each other because of Greenstockings.

Of course, Greenstockings is not her name either, that summer of first arrival. For years the childhood memory of the oldest

Tetsot'ine has told stories about Whites, and the farthest northern arm of their great lake Tucho has occasionally fumbled such
a blanched body out onto its black sand. Indeed, well beyond
the story memories of living grandmothers, it is told that children saw strange wood-chips dancing on the Desnede River,
thin, curled chips that could not have been cut by a stone or
copper axe. So sometimes, deep in the sleepy winter around
warm fires, the elders tell the story of Jumping Marten, a woman
so desirable she was stolen by enemies from the east. But she
was too wise for any man to hold, she escaped and travelled alone,
as only a woman can, until she found Stone House Whites far
away, and she was the one who brought an iron axe and a needle and tea and a small kettle to the Tetsot'ine for the first time.
Good things, just a few, very good for living.

And then, even more quietly, they tell of the one White who
came walking alone one summer from the east, guided by
Matonabbee (who had enough wives for them both), and who
wandered about making those tiny marks on paper too, and
then strangely went walking back towards the east again, still
travelling alone.

And sometimes, in the darkest winter, Keskarrah will recall
aloud the story all the Dene nations around them know but
rarely speak, of how Ageenah guided the second solitary White
down the great river Dehcho. Many of the Dene nations saw
him, and named him Long Neck, his bandy legs and ridiculous
clothes, and saw how he ate thick meat four times a day but fed
his paddle-slaves nothing but fish no bigger than a person's
hand. He made them paddle him north fast, and then immediately turn around and paddle him back south again, up Dehcho,
even harder — as if something truly terrifying had met him at

the edge of the Everlasting Ice, and he knew it had started to chase him for the rest of his life.

But now, in the regular cycle of Tetsot'ine seasons, These English have arrived, and the youngest person will discover that they and their paddle-slaves stepping so easily out of three huge birchbark canoes are impossible to forget. It will seem to them, later, that at one time they needed to think only of People, and of animals and coming weather, and food, and the prevention and curing of possible illness: that was the world of their land and they lived it. But suddenly a fireball smashed through the sky: crash! — here are Whites! Now! And immediately the world is always on fire with something else, something they have never thought about or had to do before; always, it seems, burning out of its centre and rushing, destroying itself towards all possible edges. Strangely, for ever, different.

It was Birdseye who said, much later, "I think this story may be the melting mountain again. The mountain that burst open and People had to run as far and as fast as they could to escape the ground boiling under their feet, or rocks falling from the sky. After that, everyone spoke different languages too."

Perhaps that was why she said nothing when These English called her daughter "Greenstockings" for the first time, and they found out what that meant. Somehow then Greenstockings' real name vanished from every memory, even it seemed from Birdseye, who bore her and named her first.

And Birdseye stands beside her when these paddle-slaves first stroke the lead canoe in to shore with a great, driving shout. They are standing side by side where they have never come before, on the black-sand edge of Tucho, watching the lake in its eternal heave and lift. The enormous canoe rams ashore below the crooked palisade of the new company trading post, but the lake takes it back, and then heaves it forwards again, and settles. So that all Tetsot'ine see Thick English, in his blue and gold-braided coat, place his tall boot on the black sand first.

"Look there," Birdseye says, with fear. "Look."

Greenstockings looks. Unable then to ask her mother what she sees. But her father is afraid of nothing. Keskarrah has told her out loud, grinning and rubbing his finger across his teeth, that even though he is so old only worn stumps stick out of his gums, he has never yet seen the Supreme One everyone believes is everywhere around them. "It is strange," he has said to her sometimes, staring up at the stars, or at sundogs, "that living so long, I still cannot meet anyone who understands this as clearly as I. I have met all the animals, I think, and I know many stories from so long ago, when animals talked like People. Some of those stories are mine, so I can tell them too. And I even met that first lonely White Walker, travelling with his worn-out feet, I saw him when I was a small boy. But I have never seen the Soul Everywhere. Everybody talks so much, but no one can ever say they have seen — anything."

Standing there, suddenly apprehensive, on the rock and sandy shore of the great lake with her mother and father and all their People watching, Greenstockings waits for her father to answer something to her mother. She has herself seen Tucho only once before, not here, and never crossed any arm of it. These three great canoes emerged from smudges on the far limits of the water, an edge that seems to lean above her breathing deep, breathing white with the summer rage of wind until the weight of winter will, she knows, crush it motionless into crested ice pale as an ageing woman. Keskarrah understands much, he has been given the power to know something a little, and Birdseye also has some of that — but neither of them ever talks of such things unless somehow they find words together.

So she waits for her father to speak, or ask; and watches those five pale strangers come riding in at the centre of the giant canoes, erect, motionless, not one with a paddle in his hands. On their heads sit tall, black, round boxes curled up at the side edges. One by one they are stepping so carefully over the restless line of water, onto the sand.

And Keskarrah says nothing. Not even later, when he agrees to go to the council suddenly demanded by These English, whom no one has ever seen before. He will let Bigfoot talk, the man they have agreed will speak for them this time, because they have all together decided how he will do it, and he has already learned to talk to traders in the south and is very careful. Keskarrah continues to say nothing at all in that council circle. But then, when he has sat a long time with his eyes closed, hearing Twospeaker, who came in the canoes, trying to change the White chirpings into words People can comprehend, and searching deeper inside himself, slowly, slowly he will lean forwards.

He will dare to draw, with his finger on the ground between them, a very small picture of the land. He will say to Bigfoot as he draws:

"I think, if These English are to know anything, you will have to name it. Tell them this: here we are, on Tucho, and here our greatest river begins, Dehcho, below the great bay of Tucho we call Breasts Like a Woman, flowing west and then north. And here is the other river, which flows east and then north, the

Ana-tessy. And here between them, look, is the River of Copperwoman. It flows only north, here. Do they see this? It leads north to the end of where we go, far beyond the last trees in the world. The caribou and the wolves with them go even farther north, here, every spring and summer, but we never do. Here, beyond where we go, the river bends like this, at the Copperwoman Mountains, and after certain days it becomes stinking water, here where I stood once, I was very young then, with White Walker, who knew nothing either, but did ask many questions. Tell them, if they will not walk, this is the closest river to follow if they would find our enemies, the Raw-Meat Eaters. And also, the Everlasting Ice."

And Bigfoot has been repeating all this to Twospeaker, who whistles it to These English. Keskarrah will say nothing directly to them, for he is powerful and old enough to draw the picture of the world in the sand and name a few places what they are.

But the council has not had to happen, not yet. Suddenly now, as the last White stranger steps ashore, Keskarrah does speak. He asks Birdseye, "What is it you see?"

And cold like winter water wipes over Greenstockings. Can't he see what Birdseye means? With this coming, is he suddenly become blind as well as old?

Birdseye says, "That younger one."

There are two younger ones, one as short as a boy, and when Greenstockings risks looking at her, her mother adds, "The last, the thin one."

Against the great lake Greenstockings sees that young White like a slender, wind-broken tree, walking. Keskarrah continues to chew the smoked meat he has thrust into his mouth. Finally Birdseye says,

"He's…nothing…only bone…."

"Isn't that just their skin?" Keskarrah says, chewing thoughtfully. He can still speak calmly, then. "I saw White Walker's skin long ago, and considered it a long time. It looks sodden like that, like a body coming up without blood after twelve days under water and the fish leaving it alone. But up close it's hard, almost like ours. Pretty good skin."

"It is skin…" Birdseye agrees, but hesitant. "Nevertheless his skin…isn't just skin, it's…like…bones. Or like the Snow Man."

She has said the last very quickly, and Keskarrah glances at her just as fast. After a long moment he asks,

"Then…if he's Snow Man, is bad weather following him?"

But she only sees the great lake, heaving. Snow Man? — a story of a stranger, of danger coming and going — or bones, the hard necessity of eating? But Greenstockings is so fascinated by the thin White that she forgets, for now, everything except skin — she thinks she understands skin — and soon she will discover that his skin is not at all hard, and that his hair, when he lifts the long hat that at a distance makes him look broken off, is crinkled light brown, not black and hard and straight. When weeks from now the length of him stands against Greenstockings, he will rub her one hand over his pale hair springy as caribou moss in the sun and hold the other tightly to point at himself. He will breathe quietly at her, "Hood…Hood."

And he will pull her hand all around his head, as if with her fingers in his he could draw his face into a circle, "Robert Hood," and play her fingers as though their hands were tying a string together under his beautiful chin. "Yes," he will whisper, "Ho-o-o-o-od."

Then she will suddenly understand from his intense, pale eyes that he is making a picture of his name with her hand around his face, *hood*. His skin as soft as a baby's, and yet bristly — it is very strange, that skin bleached like caribou hide in water and delicate with hair over it, sharp, not smooth. Nor bony. It will make her wonder what her mother has seen, what her father in his long, inquisitive life has truly touched. When, if ever, it has been possible for his fingers to find such skin under them: such a different creature, but perhaps a human being — a man, can she feel that through his skin, is he a man?

"Hood," the pursed red mouth will then breathe again, and she will try to shape her lips into a puckered, protruding "O" like his and puff air at him, "ooo…ooo…" but she cannot click her tongue back to sound "dd", until he laughs and laughs so happily, the skin of his face very nearly touching hers, and he will never be able to say her name at all, not even the middle of it as she can his. Though all that will be much later, when the Tetsot'ine have already led These English into their country and the paddle-slaves are very busy building that cracked winter rectangle of logs and mud, and they have finally given her a name they can say easily. None of them, except he, will ever try to say her Tetsot'ine name. Only "Greenstockings".

These English. Who also tried to name every lake and river with whatever sound slips from their mouths: Singing Lake and Aurora and Grizzle Bear and Snare lakes and Starvation River, or the names of hunters, Longleg, Baldhead, Humpy, Little Forehead, and a hundred other things, or a thousand — it is truly difficult for a few men who glance at it once to name an entire country. And perhaps they even intended to acknowledge a few of the women whose names they never learned, the women who spliced meat and tanned hides to sew endless clothing for them that first fall, when the deer crowded so thickly to the river crossings that the hunters could have lanced them far more easily than blundered about with the racket and unending busyness of guns. But since the men had been given guns and powder and lead, and told to hunt with them, they ran along the shore, across the paths of hoofs worn hollow to the water, shooting now and then instead of floating in tiny canoes on the silent water and spearing fast. It may have been that, at first, These English dared to eat only animals killed with the clumsy instruments they'd brought — though before they left the country they would eat anything, even meat other animals had hunted or left behind long ago — o yes, so gladly eat anything at all, any meat they could still lift as high as their loosening, bloody teeth.

That was what Keskarrah hated before he ever met any Whites: guns. Trader guns needed endless, slow work, and yet were never as accurate as a quick arrow. And they screamed, "Listen: I'M HERE!" for unbelievable distances in all directions. Worse still, a gun sometimes exploded in its barrel instead of out of it and shredded your hand, if not your nose or shoulder or entire arm — then you were fortunate to heal together crooked. When the hunters shot the first eighteen caribou above the rapids where the river crashed into the lake, These English named that "Hunter Lake", though with lances they might easily have taken a hundred. But the paddle-slaves were happy then, their guts packed so tight and full they carried the long portage singing. And later, when only some English came back, the names of those slaves for whom fifty songs were no more than a day's work were given to lakes and rivers everywhere north of there too: Beauparlant, Crédit, Vaillant, Bélanger, Perrault, Fontano, Samandré, Peltier. As if that would change the People's memory of their strength and dancing and laughter, or how miserably they died.

And long after that, far away to the east, a lake came to be known as "Mohawk" — where he had never been, that one paddler who was a Person from so many rivers away, Michel Terohaute.

Of course, every place already was its true and exact name. Birdseye and Keskarrah between them knew the land, each name a story complete in their heads. Keskarrah could see, there, in the shape and turn of an eddy, the broken brush at the last edge of the trees, the rocks of every place where he waited for caribou, or had been given to know and dream; and Birdseye had walked everywhere — under packs, or paddled, following or leading him, looking at each place where the fell of soft caribou and thick marten or fox turned continually into clothing for People in her hands: in their lifetime of ceaseless travel and thought, the way any Tetsot'ine must if they would live the life of this land.

The stories the land told, Keskarrah said, and the sky over it in any place, were the stories of all People who had ever lived there, and therefore they were greater than any person, or two, could comprehend, even if one could have remained in one place motionless for an entire season, either of snow or mosquitoes. But he could draw, very carefully, the places he knew through his fingers from behind his eyes onto the ground, which is where all land already lies fully and complete, though hidden. Or he would look at Birdseye, and then tenderly make those lines on birchbark with dead embers from her fire, because the seeds and roots of trees are always in the land, and the seed and root of fire live eternally within trees. Names all waiting to be breathed out again, quietly, into the air.

"Just making a sound can mean…nothing…" he will muse into the perpetual fire of the winter lodge, a fire their mothers beyond memory have carried everywhere in the flint and touchwood of their pouches. "It is for us to look. Perhaps we will recognize how everything alive is already within everything else. It is like…holding water…cup it in your hands, and it is the nature of water that very soon it will cup your hands as well."

So at the council he will make the small picture on the ground for the strangers. And the hunter Bigfoot, whom These English instantly named "chief", though he had no more authority than any other person, looked down at the immense land barely scratched between their feet, and he was deeply troubled. He said sadly, to Keskarrah alone,

"You know, if we tell them how to go north to the Everlasting Ice, they won't return."

"Yes, we know that. But what can we do, if they want to go? You've told them how the rivers could bring them back, both west and east."

"But they don't listen, and we'll never see them again."

Keskarrah said impatiently, "Of course we know that! And it doesn't matter — we never saw them before today either."

"That's true," Bigfoot agreed. "But today we have seen them, and so it's different."

Keskarrah said, "No, it can't be."

"I believe it is…different," Bigfoot insisted. Strangely, as though speaking to These English had for the first time given him the insight of debate. "We see them. How they look like strong human beings despite their silly clothes? And eyes as sharp as ours, and a flag?"

"Yes, we see that."

"Yesterday we had not seen any of it. And I would be as happy as you if we never had, but unfortunately, now we will never be able to say we haven't. If someone asks for them tomorrow, we will have to say it. And then we will also have to say, 'They are dead.'"

So Keskarrah had to tell him once more, "I'm looking. What will come and ask for them?"

Bigfoot could not find another word for that. Only great Tucho itself beyond the split palisade logs seemed to have anything to say.

Keskarrah continued very quietly, "All right, but you see they want to hear nothing except the way of the lakes and rivers to the ice. North, north, we have already offered more than they want."

Slowly Thick English, who really was their boss because he spoke without consulting anyone about anything, bent and whispered to Twospeaker, who in turn spoke to Bigfoot.

"This English John Franklin wants to know, I am supposed to say it to him, what you say to each other."

"Of course." Bigfoot looked at Keskarrah, but he refused to speak. "So-o-o," Bigfoot decided carefully, "tell him if they will not walk, there are several ways to travel north on water. We are discussing which way is best."

Keskarrah spoke out directly. "Tell them this. We have already explained the best way to go, and return."

Twospeaker agreed, "I've explained that."

"Good." Keskarrah faced Thick English. "Now we need to

know something from him. We have heard that when Whites appear, People sometimes get strange illnesses — coughs, blisters, even burning or freezing from inside. We don't know what to do with White illness, so we ask him, which of you is the one who can keep a person from dying?"

Twospeaker stared. "Do I ask that?" he said finally.

Bigfoot said, studying those stiff Whites one by one, "Not one of them looks as if he could say that."

But Keskarrah had decided. "I've never heard anyone say such words myself, but when I saw these Whites coming I dreamed of sickness like lice crawling all over, it was coming with them, but also that one of them could keep a person from dying whenever he was there. So, will one of them dare to say he can do that?"

"All right," Bigfoot said. "Ask it."

Later, when they have almost forgotten Keskarrah's question, it will be Twospeaker who explains to Greenstockings what the other young man's name means, the very short, pretty one with hair down both sides of his face. Boy English at first does not seem to know how to draw his name in the air, and when he gets hold of her hand at last he will do almost everything else with it except that. His name is easier to say than Hood's, and she laughs aloud because "Back" is right: his short back is much stronger than slender Hood's. And though when she stands beside him she can look completely over his head, he is so compactly confident and without concern that he takes her between his hands and lifts her high (no one ever sees him touch the huge double packs and massive canoes the paddle-slaves walk under day after day, carrying These English over the rock and muskeg portages to the hill above Winter Lake, where they start chopping down trees) — Back lifts her so easily over his curly head that she is forced to know, as with every man she has ever met, the power of his name: "George Back!"

But with Back she can quickly reach up, higher than his short muscled arms, and grasp two beams of the piled logs the Whites foolishly imagine will keep them warm in winter, and swing herself out of his grasp before he can finish shouting "…ack!" and kick him hard in the ribs. By then she will know where those two young English keep their names (which is dangerous), and where her mother keeps hers (which has never been dangerous for her, though it may become that), but her feet wrapped in supple moccasins are much too soft for kicking anyone memorably. Back's busy hands grapple for her again, tug her down against himself more proud than ever, and it is then she feels him shift hard between her thighs like every man always has, hard bone.

Birdseye long ago taught her how to knead leather soft and pale as a baby's face, softer even than Robert Hood's, and certainly softer than Back's. They will be wringing leather in the sunlight outside their lodge between what the Whites will call Winter and Roundrock lakes, the great trees along the esker crashing to the ground with the noise of steel axes, when her mother says to her:

"If you laugh with both of them, I think one will get killed."

"Whites don't fight over women."

"U-u-u-ugh!" Birdseye snorts. "And nothing hangs between their legs either."

Greenstockings bursts out laughing. "It doesn't just hang!"

Birdseye lifts her head quickly from the dripping leather. She rarely looks up now, because she wants to spare everyone the necessary recognition of seeing her. And Keskarrah has found no dream, nor has anyone else Who Knows Something a Little, who could divine what is happening to her beautiful face: what Eater is slowly, imperceptibly, eating her face away.

As winter approaches, pain draws her face more tightly into the emptiness where her cheek and part of her nose were at the beginning of summer. Soon white bone may be visible there, and Greenstockings fears her mother will hang a soft leather below her eyes, dreads that she will never be able to touch her mother's mouth again. The Eater is eating towards her lips.

Birdseye offers, allows Greenstockings one glance, then bends quickly, spits between her fingers on the leather as she kneads pounded caribou brain into it. Once those hands fondled Greenstockings until she cried in ecstasy, cried in ways the four men who have already fought and nearly killed themselves over her cannot find anywhere in the brief duration of their manly imaginations. Often it seems to her that men's hands are fit only to clutch knives, to claw at clubs and lances, to strip hide or flesh from dead bones, to knot into fists, perhaps — now — to grope and jerk at triggers. Broadface's left hand has become two strips of talon, the rest torn away when the gun a trader was teaching him how to shoot exploded. What can a person fondle with such a split stick for a hand, even if he's strong enough to carry a grizzly? No woman weighs as much as a bear anyway, nor needs such force if she wants to be lifted, or entered. Doing it that way is simply a story to be remembered; to be told and resmelled by other men, bragging.

Birdseye says, "Oh, he's shown you that much, has he?" the faintest breath of sarcasm in her voice, and then suddenly they are both laughing. So loudly that the other women stream about from their fires, smiling and chuckling already, crowding nearer for what they can hear.

"He has a black stick for drawing," Greenstockings tells them, "Boy English, his name is 'Back' and he can draw his own short back in one line so fast you can see it exactly, the way it bends, and then he curls the bottom end of it up, pointing down at himself, he's so proud, hooked up as he draws it almost as long!"

The women are all shouting with laughter, some behind their hands in incredulity but others open-mouthed with anticipation. For how can one know how These English will behave, so safely far from whatever land they have left that they may do anything at all as long as another English isn't looking; or what they carry in those strange clothes, doubled up perhaps or folded in pleats, and doubtless Greenstockings will be the first to find out, if she wants to. Boy English will keep pretending in his towering black officer's hat, which makes him almost as tall as the others, will continue to stride between their lodges, point everywhere imperially, order voyageurs to chop down that tree, flatten that log for the ridgepole, set that upright into place, may pretend for ever to own the whole world when his boss, Thick English, is somewhere else; but these women will never again see him without laughter flickering naked behind their eyes. And they offer Greenstockings whatever bits of advice or malice they please, especially since many of them know that, before she went with Broadface, their own men sharpened their knives to try to get the frightening power of her sixteen-year-old beauty into their lodge. If that happened, they themselves would become second wives, or third, and some of them might be happy for that too — after all, what woman wants to carry alone the weight of one man's clutching, violent necessity for attention? — so at this moment they all laugh with her:

"Such a pretty-bone Boy English!"

"You're too young for all that pretty boy!"

"He's dreaming he's a bear!"

"Back, back, bone of a back!"

Birdseye says, "But that is his name, isn't it?"

And her tone, as much as their knowledge of her ravaged face bent aside, silences them.

"Yes, it is," Angélique answers. She is a Person from south of Deninu, but her husband is Twospeaker, the mixed-blood Pierre St. Germain who speaks Tetsot'ine and French and Dogrib and English too; what he knows about Whites, Angélique knows as well. "Yes," she says again, "that is really his name, right up the middle, and maybe the thin young one could draw his name out of his bone too."

They are all puzzled. "How could he do that?" someone asks.

"In English his name can mean 'cap'."

Someone else says quickly, "Then of course he could. Every man has a cap on his bone!"

And they are laughing again, even louder because they are all laughing at the same dangly, miserable, hard thing about men, together, however it may delight or plague them.

"No." Angélique speaks so softly a moment passes before they know it. "No, they don't. Some Whites don't."

They all stare at her. Angélique continues, "My man says sometimes Whites don't have any cap there…just nothing at all. No one has seen These English yet, they always go behind something to piss, but some Whites, he says, because they think they'll be stronger then, they cut that cap off."

Into their stunned silence Birdseye says, head bent to her squishing, oozing leather, "Or it may be eaten...off."

Everyone seems to stop breathing. Into their play of words about Whites has crept the simple and continually unfathomable burden women must carry — all men. For the strangers clearly are men; Greenstockings at least has felt it and Angélique also knows. Men. In each other's eyes the women recognize the inescapable power and fear — sometimes joy, often brutality, even terror — that men forever carry about them like their cocks, limp or rigid, hanging somehow gently, possibly tender or abruptly lethal; which they bring to women as certain as the meat they hunt, offer them or thrust, even in their quietest moment at the flicker of a glance threaten to jerk out at them whether they would accept it or not: grab, ram, pound into them. Again and again, always, and leave with them as if it were a fleeting spasm; as if it were nothing more than something to forget and remember, and then shudder to watch out for again. And endure again; like passing sunshine and more black, pounding, bitter weather.

Birdseye undoubtedly knows that her small words have grown behind their eyes to help them see this. But she does not look up; she is merely silent, working at their endless women's labour. Slowly one by one the women leave, back to their necessary fires. Greenstockings picks up her scraper. Her younger sister, Greywing, helps her pull the stretching-frame with its bloody hide into the low, pale light of the curing sun. In a few days the sun will not give enough warmth to lure the night ice off the lake even by noon, though it will still darken, harden the fat layered on a hide.

Greywing has returned from her solitary tent, where, for a

full cycle of the moon, she has been initiated into womanhood, and can now for the first time begin to speak among women. "Does it matter," she asks her sister tentatively, "what their names are? You're with Broadface, won't he just…kill them both anyway?"

Greenstockings says nothing, so Angélique accepts her question. "English make knives, so I think they aren't scared of them. Maybe not even guns. No one has ever seen a White die by a gun."

Greywing chuckles a little, to cover her own daring. "Broadface wouldn't need a gun," she says. "Maybe a rock — or the heavy claw that stupid gun gave him."

Birdseye murmurs, "I heard no one has ever seen an English die of sickness either, so if their…maybe…maybe…."

She is bent so low her forehead almost touches her muscling fingers, but she stops speaking. Greenstockings grimly forces the scraper down with her two hands; the only sound is the curved bone gnawing through fat, around a hole exploded big as a fist in what was once the deer's belly, such massive holes torn by guns. Her skin remembers the length of those two young English through their stiff cloth, her own soft leather against her thigh, her belly: so different from each other, from anything she has ever felt with Broadface's long black eyes and copper skin glistening over her, his bending bones flattening her until she loosens, opening gladly. And yet, strangely, always the lurking threat of explosion — no warning, the second before you sense he's there, just smash! Her belly cramps.

Angélique continues, "But Whites have never come with their own women, and they never fight for one. They just take whom they want."

When Greenstockings looks up, Angélique is also gone. Birdseye says to Greywing,

"Perhaps there is still some water left for us in the river."

Greenstockings watches her sister lift the leather bucket. Her small shape bending, her smooth movement around and down the rocks curved to the whistling river below, beyond the trees, is like the rainbow fin of a grayling quick as a quiver of light in bright, clear water.

"Thick English," Birdseye says, "wants all our best hunters to kill animals for him. He says he will need more dead animals than anyone has ever counted."

"What do the hunters say?"

"Bigfoot says they'll hunt."

"Bigfoot?" Greenstockings cannot understand. "What? He says what we all say."

Within the shifting groups of Tetsot'ine for a time agreeing to live together, as necessity arises, one person decides finally where they will travel, where they will stop — but that implies nothing like boss. They have no word for "chief", and Greenstockings is trying to think how one person could commit others to do something they might not want to do, or stop doing at some point: the way he would order a woman he could threaten or try to beat into obedience? Why would the men do it? They would just take their families and travel on the welcoming land to where others might be who would accept their living together. Perhaps all the men do want to do it now, just kill animals for Whites?

And she feels a woman's contempt for this illogical acquiescence, this feeble agreement of all accepting what a stranger wants of them. "Soon," she sniffs, "Bigfoot will be so bigfooted even his youngest wife won't listen to him!"

But Birdseye will not laugh. "Whites have so many things. And you know men — if they could, all they would do is chase animals."

"Yes," Greenstockings says, suddenly bitter. "So many, heavy things they already need twenty gigantic paddle-slaves to carry them, and more things we women and children will have to carry for them too. And what will it help us, all this extra carrying and all the animals our great hunters kill, so busy far away? Whatever meat they get, someone has to carry it here and cook it so These English and their slaves can eat first. If we do all that work, when will we have time to eat?"

Birdseye says, still softly, "I think Thick English will hang another shiny medal around Bigfoot's neck, over the first one, and then give the hunters more tea and then whisky, and when they wake up in the morning there will be more nets for fishing and more guns and more bullets and powder piled up in front of each lodge, and every man stepping through his door will be happy to kill more animals so far away he can barely see them, agree to...."

But her voice is falling away, and Greenstockings bursts out, "Things piled up! Is that what our men think should happen? My father too?"

Birdseye does not raise her head from the leather that is twisting smoky water from her powerful hands. She says, "There are now twenty-five men here whom we have never seen before. They are very big and eat everything they can — and they all have to have clothes for the long darkness."

"Yes...and where are their women?" Greenstockings insists. "There are only three, and they belong to their slaves."

"Those three...." Birdseye hesitates. "They may also be slaves to These English."

"Three women for twenty-five men!"

Birdseye says, "I think English have so many things, they think every person is their slave."

Greenstockings looks at her mother, her scraper motionless.

"You and I are their slaves?"

"Keskarrah has said nothing."

"What will he say?"

"If all the men agree, how can he...."

"He's my father...he knows something a little...."

But Birdseye refuses to look up.

"O yes." Greenstockings can only whisper her rage to her mother, at what she realizes she has known since she first saw Thick English step ashore as if the world were rubbing its face into the sand under his feet — known but has tried to avoid thinking. "Yes! All our mighty men agree, listen to Thick English and they pile those things on us to carry. And they'll kill all the animals, so many they'll go away to avoid being killed, and we'll have to drag what they kill here to our fires and skin them for These English and cut the meat into strips and smoke it and cook it and sew their winter clothes so they won't freeze after we scrape and tan all those hides, these mighty English! Let them freeze stiff as cocks in their cloth!"

Birdseye says nothing. She refuses; as though what Greenstockings has dared to utter — these incredible pointed words hissed into the coming-winter air, which are as strange in the mouth, or the ears, of a woman as anything These English have dragged into their country — had never been spoken.

Greenstockings says, very softly, "We can go away." And

after a moment, "Broadface would come with me — if I went...."

But Birdseye is bent low, smoothing hide over her knee; she murmurs into the luminous leather even more softly, "Anger is always dangerous." Her head and voice shift, a certain awareness of age. "What is it? What have you felt?"

Greenstockings, frightened, tries to see her mother's face. Only last winter her nose was as beautiful as Greywing walking, and she herself was so empty of knowing about Whites that it was not even necessary for her to dream of imagining their aggression. But now Birdseye will not let her avoid it.

"What have you felt?" her mother insists more gently. "When you feel all over that head, those Snow Man arms and hands feeling you?"

Greenstockings understands her mother has heard every word she has ever swallowed in her thoughts, Snow Man story or not; so she waits, hiding her anger again, scraping the hide steadily around the ragged emptiness of its bullet hole until her mother is ready to help her by continuing.

They can wait for each other for days, wait for seasons and ages, since their work together will never be done as long as they live. Finally Greenstockings ventures, "Maybe...that sickness they always have is hiding...scared by our quick cold...."

"These English," Birdseye says finally, "will not admit they can keep a person from dying, but it may be true. If they have brought sickness, it is hiding." And then she adds, almost inaudibly, "Perhaps wherever their medicine man is, no one will die."

A tree is falling. Somewhere behind them, beyond the spruce-covered lodges of the People, along the sand and rock curve of esker that shelters them from the north wind, a tree falls. Its shriek, its quiet cry before it crashes, touching them like a motion in air, a whisper against the sharp, hard clang of steel they have been forced to hear for days, a new sound so brittle and ringing that sometimes when the wind turns away it slashes across the ear like the distant scream of a child. Even the eternal, gentle voice of the rapids coming out of Winter Lake is no longer reassuring. There is something Birdseye must be told.

"They both want to make my picture," Greenstockings whispers. "Draw it with their sticks on bark. Both of them...."

The fluid leather flows into stillness between Birdseye's hands.

Greenstockings is desperate to explain, quickly before her mother will speak. "It's...really no different from looking in water, water makes pictures of us, all the time, you know it does."

Slowly the leather begins to ooze again. Birdseye says, "When you look away, the water picture is gone."

Greenstockings says swiftly into her hesitation, "If no one looks at them, perhaps the pictures they make aren't there either."

"I...I don't think so. With water often you have to see deeper than you want to. But the way These English make a picture...shows more...and less...." Birdseye pauses, breathing. "Sometimes I think everything has become different. Sound, and taste, different."

The wind eddies between them, a heavy crash of English axes rolls over them from among the last great trees. Perhaps soon the trees that have always welcomed the People here to the edge of the tundra will all be dead too. Killed by These English. Laid out and skinned side by side, piled up on one another into square naked corners, trying to keep winter from cutting between them, their brown, dried blood sticking them together into walls wherever they touch.

Greenstockings whispers to her mother: "If one of them can draw what he wants, maybe their medicine man will do what you want."

And there is Keskarrah, coming towards their outdoor fire. He is old and yet she sees that he walks straight, straighter than anyone except Hood. What strange names they have — Hood — Back — no *short* back or *red* hood, just one short word to name them. As if they had no stories in them.

"…ooo…d," she practises again. If she can say it right, he will do it. Safely. "…o-o-o-o-d."

Keskarrah speaks beside her. "I've found which English it is. The one with the yellow bag he never lets anyone carry, and he's named after the sun. This paddler who is also a Person, Michel, he told me."

Greenstockings knew it could be neither Hood nor Back. The dark paddler is standing behind her father, the Mohawk from so many rivers away. Michel. He is taller than Hood, and almost twice as broad as Keskarrah. The level sunlight cuts past him, half his face brilliant like a thin, steel knife as he stares at her.

Keskarrah says, "Michel says that one's strong name is Richard Sun."

MIDSHIPMAN ROBERT HOOD

Monday July 31st 1820   Fort Providence

In the evening we divided a few gallons of rum between the Canadians and the Yellowknives, and the night was passed in mirth and revelry. The Canadians amused themselves by singing and dancing, imitating the gestures of a particular person, who placed himself in ludicrous postures, and performed extraordinary feats of activity. The gravity of the chief gave way to violent bursts of laughter, and indeed, the confusion of languages, dresses, and unartificial character had something in it more entertaining than a common masquerade. In return, he desired his young men to exhibit the Dogrib dance; and ranging themselves in a circle with their legs widely separated, they began to jump simultaneously sideways. Some, whom the potent effects of the spirits had stretched on the floor, rose from their besotted sleep and joined the circle, bouncing with uncouth alacrity, but out of time, to the great discomfiture of their sober companions.

Thursday August 3rd 1820   Great Slave Lake

At 4 a.m. we proceeded to the head of the lake channel, where we found Bigfoot and his party waiting to guide us. We were soon surrounded by a little fleet of canoes, containing the Yellowknives, their wives and children, and in company with them we entered a river 150 yards wide, with banks well covered by pines and poplars, but the naked hills behind them betrayed the barrenness of the country. We named it the Yellowknife River.

3

MIDSHIPMAN
GEORGE BACK

As the young Indian men were beginning what their chief called the Dogrib dance, Lieutenant Franklin's tent most inopportunely burst into flame and threatened to ruin the agreement the dance was to celebrate — the Indian mind being as superstitious as it is. I am not at all averse to brown, glistening muscles, especially when draped by leather and fur, but apparently the worst of the event in their eyes was the flag ablaze so ominously, rather like a beacon of uncertain signal above the black sand of the lake. I admit I ran without ceremony, fearing some base treachery, but only the flag was completely aflame, with its burning tatters falling dangerously on the tent roof. I seized the pole and scrambled down the rocks — very nearly breaking my leg — to thrust the blazing banner into the water.

What a grand fireworks of smoke and hissing that produced! Even the brown leather women, who until then had refused to be anything but silent mounds beyond the men's circle — and were thus somewhat nearer the fire — sighed magnificently in admiration. However, when the chief came pacing up, he was already in lament, a singing so dolorous and ear-piercing that our half-breed translator hesitated even more than usual before he would venture a word in English. It seemed that destroying the flag was more or less equivalent to destroying England — so the chief sang — since besides our dress uniforms that was all he had yet seen of its particular majesty.

Perhaps in our proposal we had been somewhat too strong for these primitive people. I had read the proclamation phrase by phrase for our translator so there could be no misunderstanding:

"This, our great flag, is the sign of the King of England's power, who is your king also! The King of England is your Great Father! We are not traders, we are the King's warriors, as you can see by our uniforms. We are not come to trade, but to establish good relations between us and yourselves, and to discover the resources of your country. We already know one great river to the north, but if you show us the way of the other great river to the Northern Ocean, *and* if you hunt for us as we follow it, the King will be very thankful. He will send ships bigger than a hundred voyageur canoes combined to trade with you. Then your enemies will fade away with envy at your wealth and power, and you will be richer than all your ancestors together."

They stared at us in disbelief, especially the old man who subsequently — after a deal of hesitation — scratched the map of the country on the ground. He seemed to be advising the chief, though he was much too apprehensive to say anything directly to us. (Our translator from Fort Chipewyan spoke English intelligibly enough — he had a somewhat larger vocabulary of Canadian French, though execrably muddled with Cree — but he was obviously slow in communicating what was said in either, which I gather is partly due to the paucity of the Indian language.) When Lieutenant Franklin explained further — and at more length — what we had planned to tell them, I thought the idea of the wealth we proposed was too much for their minds to grasp. They seem unable to understand anything of the principles of "property". In fact — our translator insisted — there was no word for it in their language! Ah, *primitiva gloriosa* indeed!

However, when Lieutenant Franklin tried to explain what numberless goods our great ships coming directly from England could bring them, cutting out entirely the present 2,205 miles of incalculable lake, river and rapid labour between York Factory and Fort Providence, it emerged that their hesitance did not concern wealth at all. It was the size of ships that held them speechless. A hundred of our huge voyageur canoes? Their own canoes can barely sustain four people. Thereupon Hood brought out his sketch of *Prince of Wales,* which had brought us from England, as we traded with the Esquimaux in Hudson Bay the summer before, but then, perversely, they did not for a moment notice the immensity of the vessel, but rather gave all their attention to the kayaks of the Esquimaux fleeting on the water.

"Our enemies," they groaned. "You have talked — you have traded — you have already eaten — with the Raw-Meat Eaters!"

The beak-nosed old mapmaker seemed especially disturbed and we had to expend more time than ever convincing them of our totally pacific intentions. "Our Great Father wants all his children to live at peace!" we told them emphatically. "We are all his children, we and all Indians and all Esquimaux alike, and he wants you to stop killing each other. We cannot help you be-come rich if you fight and kill each other!"

To which they — ever perverse — responded, "Then why are you come as warriors and not as traders?"

How to attempt explaining European history! What can the inhabitants of such a desolate land understand concerning the political and national philosophies of Empire? To compare their elementary hostilities to England's conflict with Napoleon, as Hood sometimes attempts to do, is ludicrous, as he would know if he had been a captive of the French for five years as I was. However, our pomp of proclamation may have been poor strategy — we might better have devoted our persuasions, as the traders do, to the simple ones of tribal pride and full bellies. God knows these natives live in a dreadful land with more than enough space quite empty around them. With no discernible social organization — and wandering about at random — why will they laboriously transport themselves through four hundred miles of vacant moss to identify a possible enemy? Not even Samuel Hearne forty years ago, in his lengthy book, could eluci-date that. Nevertheless, out of this irreducible confusion of idea and inadequate translation — however it may have emerged in their minimal language — there suddenly developed their ritual dance. What it was — other than referring somehow to their Dogrib Indian neighbours, apparently the dancing masters of the country — or why they danced, our translator could not ex-plain, nor how such a thumping ceremony would commit them to hunt for our expedition — as apparently it did!

So, whatever our strategy, happy results. I began to antici-pate that some of the females might join in, the dance being exceedingly energetic. And truly — though seated and much encumbered with heavy clothing — they were beginning to sway, rather like a field of dark corn playing under wind, when the blazing flag roused everyone, women included, for a run to our camp above the lake. After my heroics it was quickly established that our servant, John Hepburn, had built a fire before the main tent to repel the usual mosquito hordes, and being more used to smoke than clear air — his pipe was a cloud-burner — fell comfortably asleep at last, the clouds of pests held somewhat at bay, and so did not notice the thin moss catch and the flag dipping down to it under the wind until our shouts awoke him.

But the Indian mind rejects accident. The women, as saggy and wrinkled as native females invariably are — their breasts undergo great distention from an early age from long feeding of their infants, the sight of which can only be repugnant — took up the chief's lament, whereupon Lieutenant Franklin quickly had our extra flag unrolled. By good fortune it was larger than the first — though not of silk, which difference no Indian could discern — and the chief, seeing majesty wave again, subsided together with all his factotums. Doctor Richardson treated the servant for a slight burn and the dancers were especially cheered when — on further orders — Hood broached another cask of rum for them, well watered though it was. As became evident, the men — who had most willingly shared the wailing — would share neither rum nor dance with the females, but left them to look on, squat and sullen, at their own boisterous, expanding caterwaul.

Still, the old mapmaker seemed unreassured. During the dance he questioned our translator further, who repeated the name of our servant again and again rather oddly:

"Hep *Burn,* Hep *Burn,*"
together with a great deal of what seemed elaborate explanation, such as he had never yet vouchsafed us. Suddenly the grizzled oldster walked away to crouch on the folded rock by himself, staring across the lake and paying no attention to the young men trundling a circle in their tuneless chant, their pounding of the long-suffering ground. I was about to make a quick sketch of him against the great wind-swept water — truly an astonishing freshwater inland sea, we were three days crossing the narrowest parts of it, island to island — when Hood appeared beside me.

"Perhaps you shouldn't do that, Mr. Back," he said in his oracular minister's voice — so out of keeping with his gaunt, almost diaphanous appearance. "He will not like it."

Really. I know as well as he that the Indians must work for us if our expedition is not to prove impossible. I will — if such are orders — don naval dress whites (the Cumberland House dance only warranted dress blues) no matter how crushed they may be after a year's canoe travail from York Factory compressed in a Canadian voyageur pack, and stand at attention on primitive rock, facing an endless lake for an hour, until a mottled birch flotilla approaches and a chief deigns to step ashore, his shoulders draped in an enormous bear-hide — and his eyes offering not a flicker of recognition as to our existence. Though their formality outfrump the French, I will accept it: the chief may pace through the log entrance of Fort Providence and seat himself in the recently mud-smeared trading company hall — which in keeping with his imperial dignity is no larger than an English cottage kitchen — and while enthroned on dirt accept an introduction with the distant gravity of King George III himself, and I will bow as if he were in fact the sixty-year ruler of the whole earth — God save the King! But if we permit and help enact such pretentious charades for too long, I am confident disaster will strike.

I understand thoroughly the routine of our voyage — and this country as far as it has been explored and written about — and my conjectures of the coast we must map I am quite certain are correct. It is clear to us all that we are not proof against the possible treachery of a native, therefore much depends on accident and so we must work hard, anticipate what we can — and look for the best. Hope is our sheet anchor, and sailors know how to make use of that.

Our Lieutenant Franklin is nothing if not thoroughly planned, ordered and methodical. He may very well explain our Admiralty orders, and as much of the attendant purposes of Empire as he deems expedient, all of which — however translated — the chief greets with that grave dignity that invariably attends stolid incomprehension. But such laborious ceremony allows a good deal of time for me to consider this Indian and his stitched-together retinue of leather and fur and nakedness: I see strong handsome limbs, but I also see a wild people who have never seen an Englishman before, leave alone worked for one — indeed, do they know what work is? — as our Canadian voyageurs trained in the fur trade certainly do?

But the natives must obey us if we are to succeed. They must be able to find and kill enough deer to feed us and all our labouring men: five Englishmen and eighteen paddlers and two translators — to say nothing of several of their necessary attendant women — in three birchbark canoes — a minimum of twenty-five men in all travelling down the Coppermine River, which no voyageur or Englishman has ever seen — except

Samuel Hearne, now dead. And he saw only twenty miles of it at its mouth fifty years ago. It would seem much long labour remains for us even before we reach the Coppermine — and can we be certain that hesitating old man was drawing the course of exactly *that* river to the ocean? Whatever he said, via the chief and our translator? He seemed confused about a "return" river — but if we achieve our goal in the Arctic, we have no intention of returning again this way.

For when we arrive at the mouth of the Coppermine River, as we fully intend to by this autumn, we propose to explore the Great Northern Ocean — the "Everlasting Ice", as it seems these Indians call it, doubtless because they fear it — explore its shore eastward as far as Hudson Bay and the ships passing there, all by birchbark canoe. A fact we have not yet explained to our voyageurs, who are superbly trained to dance on turbulent rivers — in over 2,000 miles we have lost only one man, a sternman drowned while running a rapid, a standard hazard, we understand — but an ice-filled ocean? Lieutenant Franklin and I saw a good deal of it two years ago, north of Spitzbergen Island, and we saw more traversing it on *Prince of Wales*, and even from the deck of a 200-ton vessel icebergs are not a reassuring sight. Even for an English sailor.

And indeed, the chase of deer may in England be royal entertainment, but we are after food, not vicarious wood-and-meadow danger. Each canoe has a crew of six: bowman, sternman and paddlers. Since eating is their greatest, together with drinking their only diversion, they expect to devour eight pounds of meat per day. When you add our translators and ourselves — four officers plus servant — we presently require almost a full ton of meat a week; that is, a minimum of twenty large dressed deer. And, since we are told the deer will have migrated during the season we intend to move along the barren coast, we must now acquire at least twice as many — forty in all brought in every week — so that their meat can be dried and pounded into pemmican to supply that difficult but most crucial part of our exploration: the discovery of how to get east to Hudson Bay while mapping the northern coastline of North America.

So indeed we stood at serious attention as the seven slender Indian hunters — they are lean and agile as schoolboys — stepped forwards and Hood measured their first small bags of powder and twenty-five musket balls formally into their hands. We expect them to kill for us per week an average of six deer each.

"There are some ninety Yellowknife children and women in this band, and fewer than thirty mature hunters," Hood confides to me at the lake in his sepulchral tones. "We've now hired their best hunters — so who will feed all their families this winter?"

"They share what the others have — Indians share."

"But we've got all their best hunters!"

"Didn't you hear the chief?" I tell him bulging with native concern. "He declared, 'Never will we allow our new friends, the White warriors, to go hungry!'"

"This goes beyond hunters," Hood continues undeterred. "The three voyageur women cannot possibly skin and cut and dry all that meat before it rots — or tan all the necessary hides — even if they never sleep. The Yellowknife women will have to help them."

In our year together Hood and I have, perforce, got on well

enough, but his manner of speaking on matters he considers moral imperatives always irks me to argument. It is his insufferable rectitude — the dry echo of a small clergyman on a very small living.

"Probably Bigfoot," I say, "sees his own advantage in these arrangements. Otherwise, why would he agree?"

"A leader does not consider the disadvantages for his people?"

"Do you know what they think? Why they listen to him? He's agreed, so there's obviously something in it for him."

"I see," Hood responds, now openly snide. "You do compare him to Napoleon."

"God's Name, this greasy primitive?"

And only a cleric's progeny could produce his subsequent tone of sly unction: "Of course, I never saw the short Great Emperor, as you did, all tied up so cruelly in a donkey's pannier."

When outthought, Hood can only resort to the elementary accident of his own length. Though I outweigh him by two stone and can easily outwalk him twice in a day, as I have many times. But he must give me advice about when it may be injudicious to sketch a wrinkled Indian! Advice from him, when after a year in this wilderness he still has not learned when to keep his pistol loaded — which is always!

By August 13 we were two weeks north of Fort Providence, alone with our voyageurs and accompanied by our Indians — mostly women and children in their cockleshell canoes — as we travelled up the Yellowknife River. Though we were supposedly crossing directly through the annual deer migration route, in those two weeks our "seven very best" hunters had not yet presented us with a single mouthful of meat. Before the last portage of the day — around a rapid picturesque enough for any painter — our voyageurs suddenly, as if by bad instinct, stop and cluster into a huddle beside the canoes they have just dragged onto the rocks.

At first we think they are taking an extra moment of rest. The day has been filled with eight short lakes and seven long carries, beginning with one of two hundred yards and increasing to this one of over a thousand, up broken rock and through muskeg so tussocked and spongy that, active as I am, I am very nearly exhausted carrying my instruments and notebooks. But all their working lives these men have portaged 180-pound packs, and four of them can carry the 600-pound canoe over any rocky defile without betraying the slightest weariness. It may be their male pride — we have seen them wrestle or dance around their fires even after fourteen hours of indescribable labour — and such pride is certainly both good and highly useful to us: as Lieutenant Franklin said one night when the noise of singing from their tents kept us awake in ours, "With such spirit, we could drive these thin canoes to China." And I must say that their songs, spectral though they were in the awful silence of wilderness, did bespeak a certain courageous humanity.

Nevertheless, that hardly gives Hood an excuse to be standing there with nothing but pencil and paper in hand when suddenly they turn to what is clearly full mutiny.

They declare they have had nothing to eat for seven days except poor fish and rotten pemmican — well, we must eat exactly what they eat, so we know! — and no assurances will now convince them that the hunter smoke on the northern horizon portends anything beyond mere location. They absolutely refuse this last carry of the day unless they are first provided with fresh meat.

True, their labours have been immense — especially today — but are we to produce a herd of bullocks from our instrument cases? After being two thousand miles dependent upon them, we understand with absolute clarity that the weathercock minds of Canadians are stirred to reflection only by their bellies, and Lieutenant Franklin has me explain again, in simple French unadulterated by Cree, what he has told them again and again: he considers them his ship's crew and he has always treated them, and will always treat them, like English sailors — that is, they will do their contracted duty. If they refuse such duty, they will be immediately punished.

But it is now clear that he must go a step farther. Ever since leaving Fort Providence they have been grumbling as if they — who were hired because they were the strongest and most highly recommended of all voyageurs — are capable only of travel on rivers familiar to them. Well, he has now had quite enough of their grumbling and petulant complaint. If they do not pick up their packs immediately for this last portage of the day, he will not hesitate — as he has every right under English law — *to blow their brains out.*

Even in basic French there is satisfaction in uttering such an unambiguous phrase. The Indian women and children and old men have carried their goods exactly as far as the voyageurs in four days, and have certainly had less to eat. They are coming in off the lake in the usual bedraggled flotilla and are preparing — in their massive confusion of children and dogs and sacks of all kinds — to commence the portage without a glance of complaint. Hood of course is sitting on his heels with his sketchpad on his knee, surrounded by landscape, but he looks about when I shout to him. At my shout the Indians turn motionless, staring at us on the rocky beach, but Hood walks up very calmly, still holding his futile pencil.

We are five — but of course the servant carries no pistol. So Lieutenant Franklin, Doctor Richardson and I will only be able to execute three mutineers before the others reach us with their knives.

I must say I experience a strange sense of *déjà vu*, almost vertigo, as I check my priming. I know I must be intent on which man I must take — that enormous French Canadian or the skulking Mohawk? — why did we ever choose that glowering blackface? — but the absurdity of having survived the British Navy and the last of the Napoleonic wars and five dreadful years of French and Spanish captivity and traversing 113 degrees of longitude, all before I am twenty-four, and then getting my throat slit by Canadian half-breed louts on the shores of a desolate, nameless lake — sometimes we travel too fast to name or even see them all — is momentarily more than my mind can fathom. The huge voyageurs advance up the sand.

"Where's St. Germain?" Lieutenant Franklin asks.

Hood has pulled out his useless pistol as calmly as though he is about to polish it; perhaps he is fumbling at his powder-purse.

"He said he'd go to meet the hunters," he says.

Our translator is our most valuable man — and also a better hunter than any three Indians together — but we know his sharp and calculating mind: we instinctively think he has initated this. And even if he is not here, he may well have done so, and Lieutenant Franklin would accept the necessary responsibility of having to execute him first. But if he were here, it certainly would not end as it does: we raise and cock our pistols.

Nevertheless, the two biggest voyageurs and the Mohawk take several steps before they are aware that their sixteen *confrères* have stopped in their tracks. Dear God, they can crush us like mosquitoes between their enormous hands! But no Canadian can outface British character.

"You will all be docked three full days' pay," Lieutenant Franklin orders.

"Set up the camp here," I tell them in French, and I make no attempt to hide my disdain. "You will carry the portage tomorrow."

Dissension Lake. Lieutenant Franklin would permit no name stronger. Hood corroborated my reading of it exactly — he is well trained in mathematics — as latitude 64°, 6', 47" north, longitude 113°, 25', 0" west. And an hour later our translator and Indian hunters arrived with meat: the enormous irony, in the light of our near annihilation, was that they had killed eighteen deer along the shores of the next lake, at the end of the very portage the men had refused to carry!

Sight unseen we named that Hunter Lake, and the voyageurs spent the evening gorging themselves and laughing like the children they are — a mouthful of meat cures every ill. I do believe that the sternest possible warnings, docked pay and even cocked and levelled pistols — unfortunately we are in no position to have them whipped — mean no more to them than our daily reading of the Scriptures, since they understand not a word of English save curses. Lieutenant Franklin insists, however, that eventually the readings must have a beneficent effect — he alone remaining steadfast in such Christian hope.

But when he heard of the confrontation with levelled pistols, our translator did not laugh. Neither, I noticed, did the black-faced Mohawk. He alone had dared advance so far up the sand as to almost touch us. And he deliberately advanced upon Hood.

Though it is after ten o'clock, the light over placid Dissension Lake still lies like restless gold, a molten treasure — if only this dreadful land were that, Spanish Main golden sun and golden! — bowled among these primitive rocks. And despite the inevitable clouds of mosquitoes boiling about him like the devil of this place and all his angels, Hood sketches. As usual, he refuses to show me what he has drawn, and so I will show him nothing of my assignment either, but it is obvious he is not working on a landscape now, nor was he when those cowards momentarily defied us. A woman and a girl are going down to the lake carrying water buckets. Without a sound they float down into the level light.

It seems Hood is watching them too, for he says behind me, "Those are Keskarrah's daughters."

"Keskarrah?"

"The old man who walked with Hearne — the mapmaker."

"He has daughters that young?"

Perhaps my tone betrays me. Hood joined the navy at age fourteen, two years after me, and he must then have been as pretty a boy as any captain could wish for, but he will confess to me nothing but duty and Bible reading — why should I care about such a practising junior Franklin? His small cleric father could not have spoken in a more condemnatory tone:

"George, she is the merest child."

But I am walking towards them at the molten edge of the lake. The girl has barely lifted her bucket and stands there slender as willow, dripping light back into the water — it is the bending woman I must see. Her narrow arm reaching for water, the golden circles of her hand and bucket submerged and lapping outwards ring upon ring, her form lifting, turning, a slim darkness shaped out of blazing light. Never in my life have I seen such a stunning shape — face — if she lived in Italy she'd be burning on walls, a leather Madonna lifting water.

Midshipman Robert Hood

Sunday August 13th 1820   Yellowknife River

The woods discontinued and the rest of the country was a naked desert of coarse brown sand diversified by small rocky hills and lakes, and it was here the voyageurs gave up all hope of relief. They imagined that the Indians were cajoling us, and that in leading them into such inhospitable country, we were incurring dangers of which we were ignorant, but determined to obtain experience by sacrificing them. Their discontents broke forth into threats of desertion, which Mr. Franklin silenced by denouncing the heaviest punishment against the ringleaders. Few could have borne the hardships they endured without murmuring, but these complaints were very ill timed. We had scarcely encamped before four hunters arrived with the flesh of two reindeer, and were not again censured: the Canadians never exercising reflection unless they are hungry.

Sunday August 20th 1820   Winter Lake

We had, at length, penetrated into the native haunts of the reindeer, whose antlers were moving forests on the ridges of the hills, where they assembled to graze in security. At the western extremity of the lake we found a river fifty yards wide, which discharged from the lake in a strong rapid southwest. Half a mile below this rapid, we landed on the north bank of the river, at the most eligible place that offered itself for our winter abode.

4

SNOWSHOES

On a tiny island in the lake on whose western shore Keskarrah had assured them they would find the most northerly trees large enough to build a shelter similar to Fort Providence, the English officers began to discover the nature of "our Indians", as they labelled the Tetsot'ine in their notebooks. That August day, the air brisk as Lincolnshire midwinter, began with no more warning than an exceptionally fine paddle out into the lake, singing.

Lieutenant Franklin was deeply concerned about the trees, but he could only begin obliquely. It seemed, he confided aloud to his second in command in the centre canoe, the Hudson's Bay Company traders were relatively new in Yellowknife country, and they had certainly been very lax in establishing any sense of duty required by a work contract. After two weeks it was obvious to him that the hunters they had been forced to hire (unfortunately no other natives lived in the area) lacked almost completely the discipline necessary for efficient service to the Expedition. He did not believe that four pistols (one of them unloaded) and constant reminders of planning months ahead for meat would ever convince them of the steady, daily requirements of duty; only an extended and very firm experience of English order would ever achieve that — as it had for the voyageurs.

Doctor Richardson grunted, perhaps in agreement. With his trained Scottish thoroughness he was recording the temperature of the water. His notebooks were full of numbers, morning, noon, evening, including decimal points. But then, abruptly, he did speak.

"Money," he said, registering some final numbers.

"Money?"

"You seek out the larger issues, sir," Richardson said, smiling at his commander; at his inexorable reliability. "But most people wish to understand only what they hold in their hands. We will never control any Indians, not in this wild country, until we teach them the absolute, practical necessity of money."

"They hardly seem to require it, since they trade for what they need."

"Exactly. I believe that is the fundamental problem in the economic development of primitives. If they understood money, they would work harder to get more of it, in order to buy what they want."

Franklin shook his head. "But…it seems they want so little."

"Exactly," Richardson murmured, closing his notebook. "They must want more than they need. That is civilization."

On the ice-cold lake flashing with ripples that swished to the racing canoes, Lieutenant Franklin did not look happy at this analysis. It seemed to him not so much down to earth as

profoundly uncharitable, almost revealing an ungodly cynicism
— though his implacable optimism told him that the kindly
doctor was not at all like that. They were fifteen months out of
Gravesend, though hopefully no longer that distant from a return to it; the individual and interpersonal strains of the Expedition would gradually reveal themselves as no more difficult
than they must be, *Deo volente.*

Lieutenant Franklin twisted in his seat, looked ahead past
the driving arms of Solomon Bélanger at his back: the Yellowknives were gone. Ahead, perhaps far over various bodies
and strips of water…ahead somewhere. Their ragged flotilla,
where apparently every woman and child and man paddled or
carried whatever as inclination moved them, had gradually,
casually, outstripped his giant canoes and the voyageurs' contracted rhythm to vanish somewhere north over the rock shoulders of portages, across the endless hummocky, wet excretions of
moss. As the sun set yesterday, August 19, 1820, the Expedition
had portaged over the height of land down to this lake which,
unseen, they had already agreed to call "Winter". But the vanished Indians and the isolated, deformed pines they discovered
there along the south shore valleys did not reassure them.

Had the old man actually understood what they needed?
Such slim sticks, such wind-riven twists of indefatigable wood,
gnarled spirals, really, could not fashion a framework for canvas,
leave alone the log houses they must build. Now it was Sunday,
and they had not yet performed divine service, but the voyageurs always worked with less complaint immediately after
sleeping, especially if there was a calm lake to cross, and so he
had ordered the launch at sunrise with the prospect of service a
respite later. But despite the cheerful song of the voyageurs,

every lake vista made him more doubtful about the old man, about what they had understood him to say concerning "the last very large trees". The vacancy of tundra, the measureless Barren Lands, was already more than a threat, here all about them.

And then the island, whose low mound none of the officers had discerned against the northern shore, came into existence for them very suddenly.

It was not sight, but a distant sound above the swing of paddles that first made them aware of it. Sound they could not order, a tintinnabulation of insanities. Then, as they continued to stare over the glacial water, they could decipher motion... some things being thrown up, or leaping. Shapes skipping erratically against the sky, like sandflies on water, but which they gradually recognized to be human disportment in the midst of the water or...ah yes, that was the hump of an island: on a strip of beach people flailing, it must be their Indians since no one else could be here. They were jumping wildly about on a small island. Shrieking?

Back shouted from the lead canoe, "Carnival, sir! They've discovered an eternal spring — of rum!"

But Lieutenant Franklin did not answer him. The voyageurs' morning song had died in their throats, their broken rhythm reflecting what emerged clearly now as wailing, as aboriginal dirge, fraying out along the line of distant rock that separated the water from the immense sky.

In the last canoe, Robert Hood had been trying all morning to capture once more, on a small piece of paper, a coherent quadrant of the world through which he was being carried. But even after an exhausting year of continuously widening vistas, he was tempted to look sideways, tugged towards a periphery in the corner of his eye that, when he yielded, was still never there. Riding motionless in the canoe on this usual lake, he felt his body slowly tighten, twist; as if it were forming into a gradual spiral that might turn his head off at the neck. Like one of those pathetic little trees, enduring forever a relentless side wind so that it could only twist itself upwards year after year by eighth-of-an-inching; or like the owl in the story that turned its head in a circle, staring with intense fixity, trying to discover all around itself that perfect sphere of unbordered sameness and, at the moment of discovery that the continuous world was, nevertheless, not at all or anywhere ever the same, it had completed its own strangulation. A tree at the treeline…a headless owl….

But his sketch must stop, must have frame!

He found he could concentrate on what appeared to be a wash of river falling into the northern shore of the lake. Separating two scraggly trees, which seemed too tall to be there. Or was it simply the perspectiveless distance over water that made them appear so? He had been betrayed by this intense light distortion before: he must be careful. But a tall tree on either side — that was still a possible frame, if he drew them foreground enough.

But he had drawn that so often! Scribbling in trees where none could exist; doing it now where they did seemed mere repetition…and then his eyes discovered that the falls, instead of falling down into spray, appeared to climb out of the bristle of brush, climb up into air above their surrounding rock — like a column of ice pasted against space and darkness. Amazing.

Nevertheless, beyond any deception of light the roar of the falls emerged distinctly, and then vanished on the lake wind. But the island sound wavered over it. Those were people, certainly Yellowknives, twitching, spastic on that whaleback rock now clearly fruzzed with bushes. Hurling things that everywhere burst high in the black water.

"What is that?" Hood asked the translator, St. Germain, beside him.

"Somebody for sure dead."

"Dead?"

The English officers could not in a lifetime have imagined such grief. That was what it was, though at first Doctor Richardson was convinced it must be a witches' or (more likely) a devils' sabbath, performed with typical native perversity in the glare of high noon rather than midnight. But it was Indian grief. A distant lake had taken two hunters, one of them Bigfoot's brother-in-law, the other his wife's sister's son, and as long as the two pillars of black smoke stood beyond the falls and the mound of Dogrib Rock to the north, they knew the distant lake had refused to give the bodies back for them to mourn over and then leave properly to the animals.

"Double smoke, two men," St. Germain explained. "All their relations."

From the island the smoke was now obvious enough to the officers, even against the clouds. But their minds were overwhelmed with bellows and weeping and screams so closely about them, with lodgepoles being broken and skins ripped, kettles crushed, axes splintered, dogs throats being slit and everything, any thing or animal that came to hand, smashed and torn and bleeding, being flung everywhere into the lake. The small island blazed with the necessity of destruction. The Yellowknives were attacking their canoes, breaking the very guns with which they were to hunt.

"Why are they doing this?" Lieutenant Franklin demanded of St. Germain.

"Dead," he said stoically. "They cry, make themselves poor."

Even Richardson felt suddenly afraid. "Will they destroy everything they have, that they must have to live?"

"Maybe. Sad, very big. Always cry, dead."

Though required Empire authority might drive him to the threatened brink of execution, Lieutenant Franklin's reverence for life would not allow him to kill so much as a mosquito; but here, under his very eyes, a boy was about to slash open a terrified dog. He scrambled ashore and seized the boy's shoulder, shouting, and the boy wheeled around, might have disemboweled him if St. Germain had not knocked up his arm.

"No! No!" the translator yelled. "Don't grab — hide what you can — don't grab 'em!"

Several reluctant voyageurs stepped from the canoes, seizing what possessions they could and piling them farther from the shore, higher on the island. Hepburn trudged up and began to assist as well. No Yellowknife protested or hindered them. Richardson led St. Germain from one man to the next, persuading them that they must stop smashing the guns, which, after all, he explained, had been given them by their Great Father in England, who would be very angry if his gifts were destroyed, even in deep grief. The men dropped the firearms but continued to tear at their clothes in the frigid air, wailing; their mouths gaping, insensible holes in their suddenly grotesque heads, their eyes untouchably vacant, stunned with sorrow.

"They seem thankful if we stop them, yes," Lieutenant Franklin insisted, believing he understood something profound at last.

When the violence of their grief gradually eddied into a wailing dance, he ordered St. Germain to remain and guard what had been saved; the rest of the party must continue looking for the trees.

Richardson discovered that he had lost his notebook. St. Germain was pushing the rifles aside for him, looking for it, when Greywing came over the hump of the island dragging the slashed, sodden mass of her family's lodgeskins. The lake had given it back, she told St. Germain, wide-eyed.

Richardson could have wept. The child stood with nothing but a scrap of leather over her shoulders, and he could not keep his eyes from her slender, sturdy legs, her tiny breasts, the innocent fold of her sex, hunched together in the fierce, cold sunlight off the lake. He turned quickly then, almost wishing it were possible for him to wail as they did, beating themselves into exhaustion and emptiness. A grief to end every known grief here in this ultimate barrenness of the world, an island so tiny he felt for a moment lost as in a vacant ship on an empty ocean.

Hood appeared lugging a half-smashed canoe up the rocks, his face running tears.

"They *want* us to save their things, we aren't Yellowknives, we *can* save their things," he gasped.

"They are so..." in all his English the doctor could not find a suitable word, "...intemperate...."

"But they'll freeze, to death," Hood insisted, as if his saying it were somehow a prevention. "Marooned on this bare rock!"

"Now, now." Richardson shook himself into thinking reasonably. On this wailing island Hood's emotion was clearly inappropriate, as was his own. "We know our duty. These people have mourned before, and they still live."

"But they were hunting for us!"

"Now now," Richardson said again, and took the useless husk of the canoe in hand. "They contracted to hunt for us, that cannot harm them." The notebook was gone. Perhaps it too had, inadvertently of course, been thrown into the lake. He would make up certain details again from memory and the notes the other officers had kept, as far as that was possible. "Guard this canoe too," he said to St. Germain, unnecessarily.

"They don't leave," the translator said. "Not yet, so quick."

"How long will they remain and...grieve?"

"When they feel."

"Guard the canoe too," Richardson said again. "The children will certainly need every bit of shelter during the night."

And after a short paddle, like a blessing poured out by their encounter with unimaginable grief, at the end of the lake where the Winter River (as they called it) drained west over rapids, they found Keskarrah's forest. Exactly where, they recalled then, the old man had promised it would be. Inexplicably in these barrens a sudden island of huge intermittent spruce, as much as two feet thick and forty or fifty feet tall, rooted in the valleys and rims of muskegs and especially on the high sandy ridge of the esker that spread the river below them from Winter west to Roundrock lakes. Northeast beyond bare ridges loomed the dome of Dogrib Rock, indelibly shouldered in grey, and south across the river a massive erratic sat on a straight skyline of ridge as if balanced by primordial giants. Back shouted out, "Big Stone!" just before Hood, studying it in the evening light through the telescope, saw what he thought must be a tundra grizzly grazing moss across the slope below it. After the endless low marshes and rocks, the beauty of green vistas swirled like fingers over hills — in the distance imaginably the English winter downs — was beyond his hopes.

Doctor Richardson returned from a quick wider survey and declared the situation most suitable: stream water, many large trees, the shelter of the esker against the northern winds and its dry, coarse sand for a foundation; also, a bit farther into the trees was an extrusion of excellent white clay (amazing in a land of moss and rock) for chinking between house logs. All that, and they were on a straight line between Dogrib Rock and the Big Stone, so that even without a compass, if they were within sight of either, they could not be lost. Altogether (Richardson getting as close to excitement as a scientific Scot might be permitted) quite the proper situation to be chosen for the proposed wintering residence.

Deeply grateful, Lieutenant Franklin performed Sunday evening divine service before a great fire, the voyageurs piling on torn spruce branches still snapping with summer sap.

'Thus saith the Lord, heaven is my throne, and earth is my footstool: where is the house that ye build unto me? and where is my place of rest?... For I know your works and your thoughts: it shall come to pass that I will gather all nations and tongues, and they shall come and see my glory. And ye I will send to the isles afar off, that have not heard my fame, and ye shall declare my glory among the Gentiles.' This is the very Word of the Lord. Thanks be to God.

Robert Hood stood steady, head bowed, hands folded. Behind his eyelids he saw the children again, a few of whom he already recognized, on that rock in the windy lake, huddling under wet, torn hides supported by the splintered ribs of canoes, bent guns, sticks. In the pause after the responses he thought he could still hear that harrowing lament. Somewhere beyond the feather of wind in spruce, beyond the waterfall and the lake's deepening darkness. It seemed to him he was praying — for a revelation. How could they have existed here ages before they were known of? How would he draw a sorrow he could barely hear?

The lament was still there next morning, faint but clear as the icy air, and it carried on the wind all day as they measured out and drove stakes for the three buildings of "Fort Enterprise" into the hard sand. George Back was everywhere, gashing timber to be hewn for the houses, pointing, issuing orders. But by noon the distant sound seemed to have drifted away. It was the Mohawk voyageur, Michel Terohaute, who pointed out that the doubled black smoke beyond Dogrib Rock had been replaced by a single white column: the bodies must have been returned.

Thus informed, Lieutenant Franklin issued orders to the voyageurs: at dawn on the morrow half-crews must be prepared to portage two canoes back into the lake and bring St. Germain and the poor wretches here from their island. In the meantime, Back and two men would cross to the south side of the river immediately and set a fire there with an open view over Winter Lake. That would be a signal to Bigfoot.

Hood asked, "What...will our fire signal mean? Sir?"

"That we are coming to help them off the island. And where we are," Lieutenant Franklin said firmly. "Bigfoot understands smoke."

Daylight was almost gone before any fire was discernible

across the river on the south slope; its delicate smoke vanished without trace into the heavy clouds. Nevertheless, the flames at last leaping up beside the Big Stone, against the wispy line of setting sun, flickered with beauty; and cheeriness, Hood thought. A further touch of humanity in this surround of water and bare rock without ending.

But the wind began to lift dangerously from the west. By midnight, when Back and the two men finally returned, the entire ridge south of the river was burning like an immense, long city.

"Sir, it spread in moss, and then various small brush caught fire," Back reported, exhausted. "But there's no problem, there's no one there, it must consume itself, it has nowhere to go."

The officers and men stared at Back, the length of flaming ridge reflected in their eyes. Finally Richardson said, very quietly, "It is fortunate the river is between the fire and our trees. I found a stump today that has been growing here for 306 years."

They barely slept that night, the roar of fire magnified by the enraged wind hammering their tents. For three days they could see little; smoke enveloped them as if they had discovered a planet of flame, it was barely possible to chop down a marked tree, or to breathe. The voyageurs bringing up water from below reported that at times the fire, racing along the low trees of the opposite shore, threatened to jump the river. On the fourth night, however, a heavy rain mixed with driving sleet fell and by morning the fire was dead. All their magnificent green prospect south, Hood noted in his diary, had been metamorphosed into a hideous waste — smoking rock and bristling black poles.

"Who is dead?" Bigfoot asked Lieutenant Franklin through

St. Germain, when at last on August 26 the Tetsot'ine stepped out of the voyageur canoes onto the river rocks below the esker. And he could not seem to comprehend their explanation. "It is strange," he said. "All those trees have never burned themselves for us."

"It will get stranger," Keskarrah told him gloomily. "You may as well tell Thick English about winter immediately."

Bigfoot nodded, heavily. And told the consternated officers: there was now, of course, no possibility of anyone guiding them farther north that season. The People had nothing. As was plain for anyone to see, the lake of their grief had taken everything they had for living, and they would have to work desperately, here — if it was the will of the caribou to come south to this place and if they could, in their dreams, lure them along these paths of their autumn migration — work desperately to get enough clothing and lodgehides and dried meat prepared so that they and the English — whom they had promised to care for, and they would, of course — were to survive the winter.

For the long winter was already upon them.

Lieutenant Franklin could not believe his ears. He felt it was not particularly cold, there was still the best part of a week left in August! Finally, recognizing Bigfoot's adamance, he proposed a swift trip with a small crew to the Coppermine River, down that to the ocean, and return — three weeks in all at most. That would establish the best route for the complete, thorough exploration they must make next summer. Yes, he would reluctantly agree to such a fast trip, now.

But Bigfoot, again, simply refused. "It will be ten days for you," he said, "before you even reach the River of Copperwoman."

"What!"

"Lakes, portage so much — how you travel," St. Germain responded without waiting for Bigfoot. "Heavy, heavy."

"I said light canoes only. The two lightest, and very light packs, only two officers...."

Keskarrah's face was like an effigy contemplating the Big Stone high and black on the opposite ridge, smoking, or perhaps steaming faintly in the abrupt twilight. And Bigfoot's words, when he finally spoke again, seemed tinged with ridicule, though Hood thought it might be St. Germain's translation more than anything else. The categorical "no's" and "now's" must certainly be the translator's:

"He say, no deer now, by Copperwoman River. No deer now, by ocean. We dream here, quick, or everybody die, now. Women dry meat, scrape hides here."

Lieutenant Franklin could not comprehend. "What does he mean, 'dream here'?"

"The way they hunt."

"Dreaming?"

"Here, where deer maybe go."

"But they have guns now!"

"Guns...how to kill. Not hunt."

"What?"

"Dream, how you find 'em."

And after that St. Germain could not, or would not, explain anything except "no". It appeared the translator had become their chief, their most incomprehensible denier, with Bigfoot and Keskarrah and the other circled Yellowknives staring grim and silent across the river. At last Lieutenant Franklin could only insist:

"What do *you* say, you yourself?"

"Yes. It's so."

"But…we take temperatures five times a day, we record all the weather. Now, here, we register only a few degrees below last year, when we travelled to the end of October and our cloth clothing was quite adequate, we walked all through —"

"You, now, in Tetsot'ine place," St. Germain cut across his protest harshly. "Winter — no deer boots, spring — no feet."

Greenstockings passed them with the other carrying People. It was all so undignified, scrabbling into deliberate council as soon as they stepped ashore. Ludicrous, her father and the men behaving without calmness like Whites; the hideous, burned land must be affecting them.

Steadily she began climbing the steep esker where they often wintered for some months, though the paths were already worn raw by strange feet. The sodden bulk of lodgeskins on her back were slashed, but they were so light too, as they always were when opened in grief to release all the accumulating weight of stolid living, and she would sew them tight and warm again and she felt clean, strong enough to do anything, to carry any thing, any man who thought himself powerful enough to climb onto her. There were so many more men now and their differing skin did not matter, they would certainly want her, especially as the caribou bulls bellowed across the hills and the darkness lengthened steadily into winter. The lake beyond Dogrib Rock had not taken Broadface, who had lived with her all summer, though it might have; he had been there, and had returned with the assurance that the bodies of the two drowned hunters had been returned and properly left on the land, and Greenstockings had come out of the long paroxysm of community grief as powerfully cleansed as she always was, and there he stood facing her. Broadface. His face as ever beautifully round, glistening and long-eyed like any ravishing woman's. But a man's.

And she took him. Or he her, neither could tell which in the whistling, fierce or gentle thunderstorms they rode out together. He was looking for a son inside her, he hissed in her ear, and with his single cock's eye he would find him even if he had to look all night and all day until the geese returned, and she threw him off her as she would a blanket.

"At least your words are big," she said cruelly.

His hand found his knife, he would have instantly discovered something inside her, though not a son, if her copper skinning-knife had not already been between his legs. He knew that no man is quicker than a woman, who spends her life skinning and slicing what he merely hunts, and so he sat up, smiling.

"You're my woman."

"If you can keep me."

"You want me, you'll be moaning for me again," he promised her.

"Words," she said, smiling back a little. "Always your big words."

But she saw her mother then, above them, and she stood up. On the stony beach at the end of the island of their grief, the men were guiding the immense voyageur canoes in between rocks with great gentleness.

Perhaps Michel was one of those paddlers. She didn't look, and did not tell Broadface that the black Mohawk's eyes tracked her everywhere; why should she, that was Broadface's concern. Nor did she tell him about Boy English, who at the lake where the voyageurs had wanted to kill These English had stared at her, face and mouth fallen open as if he would eat her. She had thought then she should empty the ice bucket over his head to warn him away, but if she did, she would have to bend over to fill it again, and she remembered Broadface first catching her from behind when she was bent down like that, face to the water. He had clamped her doubled in his massive arms, her skirt already thrown up behind her before she knew he was there, and her trousers ripped down, and in an instant he had thrust himself so savagely into her that she lost every awareness except scream and a sharp, cutting agony that sliced, circled through her like a knife stabbing past any intimation of pleasure; jerking ripples, her bucket by then sunk in the lake. She could not throw him off. Held there, she had to endure whatever his body invented on the round, brutal rocks, her face open, she saw when the ripples faded, as if the black scream of pain and rage she was swallowing and swallowing would suck dry the entire lake.

But even as this slashed across her mind when Boy English stared, and beside her Greywing heaved her bucket out of the water, she knew she need not bother bending down twice for him. He was brave enough, she had seen that when they faced the voyageurs, but like every one of them this little Boy English walked across the tundra or sat in a giant canoe with his head so high, as if his stubby nose was all that had ever been there ahead of him; he would be impaled or dead before he ever knew what had always been following him, here in their country.

Hopefully that would happen before These English burned everything, or killed it, they and all their men ate so much. They fed three men just to carry the barrels of gunpowder they thought they needed to kill caribou, though the animals themselves would have given them all the sinews they could need to snare them if they had been treated properly.

"You're just a woman," Keskarrah says, watching Greenstockings touch the salve Richard Sun has given him to Birdseye's face. "And you know you are right about that."

"Just a woman," Birdseye repeats softly.

Keskarrah refuses her invitation to debate. "Every woman knows what she knows. I agree, I don't understand how we'll be able to live in our world with These English. They have such enormous canoes, they drag so much stuff along we can't make enough sounds to name it all, and there aren't enough human beings to carry it across the world if they have to walk — not even stealing every dog from our enemies would be enough. Nothing stays the way it is, everything changes when they come, and yet they mark it down as if it will always be the same and they can use it. We've known that long ridge across the river all our lives, and it refuses to stay the same the second day they're here. It burns itself black. But they don't see that."

Birdseye says nothing; her eyes are closed.

"Or any lake or river," Keskarrah continues, peering intently at the sheen of yellow salve. "They're always making marks, marks on paper that any drop of water can destroy. As if they had no memory."

Greenstockings knows she need not answer; her father is trying to think something through with talk, but she doubts if Birdseye under her fingertips is hearing that talk to help him.

"They always have to hold something in their hands, something to make marks on, or to look at things or through unknowable instruments. They aim their eyes across every lake and river with instruments that the sun distorts first, and then draw something of it onto paper, with names that mostly mean nothing. As if a lake or river is ever the same twice! When you travel and live with a river or lake, or hill, it can remain mostly like it seems, but when you look at it with your dreaming eye, you know it is never what it seemed to be when you were first awake to it. Again and again Thick English talks about the Soul Everywhere, but he himself never looks for the sun. He and his men always stare at it through something else, and I think the sun uses their instruments to blind them. To make them think living things are always the same."

He has been watching Greenstockings' fingers very carefully. "That spot," he says, pointing to a mark neither of them has seen on Birdseye's face before. She nudges the salve to find it.

Slowly he continues: "Before you were born I dreamed you'd be a woman, and that men would fight like wolves to have you — as they have. And there you were, a small bloody body not wanting to come out between your mother's legs. Where I had already been quite often." He laughs at both those happy memories, scratching himself easily. "Always wanting to be there between her legs, I did, and sometimes daring to be bloody too!"

Greenstockings stares at him. "Bloody? When a woman…?"

Keskarrah laughs even harder at the taboo he and Birdseye have found they could defy. "A man and a woman can do anything, blood or not, whenever they want to, if they're strong enough together."

Birdseye returns with a grimace, suddenly answering him earlier: "For men, women are *just* places to go, go in and go out," she says to Greenstockings, tilting her head into the firelight. The salve is smoothed like fingers along the raw, gnarled edges of her face. "That's all *just men* dream about, all the time."

Keskarrah laughs a little more, but soothingly. "I wasn't talking like that, I didn't say 'just' that way to you, you know that," he insists. Despite the ugly salve, which appears as if it will be smeared on Birdseye's beautiful skin for ever, Greenstockings has to chuckle; she has heard her parents debate so often. Keskarrah continues, "Women just come out of there, but a father is always first inside a mother, children understand that. And men of course like to go back in, as often as they can, and women like them to do it because they want it and without that long wanting nothing would be alive — women are the place of living and men want to be there too, then they are both truly alive. I think These English are human, but they are...different. As if they could travel all their lives without needing women to live."

"They don't live without women," Greenstockings says.

"How do you know?" Keskarrah asks.

She turns aside; she cannot explain to him yet what she has seen in Boy English's eyes. And thought about. She says, "They just take women anywhere they travel."

"How can they know there will be some?" Keskarrah persists. "They know nothing otherwise. If a Person isn't with them as they live and travel, they see nothing until it burns up in front of them. I've never even seen them look back to find out what anyone can see is already following them."

"Maybe," Birdseye says slowly, "maybe...."

She stops, and for an instant Greenstockings looks away from the dreadful wound whose very edge she will have to touch now, every day. She does not like the salve. She wasn't afraid when Richard Sun showed her how to spread it carefully, but she did not think of his name then, nor did she realize that looking so closely at her mother's skin every day would gradually make her see skin everywhere. And so much sickness. Growing on so many faces where she has never seen it before. When Birdseye first told her the salve wiped away the pain of the Eater, o good, so good! she was ecstatic, but it seems to her now that her mother has already become slower, weaker. That the skin she rubs is, though shining, nevertheless harder and somehow not as alive. Once she tried to ask Birdseye whether she could again fight the Eater only with pain, as she did before, but tears, like a child's, gathered in her mother's eyes and Keskarrah said roughly,

"Do what Richard Sun says."

As if he too wanted to see nothing — at least of this. As if that bit of White they are given every day for her fingertips to spread might not be as lethal for People as instruments and dreamlessness.

"What?" Keskarrah bends to Birdseye now. "Maybe what?"

"Maybe they don't need to dream. Maybe through those instruments the sun lets them see how the world is. For them always there, always the same."

Keskarrah stares at her, dumbfounded. He has never considered that the sun through glass might not deceive Whites; never imagined that something they could make and drag into the world he has always lived, travelling it into existence, might make that world more fixed than his own awareness could recognize. Greenstockings glances up and sees the possibilities of such an apprehension, with something like fear, gather in her father's eyes. Something far worse than one person's Eater.

But then, in their looking together, they are distracted by Birdseye's face. The lower bulb of her nose is no longer there.

Greenstockings remembers nuzzling her own small nose into that soft corner, and her mother's warm breath, laughter, her mother's long stroke down her knobby back with one hand while keeping her head rigid, pushing until their shared faces washed warmth over them both. Keskarrah holds the tiny box with the salve; if he does not believe in the power of These English, why does he go every day to Richard Sun for another portion, and lean so close, watching with the intensity of a touch, while she dips her finger into it and draws it around the raw edge of what is now only memory for them both? But, she realizes suddenly, what she is doing is different from the memory of lying against Birdseye's back under the furs of the animals and feeling, magnified through her own small body, her parents holding each other through a winter night when they were all the furry animals sleeping, dreaming curled together skin to skin, like seeds hidden in the long winter night, and waking into the dim morning still woven into that warmth, that soft, tensile voluptitude.

No, it seems to her now she had no body then: she was a skin of happiness folded into exquisite awareness within sleep. And the men whom she has since accepted, none, not even Broadface — not yet — has ever again helped her remember such anticipation.

Ah no, she thinks sadly, her fingers letting Birdseye know that the salve has all been placed, never again known that. As if she had already lived everything in her childhood, before she knew she was alive; and would never be more so. Her fingers at her mother's face move through the fearful backwards gap in memory. If she could feel that as an unthinking child, surely it must still be, somewhere. So, how can she think of…nothing?

But there it is. Moving into her mother; there, under her fingertips.

"Yes. Yes." Keskarrah is wrapping the tiny box in leather and hiding it in his clothes. "Tomorrow Richard Sun will give me more."

Greenstockings shudders. Her father does not seem to understand what may be the truth of that grand deceiver, the sun, not even when he says that English name. He says their families will stay here, refusing to travel with the People as they follow the caribou: theirs is now the only lodge left where These English have rooted themselves immovably on the esker above the river. And despite her gathering weakness, Birdseye still works endlessly, scraping hides, cutting the meat the hunters bring for them and These English when they have it. But Greywing is almost as fast as she at the hides, and once Greenstockings had to work streaks of fat that Birdseye seemed not to notice out of a skin before it turned hard as wood in the cold. Keskarrah refuses to hunt more than one day at a time, or dream animal dreams, but finally he has assented to Bigfoot's pleading and gone downriver along Roundrock Lake, where the other People have gone, to show them exactly where they must build the necessary pounds, exactly where he has seen the caribou trail down into their crossings. Pounds and their snares are essential now: once the lake is frozen strong enough, the animals, alert to the faintest sound or motion, will flee onto the snow-drifted ice where they can outrun any wolf, and usually not even the most skilful hunter can crawl close enough to kill them with a gun. For several days Keskarrah has gone; nevertheless he will not move their lodge with the other People to Roundrock. He returns to Fort Enterprise in darkness every evening, sometimes with a stiff hide or meat, so that every morning he can bring new salve from Richard Sun to Birdseye.

The river is still open at the caribou crossings, he tells them, but the People have not yet completed all the snaring pounds, though the lake is already skimmed with deceptive ice and the wind whips snow flurries over the eskers, trying to level the moss depressions. Strong ice, snow and snowshoes: that is the necessary sequence of travel in the lengthening darkness, and so it is not Birdseye but Greenstockings who is webbing the snow-shoe frames Keskarrah has bent out of thin steamed birch the evening Robert Hood appears, with his paper and many little pencils.

Birdseye tugs the leather down over her face. "He should not do that," she says. "No."

"I would like to draw her picture…at her woman's work. Making snowshoes," Robert Hood says in English. Very quietly, as he has learned to speak in this unimaginable land where the few sounds made by trees or rocks or water, or the occasional animal or human, vanish into silence like a snowflake touching into the swell of an ocean. He points at the young woman, gestures a fluid shape lightly in the air with his hand.

Greenstockings likes his hand, so long-boned and pale, so quick that the pencil it holds between two powerful fingertips sighs grey lines out of the bending paper. A curve of her knee, her leg, appears.

"It's too dangerous," Birdseye says.

"Why does he do that?" Keskarrah frowns, worried as well. "He can look at you, he can see you different every day, why fix you on his paper once?"

Greenstockings laughs a little. "Maybe he has no memory."

Birdseye murmurs, "Snow Man."

Greenstockings studies this man carefully for that story, and she cannot believe her mother: he is pale enough, yes, but he came to them from the south, not the north, and so how can he have brought an everlasting winter with him? And he is so thin, so stretched and gaunt, so obviously helpless, it is impossible that he have any woman or children waiting for him in the north, to whom he can be tricked into returning. She chuckles tugging the babiche tight, and holds that: would good, rich food make him strong enough…to be interesting?

But Keskarrah does not notice her; he continues to follow his inevitable man's thought: "Is he ready to fight for you?" he asks the air above her. "When a knife opens him and his guts steam on the snow, These English will be so enraged all of them will have to be killed."

"I…she is the most…beautiful woman I've ever seen…I.…"

Even very softly, Robert Hood can only say this because neither he nor they understand a single sound either can utter. He does not consider what they can obviously see; it is enough for him that the meanings of their two incomprehensible languages pass each other unscathed in the close warmth of these hide walls, their mourning slashes folded over and sewn tight against any draft, and vanish outwards into the fierce darkness before they can reach the cold mud-smeared logs of the officers' quarters, where Lieutenant Franklin and Doctor Richardson — and Midshipman Back, of course — edge closer to the fire in the centre mess and write down every English word they can think of in their journals, vanish long before they can reach the smaller house where Ordinary Seaman John Hepburn must live crowded with the twenty voyageurs and their three wives, whose various languages he cannot understand either. Years of latitudes and distance, of darkness, of cold and the absolute secret constructs of language: Robert Hood knows he has fallen into freedom. Unfathomably.

"I…if I…could touch her, there is only a…tongue, licking."

An ineffable word. And he can only repeat it: "Licking, licking."

With her bone needle Greenstockings threads the babiche through holes burned in the birch frame, tying each intricate intersection in a pattern of exact size and tension. Keskarrah's life (and therefore all of theirs) depends on how swift as a bird he can run over the valley snows where the shovel-footed caribou, whose hide threaded in her hands makes such running possible, themselves sometimes flounder and die. She too loves to run, carried by snowshoes, when winter at last smooths the hummocked, rotting muskeg and rocks and brush of ridge and valley into hard, undulating whiteness, the snowshoes, oooo, she weaves herself into a giant, winged raven lifting away, rising over island and rapids to be held on delicate eddies of curling air, spiralling, soaring to hang motionless as ash over the conical lodges of the People piled over with spruce boughs and snow, soaring on tip-lifted wings over the stumps of trees that defied the wind for centuries and are now burned or smashed down into walls for the three square English houses covered with frozen mud and hammered down like chips on the crest of the esker that opens northward into silence where the wind burrows at moss, rubs for ever over stone and lichen, whispers granular snow into rock. There, when she folds and leans down into the shelter of such rock, the sky will harden her face also, the light search through the wrinkles of her head, and she will hear the ice growing out of the ground, freezing up into her feet, branching itself through her body and out into her arms and head and ears until it bristles beyond the tips of her fingers and the innumerable points of her hair: everywhere. She cannot believe this thin, bony English can exist here: if she lets him love her, she will kill him.

But she senses Birdseye murmuring, like chant buried in her throat beyond leather, "...Snow Man, Snow Man, white as snow man...why have you come?...what follows you?...nothing but snow, nothing but woe man...."

And if Birdseye insists on seeing him as snow, why shouldn't Greenstockings love him? Hold him within herself while she can, since he is either gone or dead already? And if her mother, or father — who is staring at him now as if he were a barely discernible spoor that might lead somewhere — if either of them starts dreaming the brief footprints of what life he has left, he will turn stiff as wood. Hood's sky-blue eyes are fixed on her. He is certainly alive at this moment, bent towards her; she could thread him like this snowshoe.

Someone outside clears his throat, the lodge opening lifts and Twospeaker stoops in. Birdseye turns away instantly — she will never say a word anyone tries to translate — but Keskarrah nods happily, as if he now knows everything when an instant before he recognized only doubtful questions. He even chuckles a greeting, and Robert Hood, immediately silenced by the languages that have entered, rises and bows to Keskarrah as if he were in court. Then, formally, he requests that he may be permitted to draw a portrait of his extraordinarily beautiful daughter. And St. Germain translates.

Slowly Keskarrah rises also, shifts the huge grizzly hide tight around his shoulders and folds his arms over his chest. Under their sleeping-robes Greywing stirs, awakened by new voices. Greenstockings hears her mother murmuring again, but she is somewhere in a mist; as if the sounds being made about her are smoke and her father, planting himself like an ancient tree swaying above her, separating and merging with what may be Hood, or may be a story spirit or her endless longing. Men standing over her — and she realizes again that her father is first of all and always a man — with his eagle-beaked face pushing into anything he pleases, as men do — men always above her — will there ever be a time when their assumption over her ends, even if she slits lengthwise or crosswise every single one of their throats or their cocks? Hood's momentary seduction of her tenderness infuriates her, as Twospeaker crystallizes his pale language like familiar ice inside her ear. And her father's words:

"I will stand guard beside her so that, when the big boss across the stinking water sees her picture, he won't try to send for her."

Twospeaker laughs as he translates, but Robert Hood responds very seriously; the translator stops laughing, speaks so that his tone will not betray him.

"He says the father across the water is old, so old he never leaves his bed. But I'll tell you more, Hep-burn has told me that he's far too old and crazy, so crazy he can't wipe his own shit off his ass."

Keskarrah's eagle face does not twitch. "I think," he says, "an old White would like to have a beautiful young woman do that too, but I could be wrong. Tell him our pictures have to be made together, because if there is a beautiful daughter, a strong mother must stand beside her, and if that's impossible, it must be the father, who has already been inside the mother first."

Greenstockings listens intently to the sounds Twospeaker makes: snow squeaking under feet in the long darkness. She ties the soft babiche intersections of the snowshoe design with concentrated care: whoever crosses the brief memory these shoes will leave on snow will recognize her, and recognize her father who bent the wood, and recognize the caribou, and the birch tree, because all together in the great travelling world they have made a new creature, one winged to walk on snow, on snow where caribou are the core of all life like the moss and lichen they eat, and wolves and humans and ravens eat caribou, and moss and birch and lichen will drink every drop of their dropping blood.

When she looks up, Twospeaker is gone.

Keskarrah's burly shape under the bearskin has emerged in profile quicker than he himself ever found a line map in the dust. Robert Hood is not looking at Greenstockings yet, nor has he noticed Greywing sitting up naked among the furs, staring. Keskarrah talks, talks, as if it were his voice that is drawing his outline from the white paper.

"The lake you named 'Winter' is really a fish with its head to the east and its tail whipping up the froth of rapids just below us, the place you've tried to draw so often already. This great lake fish is trying to swim away east, as fish generally do, against the current. You can see that clearly by walking around the lake: its strong lower fin is the waterfall half-way along the north shore that in winter makes the river water climb even higher into the sky. I have seen that this lake is a fish many times walking around it, both when the lake pretends to be land but is really ice, and when it's water and cannot be walked on. Certain People can also recognize the fish from our small canoes, though it may be impossible from your big ones. That's why the last trees here grow so large: that giant fish tries to swim east, but these giant trees hold it back, no matter how hard it swims, it can't move. Of course all the trees along the south shore are burned now, gone, but I still don't think the fish can leave this winter — unless too many more trees are cut down for firewood, and if you pile up more houses, here where its tail keeps thrashing."

"Now these snowshoes she is making," Keskarrah adds thoughtfully, "they could carry you around it, when they are completely sewn. Then you might be able to see. If you drew the lake as it is you would have to see the fish, and you could name it correctly. That is, if you wanted to."

Robert Hood hears the deep rumble of the old man's voice like wind in night spruce, like aurora walking over sky. He has turned to Greenstockings, is trying to find her shape before he attempts details, and has been led astray by her exact edge, which must be…is surely, yes, under the obscuring leather and small cloths, and he wants his pencil to imagine it, yes, his fingers must imagine her shape since he cannot yet imagine physically uncovering her and actually seeing skin. How will he draw anything of her correctly if he cannot….

"O-o-o-o," he sings to himself out loud, Keskarrah's bass sustaining him like a grand organ, "you are such a woman, o-o-o-o-oh, any sea captain would forget his cabin boys and the palm trees of Africa and sail through the French and Dutch navies together to see you seated with your legs aslant, your strong fingers tying leather so hard and clean over and through and into, and your hands, God to lift that leather and see all of you, draw your woman's shape, draw it exact as feeling your skin, touching you, my fingers along every bend of…."

And he is so suddenly, vividly happy to hear himself say all this aloud while he draws. After all, he is performing the assigned duty for which he was selected from so many applicants and appointed to this expedition — knowing no one will ever know he thought this, leave alone said aloud any English word into this north air. He peers at his hand: it moves, draws this stunning woman's line from his fingertips over and over again; he can fondle her until he has found her body's exact turn, until he knows it so indelibly that when he slashes the snowshoe across her lap it seems he has hurled himself, dived across her lap stretched out and pointed, become the long, fish-like shape he aches with her to be. Thrashing.

Greenstockings has no need to look up again. She can easily hear the gathering together of Hood's body, can smell it thicken into memory while her father stands erect, speaking over the fire to protect her. Birdseye is bent beside it, hands motionless, dreaming perhaps, and Greywing pretends sleep again under the robes while she listens to this old and always new sacred story. Circled inside the lodge, Greenstockings believes Hood — who may be Snow Man, may be simply white bone — may be able to understand her fingers and her father, even if he comprehends no words and seems to be humming his own, may understand a little since he is so desperately trying to draw her, once, this instant before she is different again. But for Keskarrah speaking with such great care, she would laugh at the futility of that repeating pencil.

"The world is the way it is because it started that way," Keskarrah speaks in the ceremony of his standing. "That was when Sky came to Earth and they lay together. Their joy began then, and all day they lay together and when they separated in the evening the ground appeared, because ground is nothing more nor less than their happiness together, born between them with rocks and sand and water running. On the second day their happiness grew, and moss and little trees appeared, and fish in the water. On the third day birds began to fly across the sky and the caribou ran along the tops of the hills, waiting for their antlers to grow so they could stare at each other, and on the fourth they were so happy that everything else burst out, even that miserable mosquito, and man too, leaping around on his two legs to get away from the woman on four legs, which is bear. That was when the great bear caught him anyway and dragged him to her den so she and her cubs could lick and suck all the six star points of him before they had him for a meal, which was the only way left for him to help them. But he ran away from her to begin the great river, and with it the Everlasting Ice. That, however, is another story."

Greenstockings' hands fall motionless on the wet, knotted thongs; she has forgotten the brilliant sky eyes peering at her in the changing firelight because Hood's sound plays a skipping harmony over her father's chant, carrying her even farther into the birth of humanity:

"This story is not about eating each other, no. It is about woman and man lying together, for ever if they could so they will never be separate, but at least all day long every day, like bears who grow into each other for three days or maybe four, forgetting to eat or sleep, their bodies one, and you can touch them wherever you wish and they will lick you tenderly because they want no more than what they already have, and when they lick you they are doing that to each other and themselves. But unfortunately — "

And at this point in the story Keskarrah's tone always shifts. It does so now, with such emphasis that Robert Hood looks up at him, uncomprehending but alarmed, the pencil stopping in his hand.

"Unfortunately, man does not have an endless bone like a bear; though woman could happily hold him inside her for ever, something got mixed up for the man, somewhere, and he can't. But in that first summer when Sky and Earth lay together, there was no human woman yet, and when man escaped from the great bear he had only a shelter of brush to run to. He was alone, and lonely; he had only berries and roots and leaves to eat and when winter came he grew desperately hungry. He sank deep in the snow as he watched rabbits and caribou and ptarmigan travel so lightly on it that finally he dreamed his feet were much bigger, and he was running over snow everywhere as easily as the animals, as swiftly as wind smoothing it, whispering among birch. So at last he turned to the trees, he peeled the white, thin birch and bent them into large hoops. He stepped inside them, and he knew his feet were in the right place — but he didn't know what to do with the centre; there was no woman to see the strings of babiche possible in animal leather and so weave the webbing to hold his feet inside the wooden frames he had made.

"The bent birch lay there, empty, and every day he travelled, hunting. But in deep snow every animal ran easily from him; every day he returned with nothing, and always hungrier. Then one day he heard a noise in his shelter, so he ran as fast as he could and a ptarmigan flew out of the opening at the top before he could get inside. The next day he hunted until dark, and then from a distance he saw smoke rising from his shelter. He rushed there and the beautiful ptarmigan flew out again, but inside he saw a fire burning and his snowshoe frames drying beside it, their sad emptiness half woven over with babiche.

"'The ptarmigan has done this,' he said, amazed as the fire warmed him.

"So next morning before leaving he covered the roof opening and did not go far; he returned early, breathing as quietly as he could, sinking deep in the snow. And there he surprised the ptarmigan starting the fire again in his lonely shelter, the snowshoes lying almost complete with babiche webbing. The bird darted around, tried to fly out but could find no way to escape, and when he caught it between his hands it turned into what he had often dreamed: someone like himself but o so different!

"Woman, yes, who made everything beautiful happen, fire to cook meat and tanned hides for clothing and lying together hot as bears and children for ever, because she alone could fill the frames he had dreamed and bent. She changed when he held her, but her holding changed him as well: frame and woven centre, when she fastened the snowshoes to his feet he became a bird, flying over the soft, deep snow everywhere in the beautiful world, and she prepared the animals he captured, and they ate together, and lived. Long ago my mother told me this story of beginning," sings old Keskarrah. "O my mother, long ago my mother," he sings.

"'Greensleeves was all my joy,'" sings Robert Hood in echo, stippling the fur on Greenstockings' arm, her white-fringed deerskin he has captured,

> Greensleeves was my delight,
> Greensleeves was my heart of gold,
> And who but my Lady…?

And his sudden boyish soprano joins another melody in the round lodge where the smoke frays upwards into darkness. It is Birdseye, he realizes. Like a mound of the earth itself keening in ineffable sorrow. Beside her Greywing's head emerges from under fur, black eyes staring at him.

And then he notices Greenstockings' face, and Keskarrah stooped out of his rhetoric — both crumpling as he looks from one to the other. And though he cannot understand a word, their wide eyes speak a gathering horror.

"The Everlasting Ice holds him," keens Birdseye, heart broken. "It will never give him up, the Everlasting Ice."

DOCTOR JOHN RICHARDSON

Thursday September 7th 1820   Fort Enterprise

A heavy snowstorm prevented us from observing the eclipse. Men employed in constructing Fort Enterprise, the name given to our rising buildings. Women splicing and drying meat.

Saturday September 9th 1820   Coppermine Journey

Lieutenant Franklin and I started this morning on a pedestrian excursion to the Coppermine River, under the guidance of an old Indian named Keskarrah, and accompanied by John Hepburn and Samandré, who carried our blankets, cooking utensils, hatchets and a small supply of dried meat. By noon we reached a remarkable hill named by the Yellowknives Agnaatheth, or Dogrib Rock. In the course of the afternoon Keskarrah killed a reindeer and loaded himself with its head and skin. The frozen ground and our small quantity of bedclothes induced us to sleep without undressing, but old Keskarrah stripped himself to the skin, and having toasted his body for a short time over the embers of the fire, he crept under his deerskin and rags previously spread out as smoothly as possible, and coiling himself up in a circular form, fell asleep instantly.

Friday October 6th 1820   Fort Enterprise

Today, the officers' house being completed, we struck the tents and took up our abode in it. It is a log building fifty feet by twenty-four, the walls and roof are plastered with clay, the floors laid with planks rudely squared by the hatchet and the windows closed with parchment of reindeer skin. The clay froze as it was daubed on, and has since cracked in such a manner that the wind rushes in from every quarter. Nevertheless with the aid of warm clothing, and good fires, we expect to get comfortably over the winter.

Last night a thin film of ice formed across the river. The lake is now firmly frozen over, the reindeer wander out on it.

5

SEAMAN
JOHN HEPBURN

~

I, John Hepburn, ordinary seaman born in 1789 in Newburn, Northumberland, and lately from the Orkney Islands, speak as truthfully as I do recall of events that took place October, 1820, at Fort Enterprise, which we built on the hill above the rapids draining Winter Lake, which lies southwest by south of Obstruction Rapids on the Coppermine River in those lands far west of Hudson Bay, during the land Expedition to the shores of the Polar Sea under the command of Lieutenant John Franklin, Royal Navy.

I am a blunt seaman, but I trust my language is hereby properly composed and written for your Lordships' consideration. In giving this confidential account of the events at Fort Enterprise, it may seem strange that I do not also tell of what took place there a year later (for myself I would never call two such log buildings, and a small storage shed, a fort), or what happened on the horrid trek we had in trying to return to it after our summer exploration, horrid particularly when we succeeded after nine days in crossing the double rapids on the Coppermine. But that is not for me in my station to speak of. The proper officers have made their depositions long ago, and we few others who survived need only pray that God will give those who did not a sound and peaceful rest.

Though as seaman I served all the officers of the Expedition, I of course never quartered with them. For the first sixteen months, and even during the difficult time when the Orkneymen at Fort Chipewyan, July, 1820, refused to accompany the Expedition farther for reasons they anticipated of danger (which later proved correct), I knew nothing of bad blood between Mr. Back and Mr. Hood.

Nor suspected it, though I served both. Until October, 1820, I verify that I knew they had since our departure from England on May 23, 1819, worked companionably together. In fact, the last week of August, 1820, Lieutenant Franklin dispatched the two with a single guide and canoe to ascertain the distance and size of the Coppermine River.

That week of August was when the Indians refused to guide us farther (as it proved, wisely, for in early September winter was fully begun) and we began to build Fort Enterprise in the post-and-beam fashion of Canadian voyageurs, in whose company I slept. I would have preferred to sleep by myself, or with a companionable woman or even a dog at my feet, either one of which warms you wonderfully. But Lieutenant Franklin would allow none of that, which the traders of the country do as a 150-year custom. He performed matins strictly every evening, and divine service every Sabbath wherever we might be. At Winter Lake he attempted to use the occasion of the partial eclipse of the sun (foretold in his calendar) to prove again the superiority of Christian knowledge, and to again impress the Yellowknives with the necessity of minding the Supreme Being, who orders the operations of nature, and therefore of paying strict attention to their moral duties by obedience to His will as revealed to us. By which he meant providing provision for us. But clouds obscuring the possible eclipse all day, the desired effect was not achieved.

Moreover, the interpreter St. Germain told me that the old man, Keskarrah, who had an extraordinary influence on the band, had expressed grave doubt regarding the event. If Lieutenant Franklin could foresee the passing darkness of the sun, how was it he did not understand the approach of winter? Winter was now so much more powerful than any daily sun, he said, it was obvious the sun would very quickly be forced below the earth into total darkness. I urged St. Germain to relay this conversation to the officers, but I don't believe he did, and it was not for me to report servant talk. And the sun did lie lower and lower on the horizon until it disappeared altogether and we lived in an endless darkness for over a month (by the chronometer), relieved only by stars and moon and the aurora, or firelight. I think foretelling an eclipse is not as impressive in arctic regions as in the tropics, where day and night alternate most regularly.

Though I slept in separate quarters with the voyageurs (three of whom had their women with them for household service — and one so large she might have warmed several of us had we been allowed near her, but her husband would have none of that), any dissension between the four officers could not be kept long from me. Nevertheless, Mr. Back and Mr. Hood were so secretive that it was only on our removal from the tents into log quarters that I noticed problems. The first hint was that Lieutenant Franklin, very oddly, ordered me to place Mr. Back's bedding and kit in his own (the larger) bedroom and Mr. Hood's with Doctor Richardson in the smaller. That happened between September 30, when sleet drove the mud off the roof of the officers' quarters, despite its already being frozen hard, and October 7, when the lakes sealed over for the winter, and the repaired roof also. The young officers, who had shared one tent, now had the common mess between them, and a senior officer each to note their nightly perambulations, if any.

At first I thought it was their drawing. Since sailing from Stromness, June 16, 1819, I had noted their (I thought then friendly) rivalry, Back being more adept at landscapes, while Hood caught the grace and countenance of human figures, even animals, better. In fact, they returned from their Coppermine River journey with a co-operative sketch, where Back drew the landscape around Dogrib Rock for background and Hood an excellent white wolf turning to snarl in the foreground. (The picture is in Sir John's first book.) But their rivalry had nothing to do with their Expedition duties or possible promotion. It was the usual matter of white men in primitive lands: a woman of the country.

As Sir John writes in his book, the young woman was certainly the beauty of her tribe, and that not only for a sailor long at sea. Though the Yellowknives often treat their women with great kindness, generally they hold them in the same low estimation as the neighbouring Chipewyans (south) or Dogribs (west), to the point of considering them a kind of property that the stronger may tear from the weaker by threat or fight or killing, though the latter is seldom necessary. The women appear unconcerned by such conflicts, since the winner can usually provide better for them and their young offspring. The loser slinks about until he finds a husband weaker than himself to assault and rob of his wife or, failing that, disembowels a dog and persuades his friends to raid a distant Dogrib camp where he may more easily (Dogribs are much milder people than Yellowknives) steal another woman, hopefully a good worker and possible son-bearer. Such theft and marriage is, I was told, common, for they believe it impossible for a man to live without a wife in their country (and after three winters there I believe them), and the more powerful have two, or three. The Yellowknife Matonabbee, who guided Samuel Hearne to the Coppermine River fifty years before us, is reported to have had nine wives, though perhaps not all at once. The number depends on the hunter's ability to provide for and defend them, and when necessary several men will also share one wife, if no mature woman is available to be stolen and they agree not to fight over her.

Sir John noted in his book the endless hospitality we received from the Cree Indians of the Hudson Bay forests. I would say the Yellowknives of the far north were even more considerate and humane, especially in our great distress later where their delicacy and care cannot be overstated. During the winter we lived with them I saw many examples of tender attachment between couples, particularly between the old map-drawer and his wife, whose ulcerated face Doctor Richardson treated at that time. I call them old because their land ages people very rapidly; they were at most forty-five, since their two daughters who lived with them were, so St. Germain told me, twelve and fifteen years old. The younger would, within the year, be married if someone could persuade Keskarrah (who was feared for his powers) to surrender her.

But it was the older daughter who set Midshipman Back and Hood against each other, and it became the greater problem because of both her shaman father and her husband. For she was already married as the Yellowknives see "marriage"; that is, she had already lived with two men, and the third who had her when we arrived was, excepting only St. Germain, our best hunter, a muscled, handsome specimen of young Indian who could easily have maintained two wives if he had not wanted one so difficult to keep as Keskarrah's daughter. Not only was she strong and skilled in woman's work, but she also had an independence of mind amazing in a female. Upon the growing illness of her mother, she simply left Broadface and returned to her father's lodge, where he continued to visit her when not hunting. She was not yet sixteen years old, but already a full, mature beauty, the belle of her tribe. Our name for her was Greenstockings.

I asked St. Germain: "A woman can simply walk out of her husband's lodge?"

St. Germain shrugged. "Man has strong arms, woman strong head, she can."

When I first realized a woman was in the case, I thought it was the girl, her younger sister. She had that perfect, unused copper skin and enormous black eyes that Indian females display on the verge of womanhood, before the burdens they carry and the endless labour of their lives destroy them into wrinkles and scars. Worn faces are all one usually sees in that cold country, their sagging shapes covered by layers of worn hide, but we all saw the girl as good as naked on an island in Winter Lake when the Yellowknives bellowed their grief over the death of two hunters by destroying all their property, including their clothing. (Such is their custom of mourning, and the harshness of the country provides enough tragedy to keep them more than destitute.) No slender beauty could affect Lieutenant Franklin, who is beyond any possible reproach in his behaviour towards women, his thoughts concerned with nothing but the performance of his Christian duty and service to His Majesty's Government. The same is true of Doctor Richardson. In four years I never saw him except he had his medical kit or notebook in his hand. If he knew the female species existed, he gave little indication of it, even when he examined them for medical purposes, as he was sometimes required. Some women came to him openly suckling infants, or bared their most privy parts seemingly without shame. If it were not for the cold, I suppose Yellowknives would wear no more clothing than the inhabitants of Fiji.

You require my account as my duty, which I perform gladly, and will express here in plain honest confidence to your Lordships what I saw that winter, 1820–21. I have spoken to no one of this, not to Lieutenant Franklin, who might have asked it of me but did not, nor to Doctor Richardson, though in October, 1821, we spent those hard days alone together on the barrens and I was finally able to carry him on my back, back into Fort Enterprise. And I didn't speak of this to St. Germain either, though in that winter he became almost a friend, explaining frankly much about the Yellowknives and their land that would otherwise have remained a mystery to me. He was a mixed-blood, very shrewd and observant, and it is unfortunate he cannot give his account of these matters, which cannot be spoken of without frankness, for which I pray your Lordships' pardon.

Perhaps if Mr. Back had seen the girl as closely as I did on the island, he would have left Greenstockings to Mr. Hood. The girl was untouched, sleek as a weasel, with that quicksilver shift of leg and buttock that penetrates any man's loins. She was tiny and perfectly shaped, I thought ideal for Mr. Back. The sight of him dancing with the hefty métisses of Cumberland House and Fort Chipewyan we men always found comical, since they were half a foot taller than he and outweighed him by three or four stone. In their arms he appeared more to be climbing aboard than dancing with them, but he was extraordinarily strong and of such Napoleonic disposition (in five years as a French prisoner I believe he swallowed their Great Nation delusions as well as their language) that he considered any female taller than himself (every one over the age of twelve) a Russia to be assailed, boarded and subdued.

I suggest that Mr. Back took so little notice of the girl and pursued Greenstockings (no Indian woman needs to be pursued; she is simply, if possible, taken) because Mr. Hood, gentle and tender-hearted, forced him into seeing her as a romance because he did, and Mr. Back had to prove he could play the wooing hero as easily as the male bravado more usual in the north. I believe Greenstockings would have accommodated both without compunction, though she might have found Mr. Hood more unusual, a tall, slender man with the pale face of a saint, but very strong — so physically and spiritually strong that his innocence, which would have been amazing in a priest, had for nine of his twenty-three years survived the dedicated debauchery of life at sea with the Royal Navy.

But neither of them had the smallest notion of how, in the manner of the country, they could gain Greenstockings' favour.

Very quickly Mr. Back attempted to overcome her apparent reluctance by force (I think the darkness in that land removes
much of the anticipation from slow, tender wooing), and she
responded in good Yellowknife fashion and slit his leg for him.
Mr. Hood — who in innocence had suspected nothing until
Mr. Back returned cursing with his trousers so strategically
parted — Mr. Hood instantly challenged Mr. Back to a duel for
the honour of the lady he thought his own.

Bless me — whose honour? The woman was beautiful, especially to young men who have laboured through the endless
bush and rocks and rivers and winters of Canada, but she remained a hide-covered Indian. Mr. Hood did not consider that
the "lady", who played with knives every day of her life, could
have parted Mr. Back quite differently if she had chosen, or
that confining herself to a long opening of near cloth rather
than flesh meant she considered this exchange an initial part of
a proper courtship where blood, when it flowed — as it probably would — would simply confirm conquest.

And a duel, your Lordships. If Mr. Hood was blind to understand his "lady", his own honour blinded him to the fact
that no matter what weapons they might agree upon except
pencils, Mr. Back would kill him.

Mr. Back could not believe his ears. Mr. Hood stood before
him, rigid in furious challenge. Finally he laughed disdainfully
and said he supposed Mr. Hood must then choose the weapons
also. Mr. Hood clicked his heels and saluted. What he intended that to mean I don't know, but it did underline the formality of his action, though by gentlemen's rules, since he had
issued the challenge, Mr. Back had the right to choose weapons. But Mr. Hood was too little worldly wise to know how

deeply Mr. Back had insulted him with his disdainful reply. He instantly declared,

"Pistols."

And then they each approached me, separately, to second them.

A fine situation indeed. The Royal Navy forbids duelling, especially between junior officers, so if they approached Lieutenant Franklin or Doctor Richardson they would be immediately ordered to stop. In either case, the Expedition itself was at stake: in such a small party, in a very difficult land, each officer must perform essential duties if we were to hope for any success. But both had lost their clear sense of duty, and so I, the servant, was the only Englishman left to decide: I must act as second to both, and also as referee in a fight to the death between English officers over an Indian woman — well! — if they had been Yellowknives, one of them would have recognized his fatal disadvantage and withdrawn.

My Lords, I am not bitter against the Expedition's officers, junior or senior. I beg you not to consider me a witness too biased to be believed concerning the sad events that took place at Fort Enterprise, October, 1820, or our even more desperate attempt to return there a year later. My life has been ordinary enough for a peasant: as a 16-year-old youth from a stony farm in Northumberland, I refused to descend into the black hell of the Tyneside mines, and so was seized and impressed into the Royal Navy by the King's Men one summer evening while on my way home from the market. My mother never knew what was become of me until I was five months at sea (though she feared little else) fighting Napoleon. But our ship was captured by an American privateer and I, with four other lads (all poor like myself — the officers were held for ransom, the war making excellent business for the Americans trading men with both sides — but where would my mother have found so much as a pound to ransom me?), we five without ransom were given over to a French trading vessal. The French captain, even more convinced of the stupidity of war than we, gave us free run of his ship. One week during a storm we helped save it from foundering by working before the mast beside his men, and so a few nights later, as he tacked close to Cornwall while sailing for St. Malo, he looked steadily starboard towards France while we lowered his smallest boat larboard into the running sea off Lizard Point. What became of the others I never knew; we rowed all night trying to fight through the surf, but were forced back by the terrible seas and after two or three days I was found by a fisherman, alone, washed up like kelp on the shingle of the outermost Scilly Island, not ten feet from the open Atlantic.

That poor fisherman's family nursed me, I returned to my mother on her lonely farm and was again apprehended by the press-gang (I had never been discharged and Napoleon was apparently more of a devil than ever). But I survived that too. Why? Why did I survive our trek from the Arctic Ocean to Fort Enterprise? I do not know, but I trust in God. And also the truth of my mother's teaching:

"Once they make you say, 'a', you'll have to say 'b' as well."

Thank God she could not imagine the Royal Navy's 'c' — or 'd', though on a clear day you can see the sea from the uplands surrounding her village. But it was that first polar Expedition with Lieutenant (now Sir) John Franklin and Doctor Richardson and Midshipman (now Commander) George Back and poor, saintly Hood (lost for ever), which took me to the end of the alphabet. In 1819 I committed myself to that Expedition, and stayed though others left and thereby saved themselves much suffering and probably their lives. By the grace of God I have a steady eye and strong body; I could find and shoot even the smallest ptarmigan on the tundra when the caribou or musk oxen that might have saved us were no longer there. I could still carry the heavy hide blankets when the voyageurs (who by reason of their great packs often broke through ice into frigid water and laboured and endured even more than I) were no longer able to walk, leave alone lift their normal burdens. Only once did I despair, while hunting, but that was not on the last trek, so there is no need for your Lordships to hear of it, after all these years.

This must be said: when, by the grace of God and St. Germain's incomprehensible skill in making a cockleshell no bigger than a hat out of willow twigs and the officers' oilskins, we were able finally to cross between the raging Obstruction Rapids one by one on a line, I was able to carry Hood for a short distance through snow across the tundra. I can still feel his weight, though weak as I was he weighed nothing then. No, it seemed not so much as an empty pack.

What else we did there, or had to do, it is not my place to report. But permit my age to tell you this: I prefer to collapse carrying a good man across snow than to firing massive guns at lads who, like myself, have been stolen from our birthplace and are as ignorant as I about the grand Empire purpose of our miserable deaths; or our mutilations, body and soul. Having suffered both, I prefer starvation to war.

True, the first days of starvation bring suffering hard to describe. A woman once told me of her pain at childbirth, but that has no similarity since the intensity of it is always filled with the great hope of a sudden, happy ending. The poor in Great Britain hunger continually, but the first days of *starvation* are, I remember, not so much a matter of body pain alone as of relentless pain being pushed beyond itself into a knowledge of *hollow*, of body eating itself from inside, a beast within ravaging beast, and your knowledge of existence grows thin to the point of shell. But after the first three days, as Doctor Richardson has explained so often in his lectures, the physical pain strangely ceases. You observe another person visibly dying with you, and are at peace. The decrees of the Almighty are what they are, your anxieties are gone. The biggest problem is slowness: you are ready for death so long before it finally arrives.

Then the grand purpose of our coming to this place, this Ultimate North, no longer matters. Unlike the smash of war, in the Arctic you have always been surrendered to quiet. And gradually you recognize approaching death as a stranger whose coming grows steadily darker out of the whiteness that drifts and moans around you, and you begin to feel cold. It is a cold so dreadful you know that the winters of the Arctic have taught you nothing until now, this shell laid in ice, and you reach for anything, a frozen shrub, a useless blanket, your own leg, a frost-broken axe, pull the bones of your friend against you, anything for a prickle of passing warmth. And you see his snow-burned, flaking skin against the skin of your own face, the brown blotches of scurvy, feel his shudders reach into a space beyond bone, his eyes search the distance beyond sky or skull — and you feel a great peace. You lie thoughtless at last like a heather sheep. You have been given the greatest mercy of all, that of the gentle beasts in their dying.

I remember such a time very well, when Robert Hood looked at his right hand, the hand of his drawing. Under a clump of willows in a hollow on the tundra somewhere between Obstruction Rapids and Winter Lake. I have seen death in war, but never that way. My Lords, the heroic picture of General Wolfe dying on the Plains of Abraham is a great lie. You know this, in battle men swing from triumphant ecstasy to weeping terror, they die curled around their ripped guts and splattered with their own shit or — after the guns have stopped — from torn limbs rotting slowly towards their hearts. All those nights that I tried to warm Mr. Hood, rolled in all our clothes in our two buffalo robes — of course he was also warming me, I was starving too, though my peasant body was failing more slowly than his, tough but delicate son of a clergyman — and he whispered exalted words to me. That too is possible, sometimes, when you are starving.

Some of us suffer but are spared; I suppose, to suffer other things. I hear Mr. Hood's voice still; it sounds dry as sheep sluffing again and again among the dry husks that will never fill their bellies. Because Mr. Hood did not die beautifully. Death did not carry him peacefully into eternity. No. Despite three years of faultless duty, courage, patience, finally starvation — no dignified death, no "proper" death, no.

You have that story in your reports from the officers. I corroborate what they say. Let them stand.

Our beloved Robert, or as he sometimes joked with me of his childhood name: "Little Robin" — Hood. Ever noble, never a robber of anything. Doctor Richardson and I laid his body out in the snow under small willows behind the tent on Sunday, October 20, 1821. Left it, as the Yellowknives do, for the animals.

Permit me: I think Mr. Hood understood better than any-one the magnetic declination of the compass, naval orders, the Book of Common Prayer (which he loved to read aloud), and how that beautiful land — so cruel no human being should ever live there, yet the Yellowknives do — could make a barbaric people so humane.

I did not know this on Sunday, October 15, 1820. Then I thought Mr. Hood was simply startled into silly chivalry by a pagan slut who, if he wanted to have her, he already owned the minute he looked up and saw she existed. Then I was dis-gusted, hearing him declare:

"Pistols!"

I did not think long about acting as second to both and also their referee: I agreed, and confidentially informed Doctor Richardson of the whole matter. After a start he merely mur-mured, "Ahh, yes...yes..." as if he had expected as much, and then directed me to load both pistols carefully with powder and wadding, but no ball.

So the next morning at dawn (nearly ten o'clock in that lati-tude) I gave them the signal and they both wheeled and fired. Mr. Back was quicker, though perhaps Mr. Hood hesitated when he saw the discharge and felt nothing strike him, nor even the whistle of a ball. But he stood his ground and fired at Mr. Back from the regulation ten strides away, who was rigid with astonishment at having missed. With of course the same results. I stepped forwards then and motioned them to ap-proach. Mr. Back could barely walk, but Mr. Hood strode for-wards, relieved and obviously satisfied. I took their smoking pistols from them; sweat beaded Mr. Back's forehead in the grey morning, but he looked at me from under his bushy brows with a certain comprehension. Fortunately, before I opened my mouth, Doctor Richardson declared behind me,

"Gentlemen, this charade will suffice. Or do you prefer I inform Lieutenant Franklin?"

I think Doctor Richardson did not then believe it was a matter of honour between them. I know I didn't.

Later that day Lieutenant Franklin informed us a party was needed to walk back to Fort Providence on Great Slave Lake for the mail, and to bring forwards to Fort Enterprise the firearms and powder that were to have arrived there with the summer brigade after our leaving. If these supplies were brought forwards now on sleds, the Expedition in canoes could move on to the Polar Sea as soon as the ice broke in spring. Mr. Back immediately volunteered to lead the party.

Mr. Back walked not only to Fort Providence, but, not finding our supplies there (due to the usual disasters caused by trading company rivalry), he continued over the lake to Moose-Deer Island House and finally to Fort Chipewyan. He returned to Fort Enterprise with supplies in March 1821, having travelled through intense cold for more than a thousand miles, and that in the dark on snowshoes. A brilliant achievement, though strange for a sailor; a prefiguring of his superhuman effort that would save some of our lives a year later.

The lakes and rivers remained frozen around Fort Enterprise for nine months. By June 4, 1821, Lieutenant Franklin decided to wait no longer and we began what was the most hazardous stage of our Arctic journey: to reach the Coppermine and paddle down that unknown river to the Polar Sea, then coast and map its shores by Canadian voyageur canoe. In such a land, locked under ice to the end of June, though the sun shone almost until midnight and rose again at two, where did we suppose we would find enough water for birchbark? Doctor Richardson left first with an advance party to carry supplies to the Coppermine River, over snow on sleds and snowshoes. We followed on June 14, each of our three canoes on a sled being dragged over ice by four men assisted by two dogs. The Yellowknives travelled with us in their light, easy fashion, and seemed satisfied. They had been destitute when winter came, but they said hunting had been good (though we had all been without meat several times, sometimes for over a fortnight), and throughout our stay at Winter Lake they had not lost a single life. Not even one of them, it seemed, had been sick.

The old mapmaker, Keskarrah, however, had not wintered well, nor his wife, who could barely walk under a small pack. The girl pulled their sled with a single dog, as Greenstockings did another. She was obviously with child. And though I never saw it, I have reason to believe Robert Hood was its father. He never saw the child either.

My Lords, this is the deposition you required. God save the King!

DOCTOR JOHN RICHARDSON

Wednesday October 18th 1820   Fort Enterprise

Mr. Back set out today for Fort Providence to make arrangements respecting supplies for next summer. We have at present upwards of 100 deer in store, and about 800 lbs of suet. Bigfoot and several men arrived at the house today and warned us that the reindeer have now retired farther south into the woods and that his people must follow them.

Friday December 1st 1820   Fort Enterprise

Old Keskarrah has been nursing his wife here all winter, who is about to lose her nose by an ulcer; he and his family still remain our guests at the Fort, and intend to do so all winter. They and their visitors, who are frequent, have been a heavy drain upon our provisions. The fishery, failing, has been given up. Reindeer were not seen here October 26 to November 12; they appeared again on November 16 but remained only a few days. Keskarrah made an offering today to the Water-spirit whose wrath he apprehends to be the cause of his wife's malady. This offering consisted of an old knife, a small piece of tobacco and some trifling articles, made up into a packet and committed to the rapid (which remains open) with a long prayer.

6

MOMENTARY MERCIES
OF THE BEAR

When Greenstockings' shadow first begins to emerge from Hood's paper, the river is already motionless ice except for the smoking rapids. The winter world darkens into silver around Keskarrah's hide lodge heaped with spruce boughs and snow in the shelter of the esker. And the sharp corners of the mudded English buildings are softening a little as the ice grows over them, their green logs cracked open by the cold now furred thick as winter animals. At noon, very briefly, the sun glowers over the white folds of the scorched hills, an orange ball dancing tripled with sundogs behind Big Stone, between the black spars of trees.

Now the People have moved their lodges west with Bigfoot, nearer the new snares they have braided and set, nearer the log pounds they have piled together scraggling along the trails that

Keskarrah dreamed the caribou will wear down onto the ice of Roundrock Lake, where they will sleep every night beyond their predators' approach. Only Keskarrah's single lodge remains on the esker near the log houses, Birdseye's two dogs curled beside it in the snow. The giant ravens plod heavily from the English offal heap through deep air across the river, to roosts hidden among the pygmy spruce that had somehow refused to burn.

"At least that bird isn't wearing a necklace of caribou eyes," Keskarrah says, squinting from the doorway into the blazing silver valley, the black line of two ravens wavering through it. "As long as These English throw away enough good things for them to eat, we won't starve." He drops the hide covering, scratching himself.

Greenstockings knows the cold is flexing its young winter muscle. It wants to terrify them for the days ahead when they will be held solid and black as rock in its grip. But since that is what has happened every annual round of her life, she does not actually think about it; nor has she heard or seen anything when she sleeps, so she has nothing to say to Birdseye whenever they awake into morning darkness. Sleep now drops her into an unfathomable lake where, falling and falling, she dreams nothing. She cannot tell how deep she must go before she finds bottom and can then walk out; if ever. And she wakes to their lodge piled heavy with the stench of hides waiting to be scraped again and tanned and sewn. Never before, not even when the long killing rapids lured three canoes and two families into the hardest grief she can remember, never have they had to soften so many hard hides for so long into the coming cold. She cannot reach the top of them, sitting.

Broadface hunts and hunts, there is no winter rest and sleep-

ing for him either. On the days when he comes dragging more
frozen bodies for These English on the snow, his fingers bulge
thick with cold despite the mittens she has sewn him, fur doubled inside. Gradually his hands soften a little in the warmth of
their lodge, the skin of his face becomes almost tender while he
sits hunched forwards like an old man, eating all the delicious
animal parts that the Whites will not: brains, eyes, lungs, heart,
the long, sweet filaments of intestine fat, thick penises, nursing
udders. He scoops up the marrow she breaks out of the bones,
or bites mouthfuls of the frozen slices of mossy stomach she
cuts so thin for him that he can see the lodge fire leaping through
them. What he loves best is smoked stomach, the fat she chews
small before she spits it into an opened paunch filled with half-
digested moss and then adds blood, a little brains and water to
ferment and smoke, slowly, hanging over the fire for several
days, until he returns and sucks that into his cavernous mouth
burned black by the ice he always breathes around it.

But Broadface does not look at her. Nor turn and take her
until morning, because the men are all hunting so much to satisfy the demands of These English for fresh meat and dried
meat and pemmican for storage, firing their guns into the
pounds and waiting in ambush along the rocks of the lakeshore
and stalking the lake, and even shooting those animals who
have accepted snares as they always have. What kind of hunting
is that, Keskarrah asks him, though mildly, when a hunter no
longer touches an animal until it is dead and its life is spreading
out in the snow? He has already spoken a warning two times:
endlessly pouring grey powder and poking a ball into an iron
barrel, and flexing a finger on curled steel that can burn you
raw, if you dare touch it, is not the way numberless beautiful

caribou, who always will make it possible for human beings to live, should be forced to die. There is too much sacrifice being demanded. There is no consideration or tenderness left in so much long-distance killing; only noise and stink.

"For what purpose?" Keskarrah questions the smoke rising from the centre fire. "For huge, fat men in gigantic canoes? These strangers?"

Only Keskarrah dares think such things, and Greenstockings; but only he says them aloud. Broadface is a hunter and he does what he must, as necessity stands before him and the animal is there. He listens to Keskarrah, carefully, but says no word about the endless throats and bellies he and the other hunters rip open, the steaming guts he spills on the snow to freeze hard as his iron gun before he remembers to lift his head for a breath of gratitude. Silently he eats the food provided by the animals, the mounds of it that Greenstockings prepares for him even while she scrapes and scrapes hides and sews winter boots and leggings and coats and mittens and caps and cuts spirals of endless lacing. Within the hot, tired circle of her arms he awakes to find comfort inside her, and in the pale morning when Birdseye wakes her again he is always gone. The memory of his closed face rubbing hers, his taut, twisting legs, his hard, sullen body and mouth and hip bones and penis attached to her as if they were seared together by the very fire of intensifying cold — all this seems vaguely reassuring to her, but far less memorable than the black lake she has sunk into once more despite anything he is able to make her feel, out of which she has been pulled once more, temporarily, by her mother's hand.

Birdseye is weaker every day; the soft leather now permanently hides what the Eater continues to do to her face. Every day Keskarrah brings the salve, and with it Greenstockings touches the black edges of what has already been taken. But the salve does nothing to stop her fingers passing over the deeper blackness which opens always wider in her mother's face, and one day she recognizes that that blackness is what opens down into her sleep. She has not known such impenetrability can exist in sleep; she begins to dread that she will never plumb it completely, much less walk through it, unless Broadface… and someone else, Hood, it will be hooded Hood who may need all winter to find her picture on his paper — but that does not matter, he will find it — and she will need both of them to know how black, how deep, where the bottom of the lake is. Until now she has found no human voices there, nor any light.

So she works longer and longer, trying to avoid that sharper devastation of sleep. Sometimes in exhaustion she finds herself contemplating her hand. Her powerful pale fingers which hold scrapers, knives, dig into Broadface's muscles or play his soft balls and cock into another, more tender, pleasure. Her powerful fingers, tired though they are, feel everything, like her eyes feeling texture and shade, dimension, heft, or her nostrils knowing essence. Her fingers feel exactly the slip of Richard Sun's salve, which deadens open pain but, she suspects now, will not stop the Eater — merely hide him more secretly. And sometimes she can barely stop her fingers, the lure to touch the blackness widening in Birdseye's beloved face. She spreads the salve with extreme care, to the exact destroyed edge of skin. She cannot permit her fingers to disappear.

Keskarrah says again, moving across her personal memory of darkness, "When raven has lots to eat, he's happy. And then he won't make us as black as he is."

Clearly her father does not understand; he is lost in that long story of creating birds. Neither he nor Birdseye can help her — will it be the men? Or must it be herself?

Gradually, day by shortening day, she sees Keskarrah become the winter bear he likes to be. He dreamed some of the trails for the caribou and he is guarding Greenstockings in Hood's picture and for that, he says, Richard Sun will give them the salve that protects Birdseye. He is so strangely, thoughtlessly content about the salve, and he lies naked under his robes while the women continue in their endless work, breathing aloud sometimes of what he has seen while he sleeps, or the stories he finds wandering in his head, which he pulls into words so that they are happening somewhere, to someone they probably know, even while he speaks them. Winter is the time for stories, of course, the stories that tell why the world is the way it is and the places are where they are, and every winter he tells them again, but never in quite the same way. And some of the stories have never been heard by anyone, not even Keskarrah, because they have not told themselves to him yet and so could not be uttered until now.

However, the stories of what will come do not speak to him. He has refused the future all his life, he says that is a burden for others to carry, and now it seems he has been spared that. For which he is loudly thankful.

"I have enough to carry already," he says, looking at Birdseye but saying nothing directly to her; they both know she has her own great burdens. "Sometimes," he continues, "all the past life of the animals becomes too much for me, and all the world's endless places and so much about people, all the way back from when man was alone, no woman, and so without even a child to tell all the stories that were already happening, when man was first thinking he needed bigger feet to run on the snow if he was to live through the winter — sometimes — I don't know about anyone else, but sometimes I think the necessary order of dreams I am given is too much for one life-time."

Birdseye is silent. They all know, except perhaps Greywing, that the inevitability of the future is growing in her when she sleeps, but beyond the first two outbursts she has so far been able to contain what she knows about themselves and These English and all their paddle-slaves waiting here and eating, waiting to go north. Nevertheless they know that she cannot contain all that much longer: she will have to start telling it for the air to carry, somehow.

"I like the story of Owl, better than…." Greywing hesitates, not wishing to insult anyone; she pushes the robes close around her father and returns to her stretching skin. When her sister speaks with such a child's thoughtlessness, Greenstockings wishes she herself could still do that. But she cannot pretend any longer, as she has recently, to childlike playfulness; every night the deep lake of her foreboding deepens.

Keskarrah laughs, knowing what the girl wants and there-fore he can tease her. "O, Owl was there too when Raven said to People, 'You made me all black, and now I'll make you black too, black from starvation.' But that time Owl was good and told the People where Raven had hidden the caribou, hey! it was Owl who sang them out of their hiding, 'There they are, over there between those two thin hills, thick as maggots, those juicy, sweet maggots of the tundra,' Owl sang to People."

"I like Owl…" Greywing begins and stops, remembering

herself, remembering that a story is what it is and will not change no matter what you wish of it.

"Which one?" Keskarrah asks innocently, knowing. "There are so many stories, which one about Owl?"

But the girl is wordless now, blushing, her hand with the bone scraper barely moving. Keskarrah laughs, his eyes crinkling even more against the noon blaze of the fire, and as Greenstockings hauls down another of the heavy hides, she wishes again that the clumsy immovable houses and the medicines of These English had never paddled across great lake Tucho, that their insistence here on the esker, the loud ugliness of their voices and axes and guns walking and screaming everywhere between the silent trees, making everything jump and shiver far beyond any cold, could be dumped into a hole, as their servant does their night piss and shit every morning; and she would go personally and pick up that frozen hole they are filling and hurl it into a lake deeper than her sleep, from which they never, ever, could crawl out, they and all their endless demands and heavy words and jaws chewing and chewing and clothing and shit. Not even Hood…she would…his long pencil fingers…would he accept her throwing him away…could she, Hood?

"…I really like," their father is saying, so innocently, "is Mouse talking to Owl. Have I ever told you what she does to Owl?"

Greywing whispers, "No, no," because she wants to hear it again so very badly. And Keskarrah wants to tell it; he turns on his elbow towards her, his tone smiling like his face.

"Well, this is how their conversation starts. Mouse has just hidden herself under the corner of a rock, hidden herself there very, very fast, and Owl has had to pull out of his dive before he hits the rock and has to sit there, for her to come out, though he knows it's useless. So Mouse starts it, very politely from under the rock, 'Are you quite comfortable there? Did you bruise your wings stopping so fast? O-o-o-o, do your empty claws hurt from hitting the ground so hard, and so completely empty?' Of course, hey! Owl says nothing. Not this time, but wait, next time, as long as you're alive there's always a next time, just wait, and he clappers his beak together fiercely to let Mouse know what will certainly happen, next time. But Mouse is an excellent conversationalist, and to make sure that Owl doesn't get bored during what they both know is his long, useless waiting, she continues, very politely,

"'I've seen you eat often, and you certainly have a big mouth... for eating, but something puzzles me. I've watched for you and listened all my life, and I can't believe my eyes, perhaps my ears are deceiving me. What puzzles me, Owl, is how you shit. You shit of course out of your beautiful ass, lots of little shits, but how is it that you also shit — even bigger — out of your big mouth?'

"Owl can't do anything. He knows he would shit happily from both if only he could get hold of Mouse, but a rock is protecting her this time and Owl cannot fight rock. All he can do is talk. He has to talk.

"'O yes,' he hisses, clappering so dreadfully Mouse almost shakes the rock off her with her shivers, 'one who can only run and who would be nothing but shreds in my beak, from under a rock can have such a big mouth, such a very big mouth.'"

In the lodge they are all laughing, even Birdseye behind her soft leather. Beaks and teeth and claws usually have the last things to say, everyone knows that, so words still possible from under a good rock are doubly amusing; especially in Keskarrah's reassuring, delicate tone. Greenstockings forgets everything else; she scrapes swiftly, feeling the love of her father embrace them all, irrefutable as rock.

"Here," she says through her laughter, reaching beside the fire, "some liver to eat."

And Keskarrah accepts that and eats, his story-teller teeth savouring the tender strength of the animal that gave it.

"Where would we be," he sings softly, chewing, "without the raven and the owl, the caribou and wolf who taught us how to hunt them, the mouse who gives us wit and small discretion, the beautiful animals, all gifts, gifts."

Birdseye says, suddenly loud, "I saw the northern river last night, it was the River of Copperwoman, dressed all white like ice — "

Without moving Keskarrah glances sideways, instantly meets her eyes and, still chewing, knows he must speak very fast now, because only an old story can stop a dream from being spoken into life, even temporarily, and he must try that; who can know whose life he will save, even for a day or two days, and the first words that find him are so good, so strong, long and old, that perhaps their two daughters have not noticed. He speaks up-wards, into the smoke praying upwards:

"Hey! human beings come from…I have never heard where man comes from, though woman's story is clearer, every story seems clearer about woman than man…sometimes I think men are afraid to let their stories…they are so afraid of what they think might be their manliness…."

He hesitates, sees Birdseye still watching him, her mouth filled with words, and he plunges on, "…if man was in the world first, he must have been here alone in the summer when roots and soft stems and especially fields and bushes of berries would be ready for him to eat without cooking, no man knows how to cook everything like a woman. The creator made him so he wouldn't be scared to death with winter before he even found out how good eating and living was, before he just starved and froze black to death. Hey! I've heard it said that These English began from mud. Richard Sun told that story, white mud, I suppose, though he didn't say it exactly the way, but if that's what — "

Keskarrah stops abruptly. Words have lured him where he had no intention of going — to talk about the beginnings of Whites — but Birdseye's look above her leather has remained so intense that he cannot avoid her now, he must continue, and even as he must repeat them, the words excite him with creation again.

"Richard Sun said this to Bigfoot, I heard Twospeaker repeat it: 'You must know this, we men were made first from mud and the spit of the great Soul Everywhere.' How could I not hear that? I've never heard a story like that, about such spit, but it would be wonderful to see happening. Or feel such spit, even if you never saw it. It would be like good rain, I suppose, which in summer makes very small things grow out of the ground in every place, so that story could be told, I can't doubt that. I told Richard Sun that if I'd been spitting and playing with such mud and finding a man in it, I would have used much more and made him bigger and stronger, a lot stronger like a bear; myself."

"You're strong enough," Birdseye says, lost in his story and her own necessities momentarily forgotten. "You have words for anything, you're always so strong."

Keskarrah chuckles a little, diffidently. He cannot disagree with her now, but her praise always makes him apprehensive; he already knows her incredible strength. But now he must continue quickly.

"The white mud is good, and there's that mound of it on the north side of this esker, which These English liked so much and mixed with water and smeared all over their building — so —" he has a sudden revelation "maybe These English should really be called Whitemuds, maybe they came from this place, here they found their original mud again! Though I can't see how that could be. If they really belonged here, they would have known this place without me telling them, but obviously they know nothing here — and then our ancestors would also have known them and met them long ago, but we didn't. Richard Sun says woman Whitemud was supposed to be the companion and helper of the man. She happens out of his rib while he's sleeping, but when he wakes up and there she is, his rib a woman out of his sleep, she doesn't help him at all, she eats this one berry, which is so large it grows alone on one big tree, and then she gives it to him to eat and that makes everything in the world go completely crazy. Even the woman and the man."

The women are looking at him, puzzled, and he explains fast. "That's the part I can't understand, though I have been thinking about it. If People don't eat, they die — and Whites eat far more than People. How can one tree berry have so much power that eating it matters to everything else? For ever? Aren't there plenty of smaller berries for the man to eat? Our first man ate berries alone for a whole summer and nothing happened to him. But Richard Sun says no, that's probably because there was no woman yet. Once there is one, Whitemud man always has to eat at least as much as the woman, he can't eat less, and that one big berry she eats easily enough off the tree is too much for him. After that they both do everything all wrong.

"It's very strange," he adds thoughtfully, "hard for us to understand. Maybe it's eating *together* that's so bad for them — I've never seen a White woman, so I can't tell — maybe that's why White men never travel with one?"

Greenstockings has not heard his contemplative speculations that are tangling him further — she is thinking about the rib.

"A rib from a tree?" she asks him, smiling and ready to laugh. That's a good story. A tall tree surely has as many ribs as branches. As it is, there are never enough women in the world so men never leave them alone, but if women were as numerous as branches, the fewer men would be kept so busy running after them that at least some women would be left in peace some of the time, maybe as long as the female caribou, who with their growing calves live free from males for an entire year. She laughs aloud for happiness: what a happy story! And in her laughter catches the essence of her father's contemplations. "So — just never eat with them!"

"No no," Keskarrah, always a man, spoils it. "The rib is from the man, one rib only, that is where Whitemud woman comes from."

Greenstockings asks, "These English do have their own women, somewhere? And their first woman has a man for her mother?"

Her laughter catches in her throat, then bursts out even louder at this truly incredible story; Birdseye and Greywing answer her, and suddenly the lodge is shaking with laughter. What would such a first woman possibly look like! Even Keskarrah cannot help snorting aloud. But he stops suddenly.

"Their stories seem to be only about men, they say their Soul Everywhere is a man also," he explains gently. "I think the Whitemud story says that two men have to dream and work, really hard, to give birth to one woman."

Tears of laughter are running down the women's cheeks. Astounded, they can only cover their mouths with their hands. They are hearing such a male story that Greenstockings knows she would never have heard it, so marvellously funny, without her father's power to tell it. Did these first story men have very tiny nipples too, surrounded by a few coarse hair? How did their babies get born if they have no cunt — out of the two tiny holes in their two cocks? With nothing but a rib between them, and it bent so long and stiff as well? Her thoughts swim in laughter: if there are as many Whites somewhere beyond even the reach of the giant canoes as they insist — probably hidden under heaps of stuff they want someone to drag everywhere for them — what other fantastic stories do they have? There would be no time for anything like forgetting — only continuous laughter.

"There's trouble." Keskarrah's tone quiets them immediately. He is lying with his eyes closed, as if he has already wandered much farther than he wanted to. Indeed, as if he has betrayed himself.

"The Whitemud story," he says, "is not happy. Not like our story of the man and the ptarmigan-woman and how they make the snowshoes together. They're both the same then, and different. I've only heard a little of Richard Sun's story, but I don't think I want to hear more. It sounds dangerous."

Greenstockings looks at him, silently.

He says, "Stories are like ropes, they pull you to incomprehensible places. This rib story could drag us tighter together with Whitemuds than the endless killing of animals, which we agreed to do without a proper council — a few men quickly said 'Yes, yes' very loudly when Thick English asked it, and then no one dared say anything else. Hey! a story can tangle you up so badly you start to think different. I think these strange White-mud stories could be strong enough to tie us down — though I should be old enough by now to have heard everything at least once."

He lies motionless, contemplating the luminous darkness under his own eyelids. Searching.

"Everything," he says softly, "is becoming dangerous."

In the lengthening silence no one looks at Birdseye. But the warm lodge filled with the tight smell of life and work and thinking suddenly sparkles with all their awareness of her bent, so worn, over interminable sewing. The beloved face none of them will see again except in the dark memory of their fingers; if they dare. They are as together now as they have been; but afraid. If Keskarrah were to open his eyes, lightning and flames would circle them.

"These strangers are here now," he says with staggering sad-ness. "It must be their fault. Never before has anything been wrong with the world."

"The ice on Copperwoman's River," Birdseye speaks softly, reassuringly, "it was very fresh. So thin I could see through it, and the beautiful fins of the grayling were brushing against it, blue as veins below the rapids."

"Rapids?" Keskarrah asks, very diminished. He has spoken all he can — the most powerful story cannot stop her, so he must answer. If he does so carefully enough, he may recognize the place and they will be warned.

"Two of them, rapids, and the bare banks are without stones, a small curved lake, curved all white between them."

"Ah-h-h-h." And Keskarrah will lie as long as necessary to travel the river faster than any bird, searching for those two rapids.

But Bigfoot arrives first. He stoops into their lodge holding a long rifle in his stiff mittens, and for the first time a tall, black English hat sits on his head. He does not take that off as Birds-eye welcomes him with a gesture to seat himself near the fire. After some time Keskarrah opens one eye, then opens them both, wider.

"You're welcome," he says out loud without moving. And his tone is on such a bare edge of courtesy that the two girls almost dare show their laughter at Bigfoot's appearance. It would have been hard for Greenstockings to imagine how fur from an ordinary beaver — that's what they say it is — could enlarge and extend a man's head upwards like that, but These English have done it, somehow, because there the hat is, tall as a stump on Bigfoot's head, and as wobbly as the authority they assume he has over People just because he talks for them. How is it sewn together? What is the tiny curled edge that curves twice so gracefully around it? She has never touched one, though she thinks Boy English once was ready to lift the one on his head and place it on hers. Unfortunately before she noticed that she already had her knife at his pants, and he certainly understood nothing about playing with knives.

"Have fish found the lake nets?"

"O yes," Bigfoot answers too quickly. "Many, many."

"And caribou?"

Bigfoot gestures to the hides piled about the lodge, still too quickly. "Our women are very busy," he says. "With meat too. Their paddle-slaves remain fat."

"True." Keskarrah grins. "Those Halfmuds sit behind logs stuffing meat into their enormous mouths, no need to shoot them!"

"What, 'Halfmud'?"

"You know, These English say they are made of mud and spit."

"Ahh...yes, I have heard something...Halfmud." Bigfoot slowly gathers that into his ponderous comprehension. "Is that why they were so happy they found the white mud here?"

"I think so. And also the large trees, though ours don't have such big berries. I had heard all the White traders mix mud to smear between trees to build their houses, and I always thought they did that because they want beavers so badly, who build their houses with logs and mud rather than hides like smart People, but since I heard the story of how these Whites were made...."

Bigfoot sits motionless, confused by this confusing story.

"It seems," Keskarrah muses, staring into the fire, "they don't need the animal circle that gives us life every day. They want to live inside straight walls, as straight as round trees can make them — maybe they *have* to live inside the crossed-together corners of the trees that gave them their endless sorrow and wrong! So...they tie these big trees together...they smear them over thick with their first ancestors...and white mud is surely the best for that...then they can live here a whole winter, surrounded...sheltered by everything they've already done wrong...and all of it smeared over by the life of their ancestors — waugh!"

This reasonable explanation of White behaviour, which Keskarrah has wandered into aloud, startles his upper body up from his robes.

"That's power! No wonder Whitemuds are so strong — they always follow the power of their wrong!"

Bigfoot slowly takes off the black hat, fumbles it between his thick fingers. There is a dent all around the hair on his head, which none of them has seen before.

"The caribou," he says finally, unable to follow Keskarrah in pursuit of White wrong, "many of them seem to be going away."

"I thought so," Keskarrah says quietly, turning from what he has just understood; not wanting to think any further into what such a presence must mean for their winter's living.

"So many usually stay here, and the ice is now strong on the lake, they can avoid the wolves here, but they all seem to be leaving, going farther south into the trees...."

Keskarrah lets Bigfoot's words grow gradually smaller until they trickle into nothing. It seems to Greenstockings that her father's ancient skin glows in the firelight like a baby's, newborn. She scrapes precisely around a maggot-hole in the tensile sacrifice of hide splayed white before her: that will have to be folded over, sewn tight to keep out a spear of cold. A Whitemud baby must look like a soft maggot growing in thick caribou hide, a tender grub squeezing itself, lengthening itself out into air, glistening in light. She feels a spasm of longing in her breasts flicker double-pronged through the folded length of her legs.

"It may be like you've said," Bigfoot bumbles on. "Too many caribou have died here for us, too fast."

"They won't go on their winter paths?"

"But...you dreamed them well."

Keskarrah lifts his head. "You've heard the Whitemud story. For them everything in the world has to be wrong."

Bigfoot agrees gloomily.

"Before they found this place, Lastfire Lake took two of our hunters."

Bigfoot says, "Lakes have done that to us before."

"But not while we were hunting for strangers," Keskarrah muses. "When you work hard to feed and clothe others...." He pauses, but suddenly continues. "We are hospitable, no one with us will starve while we have something to eat, but perhaps ...perhaps at some point we...make ourselves stranger too."

The two men glance at each other quickly, then away. There cannot be words to speak about that. Not yet, nor do they want to find them.

Bigfoot says carefully, "Nevertheless you dreamed very well... the animals have fed us very well, everyone has enough so far, even winter clothing."

"Whitemuds want more."

Bigfoot says nothing, so Keskarrah says it. "They want sacks of meat for summer, they want it dried now."

"No one dries meat in dark winter."

"They don't know what we do."

"I've told them, again and again, when the sun returns there are always other caribou."

"Not along the Everlasting Ice, where they want to go."

"But why will they go there?" Bigfoot is almost shouting. "We've told them, there's nothing there but ice!"

"I know," Keskarrah says quietly. "I think we have to understand this: Whitemuds hear only what they want to hear."

Bigfoot turns the grotesque hat round and round in his hands;

Greenstockings cannot see the faintest shadow of a seam there, it is made so beautifully.

Keskarrah sinks down, props his head on one hand. His slow words walk step by step through their minds like wolves moving into the lethal curve of a hunt.

"Nothing, nothing. For them the world is always wrong because they never want it to be…the way it is."

Bigfoot snorts in agreement, "Huh! They didn't want our strong rivers, our many rapids, the quick coming of winter — they won't want the Everlasting Ice if they get there! What does it matter, what they want? The world is what it is."

Keskarrah agrees. "If I could understand them, I'd gladly tell you. But before these Whitemuds got here, I think they'd decided how the world should be."

Bigfoot stares at him, obviously lost. Keskarrah adds,

"Their first story tells them everything is always wrong. So wherever they go, they can see only how wrong the world is."

How can a place be — wrong? Despite her father's disturbing words, Greenstockings cannot help grinning at Bigfoot. He knows that hunting is easy, and a delight, but the thinking that makes it possible — and the prayer — may well be more difficult than he can ever achieve. Keskarrah has told her often: talking is never just talk, even when it happens through Twospeaker with These English. Words mirror what there is in the world, as they also anticipate it, and when she sees Bigfoot glumly ponder the hides stacked thin and high as his hunter memory beside her, she understands his dilemma. He knows as well as she that, no matter with what respect and care the women may sew them, hides remain gifts from the animals, and gifts can disappear if snatched by the unworthy; knows that hides always belong to the animals, are their clothing for ever, and that only proper acceptance, hide and human worn together, will make the new animal-person who can live protected and strong in the killing winter cold. There is no way to force animals to surrender more than they wish. If pursued unworthily, with deception, the gifts of animals will be deceptive; perhaps even deadly. That is the way they protect themselves.

Bigfoot's glance slips towards Birdseye bent over her needle, behind her hiding leather, but instantly he shifts to a minute inspection of the black hat he is turning in his hands: as if fur dragged from this country, subjected to something unknowable in English hands and returned here so unrecognizable might nevertheless be somehow less strange — less lethal — than the animals they live with. Greenstockings knows her mother has caribou hide between her fingers, the steel needle These English have given Birdseye cuts through it quick as a fish — but how long after the coat is completed and given to them will it still be there to wear? And all the women along the lake whose lodges are filled with these swift steel needles and the thick, sweet smoke of drying meat, even if they can ever make enough to satisfy the Whitemuds while they are here, how much will remain for the Whitemuds to eat when they carry it away? Clothes and meat can disappear like the animals, whose gifts they are.

Watching Bigfoot beyond her busy hands, Greenstockings ponders all this; ponders his blunt fingers stroking that seamless fur. Strange things, becoming stranger. Once they had agreed that Bigfoot had the possibility of mature, elderly wisdom, and she thought then she could easily accept being his third wife. But now he seems to have lost his discernment, his hunter balance; becoming the person everyone agreed should talk to

These English has made him by turns either foolishly arrogant or obsequious, either superbly dignified or fawning without seeming comprehension. Only after he talks to Keskarrah for some time is he the man she remembers. But his eyes always were very small, as if grown just large enough to measure everything only by their own size.

Keskarrah says carefully aloud, as if they have been speaking throughout this silence, "Not much can be said yet. You know I first thought they would go, be gone fast like those other two Whites — and these could be gone if they weren't so slow and heavy, and the winter hadn't caught them. But now...now I think...they'll be gone at last only when the ice is very thin on the River of Copperwoman, thin enough to see fish through it."

Bigfoot looks up, hopefully.

"The ice isn't very thick, not yet."

"No. But it will have be thinner...much thinner."

At the corner of her eye Greenstockings senses her mother hunched almost into a ball around her working hands. And she understands: this is the knowledge Birdseye and Keskarrah have found together and wanted to avoid, but couldn't. Almost another whole year of These English. She sees Bigfoot's head droop wearily. That may be too long even for him and his fast, preening imitation of Thick English, and she cannot help grinning at him. As if Tetsot'ine would ever put up with a man who strutted about as *boss* beyond the brief necessities of defence and raid. He must understand already that he has started acting different too fast.

There is a thickness in her head, she cannot breathe for all the talk piled like animal bodies over her. Very deliberately she unstretches herself from her finished hide, stands up slender as willow into the cone warmth of the lodge. She pulls her parka down her strong arms and over her head, picks up the leather pail and bends, quick as thinking, out into the fresh mist of snow. Black raven is nowhere in the purple sky.

The Dogrib boy, whom Bigfoot has kept as a slave since Thick English came, sits on his master's pack, clutching Birdseye's dogs close to him for warmth. One cowers as Greenstockings passes, but the bitch bares her bright teeth and she wonders once more if, when the long darkness is completely here and he sleeps behind his mud-smeared logs, Thick English will finally reach for dogs and discover warmth. Now he sleeps alone and cold every night, everyone knows he will have no woman and allows his men none; he seems to like only puppies still on the teat, before they grow old, cringing or savage in turn, and must hunt food for themselves. Like Bigfoot now, whom she once liked because it seemed then he need not be as heavy as other men. Despite his betraying little eyes.

Down the granular snow of rocks away from the square houses she will not look at, beneath the willows to the river: the hole is frozen clear as the water itself. She cannot break through with her heel. She is searching for a loose stone when she hears voices, the string of sound trailing indecipherably down towards her. She looks up from the circle of crushed wet ice, about to sink her bucket there even as it hardens again: six of them are coming down to the river. And clearly the only English is Back, leading the toboggans, packs, guns towards her — Boy English coming fast on his little snowshoes, swinging them easily, he's so strong, such a powerful walker the others half-trot to keep up.

Little Back, wrapped under his silly black hat, and his sly black eyes, like fly specks always quick to crawl over her skin.

She sensed no clean lust in him, as if sensuality for him could only be stolen from someone, hidden by deception from someone else. She has not felt his eyes on her for four days, but she feels her knife flex her mittened hand and how his blunt fingers ripped her shirt open: exactly how deep is he white, where will he fold open into red meat? She should have let her knife look more thoroughly than the skin of his pants. And his beautiful small teeth, his delicate reddening face smooth as spilled water on ice already speaking puffs of cold at her into the slanting snow that swirls suddenly out of the sky. She knows he will not touch her because others are here to see what he does, and she cannot, gladly cannot, understand a single sound or recognize the faintest picture in the white mist he blasts out at her. She should have taken one of his poking fingers.

Broadface — there he is, one of two hunters on what will obviously be a long journey. With two voyageurs harnessed to pull two toboggans with the dogs. And behind them all, grinning under her massive pack, is Little Marten, who will carry anything in any cold to roll up with Broadface beside a fire. He may have known of this travel before today, but he has told Greenstockings nothing, and from his tiny smile did not intend to meet her as they left. She looks at Boy English, his many perfect teeth, and remains silent.

"A short walk to Tucho," Broadface tells her. "For rum and White paper."

Suddenly she is very happy for them leaving on such a useless trip, days and days, a month, perhaps half a winter of snow walking. Throughout the darkness not one of these will suddenly appear at her lodge entrance — if ever again. A rock fissure may tenderly accept them, or a rapid opening to water quick as a fish gill, the cold smile clear and crystal all around them like the vanished sun, the great aurora lure them into a devastation of dreams. She should not think this, it makes her feel less than mean, so she smiles at Little Marten weighed down worse than a toboggan. Only Whites would enter the long darkness with such an interminable, annihilating walk. Only Whitemuds.

But Broadface has found his broad grin again. "You keep your hot little hole empty," he tells her. "Or I'll know it."

"O yes" — Greenstockings laughs in Boy English's uncomprehending face, passing — "and your wet stick will stay here!"

Broadface laughs aloud. "It'll be here, flying back every night, so watch out!"

"Huh! You're not Wolverine."

"You'll go crazy every night, someone who knows told me."

"Who that knows?"

"I know."

"You couldn't do that alone, and who'd help you?"

"Don't bother to cross your legs in bed, it won't help."

All the People around the waterhole are laughing. The voyageurs have dragged past too, but Back shifts around in his tiny snowshoes, smiling with benign incomprehension at these cheery native farewells. Greenstockings sees his eyes move against her, and she feels again his clumsy hand groping under her clothes for skin, beating at her nipple, his pale face hunching uncontrollably, and she breathes disdain at him and his ignorance open-mouthed, breathes it out like smoke rising above the rapids whose voice is always around them, and the People see her teasing, insulting this Boy English, always leering about and who hasn't come near her since she showed him her long, bright knife, and they laugh even harder. The sound of it spreads through air, returns from the rocks holding the frozen river with the jubilant talk of ancestors who have lived here four hundred generations, with the call of drums, with the high voices of children waiting eagerly to be born but still undecided about whom they will enter and make ecstatically happy. In her magnificent, glorious world of rock and sky and tree and ice the cold fondles Greenstockings and for an instant she sways, almost dizzy with happiness, fondles her to the very roots of her tongue. She knows Back will always find a woman and Broadface will never forget her, neither her words nor her red, moist, open mouths.

Little Marten on her snowshoes passes last, and as Greenstockings lifts the heavy water, she pauses beside her in the track.

"That Mohawk," Little Marten says softly, "from many rivers away, he's deciding to steal you."

Greenstockings considers it. "But he's a paddle-slave, to Thick English."

"What does he know? That Mohawk watches you, and has sharpened two knives."

"Does he have friends?"

"No. But he's strong enough."

Greenstockings glances up and Little Marten adds quickly,

"Bigfoot is trying to walk like Thick English now. He might not fight for a woman."

Greenstockings smiles her thanks, though it seems very odd. She has felt nothing from the Mohawk, who seems not to care about anything enough to steal it, even a woman. But now she has been warned and she says, gratefully,

"When you pick the nits out of Broadface's hair, fondle his ears. He'll fall asleep very fast then."

Little Marten laughs quietly, and Greenstockings joins her.

"If you want him to sleep," she adds.

When she has climbed the first rocks tilted against the esker, she looks back along the river towards Winter Lake. The brief flurry of snow has blown away; they are almost at the rapids, receding into a touch of dark on the stark, bent lines of the great snow world. On Hood's paper they would be nothing but tiny spots.

When had she decided she would grow so strong and smart that she could marry anyone she wanted? Or no one if she didn't? Why? She cannot remember ever deciding these things, but that is what she is living. And as her face warms in the crimson light burning along the hills she feels it must have been the four years of her mother's warm milk until Greywing was born, of Birdseye refusing to give Keskarrah any sons, so that when her blood began to flow and told her to go by herself to the isolation tent to become a woman, no male — not even a younger brother — had ever seen her naked, even by accident. So now there are men tearing at her, and will be for the rest of her life. Well — let them.

Her father passes her without looking up from his path before him in the snow. He walks steadily down the esker. She sees he is going to the rapids, to pray.

That night Keskarrah, out of his deep sleep, suddenly speaks the name of the double rapids on the River of Copperwoman, which Birdseye has already dreamed. He is speaking their name very loudly, again and again, as if he were moulding them into existence, he shouts them until the women are awake. Greenstockings hears her father's rasping breath, his cough, his shouts hammer at the lodge walls until that deadly name bursts over her white in darkness so profound she cannot at first tell if her eyes are open. And then she recognizes that the rapids are only two days' walking away, they will die very close to shelter... within reach of so many warm arms, so close —— it's a grizzly, Keskarrah shouts into the darkness, a sow grizzly come down to the opposite bank of the ice-slivered river where he stands, and she paces back and forth over water there, snaking her head to and fro as if swinging her gigantic weight into a charge through ice and moving water at him. He must sing to her, because he is without so much as a little knife or even a dog to help him welcome her visiting him on the open tundra.

"O Great Bear," Keskarrah sings, terrified, "I have never harmed you, the cooked paws of your relations or friends have never filled my stomach, only when I was dying of hunger, and then only with the deepest of gratitude, always with such enormous gratitude! Accept my renewed thankfulness now, here it is, all my gratitude, now!"

But the swing of grizzly's deadly prowl along the bank grows swifter and ever wider, she is directly in front of him now, a few steps and her wheeling turns fling her higher into the air until she blots out the sun, the sky itself turns over him her ominous darkness, and falling there he sees, like a sudden revelation, the two long rapids at either point of her turning. The double rapids, the curved lake between them slick with a white skin of ice! And then over him she rises up like a giant tree, she reveals to him her belly and chest where she suckles her young, and he must bury his face between her teats if he would get inside the violence she will now reveal to him, if he is to survive where death is already growing like depthless cold out of the land, where he would have to drive his knife, if he had one, as she embraces him. But her arms reach higher, beyond him, to lift up the coming-winter sky, and he knows the name of that place, knows that fatal place on the River of Copperwoman. And cries it aloud to the women.

"Have mercy, good Bear," the old man prays on, singing as he can, "I beg you, have mercy, go away my sweet sister, my mother, so caring when you show yourself over and beside swift water, I am begging you now, go away."

Prays and sings the bear, who has told him more than any of them wanted to know, into vanishment. Until there is only the name of the place left.

And he is awake. With him in their wide common bed of sweet hides and fur Greywing lies between Birdseye and Green-stockings, who is rigid with fear. Birdseye has not moved; there is not even the sound of her breathing to reveal she is alive, or awake. If the dreams of her mother and her father begin to follow and elaborate each other like this, Greenstockings knows that they will also have to meet at some point, and in this dark-ness she does not dare think about that. She prefers the dark-ness of her nameless lake to this place they have designated, no matter how deep, and she pulls her sister closer, the fear they must all face in the future already faintly there in the hot, fa-miliar skin she cuddles against herself.

Keskarrah says over them, "The ice is too thin to walk on. Whitemuds are always too heavy."

The heavy, heavy Whitemuds. There is a wisp of comfort for them in that. Slowly Greenstockings and Greywing turn to-gether, fold into each other's limbs as they have slept so often, the smaller girl bent around, open-mouthed between Green-stockings' breasts and legs, she curled about her as if growing that small body into her own, and slowly, gently, their hearts beat together and they seek into each other, shift, merge, become the delicacy of skin globed into one, shaped round by firm and dreamless sleep. The deep maw of the lake.

The moon rides through cloud over a rasped silver world. For months to come the ceaseless stars will dominate it, and the erratic aurora, the sun at noon vanishing from its brief smudge beyond the rocks and burned sticks of the southern horizon. Tomorrow evening, Thursday, October 19, 1820, as all the English record it in their endless notebooks, Lieutenant Franklin will see his Midshipman Hood, whom he is already convinced he loves as he would the son he does not yet know he will never have, walk away from the frozen mud-smeared triangle of buildings they call Fort Enterprise. Lieutenant Franklin will decide that his conscientious youngest officer is off for another session of sketching the natives, drawings he has already decided will form part of the extremely detailed report he must present on his return to England, to His Majesty's Government and Earl Bathurst, who appointed him to command this Expedition for the "determining of the Northern Coast of North America, and the trending of that Coast from the Mouth of the Coppermine River to the eastern extremity of that Continent" on the recommendation of the Lords Commissioners of the Admiralty; drawings as essential as the magnetic-needle readings and declensions, the endless longitudes and latitudes, the flora and fauna, the temperatures and lists of aurora borealis sightings they have each, separately, recorded so meticulously day by day despite notebooks lost and other indescribable difficulties and hardships endured.

Perhaps, as he watches his Admiralty Midshipman trudge through the dreadful cold he will soon find unbelievable, though he will be forced to endure it, the Lieutenant already has a notion that Hood's paintings and sketches will become an essential element of the book he will be prevailed upon to write, a book that will be more widely distributed and read than either Samuel Hearne's record of his amazing walk to the mouth of what he called the Coppermine River (1769–72) or Alexander Mackenzie's quick and comfortable (for him) paddle to the Arctic Ocean down what he nevertheless called "The River of Disappointment" (1789) because of course it took him where he did not want to go — always to the wrong place. The Lieutenant, who will reach a few of the right places — that is, places where he was ordered to go, though no European has ever been there before him — certainly does not suspect that the various manifestations of death he will meet on this four-year journey to the shores of the Polar Sea will make him as famous as if he were the first person to walk physically upon the moon. In searing winter darkness that he will never, quite, find acceptable (no more than years later he will find acceptable the dazzling florescence of antipodean Van Diemen's Land), John Franklin knows that, with George Back hard at work travelling as only he of the Expedition can, they who remain at Fort Enterprise "now get on very well *en famille*, not a single dispute or unpleasant word". John Richardson and he himself have "properly regulated minds" and so the possible "pleasures of (a) female companion(s)" are unnecessary to think about or acknowledge. He does not know (and if such knowledge of his future were offered him, he would refuse to consider it, as being un-Christian) that the Robert Hood he sees disappear into the spruce sheltering the one Yellowknife lodge on the esker has, in fact, left him; vanished for ever.

Doctor John Richardson

Monday December 25th 1820   Fort Enterprise

The male reindeer are now shedding their horns. The trees are intensely frozen and so hard that all the large axes are broken to pieces except one. We have frequently remarked that in the cold clear nights the moisture of the breath freezes with a considerable crackling noise.

Bigfoot with his young men and their wives are encamped near Dissension Lake, where the reindeer are again seen.

Monday January 1st 1821   Fort Enterprise

This morning the Canadians assembled and greeted us with their customary salutation on the new year. We could only treat them with a little flour and fat, and to divert their attention from their wants, which include the lack of rum for festivities, we encouraged the practice of sliding down the steep bank of the river upon sledges. These vehicles descended the snowy bank with much velocity and ran a great distance upon the ice. The officers joined in the sport, and the numerous overturns we experienced formed no small share of the amusement of the party. But on one occasion, when Lieutenant Franklin had been thrown from his seat and almost buried in the snow, a large Indian woman drove her sledge over him, and sprained his knee severely.

7
ENTERING EXHAUSTION

The name of the rapid on the River of Copperwoman silvered with ice so thin that the grayling flicker under it releases Birdseye from her unending woman's work. She begins to sleep towards that future. Into the long darkness she now lives sleeping, waking sometimes for a moment to eat a little dryfish, or drink, to go outside briefly, or have Greenstockings touch the salve Richard Sun still gives them daily to her face under the sleeping-robes.

And gradually, so gently out of her day and night sleep, words begin to rise, a faint, endless thread spun into brightness for them through the deepening winter — words that tell the incredible story of the long, long journey of the Whitemuds: what that travel has already been, and how it now hesitates here on this winter esker, and the travail it will soon continue to be, though they have not lived it yet.

The long past of what their travel has already been emerges first like pale streaks of distance unimaginably far away, with monster waterbirds, whose innumerable upraised wings they cannot quite visualize, lifting these strangers they now know over stinking water so vast only the tribal memory of snow beyond the last trees in the world can encompass it. There they are, white-winged monsters covered with lice-swarms of strangers, between massive icebergs coming like mountains through water that always rolls apart for them.

And slowly, slowly, the water turns crimson under the sun of Birdseye's dreaming, until the great sea surrenders them into heavy boats, and then quickly, into birchbark canoes too large for People, which need three men to carry one, or four lockstep, but which nevertheless dance on the frothing rivers filled with the rocks and smashing white and blue water of the quiet land the Tetsot'ine know surrounds and sustains them with life, but which these strangers do not ever want to be there. Water! they scream in every mark they scratch with birdfeathers on their papers. Calm water! Not cut into streamers by all this horrible, lethal rock, or worse, ice, this is all wrong, give us the right, the proper water! Flat, wide open, and best of all stinking!

These heavy, water-logged strangers really want no land to be here, especially not this land with ice growing down into it wherever, amidst its overwhelming rock and distance, there is a small relief of moss or sand. As if it were held in the fist of cold always, the tender green of summer at best a thin, lightning memory of surface.

But if something must be here, as it seems there must, then they would much prefer the endless plains of lakes which, if they cannot be sailed across by monster ships, can at least most easily be traversed in massive canoes driven by paddle-slaves. Then the Whitemuds can so easily sit on the water and observe the immense land pass inside the tubes they hold to their eyes, and see nothing except the folds of papers they always clutch in their hands, the tiny marks they continuously accumulate heap upon heap between straight lines, down in columns. What they lay out flat and straight and hold in their hands in these marks, which only they will know how to interpret, will be enough to guide them; that is how they know everything, and will know whatever happens to them. Sometime, somewhere, they have decided to believe this simplicity of *mark*, and they will live their lives straight to the end believing that.

But even as Birdseye weaves this continuous whisper of fact and understanding and judgement into the growing dark, the ceaseless travel of the Whitemuds begins to tire her and she forces them to move more slowly. More and more slowly from where they have been to where they plan to go, without knowing what waits for them there, and which they anticipate with both joy and fearful trepidation. Her gradual slowness teaches them to savour details, whether they wish to or not. Sometimes for an entire day she describes one single rock they must pass in the crooked river of their journey, describes every individual plain, slope, twist and crack of it, every textured grain and worn corner exactly there where, against it, the swift water smashes itself into white foam and then instantly refolds down like a glazed sheet, ribbed and smooth for that one slipping instant in which they can finally pass over it.

Or she tells them, with extreme care, of the wolf standing against the sky on the horizon of an esker beside a balanced erratic, contemplating their ponderous passage through landscape on water; she details that silver wolf exactly, to the very whisper of his jaws opening on his brilliant teeth, the shift and flow of his fur as it runs under wind. His cocked furry ears, his teeth, his tongue and his anticipating teeth.

Or caribou, female here and male there, carrying the branching lyres and immense forests of their antlers against the light of an evening lake. But there are, very quickly it seems, so few of these, and almost no running calves.

As the sun sinks completely into winter, Greenstockings watches for the lengthening line of Whitemud story that her mother's voice draws up out of darkness, waits for those giant canoes to appear at last on Tucho so she can begin to understand why they blundered into the Tetsot'ine's own brief trading journey last summer to that new trading place, Fort Providence. She wants to hear her mother tell why all the People stood there so heedlessly, as if nothing but curiosity was happening, and watched These English arrive.

But Birdseye's murmured story explains nothing about what happened to the People then — why they decided to stay and talk to these coming strangers rather than leave quickly in their tiny craft, as some of them wished; why Keskarrah dignified the White demands by drawing pictures of the land on the ground after certain of the Tesot'ine men committed themselves to become "game-killers", as Thick English would name them; or why the hunters, who have never carried more than their light weapons and themselves, now accept to drag around with them over the tired land all the heavy guns and heavy powder and heavier lead, where the heavier, deeper tracks they now leave will last longer in the sinking moss than they will be remembered. Why does Birdseye tell nothing about that first bony apparition they saw together of Hood? Or the fire, and Boy English so proud with the burnt stump of their flag scattering ashes on Tucho still hissing, as Greenstockings now recognizes it was, its blazing scream, "Watch out! Be careful!"

But no. Birdseye speaks nothing about People at the coming. Nothing of the men's broken dance after they drank what These English gave them to honour their promise, nor how some became so crazy they threw their women around as if they were frozen meat, bellowing, "Did you hear? These Whites from so far away know we're the greatest men in the world, we're the greatest game-killers, look at all these long knives, these axes, these shining guns! Now we'll kill so much meat you can roll yourself in fat with your mouth always full, chewing, chewing, buried in meat, you'll grow hot, grow round as warble slugs! You'll have enough meat, you'll see, finally!"

Men saying unspeakable things aloud, things they would be ashamed for a lifetime to hear another man say about himself. As if animals can simply be blown apart, chopped down for food because they happen to be somewhere.

Birdseye does not tell that, nor does her story linger at Tucho. Though Greenstockings remembers very well how some of the Tetsot'ine men awoke the next morning into staggers — as if their heads had burst upon awakening and blown away every memory of what they had said or done. But even when they could finally walk properly again, the men, strangely, had no memory of their unbelievable behaviour, and so for them nothing except the sweet Whitemud taste of happiness and nothing happening remained. To want again, if possible.

Broadfoot could speak as fast and sweet as any bird singing, but that evening he neither said nor sang anything; he was massively silent dancing and drinking. The Dogrib dance stumbled into disorder, and meaninglessness, finally chaos. Abruptly

Broadface fell like a tree beside Greenstockings as he tottered past, his shining new gun clutched irremovably in his split hand, and when she tried to pull him a little into shadow, away from this alarming, blank stupidity she had never before seen on his beautiful face, his mouth jerked open and he blurted out whatever stinking poison he had heard and swallowed and held within himself that day, together with everything he had eaten. And then he snored away into gentle, unawakable, stinking sleep. So she wiped his face and pulled him aside from his vomit; watched the other women suffer the inexplicable behaviour of their distorted, gradually unrecognizable men.

It seems to her now that Birdseye, in not telling this about the moment when These English came, wants every person to heal themselves so deeply and for ever over that chaos that they will all together be convinced it never happened; as if by not speaking it into story, it never can happen again. Even though everyone fears in silence that it will.

For Birdseye, asleep and dreaming, there emerges only the flit of Tetsot'ine in their tiny birchbark shells as they circle those huge paddle-slaves bellowing songs over the placid heave and breathing of small lakes; over the bright standing waves and the turning eddies where the river plunges down or is surprised into climbing over rocks, to the wash of the first long fall slanted above them. Their journey together, into the long travelling home of the People, paddles, trudges, lifts itself up the Yellowknife River, and the visitors almost shoot or knife themselves at Dissension Lake, but unfortunately they don't, and the journey trundles on through swamp and welcoming barrens, eddies and is forced by winter coming to pause here among the last great trees.

The living winter, and Birdseye is able to rest a little. It will be longer, colder, darker, she whispers, than People have ever had to live here before this coming of these strangers. Here it is, now all around them.

Here on the esker, where Birdseye gathers her strength to tell the irrevocable journey of These English yet to come. The fierce darkness thickens the wavering voice of the rapids so deeply into itself that one night before he left Broadface told Greenstockings, as he lay in her arms, that the cold came so fast he has seen a wolverine, frozen, staring at him out of its ice. No one has ever seen that before: wolverine is too smart — but there he was, caught and frozen so quick his eyes were still open. She and Greywing were then scraping, day after day scrape, rub to keep soft and sew the strong hide of deer legs endlessly into boots. Working without Birdseye now, more urgently, the rhythm of their mother's breath luring them into its whispers until both their fingers and their minds are held suspended by her lengthening pauses. They listen, and among all the destroying of trees and dragging things and endless shooting and cutting and tearing apart of anything that lives or moves, they sense themselves still alive, their own relentless round of gathering wood, cooking, hauling water, setting snares for rabbits, scraping, twisting wet hides, cutting meat, sewing — they are here, as if time were a ball rolling over itself between ice and the bottomless darkness.

And then, abruptly, one night Birdseye plunges on. Leaps ahead past the gradual return of the circular light that will eventually (they still believe) arise south of their lodge, where it will emerge from under bones and soot-scattered snow, the gurgle again of running water. She grows louder and faster, for her story has blundered ahead into summer, into the horizon reaches of tundra and barren lands circling them, into briefly green, measureless distance.

"Ahhh yes," Keskarrah murmurs that night when they all want so badly to hear every word. "Perhaps this story is becoming like the wolf's track often is, it goes farther ahead into where it will happen, on and on, until it leads into beyond, and only then can it circle back to us again."

Nevertheless, though he surmises that the story has leaped far ahead and will eventually come back to them here and now, even he is confused about what they hear. Why is Thick English trying to walk across the tundra with his Halfmuds humped under those enormous packs, over swamp and between rocks? Why are they not on the continuous rivers he drew and explained for them, why is no Everlasting Ice visible even in the hand-shaded distance towards which, as Thick English has said again and again, they will track the River of Copperwoman so that they can bring their giant ships filled with all their stuff into the People's land and make them all so loaded down with the endless things no Person has ever seen? What has happened to their giant canoes? Where is the sea? Have they left it? If so, why — when that was all they ever wanted to find?

Perhaps, Keskarrah ponders aloud between Birdseye's pauses, the story is telling itself backwards. Perhaps also, now that These English have no more canoes to float on water, the story is too exhausting for her to lay out step after ponderous step and she is dreaming another moment far ahead on the continuous circle that is their travel, has touched on it somewhere nearer to the point where the end they do not anticipate arrives at its beginning again. And perhaps that circle is smaller than they think. Because it is of course now clear that, whether they knew it or not, the trek of These English coming has always been here waiting for them. It was already waiting before they decided (as they still seem to think *they decide* everything, as if they could determine or change what will happen), before they marked down and decided what should happen, before they climbed into their ships far over the stinking water and began this coming. If that is so, the smaller circle of the story will come around soon enough until it returns to find all the People here again.

"Wait...wait," he tells his daughters, "their travel goes forwards, but the story is coming backwards, it will eventually find itself back to us here. Soon enough."

But Keskerrah's tangled conjectures comfort no one. Birdseye exists gaunt and contorted under the sleeping-robes, as if waves of pain were grinding her into the spruce boughs of her bed. And finally one day Greywing begins to cry, even more bitterly than she has so often since her mother has walked motionlessly on this lengthening journey. Keskarrah reaches his hand to the girl from out of his fur nest.

"Come," he says. "Come."

"It's so long," Greywing sobs, trying to burrow in. He pulls aside the robes and she disappears against him. "Why do we have to hear it?" Her voice a distant hollow.

Under the robes Keskarrah cuddles her, profoundly sad. "You may be right," he concedes. "These Whitemuds may be here for ever."

But he does try to reassure them, himself as much as his two daughters. "Every story is long." And adds, hopefully, "It is not necessarily sad."

Greenstockings echoes her sister, "Why do we have to hear this? If they have to live it anyway, I don't want to hear it too."

Gently Keskarrah rocks Greywing against himself.

"The White story is what it is," he says. "Story permits no lie."

Birdseye is dreaming it now. And they must listen.

A lake, the frigid edge of it, and a canoe walking upside down, six legs between stones and smooth, bent sand. A line of men following. Spoors of animals lead in every direction away from their feet, deep trails braided together into a certain impossibility by hoofs walking yesterday, walking tomorrow, never walking today.

The paws and claws that relentlessly loop around these trails of hoof-prints are a day away also. An animal watches canoe and men walking, a bird pounds steady as stone through air above them, but neither will accept being nearer than one day away from either canoe or men. Never, never again.

This is how it is, has been, will be. Before these feet felt this grain of land, they had decided it was empty; they have now been awarded that gift of emptiness to walk upon. Before they had looked through this air, these heads had decided it must be cold, so now cold fondles them with tender constancy. Malignant wind drives this snow just for them, lakeshores provide this brittle ice to slash their last, ragged canoe, rivers run with these ice-pans so beautifully white, so swift and clear at the head of rapids that, though they have been taught better, they are nevertheless tempted to try for a seemingly easy traverse. There, a mere interruption of water, the smooth head of it deceptive, the superb river poised in such elegance and folded to roar down its tight full throat of rapid, they will try crossing here because it is so narrow, they are certain they could throw a stone over it if they still had their usual strength. They *must* cross this river — and two others as well, when they meet them, though they do not yet know that those exist. As they did not know of this one either. They will be much weaker then, for the desolation of their decided ignorance clings to them as they ponderously move, an immense weight that, they may eventually realize, is heavier than anything else they carry. They will hear its relentless promise even after they have left everything else lying beside the imprints of their passing. It will say to them:

"I am your most faithful ignorance. I will go with you and be your guide, in your most need to go by your side."

They have tried, are trying so valiantly to fill this desolating emptiness. With something — anything — perhaps their staggering, closely laid footprints will be enough; or their many things that they carry to drop: an ice-broken axe, a book, a piece of round metal, rifles, a spoon, various instruments, powder, books, forks, wine glasses. Blankets. Rifles again — but last of all. They have so much to leave behind, the blind with sticks could feel along their trail, the clang and texture of all their droppings — surely these will suffice, surely bodies will not be required. Thin snow hollows and angles a drift around some thing dropped, along a drag of English or voyageur foot, then freezes instantly, a twisted calligraphy whose strangeness the curious animals will read or smell tomorrow — or yesterday. A message no one will decipher. But determined ignorance will ride on each shoulder, will whisper so softly and tenderly:

"Lo, I am with you alway, even unto the end of the world."

The canoe legs stagger, crumple two, by two, by two. The canoe smashes down again against a rock. Every animal is always a day away. Or more than a day, a week, a century, like heaven itself for ever away because rifle barrels sway, waver along the exhausted line of eyes trying desperately to see, to pray anything alive into accepting a lethal bullet. Bullets have become a mere whistle in this profligate overabundance of clear air, which accepts everything with such solicitous consideration: scream, shot, halloo, groan, cry, curse — but most tenderly it accepts silence. Will they ever hear an animal again? Eat meat — either hardened, or soft, or pounded into a mixture of filth and long hair — eat? Meat? Silence.

In a long bowl of rocks, into which wind can drive a little less snow, the canoe at last accepts a gentle fire. Small smashed pieces of it feed firelight against the cliffs, soften the roar of the rapids. A mess of rock moss and two tiny fish boils there. The vapour drifts upwards, faint as a weed bending in the muscle of a river, and eighteen men hunch together around it, try somehow to nurse warmth and smell into themselves before they can finally cup the one warm spoon they have, turn by turn, into their split and crusted mouths.

Bent across a rock, his tall, gaunt body pointing delicately towards that most dangerous river they have not yet seen but will most certainly have to cross, a man is vomiting. Who is it? Surrendering at last the last bit of his courageous ignorance back to the accepting earth?

Greenstockings cooks her favourite food for Hood. Keskarrah and Greywing sleep in a mound of robes; Birdseye breathes her implacable dream into the fur under which she has buried her face. The firelight, wavering smells, contains the cone of the lodge around them, the delicate seams of it doubled and sewn against the wind along the line of the generous animals cut open and skinned to protect them. Greenstockings stretches her bare arm, hand, fingers the deer stomach hung low in the heat of the fire braiding upwards; it swings like a bird's nest, rocking, its shadow bulges, floating on the smoky hides.

"The round, beautiful kettles you bring," she tells Hood, gently because she is not using one, "are strong, but also very heavy. They cook slower than hot stones in a bag. But they hold the heat of the food so well inside them, and there is never stone to eat then, hot stones in soup break themselves so often, you can never tell when one will do it, just split itself! and then you have to pick the biggest pieces out of the blood-soup as you eat, but there is always some left, stone cooking is hard on good teeth."

She laughs, glances up for an instant at his listening intensity, laughing. "There is such strength in stone. It cleans you, scours you clean, you're washing inside with sand whenever you shit!"

Robert Hood laughs to see her laugh, to make her laugh again, to lengthen the sound of her singing voice. Not understanding a syllable of any word she has ever spoken. And not wanting to, nor thinking about that because her obsidian eyes flame firelight at him. She is laughing, and her head and naked shoulder flicker light so variously dark and lighter against the flames; the shadows beyond her on the sloping wall move continuously, this warm circular place where she has always lived, as if the lodge were breathing. The muscles at her shoulder and neck interfolded, lengthening under her copper skin.

"There is so much to eat here," she murmurs.

The sounds she makes skim fondly about in his ears, sing, as every concentrated minute he watches her mouth, the bright tip of her tongue against her teeth, her lips — he has been trying to draw her lips for two days, to catch that bottom curve, the tilt of the corners where the sounds she makes seem to catch sometimes like a quick surprise — he does not want to understand any word she ever speaks. None. The freedom of watching, of listening with incomprehension, fills him with staggering happiness: all the reports they are duty-bound to write, the daily journal, the data piled in columns upon page after page — but in this warm place thick with indescribable smells there is no listable fact, not a single word. Never. Simply the insatiable influx of eye and uncomprehending, musical ear, of fingertips and skin. As if time could be eaten out of her hand, ingested and lived into one enveloping physical containment, all thought, all necessary decision, all duty gone. Vanishment.

"We can, together," she says, "eat it all, all the sweet and bitter things I put into it."

He feels so gloriously clean, surrounded only by release. Cocooned in warmth no one can find in their ultimately unheatable cabin that is always full of endless duty where, beside the stone-and-clay fireplace he himself built with such ox-like labour, he can never hold a pencil without mittens and the ink crystallizes between dips of the raven's quill. Frost white as leprosy he has never seen before, but read about, blossoms along his wall bed between cracked mud and log. The blades of cold slice him long and thin to his very bones, and he loves the brittle beauty of that, the darkening logs, grey mud stroked to the tracks of fingers, the bristle of hoarfrost spidering parallel lines that waver between floor and ceiling. An austerity of ice, unnecessary to number or explain or record — or struggle to mirror somehow in a lined notebook.

So he speaks softly as he sees she is listening to his happiness, trying only to enourage again the rhythm of her voice, beyond his words that she in her turn will never understand either.

"I'm so warm here with you, it's almost like…like sitting beside the fireplace in the manse kitchen in Bury, eight miles north of Manchester…though that fireplace is so huge and black and hard — I can walk to Bury in two hours, get off the eight-horse coach in Manchester and be — that's silly, you've never seen a horse! — a kind of…ridable caribou, without antlers! — but heavier, more like a movable tree than a caribou! — and my mother knits in winter and our kitchen girl bends to move the pans with their long handles around, as my mother tells her to, on the grate inside the chimney. It's higher than I am, standing, and I sit inside the chimney, the fire running low on the coals, and this is like that, not that blue fire but red — warm, warm, whenever I come in here, and it smells so different from black coal. Your hide walls are warmer than bricks baked with soot, all these orange flames of sap burning, like fresh apples in your mouth, apples from the cemetery behind St. Mary's…I wish I could put one in your mouth, how can your mouth never have felt an apple? Crisp, cracking between your beautiful teeth. And you smile, rocking that caribou gut full of whatever you've stuffed in there, I'd stuff you with anything you want...."

He leans closer to Greenstockings, his words such sibilant sound, while they both stare intently into the fire, both bent forwards but aware only (she thinks, he thinks) of each other side by side, the leaping fire that draws them together without touching. How has she always existed here? How could he not know of it? In this circle of leather and fire as distant and unimaginable as the moon. He forgets his paper at last; his pencil falls, it bristles the edge of a flame unnoticed.

"Only my mother," he whispers, "calls me 'Robin'. Only when we are alone. She knits by the fire, these long green stockings for me, or mittens, and we play verses, 'O Robin, my little Robin,' she sings, 'Who killed Cock Robin?' and I recite, 'I, says the Sparrow, with my bow and arrow, and I killed....'"

Greenstockings lays wood over the burning pencil he has forgotten; if he wants to draw more he can paint his fingers with ash. Why does he keep trying to make her outline on paper? If he wants it, why doesn't he feel it with her face between his hands? Perhaps she can tell him that — her lips, if he felt them with one hand surely his other one could find them too, even at the end of a pencil or brush. He is different, so quick to understand and so stupid, she says to him whatever she wants and even without words he often does not know anything. Her hand lifts the blazing stick as she considers that: she has never thought it before about a man; she will tell him anything, whatever has always been unspeakable, his incomprehension gives her freedom.

But he is still too stupid, despite this gentle demandlessness that drifts about him. He sits for hours watching her, or whatever is done in the lodge, even Greywing or Keskarrah as they sleep, and he asks nothing, demands nothing, forces nothing to happen with his possible male domineering. As if he isn't even a man, though he certainly is that, she has felt it. There is a quiet and patience in him, like a hunter dreaming animals to come when they want to — though she is certain he doesn't think of animals, as if he has always had more than enough to eat — in what world could that be? — but that stillness in him is not at all like every man who has watched her, a piece of something to be groped for inside his thick head but that he won't find there until he finally takes her between his hands, frees himself between her legs. She is certain he does not think like that, this stranger whom she sometimes believes she can understand. And when he isn't there in the red, smoky warmth of the lodge she moves effortlessly, turns, works in what she comprehends to be the memory of his gentle tenderness, the kind of undemand he offers her humming a desire within her…strange…strange.

In the flames she sees the tiny orange spot they are together in the great land spread out by the white darkness of the moon, the shades of the enormous lights burning over them. The People call those lights "caribou running" because stroking the hide of an animal lifts and sparkles the same fire under your hand, the lights vanishing themselves and returning on the deep night sky. She can say it?

She says slowly, aloud, "In the long dark, there are always the animals, their hoofs like quick shovels, their running in herds over the sky lights the winter darkness, and on earth they feed on the fine white moss they dig for us, to feed us from the ground they smell again, under the snow."

Hood's body intense, listening. No one intrudes with an acceptable understanding, and her happiness begins to dance with him. She says:

"They already feed our sky mothers, and our unborn children there, in the sky, the animals, and we see them most often in winter because it is then that their stomachs taste so sweet on earth, sweeter than mother's milk. I heard my mother sing when she nursed me, and my father fed me too, the only way he could when I was little, when he brought her the meat to feed me as the moss feeds the animals who feed us now, and chewed the meat tender and wet for me so I could swallow. My mother sang,

> Give me your stomach,
> Sweet animal, I am praying to you,
> Your beautiful sweet stomach
> Filled with sky-white mosses
> You have smelled out carefully for me,
> Crisp, frozen milk of earth
> Which I cannot drink by myself.
> Chew it, milk it into my mouth;
> Feed me.

And I will sing that song too. For you, I took this stomach out of the animal and poured in its blood and chewed small pieces of ribs and fat, chewed them soft mouthful by mouthful until there were enough to fill you, and spit them into the stomach until it was full, here it is, cooked and smoked too, full and wanting to be eaten, you can eat and I will eat with you, our fingers feeding each other. Or would you like it frozen and sliced so thin we will see each other through our food, your mouth full of it like mine, our chins running with juice warm and frozen? I could feed you now, should I give you my breast, should I sing?"

They both contemplate her hand pointed into the knife as it cuts the full curled stomach down from its hanging cords. And she may already be singing, as her mother once sang, cooking, or the song her father sang waiting for this animal to dream its way into his snare, into his patient hunting,

> The land around me, everywhere
> Is rich with your food,
> Such beautiful moss
> On the land holding me here,
> You will want to set your pointed feet,
> Your moist nose
> In this delicate moss, you will want to come.
> Come to me here!

And in her song, which he cannot recognize, Robert Hood sings as well, the acceptable melancholy of the English manse knit into each cell of his personal, endless longing,

> Drink to me only with thine eyes,
> And I will pledge with mine;
> Or leave a kiss within the cup,
> And I'll not look for wine.
> The thirst that from the soul doth rise,
> Doth ask...a drink...

And here the rhythm of her unintelligibilty becomes strangely tangled for him into

I, said the Fly,
With my little eye
And I saw him...

While beside them, unheeded, in her sleep far beyond anything Robert Hood will find imaginable in the quick, desperate brevity of his life, Birdseye murmurs sounds neither she nor Greenstockings fully comprehend. Though they both hear them into existence syllable by deadly syllable. Her breath brushing the fur raises no fire there that anyone can yet see; the inevitabilities already coming there still invisible, the future still hidden though already born. Like the great north lights flaming in the sky at night: always there but so rarely visible to a human eye.

A figure on a wide cliff where the River of Copperwoman plunges over itself, where the river continues to disappear north into mist. Is it a large animal lying down there, or sitting? Skulls and long bones are scattered on the cliff, human bones. One by one men appear, climbing up, burdened with black hats. And two canoes with six legs each, climbing ponderously. The figure does not move.

Hats and canoes circle, the mist from mouths moving through cloudy mosquitoes. An arm, a hand, and the figure falls over — it is an old woman dead, the braided leather rope that strangled her fear still rigid in her rigid hand. Nothing can be said here, nothing explained, nothing that can possibly advise or guide anyone. Only

briefly mosquitoes and moss, and the level tundra sloping away into an openness so long that even eyes taught
distance by the sea cannot comprehend its blue dimension from among these skulls big and little. A feud? A
raid? A war, a massacre licked clean by wind and animal,
hard in the sun and snow and so perfect but for a knife's
gouge, a splintered hollow of clubs? Bones broken and
sucked hollow as throats. Enemies. A simple comprehen-
sible word.

Endless enemies. Like the endless sea they have already spent two years searching to reach again over land
they have fervently wished, nay, prayed every night, would
finally relent and cease to be there — always before them.
The hats turn among the skulls, trying to separate various
horizons, searching to discover the prayed-for undrink-
able sea smashing itself steadily upwards upon the stones
of the ocean. Where is the trackless sea where they can,
with all their articulated skill, manipulate wind and current to carry them where — in the small words that they
carry like a bound sentence everywhere with them —
they were so comfortably ordered to go? From there, and
only from there, can they permit themselves to try to return to where they came from. Water water, where is the
water, will they be forced for ever to look for the great
stinking water?

When they have walked far enough, only a little farther, they do discover the sea. Where they recognize,
then, it has always been. And also occasional ice. True,
when with rejoicing they first discern that Royal Navy
blue, which they know instantly belongs to them — it is

always theirs everywhere on the immense globe of the earth — they decide that their great ships can sail the channels here between sandbars and shoals and strips of rock pointing north; and they are reasonably ecstatic, as behooves them. They are again at sea, all's right with the world.

In the perpetual brightness of July arctic night, both north and east ahead of them, what they consider to be the open sea glows from somewhere beyond where they can see, a strange iridescence of white as though the moon were burning like a sun just below and all along the horizon. But those may well be Northern Lights, yes, undoubtedly that is what it is, that must be recorded, another new and fascinating manifestation of the aurora borealis in conjunction with the yet-unsearched Polar Sea. They have been accumulating words about those lights since they left the Orkneys, so write it down, notes on "sea horizon glow" for further analysis, soon, when there will be time next winter.

And once they have named that iridescence, tamed it with a blurted sound, they are again content not to recognize what they can see; to ignore what the wind is breathing over them. And the icepans, small bergs, rotten chunks really, dripping and never flat but often tilted picturesquely on edge in the near water, which is never blue but black, ice always lingering a bit as if waiting for a glimpse of them when they round a cape, and then gone shyly every morning — long ago they saw true icebergs, and these are mere playthings for small animals like seals, toys to anchor terns — neither of which, oddly, they have yet spied anywhere, though they would certainly try to kill any living thing they saw and even more gladly eat if only any appeared.

And then, one morning out of silent fog, comes the Everlasting Ice.

They recognize it instantly, for it does not come to them smooth and flat the way cold would skin over English water. This ice is no skin at all; from out of the fog it is merely, implacably, itself, bristling like an emerging avalanche of jagged stone, a coming cataclysm that everywhere shades into other tinges of something that nevertheless remains grotesquely, featurelessly white, off-white with the grim age of broken bone smashed and crushed down upon itself and re-formed again out of its crushing; which, if a man stumbled into, he would have to twist, clamber, slip, as between blades or spears — no one can walk on teeth, or needles — and surely vanish pronged in three gasps. Or a tall ship to its very mast in as many minutes, shredded into splinters.

This ice does not come silently, without motion. No. Carried by its own particular wind and water destiny, it approaches muttering, or passes them faster than a man can run along the twisted sand. Where it wasn't yesterday it may be today, or not be tomorrow. In the bright, temporary disorientation of a summer midnight fog they were forced to hear it, but now they see what they heard without comprehension: out of freezing fog they see the ice grinding, crunching, groaning, cracking, eating itself from horizon and water into existence before them. Already there is barely enough open water left to launch the narrow canoes. While they stare, horrified, the ice advances, heaves itself out in long, rending groans, hesitates and backs off and sighs to a tinkle and splash like frozen bells, then heaves forwards again, groaning, gouging up the naked shingle. Already it splinters and falls into cliffs over itself, humping at them and their canoes. It is ramming ridges up under their very tents on the slender beach, black sand and stone avalanches.

Behold: ice has discovered itself to These English at last. It is seeking them out. Behold: the Everlasting Ice is advancing upon them by land.

Hood tries to feed Greenstockings with the silver spoon he has carried inside his clothes from England, but she ducks her head aside. The thick fall of her hair swings to hide her face.

"Just purse your lips a little," he says as her face emerges again, "it's hot, an 'oo' like this, then it won't clink against your beautiful...teeth."

He is almost laughing at "beautiful", which he has never said aloud to a woman before, and at his shaky hand, at the metallic weight with which he is offering her own food to her wet, open mouth. Even stranger — the gelatinous food scooped steaming from a cooked or smoked caribou stomach; as if English silver could ever place that savage concoction acceptably on white linen, lift it to perfect teeth and without a thought his mouth blurts aloud, "Haggis — Scots and haggis!"

She raises her face to him to catch the corner of his astonishment at whatever he has said. Laughter pulls her mouth wide at his exploding breath, at this game of eating, together, learning with simple silly laughter what they have both done since before consciousness. But he seems to think he is teaching her, and she will play anything as easily as parting her lips for him.

"Yes," he says, "o-o-o…round and pursed, like that, yes," moving the spoon upwards and not comprehending what he is doing, knowing nothing of how she is shaping his name as round and long between her lips to meet his spoon. Beyond him the capricious fire flares high in a strand of smoke as his hand with the laden spoon, and her eyes tighten with laughter bursting from her, as it trembles towards her — is it the fire or his excitement? — but her mouth opens to accept it for certainly he will feed her, she very nearly touches his hand with hers to slow him down, to breathe him over it slowly.

"Ho-o-o-o-o," she blows. And he has become so delicate she can touch his hand and the spoon waits for her, entering between her lips into her hollow mouth. "O-o-o-o…d." Closing around the spoon.

Robert Hood has never fed a child, and certainly never a woman. This spoon slipping along her tongue as if it were his hand has never been in anyone's mouth but his own. And hers — like his heart bursting, he wants his hand inside her mouth.

"It was given to me…" he says with extreme care, though his heart staggers. "Who fed Cock Robin…who fed…who fed…." The spoon's English shape vanishing perfectly in the red firelight of her red mouth. He lifts fingers to her lips, tips moist against her mouth, and a shadow of red along the silver curve withdrawing between her folding lips, which are all he sees, swallowing as he senses her swallow. The spoon lies uplifted between his fingers, with the complete weight of her body beside him in the fiery cone of the lodge. He cannot comprehend what is happening.

He sees himself seated beside her, his hand still up, and in the chimney corner answers his mother so eagerly,

I, said the Fish,
With my little dish,
And I caught his blood.

And he is on the wharf where the frigate H.M.S *Impérieuse* is tied, her massive guns hidden though he will hear and feel them all bellow soon enough when the immense masts shatter over him and a ripping splinter skewers a terrified sailor crouched one instant behind the smoking gun and the next flying over the sea as if he had sprouted slivered wings — but he is mumbling, avoiding something worse than that memory with mumbles, he mumbles like her mother under them, somewhere, among the furs,

"My godfather, eight years ago, on St. Bartholomew's Day just…before I went to sea…fourteen and I was…see, St. Bartholomew's knife here on the spoon handle, tradition says he was killed by a knife, it's…I dreamed a silver wolf…godfathers give you this in my land, a silver spoon and best wishes on your saint's day, its silver jaw full of long teeth, when you begin your…career, the navy for me, and so I have this…this silver…."

Her hand lifts the heavy spoon from him, her fingers hide the knife engraved along its handle. She tells him what he must hear and will never understand until it is much too late, a knowledge she already knows with an overwhelming sorrow she can never give him, necessary gift though it is.

"You must eat now," she tells him, dipping into the stomach she has cut open. "You will not die like that here. I have heard that."

She concentrates on the spoon and his bent nose, his lips opening soft and full like any woman's. And tells him further:

"My snow friend, no knife waits for you. My mother is dreaming all your travels, you can hear your journey, there, and you will die. That's what she's already said. She has not quite dreamed to your death, not yet, but I tell you your heart will never fold around a knife, not here, you will walk and walk over our land until hunger meets you, but now I feed you, now, and you may never starve either, so eat now, you may not ever be cut, nor starve, no."

And even as she speaks this, she inevitably sees what she has so far avoided. And her eyes fill with tears until finally she can look into his eyes: blurred as if seen through stony ice. For an instant she believes she recognizes that he will freeze — certainly cold will clutch and devastate him before anything else, the river may tear him apart between the ice teeth of its rapids, and when she walks there beneath her feet she will see his bulging face again, his destroyed eyes — but his eyes are before her, concentrated on her, intensely blue, studying her as he accepts each spoonful she offers him as though he would gladly swallow her too. He has never smelled or tasted anything so moistly delicious; in the officers' mess all they eat while trying to contain their endless shivering is red meat boiled or roasted by Hepburn out of every recognizability except grey slop or charcoal. He would happily eat here for ever, the Bury manse stone chimneys suddenly as trivial as twigs, if she fed him what she has fermented and cooked of caribou stomach moss and juices, bone marrow, blood, tender bits of nose and muscle and liver, a curdle of fawn's milk, the fat she has shredded and washed in her own sweet saliva. He has never sensed such texture in his mouth, this evanescence she offers him slides along his teeth, his throat.

"We hunger often," she tells him. "Often the animals are gone, they will not let us find them where they go to calve in spring or return in the fall, and sometimes even the bears or ptarmigan or rabbits or squirrels or mice avoid us like weather. All animals go where they go, we can only sing to follow them. The fish swim to us, but not always, and there may be moss to cook, it curls black on stones for winter, but if the animals don't eat it for you so you can eat it from their stomachs, you have to be careful, because it can make you shit more than you eat, and when you do that you are really eating yourself. Inside.

"I've done that often, eat myself; there is time for everyone to do that. There is a place inside my mouth that is dangerous. Every person finds that place inside them, and it only hurts for four days and after that you get thinner and soon you think so slowly, your voice comes out deeper between your bloodied, hollow cheeks, and if you bruise or cut yourself you won't heal any more, but it bleeds and hurts very little. Only if someone snares a ptarmigan and you accept a mouthful of it, then the giant hunger settling to rest in your bones wakes immediately and you want food again so much that People sometimes cannot help but eat those who have already died. Hunger then has become too much, no one can speak of it any more. People eat and vomit and eat everything again, though if those they eat have starved to death not even their bones and marrow will help, you just eat the hunger that has already eaten them. Hunger makes People crazy sometimes. I have seen them afterwards, and they are worse than dead because they are still living. But my father has lived long without going crazy and he watches ravens. 'Ravens,' he says, 'you must sing, and they will feed you. Ravens, and the compassionate wolves.'"

She cuts away a sliver of the tender smoked stomach, scoops it into the food and offers it on her spread fingers.

"The wolves," she tells him as his face approaches her hand, "taught us how to hunt these honey animals that feed us. Perhaps sometimes we are born as wolves, but they have always been our sisters and brothers, we never kill them. They will feed you too, if you are careful and let them."

Her fingers enter his mouth; his tongue curls around them slick with fat as his body tightens, coils, tightens. Slowly she begins to withdraw them, but he lingers, holding them, sucks clean every taste and lingulation of food. She is telling him:

"My father says when a person is too hungry to see land clearly, or cannot crawl around animals to turn them where an armed hunter waits in hiding like the strongest she-wolf with her teeth, when the hunter is too weak to hold his lance or bow steady, or even draw it, then ravens can lead him to what the wolves kindly leave for us. For we are all animals, we know our hunger, and when we have food we leave some for each other. Wolves will leave a head, bones, sometimes even some hide to scrape and boil, though you cannot expect the tenderest parts — remember," she says, looking directly now into Hood's eager, uncomprehending eyes, "when you are too weak to think, remember: look in the sky. Raven will be there. He will lead you to our sister wolf. Leave food for her and her little ones when you have some, and she will always leave some for you."

Hood is looking into Greenstockings' eyes and sees there, it seems, the shape of the silver wolf he dreamed — a trick of her fire perhaps — superb and powerful he remembers, its neck bent round to look at him through daggered teeth out of a jaw he shot away — why did he do that? Why did he fire that rifle, dearest God?

He dreamed he was trying to draw that wolf, always the drawing, as he has literally drawn so many, even one for Back and his prosaic background of Dogrib Rock, and he tugged at his raven quill, which was suddenly frozen tight in the inkwell, and shot the wolf's jaw away, its lower head exploded in ink and the fur ripped back completely, off its bent neck and shoulders and it was still standing there with its skinned skull and its grotesque upper jaw thrust at him like a serrated knife, bone clean and white. Why did he shoot it? How in the dream could his gun be loaded, since he has always refused that when he is awake?

Tears well in her eyes; their blackness floats him into them. Her brown hands bright as glass rise together around his face and pull him over, his head down into her lap. Surrounded so tightly by her he smells deep smoke and texture, hot animal. What she is doing he cannot think of, but is so overwhelmed with its intimacy that he would not resist even if she intended that his throat now open under her inerrant knife. She talks bent over him, her body folded about him.

"Now you will feed me," her lips tell him, her dark cheek within the length of his tongue, and he feels her powerful fingers search at the roots of his hair. She is doing for him what he has seen her and Greywing do often, and he has shuddered with longing for it to be done to him: cradling each other in their laps, they stroke each other clean of lice.

The lice are everywhere. Like sin waiting in every tree, the logs and mud roofs of their huts, every cranny of bed and blanket, the hides of every animal they eat, everything they wear, between the very pages of his notebook and snug in every fold or crevice of his body and numberless in his hair — at times he tears his hair in bristling rage and discovers nits on a single strand clustered thick as cellar onions hung stored on a delicate rope. It could be, Lieutenant Franklin has conjectured ponderously (though Doctor Richardson disagrees scientifically), that the very air of this dreadful land engenders such vermin as it engenders cold; a kind of spontaneous genesis. But now Greenstockings is picking them from him one by one, her quick fingers, which he has endlessly tried to draw tying the complex pattern of snowshoe web, strip the lice, place them cluster by scrabbling cluster between her teeth. Her full lips close, her jaw shifts and he hears the lice being crushed, and then she swallows them.

Her close face above him soothes him so completely out of his revulsion that he will remember nothing of this moment but her ethereal face. It floats golden in the firelight, serene as a madonna, offering in this filthy frozen world the ultimate hospitality of food and tender, intimate cleanliness. "Which Is Next To Godliness," his mother always said in High Church capitals, knuckling his grubby ears. Cradled here, he can only smile at the irony of what she would have refused to imagine for him: how to be next to godliness indeed.

"They live drinking your blood," Greenstockings says close against his forehead, a trace of blood curved on the curve of her lower lip. "Your sweet blood."

We are all always bloody, Robert Hood thinks. From the instant we are born bloody, everything we eat is won with blood. And bent about her hot body, clasping the full heat of it, he is

standing behind the massive ship's gun below the mast still splin-
tering above him in the continuing crash of bombardment, his
loaded pistol high as the captain has ordered and terrified beyond
himself that now, surely now one of the sailors will run, this is
too much, one will certainly try to scoot past him on the deck already washed twice with their comrades' blood and he will have
to shoot him, no, no, *execute*, the captain said, whoever deserts
his assigned post in battle is judged with instant *execution*, by
you, you are an English naval officer, your imperial duty under
oath is to stand behind that gun with two loaded pistols, one in
hand and one stuck in — he twists his face into Greenstockings'
stomach, thrusting his legs out as the soft leather yields against
him, but even there he cannot escape the thin, ascetic voice of his
father, the Right Reverend Richard Hood, B.A., LL. D., rising to
his favourite text from the high chancel at St. Mary's Church,
Bury, Lancashire, in the necessary morning lesson from St. Paul,
his categorical, logical clarity of preposterous faith:

"And all things are by the law purged with blood; and without the shedding of blood is no remission of sin. It was therefore necessary that all who ———"

He clutches Greenstockings spastically, tighter, crying aloud
to drown, disappear somehow in her smoky, yielding...he feels
his cheekbone hard against her mound; her folded legs loosen
about his face.

And he jerks up out of her arms, twists himself around to
reach his feet. "Here...here..." he hisses into her startled surprise, untying the string and stripping down the tall boots she
has sewn to care for his feet — when he walked them into the
snow he felt powerful enough to hurl aside the frozen tundra
— "My...my stockings, here...my...."

Peeling his stockings down, one and then as quickly as he can the other, and offering them to her, her brilliant eyes reflecting firelight.

And slowly she removes her moccasins. For a moment of stopped breath he sees for the first time her narrow naked foot before it enters the round mellow warmth created by his knee and leg and foot, watches her leg, her skin, slip down and fill the space only he has shaped, one leg and as slowly the other. Then she stands up, over him, long and firm in Sherwood Forest greenwood stockings, and then he can lift his two hands and touch her skin above them. And his face must tilt forwards there as his hands slide down, and turn, and feel each perfect toe spreading like fingers into the gentleness of wool, her slim, o, so vulnerable feet hidden, sheltered and safe within the interwoven circles knit so lovingly by steel in the hands of his loving mother. Forehead and skin, and lips, and tongues.

Inside the round lodge sheltered from the hard moon by tall evergreen trees below the brow of the esker, Birdseye murmurs aloud. Her exhaustion can no longer pull her story steadily into words, she can find bits of its circle only where the hard knotted threads of its facts belabour her:

> ...tracks filled. Mounds lengthen towards the horizon. Circles of twigs burned within sight of each other erased by the wind of running snow. A tent and three mounds perhaps sleeping. A fourth moving erect, massive black, the Mohawk from so many rivers away, his body blazing naked and in the snow — be careful! something is wrong, when you freeze or starve the strongest is always

the most dangerous — don't you know that? It is always the strongest who most tenderly cares for you, until he kills you — watch out!

Greywing stirs at a muffled scream, lifts her head from among Keskarrah's furs. Her mother's sleeping nest beside her is shaking, opening, shuddering into pieces.

"Everything is dangerous!" her voice cries under layers of leather. "The fire, the knife, his eye, his axe...."

Greywing shakes her father. He stirs, struggling against awareness.

"Any piece of heavy wood, his gun, his hand, his two hands...."

The lodge is clasped inside the immense, silent rock of cold that is the world. Greywing whimpers in her lonely consciousness, digging through fur for Greenstockings, along her strange woollen foot and leg, her naked thigh.

"His teeth, oh yes, watch his teeth!" Birdseye screams.

Greywing grabs at covers, exposes Greenstockings and Hood beyond her, Bone is all he can be named, asleep now; they are folded around each other slippery and naked.

"Wake up! Wake up!" She is jerking Greenstockings' head away from Hood by her long hair, their arms and breasts and stomachs separating, the intertwined lengths of their moist legs smelling sweet as animals, and they stir awake, eyes opening. "Listen — listen!"

Birdseye sings spastically over and over, *"Cock...robin... rock...robin...who...saw...him...I...said...the...fly...."*

Greywing and Greenstockings stare at Robert Hood, stunned beyond comprehension, who is staring at their mother's

open defacement rising out of the furs. He cannot believe it —
it must be the blunder of low shadows and…darkness, of the
fearsome cold as the fire dies — but his ears force him into stu-
pefaction, her breath snoring out of her opened face, her words
that he cannot but understand: as if after two years of labouring
to reach the ends of the world he had arrived there in time to
find what he most hated already waiting for him. Speaking to
him in language he is forced to understand:

"*With…my…little…eye,*" Birdseye stutters, groans in English. "*And…I…saw…him….*"

Greenstockings and Greywing shriek in fear — as if they
understood where Hood knows nothing — both reaching to
clutch him. Keskarrah heaves himself up.

"Who is dead?" he instantly asks of the darkness.

His daughters rock Hood between them, so warm against
their fine, bare skins. And then Keskarrah begins to shout, as if
to drown out Birdseye's indecipherable cries.

"Why have you come here?" he bellows at Hood with an aggression that makes his daughters huddle the stranger away between them in renewed fear. "If you are Snow Man the ice will
never thaw nor the wind stop blowing while you're here, so go
away, go north where your enemies are killing your children,
go, we can't help you, go away, go back north! Go away!"

But his beautiful daughters rock the young Whitemud
between their naked breasts, their slender arms and legs coil
around him in a tangle of grief and terror and Keskarrah knows
that this is no Snow Man, and never was. That is no way to
trick him into leaving. He can only blurt out at Hood, with deep
bitterness:

"You are strong, you could easily take one of them, and she

could save you. Should I make a picture of where you must go? To go away?"

And then, almost pathetically at Hood's stunned silence, "Will you go away?"

"...*I*...*caught*...*his*...*blood*...." Birdseye weeps in English, clawing savagely at the blackness in her ravaged face.

"Ah-h-h-h," Keskarrah groans in despair at her tone, at the unavoidable understanding that what Birdseye has discovered goes far beyond any arrivals that Tetsot'ine stories have until now explored. "Ah-h-h-h-h-h..." is all he can groan.

DOCTOR JOHN RICHARDSON

Monday January 15th 1821   Fort Enterprise

*Our men arrived from Fort Providence with 2 kegs of rum, one
barrel of powder, 2 rolls of tobacco, 60 lbs. of ball and some
clothing. They brought two Esquimaux, Augustus and Junius,
with them, who will act as our interpreters when we reach the
Polar Sea. They have been 21 days on the return march up and
the labour they have undergone is sufficiently evinced by the
collars of the sledges having worn out the shoulders of their coats.
One of the rum kegs was broached on the way up and a
considerable quantity abstracted.*

Mr. Back found it necessary to go on to Fort Chipewyan.

*In the evening the officers joined the Canadians in the hall, to
enliven their spirits by a dram of rum, and also to prevent them
from conversing upon our differences with the Indians, which
they had observed. They are most fond of dancing, with which
they continued until 2 a.m., an exercise also in a peculiar
manner serviceable to Mr. Hood. Ever ardent in his pursuits, he
had, through close attention to his drawings and other
avocations, confined himself too much to the house in winter,
and his health was impaired by his sedentary habits.*

Monday February 5th   Fort Enterprise

*Two Indians arrived from Bigfoot for a further supply of
ammunition. They are hunting south and west of the house, and
Bigfoot is displeased at not having rum sent to him. Sent him a
keg of diluted spirits and some powder and shot.*

Monday February 12th   Fort Enterprise

*The winter habitations of the Esquimaux are built of snow, and
judging from one constructed by Augustus today, they are very
comfortable dwellings. He selected a spot on the river where the
snow was about two feet deep and sufficiently compact.*

*The purity of the material of which the house was framed, the
domed elegance of its construction and the translucency of its
walls, which transmitted a very pleasant light, gave it an
appearance far superior to a marble building and one might
survey it with feelings somewhat akin to those produced by the
contemplation of a Grecian temple reared by Phidias. Both are
triumphs of art inimitable in their kinds.*

8

STOLEN WOMAN

"This happened a long time ago, when a man and a woman were living together," Keskarrah begins several nights after the voyageurs return from great Tucho without Boy English. Or Broadface and Little Marten either, who were the only People who agreed to keep up with Back travelling to Fort Chipewyan on his little snowshoes.

Though perhaps no one except Greenstockings is thinking about that journey; certainly no one in the lodge mentions it. Why should they, any more than the inevitable passages of weather? People have come to the esker from The Hook's camp because they wanted to, and from Longleg's, and Bigfoot's as well, and met where others had already arrived. Many have brought food, others have not, and there are certainly dances and talking and singing and eating whatever anyone has, and now as many as can get into the lodge sit or lie circled around Keskarrah, listening. The warmth of their many bodies together flares the fire upwards into light, glistening on winter-burned faces. Some smaller children crawl over one person to another, or fall asleep in convenient laps, under warm hands they find gentle enough.

"Maybe it was a thousand years ago," Keskarrah says at the head of the fire. "Memory can see that far, and many of you know this one about the woman and Blackfire, but hear me now.

"Blackfire was a great warrior, though no one knows his name from before then, or who his People were, and sometimes he is called 'No Fire', or 'Very Long Without Fire'. But Blackfire is his name for us because in that coldest winter, when it happened, he had a fire burning inside him that no one could see, not even in the darkness. It was his fire, one he had to carry, and it wasn't wood that made it burn either.

"It began at this time, when it is coldest, and the animals had gone away as they sometimes do for us, for no one can truly understand the way of the wind or the caribou. All the People had to live on were the good rabbits. The man who would become Blackfire was a superb hunter and he had killed the most, a great pile, and everyone brought their rabbits together to his lodge the way we do to feast, especially after long hunger when eating alone becomes worse than not eating at all. It was so hot in the lodge from women cooking that Blackfire and the other men had taken off their shirts, they were naked to the waist keeping the fires going to eat."

A murmur of assent and encouragement rustles through the lodge, and Keskarrah lifts his head higher, his voice rising:

"Then Blackfire's woman heard something, outside. She was already known everywhere as a very wise person and her names are several too. Not Copperwoman, who was stolen as well, but some call her 'Fiercely Desired Woman', or 'The One Fought Over', or 'Ravished Woman', or 'Woman Stolen Back and Forth' — but for us her name is 'She Who Delights', as her man is Blackfire.

"That day She Who Delights heard something, and stood listening so hard, it sounded like a coming thunderstorm though it was midwinter. Blackfire saw her, and came beside her in the door to look for himself. Instantly he knew what it was: an army of enemies was attacking, closing in on their camp. There was only one tiny gap left where they were not already surrounded, and he grabbed his snowshoes and threw them down to run.

"But the binding on his left shoe broke as he turned his foot into it. Immediately She Who Delights threw one of her snowshoes down for him and he was off like an arrow, the way warriors are trained to do, running for the tiny gap between the attackers. He was so fast he got through before they saw him coming and he ran for the hills, naked as he was.

"Blackfire's brother's boy, who lived in his lodge like a son, also grabbed his snowshoes to run. But he twisted his foot putting them on and couldn't get through before the gap closed. So he was the first one lanced, by the rocks below the hills, and then those enemies attacked the camp and cut and clubbed every person to death, every child and even the dogs, and they burned the camp, a fire so huge it seemed the world was burning to the last scrap of wood or bone or leather. And after they had heated themselves on that, they buried the ashes in snow so that there would be nothing to help Blackfire if they didn't find him and kill him too.

"That was the way People fought in those days: if you make

war, kill everyone. Otherwise there may never be an end to the necessary revenge.

"Yes, those enemies did what they had come for: they chased Blackfire naked into the hills and destroyed his People. But there was one Person they didn't kill, and that was She Who Delights. They captured her alive, though she fought them until they had to beat her senseless, captured alive because she was the reason for their winter journey. They had come for her, a powerful, beautiful and very wise woman. Men kill each other for women like that, they always have, and of course the war leader of the enemy strangers took her first, but then he gave her to two brothers, his strongest men. She was far too much for just one of them.

"Blackfire had hidden himself well among the rocks up on the hills. They searched everywhere there but couldn't find him, and he watched them kill his People and burn the camp. He had to see three warriors overpowering She Who Delights, but neither that nor the warriors, when they left, each one clubbing his son's body again and screaming his power, would enrage him into revealing himself. He was too smart; that fire was beginning to burn in him.

"So they carried his woman away below him, tied up like a chunk of fresh meat, and the last to leave was the war leader. Now this powerful man, White Horizon, is known to everyone. White Horizon was Blackfire's equal among these enemies, a man powerful enough to trade with him and give him shelter when they met, and so they would not kill each other. When White Horizon passed the rocks with his bloody club in his bloody hands he stopped by the boy's smashed body, but he did not hit it. He called out softly to Blackfire,

"'Come down, I'll give you warm clothes.'

"But Blackfire would not reveal himself.

"'You'll freeze to death,' White Horizon called. Still Blackfire would not answer. 'Well, I'll leave you these long beaver mittens, they'll help.'

"Then Blackfire hissed from above in the rocks, 'I tell you: when the hair grows white again around the throats of the caribou, don't sleep in your camp!'

"So White Horizon, that eternal enemy, walked away and followed his men south over the hills, and Blackfire came down and pulled on the mittens. They were so long they reached to his armpits. He piled stones over his son's mutilated body and searched for whatever could help him stay alive, but those strangers were very clever and he found nothing. He had had to watch everything being destroyed and She Who Delights raped and dragged away and yet no tears had broken from him, but when he knew that the last spark of fire in the buried ashes of the camp was dead, he sat down and cried. Without fire in the long darkness, how could he live to gain revenge?

"Something licked his face as he lay hollowed under a snowdrift: two dogs. Badly wounded, but they too had survived the attack. So he pulled a thong from She Who Delights' snowshoe, made a snare and set it, and slept tight between the dogs. And he caught a rabbit in his woman's snare. He skinned it with a cracked stone but, hungry as he was, he couldn't eat raw rabbit. Since then every Person knows, no matter how hungry you are, you can't keep raw rabbit down, you'll just vomit and become weaker. So he tore the skin into strips, wound them around his naked chest and fed the meat to the dogs, who of course have stronger stomachs. Then he started looking for People to help him.

"The snow was very deep and he could see no track, so he took the longest willow he could break off and poked it carefully into the snow, trying to discover a trail. At last, very deep down, it seemed he felt one, the slight hardness of a footprint deep down in the snow, and then he circled wider, probing, until he touched that faint hardening again. Day after day through the darkness he worked in big circles, setting the snare for rabbits and wrapping their fur around himself and feeding the meat to the dogs, who kept him alive with their warmth when he slept a little. But he was starving, and the dogs were too badly wounded; first one and then the other died.

"He could barely move, but now he was almost covered with rabbit and dog fur; and could feel the trail was just under the surface. He kept going, every day more slowly but he would not stop. Every day he remembered more names as the land showed him places where things have happened, surrounding him with the voices of his ancestors until one day, far in the distance, Blackfire saw the great rock where the Dogribs once shot Oltsintthedh full of arrows — that's another story, of two sisters being stolen — which showed him direction. And when he reached the shore of lake below the rock, he found a place where People had camped so recently that one of their fires had burned down to moss, and the grey lichen still held a spark, smouldering. He breathed on it gently, into glowing, and fed it fine strands of dry moss until it grew big enough for sticks and he could warm himself at last, and roast a deer foot left lying there by those People for someone who might be hungry.

"But he ate too fast, it knocked him out. Everyone knows now, if you've been starving, the first thing you eat will try to kill you, so be careful! When he recovered his senses, the fire was almost dead again. That really scared him. He built it up carefully and didn't try eating, just warmed himself and then followed the trail. He could see it now, without feeling for it."

Keskarrah pauses to drink the hot blood soup Greenstockings passes him. The listeners stir, nodding, the long murmurs of their attention rising in their throats, but the children have stopped running around as they usually do because all know the story is almost here now, in the lodge where they sit. Somewhere, a baby sucks.

From behind her small hiding leather Birdseye asks, "Where is raven? Wolf?"

Greenstockings knows this story her father is telling, and she could not dare ask that. Only her mother, destroyed beyond recognition...how will they ever live without her?

Keskarrah stares up into the smoky cone of the lodge. What he sees there settles into his face hard as frozen rock defying all wind-blasted snow. And he laughs, but only a little, glancing at no one, though every person is watching him. The two women, mother and daughter, understand then that this time the story will offer no brooding presence, no spirit or vision or medicine, no shimmering distance of tenderness and mercy; or beauty, beyond his cold language of deliberated theft and ravishment. The cruel gift of mittens, the gentle lichen and moss nurturing a fire — this time every foot will be twisted and freezing, every dress ripped open, every club will drip blood and every mind hatred until it is spilled out, back into the enduring land. There is no place to run from what is coming: there is only this place, there is no other home.

And if strangers, if enemies have the power to find them here, they will. With all the accumulating cruelty of their fine, murderous gifts. That too cannot be changed.

Keskarrah says softly to their circle, explaining what Birds-eye and Greenstockings understand in his cold laughter, "Raven and wolf have followed the caribou, as they do. Blackfire has to find People whom the animals have not left, and the trail climbing out of deep snow is leading him there.

"And he found something else on the lakeshore below Dogrib Rock, while he was digging around for that fire — something that guided him more surely than his willow wand. It was a needle made from the penis-bone of a marten, and he travelled as fast as he could on his snowshoes — one belonging to She Who Delights, the other the one she had completed for him — swung along the memory of that journey in snow to catch up with those People. They travelled like we do, hunters first, followed by their families and then the old men and women and last the widows with their children. He came close to them as they were putting up their lodges. At the outer edge of the camp a girl was telling her widowed mother that she had lost her needle at their last campfire, and she wanted to go back to find it. But the mother said,

"'No, don't go, it's too dark.'

"The girl asked, 'But what will I sew with?'

"'It's too dangerous, don't.'

"As the mother spoke, Blackfire came close and put his arm wearing the long beaver mitt around the girl from behind, his hand offering her nothing but the needle. Without making a sound the girl turned inside his arm and saw him. His ragged rabbit clothing almost touched her beautiful face.

"The girl said quietly to her mother, 'O, I don't have to go back. The fire has brought me my needle.'

"When the mother looked around she screamed, but just a little, because she was almost as clever as her daughter. The man was so huge, his face beaten so black from suffering and cold and starvation. Nevertheless his hands were empty except for her daughter's needle.

"'O-o-o-o,' the mother said, when she could. 'Then you can build up a fire, together.'

"That's what they called him, Blackfire. And when those People surrounded him he told them his story. O, what a wailing went up then for all he had had to endure. People understand suffering very well, how deeply and long we are forced to remember those who rob us. So Blackfire didn't have to explain what more he wanted. The widow fed him bone soup and the girl sewed him clothing with her needle and every night together their fire broke the darkness and cold into little pieces and threw them away until there was nothing left of that but the coloured lights that sing across the cold, bright sky in winter and the bears sleep, o if we could only be sleepers like bears, ah-h-h-h — but we are not bears, unfortunately, though sometimes warm in each other's arms we dream we are because, when it has finally passed, winter may seem no more than one short sleep, one warm memory before daylight and the slipping warmth of spring."

Keskarrah's voice has grown so tender in its lovely telling that both Birdseye and Greenstockings think the story will, for once, be different. Perhaps if a drum were beating it could remain good and desirable and…but of course it won't. She Who Delights is so ravishing the story cannot end here: it must stalk on to uncover the continuing rape of her endurance that is waiting, somewhere. Keskarrah's voice has already turned deeper. The name of the beautiful orphan girl tonight is The One Also Desirable, and though she has led him into a moment of tenderness — Greenstockings remembers her father told it so very differently one night, once — that will not happen tonight. Tonight, if Keskarrah follows The One Also Desirable, she will be ravished as well.

And Greenstockings feels the story breathe cold on her neck, the ice of its contradictions prickle along her back. In telling it this way, why has her father called her "She Who Delights"? Why not "Ravaged Woman"? Why not "The One for Killing"?

"Ah-h-h-h," Keskarrah sighs deeply. "A fiercely desired woman can do almost anything — but she can't change revenge. No, and perhaps she doesn't want to. Revenge is a fire she never lit in Blackfire, nor he in himself, nor in her, for a Person knows that when you have suffered such things, nothing has happened to you before that and nothing will happen to you after: nothing matters except that now you must travel, circling ahead, because somewhere that one Person is waiting for you. She will not die; she is still waiting as you are waiting for her, because we are People of this land, we know who we are. He will find the food and the friends he needs, and a needle-woman who will clothe him and heal him, and whom he will leave to travel again. That is how this land has made People.

"And, though the snow towards the south and west is still too deep even for a circling willow probe, the signs that She Who Delights has left wait patiently for him. Wherever her captors have dragged her many days before: the nick of her fingernail on a willow, the touch of her red pigment along a tall rock or in the melting snow from the bottom of her moccasin, and high along the bleak eskers where the relentless wind blinds you to everything but your own tears and the moss-spotted stones rest frozen in their hollows, there suddenly your toe will touch one and you'll feel it is loose, and you'll bend, lift it easily, and discover under it the shavings she has hidden from the sharpened killing lances of the strangers, our enemies. Your desired woman has hidden them to remind you: here, see, touch them. These killed our People, these have ravished me.

"And you will be led through the quick spring and short, flaming summer south and west between lakes and across rivers and finally the mountains almost to the greatest river itself, Dehcho, to where these faint traces of her relentless determination will end with her at last, there where every night she must lie between two of those enemies. And night and day neither demands of her any more, nor any less, than what every man demands of a woman. Only her strength and hatred will be able to distinguish between them.

"Until one day...." and Keskarrah pauses. The deep sighs of listening around him might be the great trees bending their branches lower, easing them down into cones of shelter from the driving storms yet to come. They can hear the snow outside, the silver streaking world of moonlight.

"One day, She Who Delights notices that the caribou are coming back from the north of their summer calving. These beautiful lice of the tundra flow south, the cows with their calves who have outrun the wolves and the yearlings and the growing males and the females about to be bred and the great bulls, travelling, travelling. And the great fur about their necks already hangs white as winter. It is then, when she looks across the lake where she has gone to fetch water, two enemy women always watchful beside her, that she will see some distant reeds shiver, there across the water, and know it is you. You and the friends you have found were always as certain to come for her as any stranger.

"Listen to me, all of you. Closely guarded as she is day and night, how will Blackfire take her back from White Horizon? Those enemies will hide her, or kill her if they must, the moment they know he's there, and certainly kill him too if they possibly can, because they know they'll never be free of revenge if either of them lives. How will it happen?

"Ah-h-h-h-h, beauty and wisdom are so desirable. But dangerous. She Who Delights has power, and is wise, and has decided to be beautiful. Every man knows that, knows that if he has her and lives right with her, he may become almost as powerful and wise as she — that is why she'll be stolen for as long as she lives.

"Now, knowing what she's seen across the lake, this is what She Who Delights will do: she'll throw the water from her pail, as if cleaning it, in the direction where the shortest path for Blackfire leads along the shore; she'll wear meat hidden under her clothes, to leave for him and his coming warriors when she goes to gather firewood; when they have crept close enough to watch from behind rocks on the hill above White Horizon's camp, she'll walk directly, again and again, in and out of the lodge where she lives between the two men.

"And she'll know that, when the owl calls from the sunset behind the rocks, she must place a sharp flint between her legs and turn to one of those men — which one will she choose? how can hatred decide? — turn and pull that one on top of her and hold him tighter and tighter in her strong arms until past his beating body she sees Blackfire above her and then instantly half-roll aside as his club crashes down on the head of the one she hasn't chosen but who lies waiting his turn to use her, roll aside holding the one she is bleeding with the flint she placed inside herself so powerfully that his eyes won't open even at the sound of a skull smashed beside them, will still be locked tight in the hollow of her neck when Blackfire's lance drives up into him with a scream and his body rips open to his last shriek beyond all agony or hearing.

"She will lie still, knowing that Blackfire's club was unnecessary for the ravager she holds in her arms — while that club smashes down again and again so close beside her that she's splattered, sprayed over with blood and bones. Motionless, naked, dressed and filled for once with male blood, not making a sound because there is so much screaming all around her as somewhere White Horizon dies too, and she screamed enough long ago. Motionless because she is trying to recognize this dark man working over her as the black-faced warrior and avenger and name he has suffered and lived to become, to see him exactly so that she will remember his huge, scarred, half-naked body massive in fury, his face contorted as if about to burst with hatred, lust, jealousy, desire for her.

"Lie motionless thinking: will he spear me too? Or love me? Or beat me to death?

"Knowing then she will be stolen again, and again; knowing she can never have a name other than that most dangerous one: She Who Delights."

Greenstockings circles the coals of the fire together with a long willow. She searches, searches among them, but finds no trace of guidance, only glimmering redness and a brief glower of flame that dies as it awakens. Her father is no longer speaking; a silence of People breathing this endless story that is ready to begin again. She knows Keskarrah is contemplating her sadly through a quick flame, and she feels herself surrounded; hounded home into the certain knowledge that something is stalking her.

And she has a sudden apprehension of why — growing from the depths of her mother's illness and dreaming and her own bottomless lake — why of the many stories he might have told them, this one has uttered itself just as light returns the dawn of morning. Winter living and quiet cannot hold; there are too many men here, too near Dogrib Rock, far too many strangers from far and farther away. And the caribou — they scattered, left, but then strangely returned and have been very numerous. If there were less to eat, the men would have no room in their heads for hunting women, and Keskarrah might have told the story of the Snow Man returning north to his place over the treeless tundra, trailing the ice behind him. But she knows: Hood has been changed by her mother's dream, she has not been sleeping in Snow Man's arms — where she has found delight.

Something else will now happen. And again before next winter — when the caribou return from the north of their calving and the long fur about their neck hangs white for the coming snow.

Her mother has retreated into her furs as if, despite People listening, she could still hide her dreams and ravaged face where no one knows of them. But the People in the crowded lodge have not helped her live through the darkness, beside the cracked mud and log burrows of These Whitemuds; they have

lived away from here along the interlaced paths of the caribou
worn down through snow onto Roundrock and Snare and
Dissension and Hunter lakes. Some days ago one of them may
have looked between green spruce becoming discernible in the
rising brightness, and seen three columns of smoke stand up
beyond the line of light upon the southern hills; strangely, a signal that no one anticipated, or dared to interpret.

Perhaps that is why so many have come to the esker within a
few days; have appeared this evening without saying anything
to Keskarrah other than what they blandly offer over black tea,
to sit smoking, drinking, talking less and less until all are listening. Or perhaps someone heard a bird on a snow-sifted tree call
in a voice not the oldest of them could remember, and that apprehensive message spoke itself from lodge to lodge and they
came here, some from two days' journey southwest on Snare
Lake or three from Hunter, even those hunting east past the
frozen falls and rapids beyond Lastfire Lake where the female
caribou will soon pass in their immense gathering again, on
their long travail north to their calving.

Greenstockings does not know, and the quiet faces around
their fire remain closed. Even the women bend away from her,
as if she, like her mother's face, were already missing in darkness. Perhaps that is why Keskarrah told the story of She Who
Delights, as if nothing existed besides revenge and suffering and
needles and a woman's snowshoe and lance shavings, without a
single voice from beyond, or a dreaming.

But...where then is the delight? It must be there, even if hidden. Within bodies holding each other, in tenderness, in joy
and ecstasy, forebearance, care, somewhere if she is truly that —
because how can she delight if he does not delight her as well?

Delight together. Told as Keskarrah told it, the story seems to say that all one needs to follow her is a trace of red on rock, a fingernail mark on a willow, and one or two brutal men will do whatever they want to do to one woman for ever.

Is that what she heard? Facts like accumulating snow, just falling, lying there until they are thick enough to walk upon. Is that all she will discover? The grotesque facts of desire and revenge that all of them, alive or dead, will have to hold in their empty hands? Woman...woman, will you be restolen that way?

Her name remains She Who Delights. There must be a spirit guiding, a world explicating itself out of its bits of knowledge and faith and consciousness. This story shaped to the sharp point of a lance — a story of guidance, under what loosened rock on this otherwise invisible trail has her father placed the telltale shavings, so that when she steps on it, bends and lifts it, she will find them and be truly guided? Which was the rock? Where is it? Her foot has already touched it, it is loose, it moves, but it seems she cannot lift it. Perhaps because she does not want to? But she does, yes she does, and if it is there she must do that; quickly out of this continuing darkness.

For she has determined this: her name *is* She Who Delights.

Her People rest about her in silence; even the small, unsleeping children do not move. Only the smallest look at her, lift their shining heads and great, round eyes. But she knows everyone is listening: for the approaching rush of snowshoes outside, the knife-points stabbed through the lodgeskins beside their heads, ripping down, their home bursting open, the scream of attack crushing them aside. Scream the warning! It is already too late, yes, but scream!

There are no screams. Greenstockings explodes out of depths into the darkness of air and her crushed agonizing mouth, knees like stone kneeling on her legs, of hoarse, heavy breathing above her, which she cannot see, though her eyes are staring open, it is the blackness itself that heaves her up out of her furs, away from Hood's curl and hand, not Broadface returned nor Bigfoot daring at last to take her, it is an enemy of unbelievable force like a great rock falling, smash! and arms and legs from everywhere drag her up as if she were already wrapped in ropes in her thoughtless sleep and the story had exploded against this silent, panting violence — where are the shrieks she needs, where are the knives and muscles and clubs and bursting warrior rage?

For a second she gains her balance and instantly drives her knee into the brute's crotch — enough arms do not exist to control all her limbs! — when the low shadow of the fire shifts aside from his bulk and she sees her father. Who until now has always protected her. He is not moving, not opening his mouth. Lying there, wide awake, watching.

She would shriek if she could — HELP ME! — but everything explodes at once: the brute's stagger as she crushes his balls, his fist that hammers her so hard the darkness shatters in her head, the words Keskarrah has repeated over and over about Hood spraying like stars through her pain: "Why doesn't he take you to his place, isn't he a man, doesn't he know what to do for a woman?"

Greywing screams, the sound slicing her head and body open as this enormous unrecognizable force with forty arms and fists and chests batters her and she tries to curl in tight, get inside tight against him and fumbling at him — his knife, his knife, isn't he wearing a — and Hood jerks erect at her feet, pale as upthrust bone, and crashes over instantly, his head kicked away....

Cold beyond cold awakens Greenstockings, with the driven intensity of needles. And a shoulder jolting her stomach, she knows she is hung bent double over it, is being run across snow, her head against a powerful rump, not covered with leather, cloth, towards the log houses of the Whitemuds, cold flaying her naked body, except her stockings, except where the heat of enormous hands is clawed into her like hooks, the bars of arms — not the officers' house, not one of them — if he has no knife she can hold herself limp, as if unconscious when he rapes her, so she can rip his neck out with her teeth, or find a knife, she will find a knife, there are always knives, lurking in sheaths, on strings down leggings, copper and steel and broken stone — it is the Halfmud house, he is jerking the door open, the shoulder and hands are those of the black Mohawk from far away. Michel has stolen her.

Will the Halfmuds help him keep her when Broadface returns? Michel will certainly slit Hood's throat before the sun rises. If she cannot kill him herself, she must accept whatever he does and wait for Broadface. Or whoever else dares confront him. Or Keskarrah's knowledge — if it's strong enough for someone from many rivers away — if he wants to use it. For the first time in her brief life she is uncertain of her father, always powerful enough for what he wants but — she is surrounded by the warm stench sleeping in the log house, snoring everywhere in the stinking Halfmud darkness of all of those enormous paddle-slaves asleep.

And her rage explodes her into a mistake. Michel heaves her off, down into an angle of logs, and she feels herself turning over, falling, thrown down like a pack at the end of a portage or folded slab of meat to be hacked at by whoever wants to chew bits of it, here, grab a handful and stuff your mouth, here, anybody! and she forgets the possible lethal trap of her teeth and screams at anyone alive in this house, breaks her voice, hammers it against the logs as she grabs for his leg, it is there, yes! and drives her fist up into his crotch again, screaming and screaming.

But in the darkness she does not hit him exactly where it hurts most, he grunts like some bull rutting and rams one arm between her naked thighs and still clutching her neck and hair smashes her body length against the wall, not letting go of her hair, and as her bare buttocks scrape down, hit the ground, he slams her head again and then again against the logs until her screams snap, seep out between the frozen cracks, as the crash of her head pounding bursts louder, louder…the frozen mud… dead trees…mud is not berries….

Her father's voice cradles her. Into ferocious pain, as if two rocks were grinding her head away between them, his steady smell and sound and arms hold her, she is rubbed over warm, not naked. She is being held tenderly, in agony and warmth. His querulous, mocking tone in which he conceals his deepest rage from those who do not know him:

"…I have lived long enough to know human beings…." She feels his muscles clench hard, to control himself, her erupting head squeezed so good against his stomach seeping soft, smoky hide, sweat, days and nights of sleep around the centre fire and spruce breathing warmth, gentleness. "…My daughter has always cared for me, I do not need to act like a stupid young man."

Twospeaker chirps English — she cannot open her eyes, something cold lies across them and in a wave her body vanishes, there are thick — a man's — fingers, but gentle in her hair, then short spurts of fire, oh-h-h-h-h! Her father continues without waiting politely for anyone,

"Your young man comes with papers every day, and sometimes he finds a line on them and he keeps that, and he plays with my daughter and sleeps, and then goes away again. Do you think that because you cannot say a word, no one has eyes? When you take a woman, does no one know?

"If you want to know only what you already know, why do you come here?"

It is Richard Sun, his fingers along her broken head, the sharp touches of pain. He murmurs, almost singing under his breath as salve — cold, it smells different, how many salves does he keep in his yellow bag — touches her. Twospeaker speaks, but not enough to say everything her father has said.

"When you come to our land," Keskarrah's words refuse to stop, "you cannot continue to be what you've always been. We have lived here for a very long time, much too long for that."

Greenstockings gets an eye open. Through red mist, past her father's eagle nose, a circle of heads. Hood? Hood?…where is she? Thick English, his mouth moving, his lumpy moon face. Beside Hep Burn. And a shadow of — voyageurs? — shifting behind them. She cannot see.

Lieutenant Franklin gestures for St. Germain not to translate, then asks as if seeking only basic information, as if he knows nothing, "What is this about Hood?"

Hepburn responds, very quickly, "It's our voyageur Michel, sir, the Mohawk stole the girl right from beside her pa, but I guess she wouldn't come quiet, he smashed her one an' I woke at her screaming, he brings her — "

"Hepburn," Lieutenant Franklin has heard enough and breaks in with his steady commander voice, "I am not asking for native behaviour, either Yellowknife or Mohawk. Doctor Richardson, I ask you about Midshipman Hood."

The doctor glances up; this is official, since servants are listening. His hand pauses over Greenstockings' head, gestures in the small candlelight, salve and blood glistening on his fingers.

"Sir," he says, as formally. "Midshipman Hood has given me assurances that he has every intention to marry this girl."

"Marry!"

"Yes, sir."

Greenstockings recognizes Thick English go suddenly silent; whatever it is that Richard Sun has said about her lies between them. It may be he has been told something he never wanted to know. There is a long pause before Thick English speaks again, and she closes her eyes against pain.

"How does he consider he…might marry her?"

Richardson hesitates. "I believe he was…about to speak to you about that, sir."

"In the meantime, he was living, as the traders say, 'in the fashion of the country'."

"To an extent…yes."

"To the obvious 'extent'. And you knew of it."

"Sir, I thought you also knew — "

"You understand, Doctor Richardson, that the pleasure of female companionship has no necessary connection to marriage."

"Sir...it continued...some time...."

"Several weeks?"

"Yes."

Lieutenant Franklin sighs briefly. "Thankfully, Mr. Back's journey has spared us other complications here."

Hepburn blurts out, "Sir, it wasn't for want of trying, he — "

"Thank you, Hepburn, I'm sure Doctor Richardson has already told me all that's necessary. If you know anything further, you may inform me later, and I will decide whether they are matters you need to report to me."

"Sir, I thought — " Richardson begins, but stops at his commander's frown.

"Doctor Richardson," the Lieutenant says, still formally imperial, "I will expect your clarification in that regard as well, but later. You know as well as I no English midshipman 'marries', never while on duty; nor could I ever explain such an extraordinary...connection...in these northern wilds to the Reverend Doctor Hood, his father, regarding a young man whose national and moral duties I pledged to promote and guide as I would those of my own son."

"That is understood, sir. Of course."

"Good. At the moment, I am considering this," the commander gestures at Greenstockings and Keskarrah — who wonders for whose benefit these two speak to each other in such wooden tones, for St. Germain who alone understands them? — "this 'attempted theft', as one might call it, of a person, a native woman by one of our hired voyageurs, and its very serious possible effect on our Expedition. You know the services of both the voyageurs as well as the natives are essential to our proper progress; both must be treated with firm kindness and controlled. They cannot be allowed to disrupt our intentions."

"Yes, sir. The girl is badly hurt, but with care she will survive."

"Good, then she must be treated with such care. These women, I believe, are accustomed to being beaten. Perhaps her family should be given presents and sent away, with the others, to one of the farther lakes."

"They are hard to send — Keskarrah comes to me daily for salve for his ulcerated wife, and now this...."

"Bigfoot could perhaps take them somewhere?"

Richardson says, carefully, "I believe, sir, it is Bigfoot who asks Keskarrah for advice about where to go. Yes?" He looks to St. Germain.

"Yes," the translator says. "They think, this my land, I go where I want."

"I do not think it well to move the girl far, for some time."

"Very well, take her back, both of them," Lieutenant Franklin gestures, and turns, "to their lodging. This barracks is no place to care for them."

Greenstockings feels her father tense, and hears the words rising from him: "Twospeaker. I have something to say to Thick English."

Twospeaker hesitates. "He says you should both return to your own place."

Keskarrah declares: "I have never spoken to him, but I will speak now."

Lieutenant Franklin asks, "What does he say?"

"He say it, to you."

"The middle of the night, in a barracks...is not the time nor place for a council. Tell him, tomorrow."

"No council, just say now."

"Very well" — wearily. "What?"

Keskarrah declares: "No one has died since you Whitemuds came, not yet. That is different from what we know happens in the south, so we know Richard Sun has good medicine. Now tell them: if they travel to the Everlasting Ice when the long light comes, we will not see them again."

Lieutenant Franklin nods thoughtfully to St. Germain's translation. "What does he mean?" he asks in his ponderous way. "If we go to the Polar Sea, who will die, they or we?"

Keskarrah eases Greenstockings aside; with Richard Sun's assistance in holding her, he gets slowly to his feet. He says, standing,

"The land teaches us how to live, not how to kill ourselves. We know the names of every place you will meet. And we have seen this: your journey will end at the double rapids on the River of Copperwoman."

St. Germain translates the first two sentences fast, as usual, then stops, a frown deepening over his cold- and wind-burned face. Keskarrah will not look at him, but looks steadily into the plain future of the darkness before him. So very slowly St. Germain renders the last sentence as flat and direct as he can:

"He see double rapids, Copperwoman River, finish, there land kill you."

And Lieutenant Franklin's excellent English manners cannot prevent him from smiling slightly. Which smile Keskarrah sees, and understands its arrogance perfectly.

"Tell him," Franklin says, turning to go, while his big, well-fed men stand staring, lean in their underwear about the logs that will continue to protect them enough to live through the rest of the winter, so they can sleep and wait for the light to return, and finally move on into what they have not yet seen and cannot anticipate, for reasons most of them will never comprehend, "tell him, in the name of my Expedition, I thank him for telling me this. Tell him also that I am sure, their land being so very large as we already know, that with his warning we will thankfully be able to avoid, wherever they may be, those fatal double rapids."

Keskarrah listens impassively to the translation. Then for an instant his eye catches Twospeaker's: they both know there is no escape, nor could either imagine what an escape from the inevitability of the land might be in order to want it. Obviously, these Whitemuds will be dead before they recognize this.

Keskarrah gestures at Greenstockings. "We will carry her, to our place."

And Hood is there! Materializing from the darkness behind the Halfmuds, and kneels as if Richard Sun were not there. Greenstockings hears, smells his movement: when she opens her eyes it is as if he has always been beside her, his hand on her arm, his eyes blue as sky filled with the tenderest longing and concern, his warm, weeping face leaning forwards to touch hers.

A man so gentle and delicately perceptive and intense; and ultimately useless. In the fixed conjunction of her mother's and father's power, they two have lived this strange — almost as if they were hidden, sweetly, under furs in the long darkness — lived this strange, short moment of profound difference. But the log walls built by These English and Michel's groping fists have shown her what she has always known and should have remembered: they are all men, and there are too many of them. Wherever many men are, they can exist only within a certain violence, and they will try to break you again and again. If you were to live in delight and difference with one for long, you would have to kill all the other men in the world.

Her head is still breaking. She cannot look at Hood with longing or even tenderness. There is no strength in his tears, he is so weak and useless. And stupid.

"Mr. Hood," Lieutenant Franklin orders, "get up, and stand aside."

Outside the fetid house the sky is a gasp of cold, and bright with stars. Bright enough for Greenstockings to see the narrow black spruce retreating down the esker to that known distance of silver hills. And so many People stand motionlessly on the snow, disappearing into the shadows between the houses where darkness clusters: they are watching Twospeaker and Hep Burn carry her, back. She has never felt either of them before, but they seem to have the same rock-like strength, a power of muscle, and a certain skill, and concentrated, narrow ignorance.

And then she recognizes Michel: his shape is the darkness sitting on firewood, bent forwards as if his hands were tied tight behind his back. Two huge Halfmuds hunch beside him. What will Thick English do with him now? Nothing; he is so strong and they need him to carry them to the Everlasting Ice. When Broadface returns, if he does, she will not have to think about him. If he doesn't return....

Well. In the hard cold of squeaking snow her father opens the lodgehide, and inside her hidden mother, still alive, will take her in her arms. She has been stolen for the first time. Her life will continue to circle now, in and out of whatever pain is patiently waiting for her. That is the way it is.

DOCTOR JOHN RICHARDSON

Saturday March 17th 1821   Fort Enterprise

Mr. Back arrived at last from Fort Chipewyan, having performed since he left us a journey of over 1,100 miles on foot. He brought such further stores as he could acquire from the traders, who he reports are themselves almost destitute. Mr. Franklin said he had every reason to be much pleased with his conduct.

St. Germain continues to evince great apprehensions respecting the dangers of a sea voyage. A message from The Hook and Longleg imports that if they are now sent a supply of ammunition, they would meet us in the summer on the banks of the Coppermine and bring provisions. Mr. Franklin agreed to pay them for their provisions but could not spare them any ammunition.

Friday April 27th 1821   Fort Enterprise

The movement of the reindeer north and subsequent cold weather have resulted in the pounded meat that was laid up for our summer stock being all expended. We had nothing to eat today. During the night, however, a deer was brought in which had been killed by old Keskarrah. Our men suffer much from snow blindness. Ice on the lakes about seven feet thick.

Tuesday May 8th 1821   Fort Enterprise

A fly seen today. A party of men was sent off again to get meat, and the women also sent to live at Bigfoot's encampment to diminish the consumption at the Fort.

9

GEESE

Broadface is considering the length of Greenstockings' legs hidden in wool. "Do you ever take that off?" he asks her.

"Maybe in summer," she says. "When it's warm."

"It's warm now, I saw a grey goose today."

"A caribou would be better."

"Huh!" he grunts, and refuses to speak about the caribou migration already past, or about the many lodges of People again gathered motionless around the leaking log houses on the esker, though the light is long and the snow and ice excellent for travel. "My grandmother, she once told me about geese."

"What?" Greenstockings murmurs, leaning back, stretching out, her head surrounded in his lap of warm muscle.

"It was spring, my grandmother told me, when she was little and People were starving, like we do. The men hunted every day, and they were starving so bad they had to tie brush on their bellies. But that didn't help enough. They had to move with the animals going north, save themselves that big walk back. But she was weak, she couldn't walk. Her mother said to her, 'There's nothing I can do. I'm too weak to carry you, and there's nothing to eat.'

"People were just down, there was no hope. So they left my grandmother there, they travelled away, followed the caribou like we do.

"She was little then, all alone. And after a while she heard someone singing songs about love, my grandmother said, because it was spring. Trails showing up everywhere in the sky and the melting snow, and singing, singing. Tender, quiet songs, they were all in love, travelling north. So then some came to her, she said, they walked on the ground like People. They gave her food, and they tied strings around and around her legs because she was just bones, she couldn't get up, she had no strength in her flesh. They asked her where her parents were, and she told them,

"'It's a long time since they left, I don't know, how far.'

"But they said, 'What do you mean, how far? They're just right here, see, we can see them.'

"And they left her. She felt so good, there was no weakness left inside her. They fed her, but she couldn't say what exactly, just goose grass. They were geese going north in the spring, and they told my grandmother her parents were close, so she followed them. And there they were, all the People, with lots to eat, all kinds of meat. She had been given up for dead, my grandmother once told me, but they were singing songs of love with the geese, all travelling north to meet each other — and there she was too."

Past Broadface's black mane draped about her, Greenstockings sees deep into the brilliant sky, the wisps of clouds travelling north on some wind she cannot feel. She is listening, hard, and cannot hear the great birds, but she hears the silence of small water, travelling too, of sunlight reflected hot from the craggy erratic, the long dazzling slashes of melting snow.

"It's good Michel stole you," Broadface says. "Otherwise I'd have killed Hood for you."

"And Boy English, would you have done that to him too?"

"Back," Broadface grins, his mouth crinkled in both disparagement and admiration, "he's a little shit, he dragged more stuff away from those traders, to bring back here, more stuff than they had for themselves to live through the winter, he just talked the shit out of them — but when he has what he wants he travels, fast, wo-o-o-o! his short little snowshoes travel!"

"Could you keep up?"

He looks at her along the slant of his black eyes. "I had to wait on the trail for him a few times."

And then answers her previous question, his masculinity fingered, "You're mine — he's strong, but bleeds easy enough." He grips her shoulders suddenly, his face almost touching hers. "Back fucks every woman he can, morning and evening, he wants everything he sees. Why do you think he stayed away from Thick English all winter, all that time at Fort Chipewyan? He grabs women in front of the traders, he doesn't care, he shoves his hand up between their legs when they bring him food, while they're eating."

Greenstockings is smiling up at him, feeling so warm and bright, thinking of something interesting and so she won't anger him again by mentioning Little Marten, who wouldn't leave Fort Chipewyan because she decided on a man there; she merely teases him, lightly:

"So you watched him fuck them."

"Huh, why watch him, I was busy myself."

"Falling down, drunk stiff as a log, that busy?"

"You'll scream, I'll make you," he promises her, his hard breath almost blasting into her mouth.

"Make me."

But his eyes change, he is mesmerized by her mouth. "He... likes this...to do this, to women...." And Broadface lays his lips over hers, then lunges, crushes them against her teeth. She thrusts him away.

"That hurts!"

Broadface is puzzled. "Back calls that 'kiss', he says a woman always likes it...."

"'Kiss'," she says softly, and draws him down to her. "Open your mouth," she says against his lips. "Gently...gently...."

And his eyes widen, darken into deeper black, as her tongue touches the tips of his teeth, his tongue, slips along its bending roll to the delicate lining of his cheeks — this is not anything Back could show him. She travels around his mouth again.

"That's 'kiss', she tells him. "That's 'geese flying'."

So he flies gently too, into her.

DOCTOR JOHN RICHARDSON

Monday June 4th 1821   Fort Enterprise

The snow having melted and run off the lake ice, I took charge of the advance party and we left the Fort at 4 o'clock this morning and set out for the Coppermine River, down which we intend to proceed to the Polar Sea. Besides numerous women I had 15 Canadians and Yellowknives, three conducting dog sledges, seven dragging their own sledges, and five carrying their burdens on their backs. The average pack was about 80 lbs. exclusive of personal baggage which might be rated at 40 lbs. more.

Lieutenant Franklin and the other officers and voyageurs and the remaining Indians will follow shortly, carrying the canoes and the rest of our supplies.

Our hunters killed nothing today, but just before we halted the carcass of a reindeer which had been strangled and partly eaten by a wolf was found. This afforded one meal to the party.

Saturday July 7th 1821   Coppermine River

*At 7 a.m. our united party with Bigfoot's followers encountered
The Hook's encampment situated on the summit of a sand cliff
whose base is washed by the river where it turns due north
towards the Copper Mountains. The Hook had only three hunters
with him, the rest of his band having remained at their reindeer
snares on Great Bear Lake, but his party was increased by
Longleg and Keskarrah with his family who preceded us. A
formal conference was held with The Hook when he was
decorated with a medal by Lieutenant Franklin and he cheerfully
gave us all the provision he had, sufficient to make 2 1/2 bags of
pemmican. Having completed these arrangements, we embarked
the next day at 11 a.m.*

*Here the Yellowknives all left us, except for the hunters who
will accompany us to the sea, to proceed to their summer hunting
grounds. Broadface, one of Bigfoot's hunters being enamoured of
Keskarrah's daughter, chose to go with them and The Hook to
Great Bear Lake, a vast body of water we are told lies to the west.*

Thursday July 26th 1821   Polar Sea

A great deal of ice drifted into the strait overnight. Embarked at 4 a.m. and attempted to force a passage, when the first canoe got enclosed and remained in a very perilous position, the pieces of ice crowded together and pressing strongly on its feeble sides. A partial opening, however, occurring, we landed without serious injury. Sea covered with ice as far as the eye can reach.

Since leaving the mouth of the Coppermine River we have encountered neither Indians nor Esquimaux. Our small stock of provisions is waning rapidly, and to add to the evil, part of them have become mouldy from dampness.

Saturday August 18th 1821   Point Turnagain

This then is the limit of our voyage along the coast, which has occupied us for a month, but in which we have traced the open sea only five degrees and a half eastward of the mouth of the Coppermine River. But if the length of our voyage round the much indented coast is considered, we have sailed our bark canoes upwards of 550 miles through icy sea, which is very little less than the estimated direct distance, in a straight line, between the Coppermine and Hudson Bay.

Thursday August 23rd 1821   Bathurst Inlet

The last of our pemmican gone, we embarked at 2 a.m, without breakfast and steering for Point Evrette, and we made, without the least remonstrance from the Canadians, an open traverse of 25 miles, running all the time before a strong wind and a very heavy sea. The privation of food under which our voyageurs are at present labouring absorbed every other terror, otherwise the most powerful eloquence would not have induced them to attempt such a traverse. The swell and the height of the waves was such that the mast-head of the other canoe was often hid from our view, although it was sailing within hail of us. We put ashore at last through surf on the open beach, without further injury than smashing the sides of one canoe and splitting the head of the second.

The whole party went hunting but saw no animals.

Sunday September 23rd 1821   Barren Grounds

The men found some skin and a few bones of a deer that had been devoured by wolves in spring. They lighted a fire and devoured the remains with avidity, and also ate several of their old shoes.

Our last canoe was broken today by the men falling and left behind, notwithstanding every remonstrance. They are desperate and perfectly regardless of the commands of their officers. We have now walked over the barren grounds in direct distance from Bathurst Inlet 184 and $^{1}/_{2}$ miles, though in actuality much farther due to lakes, rivers and rocky terrain.

Thursday September 27th 1821   Obstruction Rapids

The day was mild, though the strongest among us is reduced to little more than a shadow of what he had been a month ago. The Coppermine River here becomes a huge double rapids with a narrow lake between them, which we must cross to reach Fort Enterprise. But on this east bank of the double rapids no wood large enough to make rafts could be found, though the carcass of a deer was discovered in the cleft of a rock into which it had fallen in the spring. It was putrid, but not the less acceptable to us, and a fire of willows being kindled a large portion of it was devoured on the spot. The men scraped together the contents of its intestines and added them to their meal.

A raft of the largest willow that could be found, bound together as faggots, proved too little buoyant to support a man. We named the double rapids Obstruction Rapids.

Thursday October 4th 1821   Obstruction Rapids

Strong winds with snow all forenoon. The sensation of hunger is no longer felt by any of us. St. Germain embarked in the shell he had in four days of heavy snow fashioned of willows and fragments of painted canvas in which we wrapped up our bedding. To our great joy and admiration of his dexterity, he at last succeeded in reaching the opposite shore of the rapids with a double line. The shell was then drawn back, and in this manner we were all conveyed over without serious injury, though we were all wet through and no wood could be found to make a fire sufficient to dry our bedding.

We estimate we are now no more than 55 direct miles from Fort Enterprise, where we hope to meet the Indians.

10

OFFERING
STRANGE FIRE

Prayers stagger through Robert Hood, like the footprints that waver away from him through the riven snow of the tundra *what may befall me this day O God I know not but I know that nothing can*   he can no longer walk. Not even with the exhausting drag and thump the others manage to force from themselves, one foot and then the other.

But Richardson and Hepburn refused to leave him alone and motionless in this labyrinth of their disaster, within their Great Lone Empire of the Arctic Snows. The twenty-man-strong united "Expedition determined by His Majesty's Government to explore the Northern Coast of America from the Mouth of the Coppermine River to the eastern extremity of that Continent" has been forced, still very far from that geographical extremity, to attempt a return to the assumed safety of Fort Enterprise. But the Expedition has begun to break into pieces: first a translator left behind here, then a Canadian voyageur

— and then also a second — left behind there, solitary in the alarming maze of their track. And now, while Lieutenant Franklin and Mr. Back lead the remaining voyageurs onwards across the barrens, three Englishmen have stopped and wait, hunched together in this hollow beside a bare dusting of brush above snow, wait. For what? May God be willing, anything.

At noon the sunlight winks on the sloping hills everywhere around them, where their final salvation of meat may be sleeping, hidden. They have learned from the astounding brevity of arctic summer that motionlessness is of all possible postures most dangerous, but what can they do? Hood cannot walk, no one has the strength to carry him. Three men so feeble they can barely erect a small tent —

And suddenly there is a fourth! Of all the men in the Expedition, the Mohawk voyageur, Michel, has returned to them from those who have gone ahead. Michel Terohaute! as George Back with his French quibbles always mocked him among the officers — certainly never to his black face — o high and lofty land, who is like God indeed!

Michel with a written message from Lieutenant Franklin, informing them that he has sent Mr. Back ahead with St. Germain and the two strongest Canadians, and that he with eight others (I. Perrault stopped to rest near some bushes earlier) are proceeding as best they can. However, J-B. Bélanger and Michel T. can no longer keep up even with them, still toiling as directly as the terrain permits via compass towards the hope of Fort Enterprise — they are, he is confident, now very nearly within sight of Dogrib Rock — and the meat the Indians have surely cached there for their sustenance, and so these two are returning to Doctor Richardson's group to assist as they can and await rescue with them. Lieutenant Franklin affirms that Mr. Back will send meat back to them as soon as he and his men, who may very well by now have already reached Fort Enterprise, when they find "the Yellowknives who alone can save us all."

Richardson hesitates in his eager reading of the muddled note, but cannot avoid declaiming the final phrase of most uncharacteristic recognition into the rigid air. In fact, he repeats it, so strangely convincing, "…the Yellowknives who alone can save us all." And looks at the Indian from far away, Michel, standing there alone: J-B. Bélanger is not with him. And this message, barely decipherable on a page torn from the back of the Lieutenant's Bible, the letters as if drawn one after the other by a concentrating child. Only Michel, looking fixedly at Richardson and Hepburn, then an instant at Hood covered flat in the shelter — Bélanger supposed to come too? The paper says? The Canadian didn't follow, he never see him, never for two days, he come along the track, back to them, never see him once.

Turning before them, Michel seems suddenly very powerful: so deliberately intense and muscled it is obvious that he could walk wherever he pleased. Perhaps it is because he carries only his bedding and a long rifle with powder and shot — which Lieutenant Franklin has now assigned to him, he says. But beyond specific hunting forays, no voyageur has ever before been permitted a loaded rifle; especially not this one.

And even more unbelievably he has brought meat, both a ptarmigan and a hare! For them, who for days now have eaten only bits of boiled leather or painfully scraped-off lichen, burning or cooking that while it somehow remained as repulsively inedible as ever. Hepburn exclaims, gnawing his mouthful of meat,

"O God, maybe this one won't tell lies, like all the others."

Resting, they have continuously discussed food as the hungry will, making sounds to vary the moan of wind among small brush, their tent too thin to be worthy of assault.

"If we could see sky," Hood on his back could still speak with some precision, "we might see...ravens. Ravens always eat."

"They will reach the Fort," Richardson asserted calmly, "and the Indians. They always have food."

"Not always, I think."

"This is their place."

"Yes," Hood mused, "it *is* their place.... 'And dwelt at a place by the brook Cherith, and the ravens brought Elijah bread and flesh in the evening, and he drank from the brook.'"

Hepburn chuckled, "Sir, if only you were a prophet in Israel!"

"'And the barrel of meal wasted not, neither did the cruse of oil fail, according to the word of the Lord, which he spake.'"

"I don't want so much." Hepburn could say things the officers could not. "Just one wee pig, one of the suckers that almost knocked you down, sir, in the mud of Stromness. I'd slit its throat an' we'd drink blood an' eat its liver raw, like the Indians say, because it gives such quick strength, o, I'd fry its fat so crisp an' tender we'd dance the flings in a week!"

"My teeth seem rather loose," Hood murmured, "for fat crackling."

"Aye sir," Hepburn said quickly, "but our Orkney women fry them somehow crisp an' tender, I don't know how, maybe because there's always three of them for every man returning home from the sea. It do make the juices run."

"Ah-h-h-h," Hood sighed, "the fat pigs...."

"I think Orkney women always prefer a man hoisting sail, sir, to any amount of pigs."

"I'd gladly forgo pigs for a great hot fire. If this tent was on fire, I'd dance your fling."

"Aye, so we would, all the three of us!"

Hood was chanting some scrap of memory: "Three men bound in the midst of the burning fiery furnace, walking loose in the midst of the fire — set the tent on fire again, Hep Burn, according to your glorious name, as you did on the shore of the lake, the one they call Like a Woman's Breasts, and we three Shadrack, Meshack and To Bed We Go will walk loose in the midst of it, nor was an hair of our head singed, nor the smell of fire passed on us!"

Even Doctor Richardson, carefully Presbyterian, could join what seemed to him such biblical cheeriness: "My friend, we then need a fourth — there were *four* men in the fiery furnace."

"Yes! Also an angel, I pray, sweet angel, come! Carry us into the great, fiery furnace, the Yellowknives call it 'Like a Woman's Breasts', o, soft breasts, blessed be God!"

Yesterday Hood could play that aloud; today with a mouthful of food he cannot count four, and his debilitated mind drifts, shimmers, trying to focus on Michel; he looms somewhere in his past like some mountain, but he cannot find it, the winter so endless at Fort Enterprise, it seems more a blackness already exploded long ago, and for an instant his mind focuses — yes, Michel is the only Indian voyageur.

What induced a Mohawk to hire himself into such miserable drudgery as year by year paddling furs up the unmerciful rivers of Canadian rocks and plains? With his axe of a face he should be staring down another warrior somewhere in *I adore Thy eternal and inscrutable designs I submit to* this frozen desert, his courage as naked as the hatred on his full and twisted lips. And somewhere he exposed that hatred, during a winter, Hood is certain, though whatever it was straggles away in the present instant of freezing — yet here he is, an Indian shouldered up out of the frozen earth and offering small meat, scrawny juices, to ruin once again Hood's accepted somnolence of starvation.

He is not a Yellowknife.

And again Hood's mind trips against some anger, a lurch of what must have been rage. To destroy his peace Michel has destroyed his fast — Michel did it before in winter too, yes, in an earlier winter, he certainly destroyed something that Hood cannot now quite remember, he has avoided every thought of it for so long, but this is a devil and he has returned, forced him to this renewed sacrilege of EAT. Meat in his mouth, shreds to feebly suck at but never uncatch between loosened teeth, sinning his stomach into a grotesque memory of longing for satiation. His teeth seem to shift, for his spastic tongue, pushing them tastes sweetly of blood. Can you live sucking your own teeth for their blood?

Before the Coppermine River, ten days, fourteen days, all of September or whatever — before they finally arrived here at the double rapids, which they have called Obstruction, which destroyed their last bits of strength — then Michel was a good hunter — or was it J-B. Bélanger, who should now be here too, with all his small prayers and charms luring the animals out of their unwillingness, to offer themselves a sacrifice for their pathetic hunger? But now Michel's apparent strength is not enough, so he says, to hold a wavering rifle into steadiness, hardly enough for a ptarmigan, which will sit until you step on it, and to kill a caribou — well, since Obstruction Rapids not a

single one has shown itself, not even on the skyline of the farthest esker, though once herds moved like distant mirages of
forests, always fading when pursued — he would have to be
close enough, he declares so loudly, to lean forwards and break
a caribou's neck with an axe   *we'll shoot at a wren says Robin to
Bobbin*   but the note says Belanger was coming too.

Jean-Baptiste Bélanger, *"le rouge"* for his skin, crossed himself so swiftly, praying open-mouthed while he paddled in terror, the canoe smashing across or into the ridges of the sea, ice
sailing by like knives, his clothes tattered with charms, his enormous hands clenched ready for death on the birch paddle bending. Did Bélanger *le rouge* begin to follow Michel back to them,
and stagger into motionlessness like the three others — or four
— who have already stopped walking, somewhere after Obstruction Rapids? Those who still rest where they stopped —
rest how? With the ravens or the wolves? Yes, "rest", Lieutenant
Franklin told them, never "wait", but "rest, wrap yourself tight
in your sleeping-hide and rest, we will return with help…help"
— Hood remembers that very distinctly. Rest for help.

He lies in his sleeping-hide. Buffalo, rigid with cold, but pli-
able, with the heavy smell of prairie he has never seen. Someone
once suggested he should not have had this warmth carried for
him so far on forlorn seas and tundra; also, never wear caribou
and seal skins at the same time — superstitious natives — was a
curse carried for him into this north, lying under prairie hide in
this barren land?

Rest, o rest. It was said, so gently, sadly, to each one, Mathew
Péloquin, Régiste Vaillant, little Junius the other Esquimau
translator, who served them at table so proudly at the Fort. And
now Ignace Perrault too. Rest, we will return. With help.

Presumably they are all somewhere — like Bélanger too? — still resting, breathing in the official Expedition decision of an expectation of strength and of food. What happens to them when their arms, their eyelids, stop moving like their feet? Will the animals come? Yes. Always too late, but the warm animals are certain to come. Someone once told him that too.

And did the solicitous animals show Michel this hollow of gnarled trees, this larger possibility of fire? Why did Michel carry him here away from their brush shelter; Michel hates all the officers, he has at least since the long winter certainly hated Hood, about something, something so enormous he may never again be able to remember   *we will go to the woods says Michael to Robin*   why did he not continue walking with Lieutenant Franklin's group — or are they already all dead before they ever got a glimpse of the great monolith, Dogrib Rock, those eternal enemies of the Yellowknives?

No, he brought the Bible note, that was certainly the commander's starvation writing. When Michel left it, that group must still have been struggling to reach Fort Enterprise — o, Greenstockings will be there! the fire burning in that endlessly warm round lodge, with caribou heart and brain bubbling in her kettle, stuffed stomach turning in smoke there and the heat of her long brown body   *dear God my God nothing can happen to me which Thou hast not foreseen ruled willed ordained from all eternity bless her bless her that woman more gentle and tender* Why has he, so powerful, come?

Perhaps they are already all dead.

And Michel, of course, does not know how to find the Fort from the tundra, and the necessary Yellowknife food that alone can save them all. He is the wrong kind of Indian, from far too far away, there are great differences in Indians — this one knows no directions here if he cannot see Dogrib Rock.

Michel squats at the tent opening, beside the green miserable fire, his rifle in his lap. He was always somehow lost crossing treeless rivers — sea coasts and rivers without trees were a White curse, he told them. When the Expedition stumbled upon the first bristle of waist-high spruce after finally leaving the ocean, it was Michel who walked to them, kneeled, pulled their needles against his emaciated face burned even blacker. Breathed them in like a child.

Trees, these tufted sticks! A single English oak contains more wood than all the twigs bundled together from here to the Polar Ocean. In the blur of his starving eyes floating with blotches, Hood sees through the tent doorway a convulsion of stringy erectiles trying to be green in the blasted withering of wind and snow that tears at them; sees a blister of grey snakes frozen upright.

Robin and Bobbin two big-bellied men
They ate more meat than threescore and ten
They ate a cow they ate a calf
An ox and a....

The spruce-twig flames slowly, slowly burn themselves down through early October and long September snow, sink towards the permafrost, frozen since before time. Michel lugged him here like any weary ox, though he hates him — why? Robert Hood's shredded mind shimmers over hatred scattered like ash upon his past. They will insist on his trying to stand again, perhaps even walk. He grasps with a sudden clarity: we must force this Mohawk to carry me all the way, I can still see the compass,

I would read it backwards on his back pointing back along the
trail we have travelled, the needle wouldn't waver any more that
way than the daily compass point shivers through his mind, it
will guide him backwards into gentle summer, all the numbers
and calculations shredding away, and he remembers and forgets
again that Richardson can calculate true north as well as he,
this infallible point on which their lives swing erratically, as if it
too were staggering across the magnetic landscape without
destination, a discovery of direction from the abysmal height
of the stars. Michel can drag him on his buffalo robe — they
could freeze it solid in water like the Esquimaux and say it is a
sled and harness Michel like any black dog and he will write
out the calculations, fill all the pages he still has, they are all
somewhere safe, pages with numbers and formulas and the
exact mathematical sequences of magnetic declension he knows
better than the beat of his blood, numbers upon and over numbers until Dogrib Rock is forced to emerge out of those precise
numbers, its grey plateau exact as distance, and beyond that the
black treeline is drawn along the esker that for ever shelters the
cone of Keskarrah's lodge — Keskarrah!

The old man blazes in Hood's memory, branches piled in
warm green bedding over his lodge and under the hides, where
smoke drifts up and arms fold him into the warmth of breasts
the apple taste of her nipples, o sweetest sweetest

How sweet the name of Jesus feels
In a believer's ear

the huge green trees flaming with heat, the great numbering
trees! If he could only draw Lieutenant Franklin there, and

Back with the Yellowknives — Greenstockings! her arms, her everlasting arms.

> An ox and a half
> They ate a church and they ate a steeple
> They ate all the

There they are, the tall spars of trees left against the sky beyond Dogrib Rock. Hepburn bends over the smoky fire of twigs trying to heat the horrible *tripe de roche* that scours Hood's mouth and throat bloody. Perhaps in his relentless, solicitous effort to feed him, Hepburn will now cure him with smoke — only the lichens do not hide themselves from their ponderous search. If he swallows them smoked, his bowels will at last tear themselves completely out of his anus, their final convulsion rip them loose from his twisted skeleton. When he touches himself he feels bone; and pain everywhere, like snow.

Is there skin? He can see a little, sometimes, on what must be his own hand. He can smell it, he has never stunk like this, strong as urine running the gutter of manse stable. He can no longer feel lice; perhaps they have fled like rats from a dying ship. And Hepburn is there sifting through smoke, stinking stronger than smoke, and Michel is gone, always gone. Hunting. They three grow steadily colder while they wait, motionless, or search for something edible in a land where whatever it is they know, or do not know, is killing them.

All he can see and feel beyond snow and wind is rocks — so eat rock broth, cooked or fried and impossible to burn black, skim the thick, yellow stonefat off a lovely soft-boiled rock. When Michel returns from his hopeless hunting he will lie down against him again, naked, that huge Mohawk back still muscled, so much warmer than Richardson's, if only he dared to take it in his arms   *who said that to me? I will kill you who is saying it?*   Hood's lips are crusted-over crusts of sores, something jagged as crushed paper drifts in his torn mouth, what he can swallow is a faint slip of blood along his throat; his own blood, he is swallowing himself from that dangerous place in the mouth he has heard of. He feels nothing of feet.

But there is a small bump, down the length of woolly hide, he can still make that out — but he feels nothing. His long green woolly feet, his wrong sealskin feet — they have gone away. His all-a-greenwood feet were left behind. Ah-h-h-h, they are useless anyway, all useless: books, instruments, smashed canoes, feet, whole bodies on a trail of uselessness sprawled over tundra, too bony to eat. Where do they rest without him?

Little Robin Redbreast went for a walk
He sat upon a little pole and ate his little

Until Greenstockings kneads them supple as the caribou leather covering her breast and tongues them, each toe warm as milk, into the haven of her nest and body

…and the storm of life is past
Safe into that haven guide
O receive my soul.…

"Mr. Hood."
Doctor Richardson's voice. From beneath the other buffalo hide carried for two years from the North Saskatchewan River

plains by Canadians. Richardson can still walk, or crawl a little, but mostly he lies beside Hood; he may never recover from attempting to swim the Coppermine River with a line for them to cross on. That was when George Back first seemed to realize — Back never understood anything unless he said it aloud and, since Lieutenant Franklin's structure of naval command permitted them very few spoken words, though in desperation they might write more on notes, where they could be lost or by mutual consent or order destroyed before they were fully copied into their daily journals, a thoughtless, wordless Back was Franklin's perfect officer — "We could all die here," Back said *sotto voce*, astonished into discovery by the voyageurs trying to warm Richardson back into life, "on the wrong side of this bloody rapid."

Because after five strokes Richardson's arms stopped in the water, bent down into whirls smooth as glass, apparently inert, and when he turned on his back, after ten more strokes his legs stopped too, and they desperately hauled him back for dead, though they found he was not quite that, yet. But when they stripped to warm him, they stared, dumbfounded at the revelation of his body. *"Ah Dieu,"* the voyageurs groaned, *"que nous sommes maigres!"* Enclosing Richardson between their naked bodies, unable to see their own bone cages by the seething water.

As if they had clawed over thousands of miles of sea and land and sea and back over the land again, to discover no more than each other's walking skeletons.

They named that — what? — Burnside River? — which he recognized when he accumulated the numbers for it, recognized like a word leaping into reality at the tip of his pencil on squared paper, that it was the river her father   *O God her father*

our father which art in heaven   drew on the ground when they
first arrived on the shore of the great crashing lake. Keskarrah
had called it the Ana–tessy, named it the closest and easiest river
for their return if they must return from the east — that was
what Keskarrah meant! Their return made easily by water, floating canoes, revealed at their feet in the dust a year ago. But they
then recognized nothing of their possible salvation, and Hood's
numbers told him too late that if only they had found this
river's mouth on Bathurst Inlet, it would have saved them seven
days of starvation walking and perhaps saved the canoes and
also all…or was that rapid at last and truly the Coppermine?
No, only a single wash of white water — God our father which
art in heaven a land so enormous, graspable only through the
confusion of after-the-fact numbers that foretold nothing, no,
those huge single rapids where all of Lieutenant Franklin's instruments and notebooks vanished in glaze, the ice there barely
crusted the edges, that *was* the Burnside River, not yet running
in icepans, and they named them Bélanger Rapids after Jean-
Baptiste *le rouge*, which was all they saw of that river, the
Burnside, which he recognized too late as Ana–tessy and where
their second canoe smashed down off the shoulders of the
voyageurs into tiny shards of fire — to save the canoes and
themselves at least seven days they should have come up that
river of return — but they did not. No, when they at last
crossed it the Canadians had already carried two canoes for 107
direct miles over the barrens since they left the 200-foot falls
and the river they called Hood. Ah-h-h-h, Hood, his father's
name. Drawn long across this land…somewhere.

  "Mr. Hood," Richardson murmurs again. "Do you wish to
read?"

"Thank you, Doctor Richardson. No. If you do, please."

The winter light has inevitably drawn their ritual of morning and vesper readings, as they try to remember them from the lectionary of the Book of Common Prayer, closer and closer together. Soon only firelight can show them what   *I promise I will I will*   text they should read, their only chronometer tell them when. And even that instrument will mean nothing when in their gathering debilitation they lose the sequence of morning and evening to the continual darkness coming steadily on. A low line of light somewhere, is it growing or waning? They cannot remember, however long any of them will still breathe to see it.

" '…and there came a fire out from before the Lord,' " Richardson reads in the slow, stentorian rhythm of King James, the ritual comfort of its Judeo-British confidence, " 'and consumed upon the altar the burnt offering and the fat: which when all the people saw, they shouted, and fell on their faces.' "

"So would I," Hepburn says outside. "Seeing good fat burn."

Richardson glances towards him without the effort of moving his head, then continues, his voice so magnificently roughed and deepened by starvation:

"Leviticus, chapter ten: 'And Nadab and Abihu, the sons of Aaron, took either of them his censer, and put fire therein, and put incense thereon, and offered strange fire before the Lord, which he commanded them not. And there went out fire from the Lord, and devoured them, and they….' "

Hood is contemplating his stinking arm: he can smell it better than see it; for some reason it is uncovered. Though he does not feel it cold. He does not feel hunger either, but he continually thinks, eat, his English duty is EAT…his stinking arm reminds him: they are four men and each has two arms. Surely one is sufficient for any man — for walking, two legs are essential — a contribution of an arm, only one each, with all its bones — but the hand. Attached to the arm, so particular, the hand, the most personal and intimate body part one knows of one's self.

"'...they died before the Lord,'" Richardson stumbles on. "'Then Moses said unto Aaron, This is it that the Lord spake, saying, I will be sanctified in them that come nigh me, and before all the people I will be glorified. And Aaron held his peace.'"

Who could masticate his own hand?

Michel is outside, over the fire. No one has heard or seen him return, they are so far away in the blessed garden of Sinai, and when he lifts his axe together with something else, Hood sees only a black blur, but Hepburn lurches to his knees.

"Meat!" he gasps. "He's brought red meat!"

They cannot believe they are drinking the pale blood soup Michel cooks over dry sticks; their loose teeth ache gnawing stringy meat from shreds of bone. Hood eats at last, but eating is such a labour, such laborious duty, that when he swallows the hunger inside him awakens, ravages him instantly. He knows there is not enough to drive his hunger beyond itself. His excoriated mouth.

"So bitter and lean," Hepburn says, "but to God be all praise!"

"Perhaps, 'twere better, to fast," Hood murmurs. "Before, the Lord."

Richardson says, "Aye, praise Him," to Hepburn, studying with his unhurried eye the bone whose marrow he is sucking. "This wolf...it must have been very near death...too."

Wolf is not to be eaten, Hood knows that, and the gristle tells him too; wolf is brother and sister, wolf will feed you but is not to be eaten!

"Raven," Michel mutters, and gestures his mittened hand into flapping distance. "See raven, big rocks, wolf freeze. Raven…eat."

"How would a wolf die?" Richardson asks, quietly scientific.

Suddenly Michel is shouting. "Caribou! Old wolf, horn," and he thrusts his hands out, head curved down, jabbing, "old wolf, worn out, no good, big caribou!"

Richardson continues, "And you took your axe with you, this morning?"

"Raven! Meat freeze, chop!" Michel is so wildly furious he seems about to reach for their single axe again, chop them all into edible pieces.

Richardson maintains his level politeness, "Of course, I know frozen meat is too hard for a knife, of course."

How can Michel waste strength on anger? Hood lifts his boiled bone with its strange bristle of dark ragged meat to Hepburn, sitting at the tent opening beside his bedroll. Gnawing is impossible; the pain in his head has grown into his stomach, an unfathomable and unuttered loneliness. Michel's wolf dripping like a strange memory of pork in his mouth.

"Fast before, the Lord…."

"Sir," Hepburn says gently. "It's your little share, you must eat, sir. You must."

The ravens and the wolves shall feed thee   He has always known that, wolves and ravens. But who told him first, who told him so indelibly what he now instantly thinks whenever a bird — any bird, blue or black or white — moves though air?

Where it may rise and where it rests there indeed is God's good
plenty   *how shall we boil her says Michael to Robin*

    the church
    they ate the steeple
    they ate all the…the priest and all the people

but until this unutterable north he has always had enough to
eat. The only ravens he knew were that fringe of small rooks
above the pasture trees   *here's parson rook a-reading his book*
and of course Elijah in his father's absolute sermons bent forwards over the pulpit, such a consolation without the least
touch of cold or green wool or seal-skin-cursed feet or the rip of
hunger like blood leaking inside in your body

    In the brewer's big pan
    Says John all alone
    In the brewer's big pan says everyone
    And we'll have enough over to give eyes to the blind
    And legs to the lame and pluck for the poor
    In the brewer's big pan says every

All alone. As the light shrinks over the brush and their tent
hardens smaller into drifts only one point of distance remains:
that place where the eskers once opened west to God only
knows what farther lakes. His eyes blinded by starvation, that
opening is carved in Robert Hood's memory; it rests on the
mosquito-smeared canvas ceaselessly pounding about him —
could he lick that for sustenance, those thin memories of their
own healthy blood dried and carried and crushed? — whistling

with snow under wind. And he feels that notch of land roll along the back of his aching eye, never a human figure in it even when he hears Hepburn drag himself away for *tripe de roche* he has somehow missed until now under crusted snow, when Richardson again moves the little distance he can, feeding that minuscule, useless fire.

Every day Michel hunts.

So he says. He vanishes into the spaces Hood can no longer see and then they are so kindly three again, quiet, gentle, stinking like labouring horses though they have not so much as moved, so delicately thoughtful of each other, their manners as reassuring and immovable as the starvation that they now acknowledge without a word is eating them.

But then Michel is there again, moving so hard, hammering frozen wood together beside the tent, so dreadfully alive and loud. Never bringing more meat. How can one man hunt, alone and starving? he roars as if he had found coherent English in his craving gut. He smashes firewood too impossibly fast for Richardson to prop in the fire, he seems stronger than ever, his high voice often bellowing some grotesque language. Richardson is now convinced: Lieutenant Franklin and his party have not reached Fort Enterprise.

What! Michel is enraged. It seems he is outside, suddenly arrived in silence, and has overheard that remark, them talking White again! He yells he will leave for Fort Enterprise right now, he should never have come back to care for them, they cannot walk and he will not carry them, he will take the compass and go himself — teach him how to read it and he will go, he says, his tone changing, quickly quiet, he will go and find the Yellowknives and bring food back to them, he has taken care of them for days, he will save them if they teach him how to follow the compass, save them for certain now, teach him the instrument.

You need at least two to hunt, he says, as any wolf will show you. Every animal stays far away from me alone, there is just the stink of death here.

And he will die first, hunting every day as he does, and when he is dead he knows what they will do. They will eat him, the way they ate his brother on the Ottawa River, that is what Whites do to Mohawks, if you can't help them they just tear you apart and eat you — bones and all!

The three Englishmen stare at him. At his preposterous — he cannot know what he is saying — unthinkable words. Finally Hood gestures to Richardson, who bends to him.

"He is right," Hood is able to whisper, and Richardson jerks in consternation. "Not...eating. But you must, find help. Can you walk?"

Richardson smiles wanly. "Perhaps in a day, to that stone."

"Then Hepburn must go, he is the only one left, with Michel, to reach — Enterprise, if possible."

"Lieutenant Franklin and Mr. Back will never desert — "

Hood talks between breaths. "Of course, but perhaps... something has, happened, and you cannot...Hepburn, perhaps he, some strength, we must not, sacrifice, him too."

Slowly Naval Surgeon John Richardson's eyes sink into themselves. It may be that Mohawk voyageur Michel Terohaute's unthinkable outburst has permitted Midshipman Robert Hood for the first time — it is not for Seaman John Hepburn to say such things to his superiors — permitted Hood to utter at last that impossible word: *sacrifice*. Perhaps if for two months they had been heaved about in a longboat at sea, the four naval officers of the Expedition could have confessed that necessity earlier, but perversely their duty on land among these numberless rivers and rocks and shorelines and lakes since leaving the shores of Hudson Bay have helped them discover very little English vocabulary. Land. Frozen so motionless, it does not storm and heave like the sea whose travail it is their heritage to know; it can be travelled upon, of course, but it is nevertheless also as unending as the sea. Wherever they walk, they are encircled by undifferentiated namelessness.

Thus marooned, land-cornered, this senior and junior naval officer left behind know they retain nothing; except perhaps a slight courage. It is unnecessary to speak. One last attempt must be made.

An attempt possible only by their English seaman-servant from Northumberland and the Orkney Islands, who is still capable of some travel. At first John Hepburn refuses to leave Hood; but he does finally, in tears, agree to try. Of course he cannot do so without Michel, who has already chopped a large heap of small brush to sustain the fire. Michel will go whether they give him the compass or not; and he adds, that strange blackness sharpening his frost-ruined face again, Hepburn must keep up with him. He will certainly not sit and freeze here, and be eaten.

"Why does he," Hood says in his starvation slowness, "talk like...that?"

He feels the one warm spot on his freezing body: the back of the native, as Lieutenant Franklin has always called him, breathing perceptibly against his back. Once he stretches out under the robe with his face to the wall of the tent, Michel slips

instantly into the heaven of painless sleep; which is now all that
Hood himself longs for.

Richardson shakes his head. And Hepburn suddenly responds, without being asked.

"He's right enough, sir. I heard plenty of sailor stories."

"Of, what?"

"Oh," Hepburn hesitates, "on that American privateer we
were often in trouble for food. Then the strongest is the worst,
real dangerous."

"For what reason would that be?" Richardson is trying to
leaf through his small Bible with gloved fingers; the stiff pages
stick.

"The strongest, they can…kill you, first."

"First?"

"When you're too weak…to protect yourself."

Richardson says steadily, "One would expect the strong, as
good Christians, to aid the weak."

"Aye sir, Christians, they expect lots…."

"Americans, and war business, well…but I cannot think
that of Englishmen, not even those of common station."

"Hunger does bloody things, sir. I've seen it."

"What have you — " Richardson stops abruptly, then continues as well as he can with his usual levelness. "So. Mr.
Franklin was wise also in that, to send the strongest voyageurs
ahead with Mr. Back for help. A leader must always…con-
trol…men, before they are uncontrollable. By force, yes, if
necessary."

Richardson looks at them both: in the spastic firelight Hepburn is clumsily sewing a tear over his knee, Hood is almost invisible under his robe against the high mound of the sleeping

Indian. Back — the smallest but strongest officer, with good French and certainly the quickest gun. And ruthless.

"The strong know that, and may therefore have reason to fear the desperation of the weak…but…" Richardson's tone for an instant becomes the doctor's again, analysing carefully, "such…flesh…would sustain nothing. Really, since it itself is starving. It would provide no nourishment. And if it suffered from scurvy.…" He shrugs. "Less than useless."

"A starving man don't think of much but eating, sir."

"I understand. But we," Richardson says, steady and careful, "are Christians…you are not like that, Hepburn."

"No, no," Hood echoes him.

Hepburn says nothing; he is certainly stronger than the other two. "I was born on a croft," he once told these two officers at Fort Enterprise. "I knew enough hunger waiting at the next corner, and people starve in the Orkneys." Though he has not mentioned any of that since they started to walk away from the ocean.

And now it may be that they are all three weeping. If Michel were awake and if he, after two years of working for them, had some understanding of what it was these strangers wanted so badly to find that it made them drag themselves so mercilessly over oceans and lands, a trek on which they expected every inhabitant they met to be similarly sacrificial and assist them for nothing more than what they had already decided was "proper compensation", yes, to slave for them to the very point of death, perhaps then Michel too would be weeping. However, it is Hepburn who sobs aloud.

"'After the doings of the land of Egypt,'" Richardson begins reading again, "'wherein ye dwelt, shall ye not do: and after the doings of the land of Canaan, whither I bring you, shall ye not do…. Ye shall therefore keep my statutes, and my judgements: which if a man do, he shall live in them: I am the Lord your God.'"

And his hunger-gravelled voice declares further: "'None of you shall approach to any that is near of kin to him, to uncover their nakedness…. The nakedness of thy father, or the nakedness of thy mother; shalt thou not uncover: she is thy mother, thou shalt not uncover her nakedness…. The nakedness of thy sister, the daughter of thy father, or daughter of thy mother, whether she be born at home, or born abroad, even their nakedness shalt thou not uncover. The nakedness of thy son's daughter, or of thy daughter's daughter, even their nakedness….'"

Richardson's cathedral solemnity begins to falter: "'…thy mother's sister's daughter or…thou shalt not uncover the nakedness of thy brother's wife: it is thy brother's brother's…brother's naked….'"

And stumbles to a stop. Hood is laughing.

The other two are suddenly aware of it but for a moment cannot understand what he is doing, his cavernous skull agape with such staggered jerks of his bony skeleton that Michel grunts and seems about to turn on him, flinging his bare arm — once so huge with muscles but now stretched into ropes — about the air before huddling down again, twisting the buffalo hide even farther over himself so that suddenly Hood's bare leg and seal-skin feet lie exposed. A crossing of blotched blue sticks.

Richardson leans to him and tugs the hide back, tucks it under again.

"My f-f-father," Hood stutters between the feeble hiccups left in his skeleton, "never read…that…vespers!"

"I have...lost the readings...I'm just following Leviticus, and this doesn't seem appropri — " Richardson does not conclude. Hepburn is crawling past them.

"Maybe morning readings, sir." He is almost outside. "The light, it's coming up, I think."

It may be, barely visible as Hepburn crawls out of sight, light like a line painted deeply south-east by south all along the tundra's edge. Richardson lays the little Bible aside, fumbles with his calendar notebook.

"Then it must be Sunday. October 20," he says at last. "Fourteen days since Mr. Franklin left us. Or is it Saturday?"

"One must...never...father instructed us," Hood is still twitching a little, "travel on...Sundays!"

Though they have of necessity, so often. Is it the twentieth Sunday after Trinity? If it is Sunday. Hood sees this number with staggering clarity arise with the meagre dawn, and the ridiculous laughter that stretched him flat and gasping suddenly explodes again with his father reading that ponderous text so long after Trinity, they should be somewhere in the Prophets, always on Sunday; like the arrangement of their familial decorum into ritual goodness before they all trail after his black robes into St. Mary's, first the comforting wife and mother, she of all true gentleness, and then the three upright downright sons, Richard Jr. and Robert-robin and Georgy-porgy the blessed king for ever, and then the virtuous girls, Catherine... a parade of Anglican clerical perfection. Robert Hood's mind is sodden with texts, touch him and he floods, his doors wrenched open and the rivers of sacred English words dammed up in his memory stream out, all of them into this arctic dawn, visible and blaring out loud   *surely there is a vein for silver and*

a place for gold he setteth an end to darkness and searcheth out the
stones of darkness and the shadow of death but where shall wisdom
be found the depth saith it is not me the topaz of Canaan shall not
and he looketh to the ends of the earth for I mourn for my love
here's a pretty dove he putteth forth his hand upon the rock he over-
turneth them by their roots doest thou do well and also much cattle
to be angry yea I do even unto death I do well that cannot discern
my right hand from my left to be very angry and also much cattle
yea I do

"Doctor Richardson?" Hood whispers; who knows how far
Hepburn has managed to drag himself.

"What?" the doctor responds, as closely confidential.

"Is there, anything, about a daughter's...nakedness, or a
son's?"

Richardson shudders. He has assumed that in their suffering
together they have already spoken of everything necessary; for
him at least starvation (and so he thought for them both) was
their complete and mutual confessor. But never this; what
childhood abomination has Leviticus led this poor boy's dying
memory back into? Truly there are more things in heaven and
on earth — he cannot deny his friend anything, not now.

"Not here," he says finally, searching to focus in chapter
eighteen. "What is it...?"

"My daughter," whispers Hood, "or it may be, my son. Will
need washing, their nakedness, their soft nak — "

"My dearest Robert!" Richardson interrupts before he can
say more — but does not know how to continue. And Hood
seems suspended on one elbow, staring at him as if he would
drag assurance out of his very eyes. "Of course, of course the
mother...washes...."

"O yes," Hood exclaims, "yes, she'll wash, o Greenstockings is, very clean, she smells quick as firelight, moss, woodsmoke, that is, Doctor Richardson, the purest, and cleanest, when the child is born she's absolutely clean…" — sitting up now, a structure of bruised bones shouting as if it still had the strength to walk wherever its eyes led, its still fingers shivered in anticipation of those delicately turned numbers spreading like columns of trees over pages, the shimmering paint and brushes were clenched between its teeth — "sand and smoke and ashes is the sweetest washing, I've seen her wash herself, and the girl, clean as my mother dreamed in the manse, when I take her, and my daughter back to England, or my son, she will show my mother her washing, there is always uncleanness, my father read that, it is there, you should read that, 'If a woman have conceived seed, and borne a man child: then she shall be unclean seven days,' that is what he preached, from the high pulpit, seven days! 'But if she bear a maid child, then she shall be unclean fourteen days, as in her separation: and she shall continue in the blood of her purifying threescore and six days'! Greenstockings! Read it!"

Hood's voice, ravaged by hunger, roars about the blotched tent and breaks off as he collapses against Michel, who stirs but refuses to awaken; he will never waken for a White scream. Richardson grasps a wrist, which is mere bone. Hepburn scrabbles at the door,

"What, sir? Sir!"

"No," Richardson says quietly. "Not yet. He fainted. Leave him, just fainted. Unfortunately."

"He said…a name?"

Richardson quietly covers his skeletal friend again. "He has

not said her name aloud for nine months" is all he says to
Hepburn, weeping again. And he lifts his Bible, bends to it,
knowing he read those words — how could Hood remember
them so perfectly — as recently as yesterday perhaps, or last
week: and finds them under the tip of his finger — Leviticus,
chapter twelve:

"And the Lord spake unto Moses saying…Who shall offer it
before the Lord, and make an atonement…if she be not able to
bring a lamb…two young pigeons…and she shall be clean."

A brace of ptarmigan then, will that suffice? And blood, of
course; always sufficient blood.

Not spoken her name since that dreadful January night —
nine months? certainly nine. Not even later, in July when they
left the Indians on the Coppermine River, just before they came
to the useless mountains that revealed no copper at all — it is all
somewhere in his notes — in July that dangerous woman whose
beauty caused all those fights vanished with the pretty-faced
hunter. Or was it with that one from the huge lake they said was
in the north-west, Great Bear Lake, with that other Yellowknife,
The Hook? They had hung him with medals — it is all detailed
in his notes, facts upon dangerous facts. And in his memory. In
his report he will arrange and edit them properly, as always, so
they will make proper and decent, acceptable sense.

A very short chapter of Bible. Eight priestly verses for Greenstockings.

Or should he burn his notes? Sacrifice must be made. Not
necessarily blood, but burnt sacrifice most surely. If he cannot
write his report properly, as Lieutenant Franklin advises him,
the notes must be burned. When he is about to die, that must
also be done. Things have taken place that would not be under-

stood properly, they may be there in memories, like ineradicable teeth, and whoever survives, whoever, must write the acceptable account of what can be properly reported; and crush, burn his memory.

Hepburn is studying Richardson as though reading his thoughts on the grey Sunday (Saturday?) morning light.

"He's good," the sailor says suddenly, "on my honour, sir. That's all I know of Mr. Hood."

Richardson looks at Hood's flatness of bones; if he is no longer in a faint, he is sleeping. Who would want him to awaken in this horrid place? He has paid more than double for all his sins.

"Yes. As Englishmen," Richardson softly includes Hepburn, "we hold for ever sacred the memory of our blessed, our glorious dead."

But when Michel sits up, Hood is immediately conscious, one unawareness breaking the other. His mind still teems with inchoate phrases and he gropes for Richardson's Bible, he will find the exact places, the exact words and every detail of punctuation as they go on and on beyond what he has or will ever read *unto the least jot and tittle* every iota frozen aloud into him that he is now condemned to recall here in this mocking inescapable land, they burst blazing as ice inside his head *but God prepared a worm I will when the morning rose the next day and they wander for lack of food knowest thou knowest thou bring forth Canaan the wrens so small who bore Cock Robin's pall in his season canst thou kill I will guide Arcturus with his sons canst thou provide raven his food thou kill when his young ones cry unto God for food canst thou knowest kill thou kill kill* but he cannot see anything.

Raven could brush the snow from him and he would not be able to see a speck of his blackness. Hood feels icy paper against his nose and sees nothing; a possible dance of snowstorm. Is it? Soundlessly, without wind? He puts his hand to his face: yes, his eyes are open. It is the book.

He realizes he no longer has dimension. He is a sheet laid between frozen hides, become his own pencilled calculation so thin it cannot be seen, a hide 'twere better 'twere scrapped clean of hair and eaten, and therefore he must explain to Michel, yes, he must, he has Richardson's Bible in his hands and sometimes he finds places where the words he can see for an instant collide with his memory. Richardson and Hepburn are somewhere nearby, scratching through snow for rocks again, and when Hood tilts up, the grey mist of his seeing gradually blurs into a gathering sharpness. He begins to see the thick words at the tops of pages, "Job", "Romans", "Daniel" — it is truly Bible but the small light rising towards noon reveals words he does not really need to see, dragging through his mind   *if then God so clothe the grass which today kill will wander in the field provide yourselves with kill bags which wax not old and he shall surely kill come in the second watch or in the third*   and what he must explain to Michel, Michel who squats in the tent doorway behind him, cleaning his long rifle so thoroughly for tomorrow, certainly tomorrow those two will start for Fort Enterprise, yes, but what he must explain to the Mohawk very carefully is that he will *not* show *him* how to use the compass!

Only English Hepburn can carry that beautiful English copper, no savage can be entrusted with this civilized mysterium, this floating spirit whose pointer, when properly followed through the delicate labyrinth of numbers, leads always to the ridiculous play fort where their salvation sleepeth. Unless the ravens and the wolves come wandering here for lack of food, and they have not seen a track for seven days, the animals would now have to come driving an entire herd of caribou through the western notch of the eskers and offer to kill them at their feet if they were to have enough

> robbin-a-bobbin
> he bent his bow
> shot at a pigeon and killed a crow
> shot at another
> and killed his

"What?" Michel roars behind him. "You say what?"

Robert Hood can almost turn his head; for a moment he finds the strength to look back.

The Mohawk is directly behind him in the tent entrance, his body bent to him as if to take him in his long arms as he holds the rifle in both hands high across his chest. Perhaps he expects an attack; with a slight twist he could thrust the weapon against Hood. But Michel is not doing that, not yet. He leans closer and closer, hissing a small circle of English words that abruptly explode like a black January memory:

"I tell you, I kill you, all the time, I tell you, I kill you, before you die, I tell you I kill, you...."

But Hood cannot hold it. Neither that January night nor the words that have whispered themselves into this landscape week after week through winter and spring and the exhaustion of summer, until he recognizes them like starvation, the penitence of his fast eating him cell by cell down to the last frayed

whisper of what he once knew he could not possibly have
dreamed in this land of goodness, of beauty, of tenderness and
love   *I will kill you*   For nine months these words have eaten
him   *before you die*   When you have exhausted the last jot and
tittle of suffering, when it is no longer possible for you to feel
either God or country or duty, just before you die, at the instant of your last despair   *I will kill you*

> a sighing and sobbing
> To hear the bell toll
> For poor Cock Robin

Why? Why? Oh-h-h-h-h-h, he cannot even groan himself,
the sound he hears Birdseye groaning somewhere is his skeleton
body sinking to this earth, bowed under the heavy, heavy memories that have always pulled him, he realizes now, down; those
follow-my-leader memories rooted and growing in him all his
life — he was such a silly, gullible child, a child who thought he
knew everything because he knew only the confident, simple
world of English games, and endlessly elaborated, confident
duty, words

> robbin-a-bobbin a bendy bow
> shoot at his brother and kill a crow
> shoot again and kill a wren and

There is a spot of round, hard ice against the back of his
head, so round and small, surely the fine, reassuring solidity of
English steel against his hair   *just when you die I will*   as comforting as a child's prayer of forgiveness, and he leans back hard

into it, pushes himself up against it harder with his last bit of fervent strength, perhaps that at least can be properly, firmly fixed

and that will be all for gentle

The last syllable may be floating, trying to float, there   *men...
men...men*   And young Robert Hood never able to complete it.

Doctor John Richardson

October 24th & October 25th 1821   Brush Shelter

On the two following days after Michel's death we had mild but thick snowy weather, and as the view was too limited for us to preserve a straight course, we remained encamped among a few dwarf pines about five miles from the tent. Hepburn found a species of cornicularia, a kind of lichen, that was possible to eat when moistened and toasted over the fire; and we had a good many pieces of singed buffalo hide that had belonged to Mr. Hood remaining.

Up to the period of his attack upon us, Michel's conduct had been good and respectful to the officers, and in a conversation between Lieutenant Franklin, Mr. Hood, and myself, at Obstruction Rapids, it had been proposed to give him a reward upon our arrival at a trading post. His principles, however, unsupported by a belief in the divine truths of Christianity, were unable to withstand the pressure of severe distress. His countrymen, the Mohawk-Iroquois, are generally Christians, but he was totally uninstructed and ignorant of the duties inculcated by Christianity; and from his long residence in this part of the country seemed to have imbibed, and retained, the rules of conduct which the Indians here prescribe to themselves.

II

Out of the Lake

Greenstockings kneels in her small shelter, the pad of moss between her knees. When hard pain swells through her again she tilts forwards, arms braced, her stomach mounded immense and heavy holding her erect against her doubled thighs. Will this stubborn, powerful child ever deign to let go of her?

The lowering sun rises into the second day. She has stared down hour by hour at this moist lace of matted green and brown stems beneath her, her forehead propped exhausted on the stone ground. When she can think, she hears the lake of the great bear, Sahtú, breathe against the rocks below, and she feels her happiness multiplied by the length and depth of that deep, black water she knows she has climbed out of, at last.

The water is with her, snuffling between the split erosions of Sahtú's cliffs, the mountainous bristle of grey stone that looms above her. Called Forbidden Rock since the prophecy — which not even her father is old enough to have heard the Prophet tell People, though he says he once saw him as a little boy, looked up and saw bent over him an ancient man with both eyes blind, so enormous and deep from a lifetime of looking inside himself that along the blade of his nose his face had grown into a skeleton cross. Since that prophecy of vision, no one dares to paddle a canoe in front of the Rock where it thrusts itself out of the lake, glistening like diluvial ice spired upwards into granite. So two days ago, when the Tetsot'ine came paddling south along the east side of the lake, they camped for night at their usual place in order to carry the long portage behind Forbidden Rock and thus avoid the deepwater danger before it; that night this child within her gave its first great heave of intention.

But why choose this dangerous place? "Why," she asks, her fingertips tracing its curl once more, and feeling reluctance flutter like breath through her distended skin, "why if you truly wish to cry here first, why now abuse me and refuse to be born so I can comfort you?"

Keskarrah smiled at her when she left, and she understood him: it seems your child is like you — contrary.

And she smiles, remembering; eases herself down again, onto the length of her left side and pulls the marten-skin robe Greywing brought over her nakedness. The small animals are always ready and warm, their soft tenderness a wrap of comfort. The camp with all her People is beyond a ridge; they are living as easily as they can, this waiting a mere hesitation in their continual travel as they follow the animals, and she cannot hear them, only the slim trees whispering into the sigh of the lake. She is surrounded by waiting, and abysmally alone. If a she-wolf came now, delicate furred feet silent from rock or deep water — as she did for Copperwoman, yes come, come — she would greet her with happiness,

"Come my sister, come my mother, you have birthed so many children, come and welcome this one fearful of the world, come sing it into courage."

The strength of the she-wolf fondles her, the wolf's long tongue wipes away the tears along the edges of her eyes, and she feels through the ground a faint, steady beat; she is two bodies curled in and around, tight together, and gradually taken into the rhythmic, sacred power of drum. They are there, they are here, Birdseye can no longer walk, but in their veneration for her the People are carrying her, out of the exhaustion of her year-long travail, south into the winter trees to wherever she wants to stop breathing even while this little one begins; and Keskarrah is a man, he cannot help Greenstockings, nor can Broadface, hunting and hunting. But their care and love for her beat like blood in the land. Especially here in this place of fearful vision, in the beaked shadow of Forbidden Rock.

And she thinks continuously of the child, a soft heavy stone turning inside her, refusing and refusing so stubbornly hard. That too is its good and separate will, hers no longer, and her mind flares into light, she sees it already running down to water, where waves curl forwards and race back, or through flowers on tundra, and leaping over worn round rocks and tussocks of moss, such long legs and belly tight with caribou meat, mouth open in breath and laughter. She can see that, land and child and sky, carrying her, as the rigid, battering pain heaves her up onto her knees again, rocks her groans into a piercing vision of — is it herself? running as she once did? is it Greywing? is it this hard child of living stone? already grown after it has been carried for several years more at her breast and on her back? and running free in a strength possible only because she has given to it her own continual work, her intense and willing slavery? After this difficult but ultimately mere moment of birthing.

Like the moment her blood told her she was becoming a woman. "Don't hide that, when it comes," Birdseye warned her. "You'll be shy, but don't ever hide it, it's too powerful and dangerous, men can die if they touch you." But it came so quickly and she had to retreat into her place of separation, wait alone where the women told her to hide under a tree, two days without eating, until an old woman came laughing with a great cape of fur to cover her sitting with her knees pulled tight against her stomach — so hard and flat then, she couldn't do that now! — and she clasped herself, sat looking over her knees for days inside that tent of fur, so warmly hooded — patience then, and wonderful rest, waiting while her body travelled within itself in its own indelible way, and other women brought her water to drink through a bone straw, but spilled most of it to make her life strong, and Greywing and other small children came with food — dry meat, but no berries whose juice is too close to blood — and she took a single bite and gave them the rest so she would always be generous — she was so patient then, at rest while the moon went through its whole cycle, and happy at the dark slip of her unstoppable womanhood. When Birdseye's face was still beautiful, and whole.

Below her the waters of Sahtú brush dark in a long wedge under wind, swift as clouds streak towards the horizon where there is no shoreline; she has no fear of this immense lake, even when the shoulder of the rock beneath her trembles.

Not like drum, but a solid shudder. As if Forbidden Rock had spoken to the massive water, and earth which alone can contain the bottomless lake, were alert and listening too. Were considering flood, or perhaps explosion. Can a lake melt like a mountain and rain water like rocks from the sky? Greenstockings is suddenly afraid in her exhaustion. If Keskarrah were with her, he would tell her that story too, the difficult story of final deluge or volcano being spoken beneath her. What can flood them? overwhelm them? their land held so firmly in bowls of water and ice?

Before this child insisted that this was its place, she has never dared kneel here to feel this sound, nor heard this subterranean beat through her body. Though she has heard her father tell the prophecy many times:

"The Prophet was so old when I saw him, and I was only a little boy, that he had already seen everything twice, everything in the world with the one milky eye nearest his heart, and his right eye was closed, he never opened it because that way he could look inwards most clearly. When you have been given power to do that, you often see more than you want to know. It scares you to know something a little. Once, long before we had even heard of Whites, he knew something one night, here, when People stopped to continue their journey next morning, and he sang to his drum all night so that they had to stay up without sleep and listen. And in the morning he told them.

"'I thought I heard,' the Prophet said, 'that harm would come over us, like rain running, so I sang. Listen, singing I saw strange people come to this place, people pale as meat drowned in water, with unbelievable clothes. They went into the hard belly of this rock, into a hole they pounded there, right into the folded rock. They had tools harder than rock and they tore a hole out of it with a terrible noise, the rock screamed night and day louder than anything we could have explained, you had to hear it two days' paddling away across the lake.

"'Out of that hole they pulled long sticks of rock as thin as arms, and so dangerous they shone, they melted your hand into burning air if you touched them. Then huge birds sailed down on their grey bellies onto Sahtú, and swallowed the sticks pulled from the mountain and flew away again, bellowing up from the water and roaring south, roaring who can understand where. But I saw that, it will come. Rock groans continuously. And when Rock groans it is warning us: be careful! Be careful. Strange people, more and more, strange fire, be careful!'"

Why, when the world is immeasurable and land endless, why does this child groan to be born here, and yet refuse? Forbidden Rock continually speaks what no one, not even the wisest, has yet comprehended beyond warning. And now she must wait here, cry with the earth and its inconceivable necessity of endurance.

She sees motion between hides above her: two ravens, riding light there. Long wings hold them above air it seems, the small density of their bodies blazing on the bright sky. She surrenders her heaviness to them, they soar over green summer land quick with flowers, the blue line of twisted rivers, and high stone rivers of eskers streaming their ridges north along the flat land into the white froth of rapids, lakes foaming into green lakes. The black movement of ravens intersects inland. Are they flowing into each other, are they doubled into one mellifluous sky warmth of People curved around and into each other skin upon skin? They open, sail wide and merge again. O to be raven, o to ride north on wind, to look down along the floating spine of the world.

Under her patient woman's hood she drank the water she was given, but only one sip through a swan bone; she wore the stick necklace to scratch her heavy hair; she wore ptarmigan feathers tied below her knee so she would run all her life. And goose feathers in her hands to make her tireless, brushing them along her folded legs, blowing through them with a puff of breath like breathing out, "o-o-o-o-o" — the centre of his green name she could not yet dream was already coming — "o-o-o-o-o."

And she remains on the grained rock. Past her knees, where the sheltering hides do not touch the ground, Greenstockings sees Greywing's lovely head, body emerge in the saddle of the ridge. She is a woman, men are watching her, and when the deer grunt their rut in the valleys the men will dare each other to ask Keskarrah for her fresh warmth, take her, find her lust or accommodating gentleness. If she lets them. She is coming with food, her long strides as strong as the voice of the rock, she fears nothing here or anywhere. But behind her another shape, an old woman, The Hook's mother. Even as Greenstockings sees this, pain lengthens through her body again, stretches her long and groaning.

But she struggles onto her knees as she has been instructed, gasping, pushing down and pushing because her body is tearing at itself, because the child will not move, there is space for more than a man between her legs but the child refuses and the old woman is beside her, one strong hand warm on her back and the other caressing her stomach, chanting under her breath,

It is time to breathe, little child,
Come out, come out,
It is time to eat, little child,
Come out, come out, bite the sweet air,

and Greywing wipes her face with fingers of water, catching her
cries in a wet hand, the ground rhythm still rocking her, throb-
bing in her ears with her mouth gaping for air, the water and
blood pushes a thick line down her thighs into the patient
moss. She clutches the two rooted trees bent over her, heaving,
heaving down until she will split and all her muscles lock in
cramp together, down, down. But the child refuses.

When the pain has relented a little, the old woman eases her
against herself, heavily onto her right side; looking away from
the lake between hides, up into spruce and shouldered rocks.
Her face shines bent over Greenstockings, her eyes and mouth
hunched as if in its folds her ancient skin sheltered goodness.

"Almost ready now to show you its face, this one," she says,
chuckling a little. "But it is fearful, coming here from so many
rivers away."

"From farther than that," Greenstockings whispers through
her teeth.

"O-o-o-o, over stinking water," the old voice so quiet, as if
too gentle to know. "It's very strong, come such a long journey."

"Will it be…worn out?"

The old woman's hand searches hard under the furs Greywing has folded over her, exploring her belly that shimmers,
teeters over an awesome recognition of coming pain.

"No, no," she says, her other hand firm as rock against the
small of Greenstockings' back, so exactly placed, so precisely
comforting. "No, this one is very strong, you can feel that. It
will live longer than you both lying together."

And for one shiver she knows thin Robert Hood again, his
arms locked around her, alive or dead they will never let each
other go, her legs hooked over each other into the fold of his

narrow buttocks and pulling, holding him rigid, rooted inside herself as her shoulders suck in his hands and their faces are face upon face, her child must be, it will be, it started with him, the hovering, distended agony of her womb declares this to her: yes!

"...a baby's cry beside great Sahtú," the old woman chants her ancient birthing story, both hands fondling and circling her great gift now. "O, that is strong, it will come, come, girls cannot find such a beautiful child, no, not many fine girls, but a woman can, you can, you must look small, small and there it will be in the split print of a caribou's hoof, that passing goodness in moss, perfect and small, no bigger than a thumb, crying for you!"

While Greywing cradles her head on her folded thighs; wipes her sweating face and feeds her blood soup. And tries to tell her other stories, talking of People now as they rest and wait, for today at least.

"The Hook talks with our father, like Bigfoot talked when he came, they sit all day and eat and talk. The Hook says, 'We have to go farther south, to the traders,' and our father says, 'There are fine caribou here, we're moving south as they move,' and The Hook says, 'Our guns can't shoot without powder,' and our father, 'Of course, but are there no trees left for pounds, no braided gut for snares, no rivers for spearing?' and The Hook laughs, 'Bigfoot is near the traders, if we don't go he'll get all the guns!' and our father laughs right back at him, 'And get a bigger head too! Can't you see, I left him to go with you? We have enough hatchets and needles and pots to carry now, if we hammer the guns we have into spearheads we don't need to visit those traders for two years, or if we're lucky, three.'"

Greenstockings has to smile; hearing in Greywing's voice her father's delicate needling, so exact in its explications of the land for hunters who, caribou thick around them or travelling just over the next ridge, nevertheless still cannot think further than "Kill! Kill!"

"You've seen the contradictions of the traders," Keskarrah debates. "They want us to hunt caribou, as we have always lived, because they need that meat to eat too, it is too far for them to carry food from the stinking water — but they want us to *live different* too. They really want us to use up our lives killing small animals, as many as we can."

The Hook says, "Small animals live here, lots of them, the traders want only their skin."

"But who eats fox, or marten, unless they're starving?"

The Hook cannot answer that; he doesn't really think that tramping through snow and collecting small bodies contorted hard as rock in traps, or finding the stumps of gnawed legs, is worthy of a hunter who has travelled with the forests of caribou along ridges and down to the glacial lakes. After waiting politely, Keskarrah continues,

"Caribou have always given us what we need to live, why kill every small animal? To please Whites? Why? And destroy ourselves in winter and summer walking the tundra like loaded dogs to the traders with their fur? To get powder for guns? If we don't use their guns, we won't have to carry powder or lead. Iron knives and needles are very good, of course, and kettles, but Copperwoman has always given us fine copper ones."

"But if others have White things," The Hook insists shrewdly, "we have to have them too."

"Why?"

"Guns are for killing, they can kill us too, very well. If our enemies have guns...."

Keskarrah waggles his hands as if batting away the last groggy mosquitoes of summer. "We already know enough ways of killing, we don't need more."

"Bigfoot wants to hunt only with guns, it's so easy...."

"We all know that. And we also know that last winter he kept sending his young men to Thick English: 'Give us more powder, so we can hunt!' We have to beg Whitemuds for their things so we can live in our own land? Huh!"

For a moment Keskarrah's disgust splatters about his lodge like spit; not even The Hook can find a word to say, though his mouth is open.

Keskarrah is staring up, the fire's smoke ascending faint as prayer.

"People I think can kill themselves, trying to carry too much," he says. "And also, there is Whitesickness. Traders won't trade you that, o no, they don't offer you sickness for furs or food, but often a person receives it anyway. As a gift, I suppose... something from Whites, a little extra. When I was a boy more than half the southern Pointed Skin and Cree people were killed by a blistering, bleeding sickness that no medicine could stop. Wolves and rocks didn't give them that, neither did caribou. And the very best trader guns couldn't kill it either."

Hearing Greywing tell her this, Greenstockings almost forgets her body. Earlier that summer, at the place on the River of Copperwoman where, if you wait quietly at dawn, you can sometimes smell the sea, Greenstockings recognized that Bigfoot's head had finally swollen too large for him to wear the black Whitemud hat any longer. It happened when Thick English

gave The Hook a shiny medal to hang around his neck, and he
in turn gave him every bit of meat his People had; while Bigfoot watched, his face blacker than the sun could burn it. Then,
for the first time she heard Bigfoot interrupt her father while he
was still speaking:

"These English," Bigfoot declared then, glaring across the
river north to the distant haze of Copperwoman Mountains,
"have brought us no sickness. Only many good gifts."

Deliberately her father waited; to be certain Bigfoot was finished.

"Gifts." Keskarrah spoke finally, and continued with stunning directness, "Gifts. Given to every person who does exactly
what they say. Who works for them like the Halfmuds. Gifts
we then have to carry."

"We smoke their tobacco," Bigfoot argued, but could not
look at him; Keskarrah persisted,

"And beyond good smoking, how have these 'gifts' helped
us?"

"No one has died."

"Two hunters died."

"The lake took them. And we lived without sickness through
the winter."

Keskarrah smiled slightly. "We haven't lived well with our
ancestors through a winter before?"

"They've come to us, they're our guests!"

"That's true. And we are such People who know well in our
hearts how to welcome guests. But no one changes their whole
life, for guests."

Bigfoot said then, very strong, "It is as I said when they came:
they are here now, we can't change that."

"I know," Keskarrah answered, suddenly sad. "And These English may go away, or die, hopefully before they find whatever it is they want here. The land will take care of them, I think Copperwoman will give them less copper for their giant boats than she gives us. But the White traders stay with us because they've found what they want — fur. And they are finding ways to make us want what they have, all this Whitemud stuff piled up, I think it can make a person avaricious to have more of it, just a little, more, and finally like Whitemuds you have so much you have to force other People to carry it for you because otherwise someone will steal it from you."

"Stealing…we've always stolen women."

"A good woman doesn't come from Whitemuds."

"But a person needs one to live."

"Yes…as a person needs a good man to live."

"Sometimes you have to steal one."

"Yes, men sometimes do that, and often they don't — men and women find each other otherwise, and both want what they have found. And," he added thoughtfully, "some old men tell a stealing story, again and again. As if they didn't know any better."

Keskarrah and Bigfoot looked at each other steadily, reading each other's tone correctly there on the gravel ridges of the River of Copperwoman. Beside the voyageur canoes piled high with Whitemud things, The Hook was talking with Thick English, and from a distance the large medal around his neck glinted in the sun very much like the one Bigfoot had been given a year earlier on the blacksand shores of Tucho — when the flag had burned like a beacon, though they had not then understood what it signalled. But they were thinking about that now as well.

Keskarrah turned away; for a time he contemplated the Copperwoman Mountains on the northern horizon. He said at last, even more sadly,

"Copperwoman was stolen. But stolen by enemies, and out of that she gave us a great gift beyond her story, as you know. A man may think he has power over a woman, but if he takes a woman who doesn't want him, she can make his life taste like dogshit. Even if he tries to beat her twice a day."

Bigfoot was also considering Copperwoman's story, sinking year by year into those mountains, escaping deeper and deeper into the memory of her abuse. Taking her gift of copper with her.

"If These English find her," Keskarrah concluded, "very soon not even the top of her hair will be there for us."

Bigfoot finally asked, abruptly small again, "But…what do you say? What can we do with these strangers?"

Keskarrah answered, strangely, "I don't understand."

As Bigfoot waited, the wind breathing.

Keskarrah murmured, "I think…it will have to be the land. Birdseye is alive, but these Whitemuds have stolen her nevertheless. She saw them too clearly, and dreamed what they will do, and now she is empty. We must pray that the land will take them, before they steal us all."

In her confinement under the bent trees Greenstockings feels again the power of her father standing over her as she weaves the snowshoe, protecting her from a great danger only he can see at the tip of Hood's black pencil. Hood who is gone, for ever. Perhaps her father should have been protecting Birdseye then as well — if that had been possible. It is obvious that Bigfoot, at the river, could not understand, nor does Greenstockings, now afloat on her distended stomach, memory opening her eyes into her sister's upside-down face. Leaning down to her, and weeping.

"Our mother," Greywing breathes, "our mother."

And Greenstockings discovers the strangest thought: White Horizon's men could never have held She Who Delights without other women helping them.

Greywing murmurs, "She's waiting for this one…waiting…."

Greenstockings whispers, "I wish she were here."

They are crying together, sister cradled into sister by their grief for their mother. And the old woman can only hold them both between her large, work-ravaged hands, crooning to them as she croons to the unborn child,

Come out, little child, come out,
A hoof-print is waiting to welcome you, come,
Now is the time to breathe sweetly.

The sisters know they will always have mothers to love and comfort them, but they have been mourning Birdseye's cavernous death for so long now, the deadly salve from Richard Sun that somehow numbed her alive through the winter nevertheless so deadened her that now, after the brief summer without it, she must be carried on through this length and burden of dreamless dying without the final mercy of death.

Greenstockings knows now that the last time they saw the English on the gravel along the River of Copperwoman, Keskarrah reached a hard decision; just a day ago, as they paddled south on great Sahtú towards Forbidden Rock he explained that decision to her, because her memory of the coming and going of these strangers will live far beyond his own.

"I dared to ask them," Keskarrah said to her as their small canoe searched through the waves in the scattered flotilla following The Hook. "You heard me ask it: 'Who among you can keep a human being from dying?' I asked that, but I was foolish. I had lived so many years with Birdseye, I didn't need to hear her dream their future for a whole winter to understand. I should have known that to ask like Whitemuds ask — for everything at once — is far too dangerous."

"But what could you have known?" Greenstockings asked him, paddling steadily with the waves that carried them where they wished to go.

"I was foolish, I thought sickness was no more than blisters, bleeding perhaps, and some People lost in their bodies. Or even Eaters eating parts of us. But that's not it — the sickness they bring is a *spirit*, of *things*. It is connected somehow to this endless killing of more and more small animals, and this shining little shit they hang around People's necks where nothing so bright has ever hung before. Look, The Hook can never take it off or he'll lose it, and so even the sun plays with it every day. Behind their quick kindness, These English are deadly. Their coming will destroy us."

"Hood didn't destroy me."

Keskarrah turned his long, worn face back to her; the water carrying them like birds in the tiny shell they built for this travelling and that they would leave at the last portage for the next traveller, or to rot back into the land.

"That's true," he said. "You were strong enough to have him for a little while. Until the right enemy came and stole you."

Greywing says softly into Greenstockings' memory of her redemption from the Whitemuds, sweet breath against her face,

"The People have to go south with the animals, tomorrow. But I'll wait with you."

The old woman is gone. They both know Keskarrah must move with the People, who can carry Birdseye over the portages, or their family will be left impossibly solitary for the winter. Shaking herself back into her large, simmering body, Greenstockings sighs with a great happiness. There is only physical pain here, pain easy to accept, easy to bear, and out of it a child wants to be born. She exclaims:

"We can follow them later, together, you and I and this one."

"Broadface says nothing, he's still thinking. But he's looking at me."

Greenstockings gasps, on the edge of laughter. "He wants you? I know it!"

Greywing smiles. "He wants me — so he can have us both."

"No, he'll drag you off and leave me...."

"No!" Greywing hisses fiercely. "Both, or he won't have me! He brags he's such a great hunter, well, let him hunt for two — three! And he won't kill this one, no matter what it looks like. I told him."

Greywing's young hands cradle her sister's head in her lap, clasping her in a confidence strong enough to confront any man or mystery of this child that has rooted itself in Greenstockings' body with its own particular coiled stubbornness.

And then, in a threatened gathering of pain, laughter catches her into another gasp. "I can teach you, what Broadface likes, what he thinks he doesn't...he'll be so busy...."

"...we can do what we please!"

The echo of their laughter bursting out together in the tiny shelter remains long after Greywing has gone to convince Broadface that he has convinced himself that he is hunter enough to have both of Birdseye's strong, beautiful daughters. She will remind him that not even The Hook or Bigfoot with their shiny medals dared attempt as much. For a time Greenstockings can lie peacefully, almost asleep on the surface of her coming great pain, as a gull rides the lifting water. When the white she-wolf comes, she will give her the thick sweet afterbirth.

And soon she is certain she hears sniffing behind her, the quick pad of feet. But she does not turn, does not lift her belly around to see the animal, or the surface of the bottomless lake, or Forbidden Rock talking eternally within itself. She rests completely upon the earth, her body opening to offer birth to this strange, wilful child. And she feels herself becoming Copperwoman: the worn trail made by the caribou travelling north to the sea plain of their birthing is before her, and now the wolf has come to lead her through that water and swamp and rock, five nights she will follow, though the water rises to her armpits and over her shoulders, until she reaches the land of her People where she can rest. And there in the morning she will see the copper mountain shining above her like the shoulder of the sun rising, a green gift for every generation of her People; and she will search for them and mark her path with the gleaming metal she drops to lead them back to the incredible copper gift of knives and awls and spear points and needles and ice chisels and bracelets and shields and hair clasps and hatchets and rings and arrowheads and kettles and needles, the green and yellow copper lying under their eyes in the shapes and parts of all the burnished animals they must hunt to live, the life to which they give their bodies back when they themselves must die.

Slowly, carefully, Greenstockings turns her laden body, lifts herself to her knees. She raises her hands to clutch the bent green trees of her shelter and begins to rock, slowly, steadily, until at last she feels the living strength of the child that has grown inside her spread through her, enormously. She groans in prayer, and the child groans together with her. To the long drum rhythm of the earth; to the groan of Forbidden Rock out of which they all know someday Whitemuds will rain horror on the world. Know because their prophet listening to the voice of the earth has already told them. But this child will be born strong nevertheless; no Whitemud can stop it.

Doctor John Richardson

Sunday October 28th 1821   Dogrib Rock

We attempted to keep a straight course, but, owing to the depth of the snow in the valleys, did not reach the rock until late in the afternoon. We did not like to pass a second night without fire, and though scarcely able to drag our limbs after us, we pushed on to a clump of pines and arrived at them in the dusk of evening. During the last few hundred yards, our track lay over some large stones, among which I fell down upwards of twenty times, and became at length so exhausted that I was unable to stand. If Hepburn had not exerted himself far beyond his strength, and speedily made the encampment and kindled a fire, I must have perished on the spot. That night we had plenty of dry wood.

12

EATING STARVATION

The Reverend Dr. Richard Hood,
St. Mary's Church,
Bury, Lancashire, England

Fort Enterprise, the Arctic Regions,
Tuesday, October 30th, 1821

Reverend Sir:
I write to you, Sir, to whom I am a stranger, as the father of my departed friend Midshipman Robert Hood, now blessed for ever.

I trust you will excuse the clumsy letters which is all I am able to make in the urgency of writing to you immediately, upon our arrival after indescribable hardship at Fort Enterprise yesterday, when you understand that I may not be able to send this letter to you personally, or that it may never reach you despite my efforts, because of the grievous disappointment we have here experienced.

Despite our struggle to return to Fort Enterprise, there was here no supply of provisions, neither for Mr. Back and his men, who arrived first, nor for Lieutenant Franklin's party, nor for Hepburn and myself who arrived last by several weeks, supplies so solemnly promised us by the Indians when they left us last summer, the natural fickleness of which people renders them expert in finding any number of reasons for changing an arrangement however desperately important.

But let me spare reproach where it cannot be remedied. At this point your dear son would require me to add that, on the basis of our year's experience with them, the Yellowknives may themselves have suffered some grievous deaths during the summer, such as by the oversetting of a canoe, whereupon the rest would have thrown away their clothing, broken their guns and mourned themselves into a debilitating weakness, which is their habitual and most inappropriate mode of expressing their grief, since thereby they curtail themselves of every means to continue procuring food for themselves in this desperate country.

Through the protection of Almighty God I have escaped until now, and feel my first duty the more keenly is to leave behind while I can, for you and your grieving family, a reassurance and whatever word of comfort is possible concerning your beloved son's last hours, to which I was witness. Lieutenant Franklin endeavours to outline the Overland Expedition's report, and the rough notes of my journals will be added to those official ones, together with these words, for I presently feel my first duty is to you.

We have, throughout the Expedition, been indebted to Lieutenant Franklin for the excellent example he set us in the strict and regular performance of his religious duties. Your son, I firmly believe, had never suffered the principles of religion to be absent from his mind, and to the last he was poring over the Scriptures.

But it was during our perilous march just past across the Barren Grounds from the sea that he and I unbosomed ourselves to each other, and our conversation tended to excite in us mutually a firm reliance on the wisdom and beneficence of the decrees of the Almighty.

Our sufferings were never acute during the march; the sensation of hunger ceases after the third day of privation, and with the decay of strength, the love of life also decays; we could calmly contemplate the approach of death, and our feelings were excited only by the idea of the grief of our relatives.

It was of you, Sir, that your talented son thought and spoke most in the latter days of his life, and when obliged by weakness to abandon everything else, he clung to his Prayerbook, from which the service was daily read with studious devotion.

He delighted also, morning and evening and throughout the day, in repeating the prayer of the Princess Elizabeth of France presented to him by a lady previous to the Expedition leaving London, which he repeated so often aloud that the words are perceptibly in my mind whenever I think of him, which is daily since he preceded me:

"What may befall me this day, O God, I know not. But I do know that nothing can happen to me which Thou hast not foreseen, ruled, willed and ordained from all eternity, and that suffices me. I adore Thy eternal and inscrutable designs, I accept all, I make unto Thee a sacrifice of all, with patience under suffering and with perfect submission."

The prayer is longer, but you also will have the text — I cannot write more today, and am confident, Reverend Sir, that your son rejoices in Heaven's blessedness.

Your sincere friend,
John Richardson

Wednesday, October 31st

I will try to continue, Sir, so that the narrative of our journey may possibly be recorded.

The cold was today severe, but I resolved to remove myself from the suffering in our desolate building and endeavour to kill some partridges, which run everywhere. They are so perfectly adapted to this extreme climate that one could easily commit the sin of envying them the beneficence they have received from the Creator.

I was, however, unable to steady my arm enough to dispatch one, being too dim-sighted with famine, but while I was endeavouring this, a large herd of reindeer, perhaps thirty or more, passed close before me, indeed, under my very gun as I supported it against the bole of a tree. I could not hold the gun straight, though I fired, and may have hit one, but was unable to pursue them when they fled; indeed I had not enough strength to ascertain whether any left a drop of blood behind, which I would have eaten from the snow.

Hepburn might have wounded one of so many had he been there, but he was hunting farther along the ridge. His sources of strength are astonishing. When after the death of your son our track lay over some large stones, among which I often fell, he transported me over them and speedily kindled a fire or I must have perished on the spot. Today Hepburn saw not a single animal, not so much as a ptarmigan.

Such heavy disappointment.

The men of Lieutenant Franklin's small party, whom we found with him when we entered the main house at Fort Enterprise, the greatest part of which had already been pulled down by them for firewood, were all even more wretchedly weak than ourselves. Lieutenant Franklin had endeavoured to feed them by raising reindeer skins from under the snow, where the Indians flung their worn bedding when they left with us the previous spring; these are for the most part rotten and thin, and he can bring in no more than two a day although the distance he drags them does not exceed twenty yards, but those that contain the hibernating larvae of the warble fly are most prized by us for food. The voyageurs Peltier and Samandré can no longer move from their blankets, their loss of flesh producing huge sores where their small weight rests, and our secondary Indian translator, Adam, is much distressed with oedematous swellings. I have now made several scarifications in his scrotum, abdomen and legs, which have eased him of a large quantity of water.

We sup on singed skins, a soup of pounded bone, which is so acrid as to excoriate the mouth, and a soft larva each for an amen. Moment by moment we pray that Mr. Back with St. Germain may locate the Indians very soon, who before God remain our last hope.

I must explain, Reverend Sir, that your son, though debilitated by perfect famine, did not expire of it. He was the finest navigator among us, and in our march from the Northern Ocean after August 25, which soon became desperate because the untimely coming of winter had driven the reindeer, which were to have been our source of food, south before us, your son was always in second position with the compass, immediately behind the leader, a voyageur who every hour took turn and turn about with his fellows breaking trail through the snow. Such a position was necessary for him to keep us on the most direct route for Fort Enterprise crossing the featureless tundra, but you will understand that he exhausted himself following in that single track, and when he finally admitted that he could no longer continue in that position, and I took his place, he was already greatly weakened.

Also, the *tripe de roche* that we scraped from the rocks, unpalatable and feeble as it was, became our main source of food, and was nauseous to all, but caused him the greater pain of bowels. After a time it was necessary to eat our extra skin footwear, but then we had none to put on at night, and those we wore wet from the day's exertions froze on our feet as we slept.

No language that I can use will convey a just idea of that painful journey. I shall merely mention that in traversing the tundra we had to coast four lakes and cross three huge rivers never before seen, and when after nine days we managed to cross the Coppermine River at the double rapids, every reserve of strength your son had was gone. He could no longer walk and there was no one who could carry him. We would not leave him alone while the rest continued, as we permitted the voyageurs to do when they weakened. We finally crossed the river on October 4, and on October 7 Hepburn and I remained with your son while Lieutenant Franklin and the rest of our party continued towards Fort Enterprise as best they could. A day later Mr. Back, with the translator St. Germain and several strong Canadians, struck out ahead to seek help of the Indians. To date we know nothing of the progress of Mr. Back's party, but we do know that eight men have been left behind.

This includes the Mohawk Indian voyageur, Michel Terohaute. It was he who killed your son Robert, who did not die of famine. Michel shot him, and he was instantly, painlessly gone.

I can offer no consolation to you for such an inexpressible loss. But my prayer is directed to Him Who alone is able to pour balm on the broken heart, for I have every confidence that your son is in His presence in Whom we will all and for ever rejoice. I shall endeavour to continue this narrative, as I am able.

Sunday, November 4th

Towards evening on November 1 Joseph Peltier became quite speechless, and passed away without a sound during the night.

François Samandré, whose strength throughout the day appeared to be greater, as if he were terrified at the fate of his companion, grew very low and lived only until the morning.

We have removed the deceased as far as we can from the fireplace, but are incapable of laying them outside the house, and spend what strength we have bringing in wood we remove from the nearest walls of the storehouse, which barely suffices to keep the fire going.

Hepburn's limbs have now begun to swell, and the incisions in Adam's legs have been renewed. Lieutenant Franklin found one more reindeer skin today, but unfortunately without larvae.

The weather is comparatively mild. The view down Winter River as beheld from the house, at all times beautiful, was uncommonly so today.

I must conclude in haste, no help has come. We have heard nothing from Mr. Back, but know that ten of our twenty Expedition members no longer live.

Lieutenant Franklin assures me that on October 9 last, when the Canadians Bélanger and Perrault were unable to continue with his party and turned back with Michel to rejoin us because of weakness, it was Bélanger who carried the rifle and ammunition. But Michel alone came to us with the note from Lieutenant Franklin, carrying the rifle, and seemed surprised that both Perrault and Bélanger were mentioned in it as being with him. He insisted, angrily, that he had not seen either, nor had they come with him.

To us Michel appeared then to be, despite Lieutenant Franklin's note concerning his weakness, very strong and he went out great distances to hunt every day, though it appeared he shot nothing. He once fed us the flesh of a wolf that had, he said, been killed by the stroke of a deer's horn. We believed his story then, but afterwards became convinced from circumstances, the detail of which you may be spared, that what he brought us, and used privately for himself when he went away for several days at a time, must have been some portion of the two lost men. He may have murdered them, or found their bodies in the snow, but Lieutenant Franklin conjectures that Michel having first destroyed Bélanger to obtain the rifle, completed his crime by Perrault's death to screen himself from detection.

His subsequent conduct showed that he was certainly capable of committing such a deed.

I can only hurry on with memories too painful, and with strength too far gone, and trust that somehow through God's grace these words may reach you with some small comfort of fact. The fire in the fireplace built so well the previous year from clay and stones by your talented son throws a most grateful heat, but we are too weak to keep it fed and suffer much from cold, though we wear every particle of clothing we have left, indeed have not removed any in two months.

Your son died instantly. After our morning devotions on Sunday, October 20, Hepburn and I were at some distance, endeavouring to gather wood, while your son was sitting up in his blankets near the fire. I heard him speak loudly several times, as in admonishment, to Michel, who was readying his outfit to advance on the Fort with Hepburn. Then I was startled to hear the report of a gun.

When I arrived, I found your dear son lying lifeless, a ball having, it appeared, entered at his forehead. I was at first horror-struck, that in a fit of despondency he had hurried himself into the presence of his Almighty Judge, by an act of his own hand. But the conduct of Michel soon excited other suspicions, which were confirmed, when upon examination, I discovered that the shot had entered the back part of the head and passed out at the forehead, and that the muzzle of the gun had been applied so close as to set fire to the nightcap behind. The fired rifle, which was of the longest, could not have been placed in a position to inflict such a wound, except by a second party. Michel now held a shorter gun in his hand, and upon my enquiry, replied that Mr. Hood had called him into the tent to clean the short gun, and that while his back was turned the long gun had gone off.

Hepburn had now arrived and Michel moved with the short gun between us, declaring himself incapable of committing any act as would endanger Mr. Hood, the gun must have gone off accidentally. Hepburn tried to speak, but Michel turned angrily towards him and demanded if he accused him of murder. He was very strong and held the loaded gun, it was unsafe for us to say anything to each other on the subject in his presence, as he understood English well enough.

I am, however, perfectly convinced that he committed the desperate act. He had insisted we must try to reach Fort Enterprise, but knew we would never leave your son behind as long as he was alive.

The loss of such a distinguished officer of such varied talents and application, to say nothing of the bosom friend he became to me, I cannot express to you. Daily we had expected the worst, and yet we never did despair. Had my poor friend been spared to revisit his native land, his variety of talent in scientific observations, together with his maps and drawings, which have been the admiration of everyone who has seen them, must have rendered him a distinguished ornament to his profession, and I should look back to this period, where we never spoke but with cheerfulness, with unalloyed delight.

The Bible was lying open beside the body, as if it had fallen from his hand, and it is certain he was reading it at the instant of his death. *Blessed are they that die in the Lord, for their works follow after them.* Amen.

We wrapped and removed the body into a clump of willows behind the tent and, returning to the fire, read the funeral service in addition to the evening prayers, and also some of the forms of prayer to be used at sea, as were appropriate, for truly our eternal Lord has here spread out and compassed these lands like "the waters with bounds until day and night come to an end." We passed the night in the tent together without rest, everyone being on his guard.

Reverend Sir, the sailor Hepburn and I were in great perplexity. We were ill and very nearly destroyed by famine, our friend whom we had nursed for weeks as best we could now lay murdered, we were convinced of it, though we could not communicate beyond glances, by the man who purported to have returned to save us and who now for the first time addressed us with such a tone of superiority and blatant behaviour as evinced he considered us completely in his power. He kept himself always armed and between us, and would allow us no conversation, giving vent to various expressions of hatred towards white people, some of whom he said had killed and eaten his uncle and two brothers on the Ottawa River as they had devoured Mohawks for two hundred years. Such dreadful stories of course abound in the Canadas where he originated, though we have heard very few here in the north, indeed it seems the natives here abominate such abhorrent customs. In our weakness we could not by any device escape him, and knew he would attempt to destroy us at the first opportunity that offered, and that all that restrained him from doing so immediately was his ignorance of the way to the Fort.

We could not therefore mourn your son properly as befits a beloved brother in Christ. We determined on trying for the Fort, and left that horrid place the following day. Four days later we at last sighted the Dogrib Rock, though it was no more than fifteen miles, and it was here that Michel left us for the first moment alone, saying he wished to gather some *tripe de roche*. Hepburn instantly confirmed me in the opinion about the circumstances of poor Hood's murder, and that there was no safety for us except in Michel's death, and I was thoroughly convinced of the necessity of such a dreadful act. Immediately upon Michel's coming up, I put an end to his life by shooting him through the head with a small pistol I carried concealed throughout the Expedition.

We discovered then that Michel had gathered no *tripe de roche*, but had halted for the purpose of putting his gun in order with the intention of attacking us, as we had suspected.

Hepburn and I were another six days before we staggered into Fort Enterprise, though we had less than twelve miles to travel, where we had the melancholy satisfaction of embracing Lieutenant Franklin and his companions, the wretchedness of whose abode it is impossible for me to describe.

We weep with you, Sir, and with your family for a gentle, tender-hearted son and brother now lost. His talents shed a lustre upon the Expedition, even as the memory of his blessed spirit has given me the strength to write these clumsy words with much crossing out, which I pray God in mercy may in the manner best known to Himself reach you, to offer a few moments of consolation to you in your inexpressible loss.

It is evening and we three are still alive at Fort Enterprise, together with Adam, the Indian translator, very low. We have made up an outline report and a packet of letters to our loved ones. Fear of death has long held no meaning for us. We pray now for peace to die in the Lord. With the highest esteem, I am, Reverend Sir,

> Your very sincere friend,
> John Richardson

The name for it is "long pig", you ever heard of that?

Ask any English tar an' he'll tell you. Give him a drink, an' he'll tell you more than you can stomach, ha-ha!

Stomach all right it is, an' was, all of them bloody big Canadian paddlers dead, just dropped an' dead on that trek from the Northern Ocean over all those rivers an' barrens an' snowdrifts an' rocks an' that big double rapid on the Coppermine, Obstruction Rapids, what took us nine days trying to get across till St. Germain, who could do anything, made that cup out of canvas an' we pulled ourselves across one by one — the rapids really finished us. But those Canadians were dead, an' our English officers alive — except poor Hood shot when he lies dying already, our officers live to come home an' every one of them quick as winking Knights of the Garter an' famous.

An' me too, alive, the one yattering tar daft enough to go every step with them when even the Orkneymen — God be blessed, quick Orkneymen! — know enough to run early in the hard going, me a sailor of the bottom class given a soft lick on the London docks all those years, an' now more than soft in the sweet air of Van Dieman's Land, sweet if you ain't a gaolbird here, all because I come alive out of that trek, you think ten Canadian voyageurs are falling down dead because they were *weaker* than us? Ha!

You hear me now, I lived with those Canadians for three years, an' ate an' slept with them too. More than I wanted, but that's the English way, the servants sleep together whether they can talk to each other or not, I saw those buggers work, blessed be God! work strong as any ox an' so fast on their feet or with their hands you couldn't see them move, that quick, an' when the rapids there come roar a white wash down a canyon bend they'd never seen before an' those great canoes thin as paper an' loaded deep to the gunnels, you should of heard them laugh, riding that, where one wrong stroke an' it all goes smash! riding it like ducks light an' sailing. Or seen them paddle across a lake singing to a rhythm that would break your back before your lungs, sixty strokes every minute between pipes, that's a hour steady without a stop! I seen them naked, many a time, they had shoulders an' chests like a great Scots Clydesdale.

An' only two of them lived, that's all. Two of the eleven, or twelve — talk about disciples, ha! One alive was Solomon Bélanger, *le gros* they called him, his brother *le rouge* was...well, left behind to "rest", like we said to them then. But Bélanger *le gros* was so strong he walked through snow from Fort Providence to Enterprise in five days with mail in November, 1820, more than one hundred and fifty miles of devil's winter, the last thirty-six hours without stopping, straight into a snowstorm an' come in, we had to break the ice off his face to know who it was. An' a year later it was him found the Indian track for Mr. Back that saved us all, an' us in the Fort giving up, mostly dead.

He was one that lived, an' Joseph Benoît the other, a square hulk as wide as he was tall, an' so thick no one could lock his arms round him to throw him. I never knew which was stronger, Joseph was the only one ever dared to say a word back at Solomon, though once he didn't blow his breath talking, he just grabs *le gros* by his leather pants an' shirt an' hoists him over his head an' throws him in the Yellowknife River. I think Joseph could have taken *le gros* if he had wanted to. I saw them dance around the fire watching each other close enough, like two old dogs who've known each other for ever, you know, circling and pissing in the same spot, one beside the other.

Those two the only ones, the other ten dead. What for?

Ah-h-h-h God... I think there were times John Franklin thought they died because they cursed so much, those Canadians. It seems to me a good easy vice for working men, it don't take time from work, nor energy, an' costs nothing, but the Lieutenant thought their cursing was so *sinful*. He couldn't even understand their Cree French! The name of God an' all His shining attributes an' history was there plain enough, known or unknown, an' every blistering part of the Lord's body uttered in vain, though the way they said it they sure didn't figure it was *vain*. I don't know if they ever cursed him — Sir John — he just a lowly lieutenant then, an' near the end they were even past cursing after five hundred miles in those paper canoes in an ocean always nearer ice than water. Mr. Back, Sir George now, mostly never translated everything they said, though sometimes I thought he explained more than needful, a raunchy little midshipman hard as a rock an' needing something, anything I guess, with no women inside a month's walking to titter him up like they always did. But when we left those Canadians behind in the snow, one skeleton after the other with a thin blanket an' mouth bleeding scurvy, those poor buggers were all praying like the true Christians they was raised to be, not one of them wasn't.

Why ten of twelve, falling down? I'll tell you: they had carried so much of our useless stuff — useless for staying alive, if that's what you're after in that country, an' what else can you chase there once you're forced to get down to it? — carrying so much stuff even on foot in bloody big packs even after all the canoes were smashed, that strong as they were, they got caught on a neat point: what between starving an' dropping of scurvy an' freezing, they were just *worked* to death.

On that Expedition I worked as hard as any Indian dog I ever saw, an' I expected that being the only servant so called to four officers who ate what we ate — if there was anything — they worked hard too as officers go, an' walked every step like us after the canoes were gone an' carrying their own notebooks an' instruments, but I tell you I never worked like those voyageurs piled high as donkeys. An' when the Doctor an' me were left alone to get to Fort Enterprise, Hood an' Michel both dead, shot — o, the Doctor he had a good hand then, still steady enough with a barrel notched in the ear to make the one shot he had time for, that shot neat an' quick as threading a needle with one stroke an' Michel was in Mohawk heaven or hell, let him rest in peace or heat, whichever he found. But we did that together, me an' him. You don't think one of us could of done it alone?

The Doctor has reported, "Immediately on Michel's coming up, I put an end to his life by shooting him through the head with a pistol."

That's right. The Doctor cannot lie, I tell you, he doesn't. But you think he just walks up to that big bastard with a loaded pistol, even when he's never let him see he's got it, an' that Mohawk ready to kill us as he is just stands there, smiling till the Doc gets it all primed ready — "Just stand at attention, my good man" — an' lays it up between his eyes an' neatly blows his brains out? A clean, legal, proper — execution? Hah! Life on the polar Barrens ain't no Admiralty report, nor a thick book neither like Sir John's, so "picturesque", as they call all those pictures and nice words put so nicely together to cost ten guineas.

Listen to me, once we see that Dogrib Rock, we just have to get to it to see the Big Stone, south-west, an' Fort Enterprise is on the straight line between. When we see that, we know: Michel doesn't need us no more, nor our compass, which he always thought floating magic an' couldn't read anyhow an' we would never explain. We have to move quick now, because he sure as hell will.

So when he comes up with his rifle all primed to shoot us one after the other, an' leave us for the wolves if they'll have us, I walk straight at him as if I'm looking for brush for a fire an' he brings up the rifle but not really expecting anything, my hands are empty, we'd been so quiet an' convenient just getting weaker while he somehow stays so strong, we never say nothing about where he goes day after day an' never brings back nothing to eat, though he always seems satisfied when he tells us there's nothing to hunt, an' lies down to sleep pretty easy with his loaded rifle, or even when he cursed "the French" as he called all Whites for stealing land from his people an' using them for everything — even food! The shit Whites ate his three brothers one winter on the Ottawa River! Though I've heard it said his people were that cruel, an' some priests say addicted themselves to the habit of eating human flesh — no, I don't say nothing to him, not a word, then.

I just walk close past him, he not quite suspecting me yet, but alert, an' stumble hard as I can into him, I knock him down ramming against him an' would of got his first bullet in my gut — would've if I'd been normal big-gutted, he sure as hell fired — but the bullet grazes my hip an' I crush him deeper in the snow, I bury him with all the weight and strength I've got, I'm screaming it's him or me, an' the Doctor gets there an' pokes the pistol in his ear an' fires.

Execution — but you can see we didn't have time for prayer, not then. Though I heard him call himself a Christian. He thrashed under me pretty hard, but never moved after.

God be praised for saving us by our own hand; an' we're three days snowbound, the Doctor reported. That's true, there was lots of snow, falling an' drifting, an' we were too exhausted after that to move, I can tell you. He cleaned my wound with snow an' sewed it with thin boiled babiche from Michel's pants or I'd of bled to death, my hip didn't heal till spring when I had some fat again. Michel froze fast right there in the snow where I dropped on him, an' in those three days, "snowbound", I ate a lot of him.

Very careful, he so strong from the voyageurs he'd fed off, Canadians, as we called them, feeding a Canadian — an' him an Indian — feeding me, a circle the way we'd done it anyways for two years, though this was slightly more personal, you might say, taking care of each other, me starting with slices off his good muscle, arm or thigh, the way the Doctor told me it would work, slow, slow, a little broth first, then boiled, then roasted, otherwise you vomit an' destroy yourself worse.

The Doctor himself wouldn't have any of him, he was drinking only country tea with bits of Mr. Hood's singed an' boiled buffalo hide to eat. That man's so strong in his head, an' tough, o, a Scot beyond all Scots, give him oats — which are real hard to find on the tundra — or nothing, with principle enough to curl your hair a fine Christian grey, though at the time he wasn't thirty-five. What he ate earlier, which Michel brought, wasn't his responsibility, he said, though he suspected something, it was the shape of the bones. An' he reported to the Lieutenant that I "exerted myself far beyond my strength" so that we did finally reach Enterprise an' found the four that's left there starving worse than us. Where did I get the strength to hunt an' carry the gun an' a bit of powder an' bullets an' hatchet an' bedding hide we hadn't eaten, an' lug the Doctor too, which he did not report, not exactly? On my bloody back!

His heels draggin' two furrows behind me, though there was nothing to sow in that godforsaken snow. Sir John wrote in his book for anyone to see who can read an' has ten guineas, "John Hepburn, an English seaman, and our only attendant, to whom in the latter part of our journey we owe, under Divine Providence, the preservation of the lives of some of our party." How lucky, me of the bottom class somehow had all this amazing strength to offer them.

Believe that, an' I won't mock you. But I say, if you care for them, you serve. An' I cared for them, every one, even Back, who could outwalk anybody except Solomon an' wouldn't let nothing stop him finding those Yellowknives again an' talking them dizzy until they brought us meat an' saved us — though I wasn't there an' I've got nothing to say about how he an' St. Germain an' Bélanger *le gros* lived long enough walking to find them, I wasn't with them an' I'd never ask. Back reported they left Gabriel Beauparlant — he always called him his servant — to "rest" in the snow somewhere near Roundrock Lake, an' his body was never found, like none of them was, who'd go find them? — God, Back would've eaten anything an' walked into blazing hell to save us, I know that an' I served him, before an' after, just as well as I served young "Robin" Hood, poor churchly bugger, he at least got some good loving in that hard country, for a little while, till it got all bust up. It's not for me to talk about. If you care for them, you do what's needed so they can return home with their great principles safe an' precious as the crown jewels of England. How many English servants, you think, have had the strength to save the upper class their shining Christian principles? Or, if they couldn't save them, have never said a word about it neither?

"Long pig." It's a good name. The Fiji Islanders with their curly hair sticking out call it that, an' English sailors too, since they started talking about it after Captain Cook. That's the exact taste of it, I tell you we're closer to the suffering beasts than you'd think, an' plenty of Englishmen know it; more than may tell you. An' they've drunk each other's piss too in the rotten tubs they sail off in, that bust up so easy in all the storms an' rocks of the whole bleedin' world. You want principles? The big world's bloody harder than any "principles".

Listen to me, I been on every ocean in the world, ships good an' ships bad an' ships worse than that, an' even in canoes in the worst of all, the Polar Ocean. Meat is…meat. If I have to I'll eat anything. Even bacon, though I can't stand the smell of it, always stinks too Mohawk to me, ha-ha! "Long pig" — stand an English tar to a few pints an' he'll tell you that, long pig it is. An' any officer'll tell you the same, if he don't lie.

DOCTOR JOHN RICHARDSON

Wednesday November 7th 1821   Fort Enterprise

In the morning we heard the report of a musket, and soon after a great shout, and on looking out beheld three Indians with sledges below on the river. I imparted this joyful intelligence to Lieutenant Franklin, who immediately returned thanks to the Almighty, but poor Adam could scarcely comprehend it.

The Indians, The Rat, Crookedfoot and Boudelkell, had been sent from Bigfoot by Mr. Back with dried meat and fat. We devoured their food, and they incautiously permitted us to eat as much as we could; in consequence, with the exception of Adam, we suffered dreadfully from distention of the abdomen, and had no rest during the night. The Indians were unwilling to remain in the house where the bodies of our deceased companions remained exposed, but Hepburn and I were now able to drag them out a short distance and cover them with snow.

Friday November 16th 1821   Travelling

Our feelings on being at last able to quit the Fort, where we had formerly enjoyed much comfort, if not happiness, and latterly experienced such a degree of misery scarcely to be paralleled, may be more easily conceived than described. The Indians treated us with the utmost tenderness, gave us their snowshoes and walked without themselves, keeping by our sides that they might lift us when we fell.

About three miles distant from the house we encamped, as I was unable to continue. The Indians cooked for and fed us as if we had been children, evincing a degree of humanity that would have done honour to the most civilized of nations.

13

THE SPLIT-FOOTED
CARIBOU

Then, suddenly as always, the caribou appeared like the wandering wind they were upon the shores of the lake beyond the Tetsot'ine camp, and in the sky between stones along the high ridges. When all the hunters went to them, quickly and with great care, they were welcomed by so many bodies steaming open in the darkening winter that everyone knew they could eat for at least four days, and sleep full-gutted for another four. And they sang:

> How glorious to see,
> How unutterable, the great animals
> Who live by voices we may never hear.
> Another People like ourselves, splendid
> And complete, always travelling, always held
> Like we are in the magnificence and travail
> Of the long land.

But the very next morning, the men ordered the women to take half the meat they hadn't yet eaten and go, pile it up in Bigfoot's lodge.

Why? Because Boy English had appeared out the north. Even more abruptly than the animals, more or less dead from hunger, with Twospeaker and an emaciated voyageur half-carrying him, and starving as well — and obviously, wherever and whenever Whites appear they always need food, right now, food! When the women heard what the men said they cried aloud in protest; all the children, with most of the dogs, soon joined them.

Every woman had gone out the day before in such laughter and happiness, praying gratitude with singing, onto the lake to bring in the considerate animals the men had hunted. Draping ribs in pairs over their shoulders, the legs and hides, barely frozen, stacked carefully on their sleds, the children pushing caribou heads by their giant racks before them over the wind-swept ice, steering them with shouts of laughter to the crested tops of drifts, riding them down. And the feasting all night, at last everyone was again stuffed tight with heart, liver, intestines, the marvellous sponginess of brains and cooked stomach — and the men and larger boys had eaten their fat, bloody fill of penises and scrotums and udders and wombs, torn them apart with laughing teeth and swallowed them as thick as they could to make sure no woman came near these special gifts from the animals and so destroyed the next hunt — for who could say, today and tomorrow and the day after, when there might again be nothing on the lake, not a caribou anywhere within dreaming. But now all these racks of ribs, these haunches like massive frozen clubs striated with fat, these tongues — why must an

English with his two bony slaves come again from the dead and receive all the delicious tongues?

Fifty-nine tongues, someone counted through her enraged tears, many of them taken from caches to celebrate the tender returning-winter concern of the animals. Why could These English, even when hunger twisted their guts tight and chopped their faces down to bone, eat nothing but the tastiest, the most celebratory parts? Always returning, these Whitemuds, how often could that happen, every year now for ever returning and returning; if they were fed now and went south to the traders, would they blunder back north next summer again only to come starving again a winter later? The women had thought they were rid of them last summer when they trudged off, their overburdened slaves hauling canoes across rotting ice north and east to where every person knew the Raw-Meat Eaters lived on the Everlasting Ice of the stinking water, whatever it was they wanted to do when they got there — look at its endlessness? Any fool could see the limits of that in one turning glance, had they no eyes, how long did it take them to see?

And they said then they wanted to go away east, east, not come back here — so why hadn't they? Because there were no animals to eat there, and no People to hunt for them while they travelled — but they had been told that! Couldn't they hear what they were told?

But that doesn't matter now, because here they are again. Just as the long darkness closes in, one of them comes staggering back, somehow, though most of their slaves, he admits, are already dead — but every English is still alive, yes! — well, everyone knows why These English will live longest — but we must hurry, food, quick!

What child doesn't know, the women cry to the air blazing in the brief noon sun, that in winter everyone needs food? How stupid can you be?

And everyone dies. We ourselves are always dying. When the caribou and the rabbits vanish, to whom can we run and cry pathetically, "I am here, feed me or I die!" Who pulls us out of vicious rapids or sews our clothes? Who kills himself carrying us around portages and over snow?

But These English come staggering out of the winter and announce, "Look! We're here! Behold how we suffer, we're almost dead! We've eaten the pants you sewed us, our hairy legs are freezing, quick, Thick English is naked, his name is become He Cannot Walk Because He Has Eaten His Boots! Feed us!"

But Broadface says to Greywing, "You, carry this good meat to Bigfoot."

"What I once heard," Keskarrah says to them all, "I found hard to believe, then, but now I know it is wrong. These English can't keep death from us, nor from themselves."

Greywing looks at Broadface, laughing. "Those Whitemud mouths are too stupid," she says, "they can't chew good brains," and she jerks forwards, her hand catching, as it were, her own vomit; Broadface laughs with her. Greenstockings thinks: they do that best together, laughing at someone.

"We couldn't, of course," Keskarrah continues, eyes closed, as if he had heard nothing, nor any wailing outside, "withhold food from anyone if we have some, especially from those to whom we have already given hospitality. And accepting a gift is an obligation as well, even after you recognize it has become dangerous. Richard Sun's gift — dangerous or not, I accepted it — we all accepted and gave hospitality...." He opens his eyes to Greywing, who is no longer laughing; as if he were about to enter a memory of weeping. Then he looks at Greenstockings.

"Perhaps," he concludes, "you accepted something once too, from this Boy English who has now arrived starving so well."

Broadface stiffens, and Greenstockings says deliberately, "No. I accepted nothing but a little laughter from him — I thought about more, but only once."

"Ah-h-h-h," and Keskarrah sighs heavily. "Doing is very simple, we all do things. But thinking — even once — that offers many more possibilities."

And it may be that Birdseye is still in the lodge with them, her body still taking a breath at such long intervals that, bent closely over her and watching intensely, Greenstockings is convinced: yes, surely now, with this lengthening pause her mother will at last, mercifully, forget completely how to breathe. But Birdseye is not there; there is no one to answer Keskarrah if Greenstockings will not.

Broadface stirs his big body with impatience, as always, but it will be a long time before he dares to interrupt the father of his wives. He can only order the youngest, even more loudly,

"You will carry meat!"

and gesture with as much dignity as he has at the share of animal bodies he hunted. What of it Greywing will pick up is her decision.

While outside the wailing dialogues of the women move on towards Bigfoot's lodge, the shrilling of dogs excited by so much passing meat drifts along the ice of the lake the English will later name "Greenstockings", where the Yellowknife River (they already named that the summer before) continues its long, stony descent, now chewing its paths through ice towards distant

Tucho. And already Crookedfoot and The Rat and Boudelkell have left; Bigfoot sent them immediately in the night when Boy English arrived, with a sled of meat in case Thick English really was still alive in the log and mud house they lived in last winter, but several People have been suddenly lost in both Bigfoot's and The Hook's camps during the past month and they are all quite destitute, so impoverished that Keskarrah has almost stopped dreaming the hunt of the animals altogether.

"Where do the animals go? Where will their trails be for our snares?" The Hook and Bigfoot have kept urging him.

Keskarrah has responded very deliberately, lying as it seems comatose in his bare furs whenever the large winter camp is not moving.

"We have always dreamed, praying as the drum speaks," he says finally. "That is our way. But now someone has to think as well. There may be others now who must start to dream; it has come to me after this hard beginning winter that I must dare to think only."

And they understand that he says this because of Birdseye; why, when they wait for him silently, he suddenly speaks of something else, as if their present hunger were no more than a mere hesitation in their lifelong travel.

But despite their mournings and Keskarrah's refusals since they joined Bigfoot travelling from great Sahtú, the many People all gathered together now have been eating no more poorly than they often do after a slim summer, when the caribou rut and can still dig easily through the first snow. However, since they arrived severally with The Hook, Bigfoot has continued moving steadily south, towards the traders' fort on Tucho. There, he reminds them, promises are waiting from Thick English, promises he wrote down to stand for ever on paper before he left north: there they are to receive every White thing they want for all the food and clothing they have already given the Expedition. That promise is there, he insists, waiting to help them, and they must get it before the traders hear that Thick English is dead.

And they are travelling right, they are still within the winter feeding range of the caribou. But the farther south they move, the less Keskarrah has helped them hunt, the more certainly lured out of mourning into disturbing, uttered thought.

"I know there is less danger when an old man thinks," he says now, as his beautiful daughters look at him, trying to smile a little.

Greenstockings answers him. "It may be time for young women to try to do that too."

Keskarrah looks at her intently. "You think so?"

"People die, others are born...."

"And some," he agrees slowly, carefully, "may begin to feel they know something a little."

Greenstockings cannot speak about that; Keskarrah accepts her silence, and continues,

"I've done everything, and perhaps dreamed enough, so I have to risk thinking. These English won't eat the best the animals give us, they don't want heart or marrow or eyes, lungs, those particular parts full of wisdom and endurance, so different between one's teeth. They just want fat — our cold has finally taught them to eat fat — and of course the red meat, which is all they have ever wanted. And these fat ribs hanging there," he gestures gently, "may well be waiting for Hep Burn to burn them. If he is still alive. It's possible the good animals will give us more."

"Burn, burn." Greywing laughs fully at last, the only word they need for Hep Burn's cooking, his dedicated capability of charcoal. She hooks the great double-bowed rack of ribs down from over the fire, and follows Broadface out.

Greenstockings smiles at her emaciated father, at his gentle release of them and their ultimate kindness of food. She ducks out into the gasping cold, the hard door covering falls shut with a crack behind her. She will go see them too, but empty-handed.

The brittle normality of darkening snow. Squeaking underfoot. No one has spoken aloud to her of Richard Sun since he took his salve with him last summer. Nor ever, after she was stolen and Michel tied like a dog to his log bed until Broadface returned, of Hood. The dead deserve the respect of silence, whether they are still walking or not. What was left of his destroyed body has fed the wolves, after the ravens opened whatever thin snow he was wrapped in and took his eyes, his lips and tongue, all those gentle parts of him that they love first and best, the delicacy of spirit he once revealed to her so briefly. The noon winter sun rests like a golden mouth of crystals opening just beyond the ice of the lake, away from the lengthening land that stretches farther and farther north between him and her own continuous travel, south, with child and People.

And though the ravens have their territory, nevertheless they fly steadily, continuously, everywhere north to him in the level light, he has also nurtured them, for a moment, and they lift her high on the invisible lines of their flight until she sees the long narrow rift of her lake below, with Singing Lake and Aurora and Winter, Little Marten (which is the People's name for it, remembering the numberless women who are always martens, quick and smooth and warm at their eternal work and caring, just like the animals who give up their lives with their skins), and Lastfire Lake where the caribou cows carrying their unborn calves with their yearlings will cross again in the lengthening light, travelling north to their birthing, each lake reaches out tenderly with bent little streams of fingers crushed solid at the rapids and outlined by grey brush and rocks and shadowed hollows for which not even every English in the world will ever find enough names, where water will trickle into the tentative light of spring below small willows at the double rapids on the River of Copperwoman, where the grizzly roared its warning to Keskarrah, and Birdseye saw him lie, staring up into the brightening sky wrapped in one last, useless blanket: Greenstockings feels desire rise within her again, great black wings rising.

It was Birdseye who told her very early, even before The Hook's mother repeated it as she waited at Forbidden Rock: "It's hard to find a child who will become a person Who Knows Something a Little. They're too hard to see. You can look and look in every hoof-print you cross, but you won't find one."

Greenstockings would not accept that. "I'm old enough," she declared, resisting this "age and suffering wisdom" her parents always insist upon. "If this child is one, I'll find it."

Birdseye continued, as if not hearing her refusal, "An old woman like me would find one. It wouldn't hurt anyone, being born in a caribou track, and no bigger than a thumb."

Greenstockings feels the child's strong sucking as she holds it to her breast under her clothing. It came to her, she found it in the death of her mother, and with that memory of her mother's story she is lifted high and far, the great black bird lifts her away, not so far really, the path in air level and certain as a thong pulling her to that last measure of snow where he now is, not Snow Man, as her mother feared the first time she saw him, but drawn into the snow, now an abstract assemblage of bone. Scattered.

"Remember that tiny child," her mother told her. "When it is alive, look hard for it. Then you'll live well, as long as necessary."

She has screamed enough this year past, even during those months when she saw him only at a distance and without so much as a gesture, their perpetual exiles fixed for each other, when sometimes she closed her eyes and still enfolded him as tightly as ever, as completely as she could within herself. The mouth of the child is a hot, rhythmic grip about her nipple — she will find the knowing in this child, she knows she will. So she follows her sister and their common husband easily, confidently, through the hard trampled snow between small spruce, lodges and the tiny fires of their People towards Bigfoot's lodge.

From just inside the entrance, through the press of heads and bodies there, she can barely see the top hair of Boy English standing, but all of Twospeaker's head. Bigfoot must be seated beside his fire, she can hear his voice talk in his new English way, alone, no elders and not even The Hook agreeing with him about what to say. The way in which, Keskarrah in his bed has mused, Bigfoot will either make the Yellowknives more aggressively powerful than they have ever been within the long memory of People, or he may, together with These English who come and go and the Dogribs and the Raw-Meat Eaters who are, of course, enemies between the lakes and along the stinking water, Bigfoot may destroy them. Perhaps completely. Keskarrah cannot decide yet which it will be, power or annihilation, but he thinks it must be either one or the other:

"It's not the way of People to have one big boss who gives orders and everyone obeys them. That's useful during the temporary necessities of defence or war — one man telling every man what to do and everyone running around to do it — and perhaps we should consider ourselves at war now — but all the time? Who can endure that? It's not the way of the land."

What Bigfoot is saying now in his lodge in the silence of listening People does not sound more than normally dangerous. In fact, Greenstockings is certain it is what Keskarrah would say if he had bothered to get up, if he had ever agreed, as Bigfoot has, to care for all These English still alive and their slaves one more time. Perhaps because Keskarrah would indeed consider this war.

"Three of our best hunters have already gone with meat to Winter Lake," Bigfoot says carefully to Twospeaker making impenetrable sounds after him, "and we understand, they'll need more food if five or six are still alive. We know that, we've come the long journey back from starvation many times. But listen, and you hear People crying. We don't cry because we have nothing else to do. We cry because the animals have not been happy with us. It may be we asked them for too much last winter, but only yesterday did we have enough to eat for ourselves, and who knows what will come out of the north tomorrow. Our children cry, and there are traders on great Tucho who also want to eat. They beg as well, 'Bring us food!' They can't live without us and the animals either.

"But you've come to us now, very hungry, and we're the only People who know your way and also the way of the animals. We learned last winter that knowing both animals and Whites is hard — that it can kill you."

Boy English says something quickly, and St. Germain talks fast after him. "He says he knows about the stubborn traders, and the Commander knows it too, but he says the traders will take the meat you give him off your debt with them. He will make sure of that, if you help him; the traders will give you even more credit."

"I owe no trader anything. The owing is on the other side."

"He says, all that will be given, absolutely, everything already promised and written, and for what you give now he will pay double. For everything. See, he says, I write it exactly, here, for everything you give now, for every one piece of meat, the traders give you two. That is how I write it, here."

"The things the traders have left in their buildings can't be eaten."

"Perhaps they have, some things…."

"We know what we know. The traders themselves have nothing to eat unless we bring it to them."

"I know that, and he knows it too," Twospeaker gestures to Back's emaciated face poised and listening, "but These English are dying up north, they may be mostly dead already, so he promises two for one, to go."

"Yes," Bigfoot answers, "that is the way you always explain it, and we always believe you. But," he looks at Back, pausing for the language to catch up, "last summer when you were trying to paddle canoes through the ice, the traders gave us nothing for your promise papers. They said they had nothing to give."

"Sometimes, when the long canoes don't come from the Bay in the summer, but — "

"Paper," Bigfoot interrupts, "it may be good for them to eat across the stinking water, but here it tastes like shit."

"Listen," Twospeaker frowns, listening to Back, "he says the long canoes will come with goods, they *will come*!"

"Oh, they will come...if not this summer then the next. But, you know, we're People, we live every single day. It might be good if we were bears sleeping all winter, but unfortunately we don't."

There is a long moment of silence; then Bigfoot touches the centre of his argument with exaggerated humility:

"We are poor People, who understand very little, and we believe your papers — but perhaps the traders don't believe them."

Boy English's voice becomes very quiet, very patient, and Twospeaker, his gaunt face as hollow as a broken tree, says it softly after him, "The Commander says the traders will obey the papers. Otherwise our Great Father across the water, who is over all, will punish them severely. But first, right now, we must save your friend the Commander!"

"Ah-h, Thick English...." Bigfoot nods, hesitating.

Greenstockings can see him now; he is not wearing that tall Whitemud black hat for this singular council where more women and children than men listen and only three speak, one of them chirping. Nor the shiny medals around his neck: Bigfoot must have at least two, or perhaps three, not one of which will fill anyone's stomach. She cannot help but smile as Bigfoot's tone and language broaden even more; almost like her father when he gazes over distance, or thoughtfully at coming stars.

"We know of course that your Great Father will do what you say to him, but he is very far away, perhaps as much as two years, going and coming back, two years or is it four? And some of us have thought, though it couldn't have been me who you know has always been your friend, that perhaps when he punishes the traders severely in two years, or four, for what they do to us now, most of us may not be alive to be thankful for it. As you know, life is hard for People so far away from your Great Father, and so ignorant in this hard place where we have always lived."

And suddenly The Hook stands. Greenstockings cannot see whether he is wearing his medal. He speaks loudly, and straight, "We have heard that Father is so old he may already be dead. Does he die?"

"If he dies," St. Germain translates Back's reply quickly, "there is always his son, who is instantly Father after him."

It is Bigfoot who continues the debate with a long release of breath, "O-o-o-o — a son." He pauses, looking around, pondering the problems of sons and fathers. "White fathers are always followed by sons?"

"Yes."

"And these sons always finish what their fathers start?"

For the first time Boy English hesitates. It may be he has finally comprehended the profound irony of this consult. But he speaks confidently nevertheless, and St. Germain says it after him,

"Yes. They do."

"Ah-h-h-h-h-h," Bigfoot breathes deeply, and Greenstockings could laugh aloud. He has listened more carefully to her father than she thought. "We have good children, who always care for their parents, but even we can't always trust children to do what their fathers say."

It is the women who mutter angry agreement; the men who surround Bigfoot offer only their shuffling expressionlessness, their cold-blotched faces rigid. They recognize necessary debate, and savour it, but they already know what must happen.

Bigfoot continues: "However, if you told us now that your enormous canoes, the ones pushed by wind, would come into our country from the north, along the River of Copperwoman, then the traders at the Fort might of course behave differently."

Boy English responds hastily, "That is not for me to say, anything about that. We found very much ice in the north, and great rocks in the river."

"Of course," Bigfoot agrees with him solemnly. "We suggested that to you before you went. And perhaps you did not find enough of Copperwoman either?"

Boy English answers nothing; perhaps he does not understand, and quickly Bigfoot continues as if that incomprehension is not, for the moment anyway, important.

"What I say is, if the traders, who have tried for some years to live in our country and persuade us to kill animals for furs, if they don't honour your papers while you are still here, what will they do when you leave? Or if you…."

He does not complete "die here", though everyone understands that, but perhaps Twospeaker explains it because Boy English insists immediately,

"I am alive. Look, I am the King's officer and I stand here to tell you. You will get all we have promised before and what I promise now. But I must save the Commander. He gave you medals, he gave you many presents for your hospitality, and you promised him you would — "

Twospeaker stops as Boy English interrupts himself, listens, and continues. "He means the Commander has given you all his hand and he trusts you, every one. He says, 'Bigfoot and his People are good. They will never let me die in their country.'"

Bigfoot responds quietly, "We know ourselves, in our hearts."

Boy English repeats, "He trusts you."

Bigfoot continues, "I don't speak for myself. I myself owe nothing to any Whites, at any fort, but my People are owed many things, as it says in those papers written by you. And if we wished to, we could punish the traders very quickly, we wouldn't have to wait for years. But I have decided. I will give more food for your Commander. He is my friend, half of what I have."

Greenstockings sees his hand for a moment, near Boy English's head, gesturing. And Bigfoot's youngest wife moves in the crowd, a tied burden of frozen tongues and fat bundled in hide dressed ready for moccasins or leggings on her shoulder. At least he has not had his Dogrib slave come carrying this gift, though of course Boy English would not understand that as an even subtler dissatisfaction and insult.

Other men are gesturing, and more women with bundles stand to move forwards between People even as they wail, wail gently higher and higher, as if they were mourning a child that the sky or the land or the water had taken; as they are, since it is food their children cannot eat because they must bring it here and stack it before Boy English. The stone-faced men say nothing to stop this rising keen; it is the right of sorrow to utter itself.

Greenstockings turns away. She will not watch Greywing throw down, at Broadface's gesture, the double-rack of ribs; she will not see George Back's exhausted eyes study her sister's face, flicker up legs bending for an instant before him in tight leather.

The sun is almost gone again beyond the southern horizon when she meets him. He stands bent, silently watching his slaves who helped drag him here and several hunters tie down the mass of meat that they with their dogs will pull to Winter Lake on four sleds. He does not straighten or turn, so she can consider carefully how he stands, curved old and even smaller than she remembers, study how hunger has chopped his face down to bone like an old copper axe striking clumsily, feebly, at a frozen tree. A year ago he looked so different.

After she and Greywing came into camp with the child, Birdseye gathered and saved her strength, after such a long dying, and after four silent days she walked alone into the first winter snow. Greenstockings refuses to remember the place, she will never allow anyone to name it. This pathetic White thing once laughed when Richard Sun gave her father that deadly salve; and Thick English laughed too. Did Hood? Her father will tell her, if she ever asks him.

Boy English glances around, and sees her. His eyes are black, empty. It seems to her he may have been spared the decision of having to eat his paddle-slaves — perhaps because they died too far away from him, because he could still leave them, walk away fast enough before they froze into forgotten sticks.

But under her look she sees his face change; it may be his legs remained strong enough to bring him back to them; perhaps he was a man who could demand even death as a service, and so he could reach her People, alone with the last and strongest of his slaves. She hears Birdseye's voice speaking to her again, in that strange, abstracted tone, of what may be happening past or future, telling her everything she will encounter sooner or later. Her life already exists, everywhere, in the words with which her mother has surrounded her, so she watches Back's ragged lips move without fear, his face peeled by hunger and by sunlight dancing its quick irony on the snow. His face begins to thaw, to flicker a little as he stares back at her through Twospeaker's obedient words:

"He says, the ravens guided us, and the wolves fed us on Roundrock Lake. He says I should tell you: ten days we had to rest there and ate the meat they left us; we were dying, and wouldn't have found your camp, or reached it without the wolves."

"Is that all you ate?"

Twospeaker stares at her a moment, but does not translate. He recovers, and says to her, "He...he says it's...just like that, like you once told Hood."

"What does he know? Hood is dead," she tells Back. And considers Twospeaker, who glares at her but still refuses to translate.

"You won't tell These English," she says to him, "what a woman says?"

Finally he responds, fiercely, "I will not say that. You know nothing."

"It's true. It doesn't matter if you won't say it."

"And your father's dream almost killed us all, at the double rapids."

"He warned you, don't go there."

"We had to!"

She has always thought Twospeaker was smarter than These English, but such a response to a dream is not worth laughing at. There is a gleam of implacable White rigidity, of stupid obedience in his eyes that suddenly explains why his wife has left him. He stands glaring, with an abrupt demand, though Boy English has said nothing:

"Are you holding his child?"

Greenstockings hears him, and sees Boy English looking from her to him urgently, but she is listening to Birdseye even as she is aware of her tiny child asleep under her clothes, their naked bodies warm against each other. It is her mother who tells her, like the straight, black flight of a raven through the trackless sky, that Richard Sun will come, and Hep Burn too, together with their boss Thick English, all dragged torturously away from death by this animal food they are giving. And it will be Hep Burn who dares to tell her without words how Hood was killed before he died, how Michel who stole her once was killed and was of necessity eaten, as the living always somehow eat those they kill, animal and person always the same. It will be Hep Burn who reveals These English for her to understand, not like Hood for ever careful with slender marks ventured over and over on paper, but drawing with a long articulate stick and using the snow as if their winter world were a page too small to explicate the tangled story of this White coming, drawing people like sticks for her along the snow doing all the kind and deadly things necessary, everything Birdseye has already told her they will do.

It is Hep Burn to whom she will reveal this sleeping daughter, her black hair and her perpetually open eyes of mystery: one deep brown and the other blue. Hep Burn will dare to draw in snow, and therefore see, and will not utter a word about either for thirty years, or forty. She already knows that.

Birdseye. Her eaten face so horrifically open, hard, crusted. A black hole of enduring. This beautiful child, who will always have a perfect, untouched face.

Boy English has said something now to Twospeaker, even as he tries to tear again at her clothes with his glittering eyes. Hunger will never kill that in him, until he is dead altogether.

But she has already forgotten Back because she knows, though she does not yet comprehend it, that she will see him again; he will return to her land somehow, again and again. He will be here with Thick English and Richard Sun again after a few summers, and on great Sahtú, where they will then winter, he will draw on paper a picture of Broadface — not daring to do what Hood has once done to her image — and years later, when this daughter is as old as Greywing now and four other children sleep in their ageing lodge, though three others will have died, he will come a third time as the only boss of his own labouring paddle-slaves, and they will meet each other at the Muskox Rapids on the River of Big Fish, a river whose tortuous and completely treeless route to the icy sea he does not yet know exists, because Keskarrah has not bothered to tell him what he is too ignorant to ask for. He will name the river after himself, and they will see each other again, laugh a little sadly, and say nothing.

A few of these her People will still be alive with her then, including Bigfoot. But sickness, strange and various sicknesses beyond anything they have ever known in the past generations of all their stories, will continue to kill so many of them, and the endless thefts and raids the few men will be so strongly tempted to increase against their nearest enemies, the Dogribs will destroy them as a People — after all, the Tetsot'ine have so many guns, so much powder and shot from trapping so many small furs, of which the traders always want more! always more! so they need less time to hunt and have more than enough time to plan wars, since there are always fewer People to feed and it is of course so much more manly and exciting to use guns to steal food and wives and clothing and dogs and territory from

enemies than to work for them in the slow, considerate ways of
the living land, and they have this endless source of powerful
weapons if they just kill enough animals — and those enemies
they do not kill they can certainly try to enslave and force to
labour for them like Whites do paddle-slaves — sickness and
the men's unrelenting aggression will destroy Greenstockings'
People.

But she cannot now ponder these recognitions. Nor think
that Doctor John Richardson, the deliberate executioner who
will continue to live and grow famous because of this food they
are sending him at Fort Enterprise, will in twenty-seven years
again pass through their land in a swift, scientific canoe and
record carefully on squared paper the Dogrib stories of Tetsot'ine destruction.

Greenstockings, not looking at Back, does not consider this
knowledge she already understands, though it would not surprise her if she thought of it, having of necessity watched men
and women so closely with her mother dreaming, and listened
to her father think, voice his scathing comments on following
the male excitement of raids rather than the ecstatic dreams of
good animals, the iron ignorance of guns. Who will be left to
remember them in the long winter evenings? Will she be there
to tell stories of when animals talked like People, or they could
still sense with willow sticks the texture of footprints leading
them true and deep beneath the snow, or circle sleeping into a
recognition of future, will she be left to tell her last grandchil-
dren those stories in a starry night? Her memory holds this already, and more than she can now utter into awareness of the
past and the future; it has been taught to her for ever by her
mother and her father. But now, at this moment....

Greenstockings considers Twospeaker. This man who can speak with four voices and is a hunter of enormous strength; who long ago asked the ravens and wolves to teach him; who, oddly, has given two years and very nearly his life to These English. For what? His wife, Angélique, has gone away, south, where there are other men. Very nearly given his life for a few passing gifts — why would anyone bother following such bent little Whites when there is such a large land to walk on wherever the light leads? She cannot, she will never want to understand this.

Now there is nothing more she needs to tell him for Boy English. These English will always, eventually, find whatever it is they want, though it may require centuries, however many of them die.

She says, "I found this child in a caribou hoof-print."

"That old story," Twospeaker hisses at her. "Show him! He'll know whose child it is, when he sees it."

Little Boy English. All the Whitemud layers that hunger has skinned off him he will now put back on, thicker than ever, because he will be so famous when he returns to his proper place over the stinking water. But Hood will remain here, alive in every wolf and raven she sees, for ever.

She tells Twospeaker, "Maybe it fell from the sky, maybe it's no bigger than a thumb."

"Whose child is it!"

So she tells him: "Mine."

Back, like Twospeaker, stares at her.

"Do you hear me?" she confronts them. "Mine."

And she turns, leaves them both as the arctic light darkens around her in its impenetrable, life-giving cold.

Acknowledgements

Greenstockings' story began for me in the vast land below the Arctic Circle, along the delicate treeline that emerges and vanishes between the Coppermine River and Winter Lake. On the high esker west of that lake are the stumps of white spruce, the hollows, the few fireplace stones that mark the existence of Fort Enterprise (1820–21). The site is about 250 kilometres north of the city of Yellowknife by Twin Otter; it's much farther by canoe.

The most helpful Dene texts I found were George Blondin's *When the World was New* (Yellowknife: Outcrop, 1990), and *The Book of Dene* (Yellowknife: Department of Education, 1976). The latter gathering is the work of Emile Petitot, O.M.I., who for twenty years (1862–1882) lived as a priest with the Dene and listened carefully to their stories. The narrative in chapter 9, "Geese", comes from *Ted Trindell: Métis Witness to the North* (Vancouver: Tillacum Library, 1986), edited by Jean Morrisset and Rose-Marie Pelletier. Particularly stimulating was the fine book *Life Lived Like a Story*, compiled by Julie Cruikshank in collaboration with Angela Sidney, Kitty Smith and Annie Ned (Vancouver: UBC Press, 1990).

For the specific version of the stolen woman story told in chapter 8 I am indebted to William Ittza of Fort McPherson, NWT., as recorded (1947) and later published by Richard Slobodin in volume 1 of *Proceedings: Northern Athapaskan Conference* (Ottawa: National Museum of Man, 1975).

The White texts of first encounter that I used most were John Franklin's *Narrative of a Journey to the Shores of the Polar Sea, in the Years 1819, 20, 21, 22* (London: John Murray, 1823), and Samuel Hearne's *A Journey from Prince of Wales's Fort in Hudson Bay to the Northern Ocean in the Years 1769, 1770, 1771 & 1772* (London: Strahan and Cadell, 1795). Informative also was Richard King's *Narrative of a Journey to the Shores of the Arctic Ocean, in 1833, 1834 and 1835* (2 volumes, London: Richard Bentley, 1836). Critical for recreating John Hepburn's memory was volume 1 of Joseph-René Bellot's *Memoirs* (London: Hurst and Blackett, 1855). Most helpful of all were two first-expedition journals, excellently edited by C. Stuart Houston: *To the Arctic By Canoe, 1819–1921: The Journal and Paintings of Robert Hood, Midshipman with Franklin* (Montreal: Arctic Institute of North America, 1974), and *Arctic Ordeal: the Journal of John Richardson, Surgeon-Naturalist with Franklin, 1820–1822* (Kingston: McGill-Queen's University Press, 1984). My debt is obvious in the journal entries used throughout.

I would like to express particular thanks to Ian S. MacLaren for making his research on George Back available to me before publication. Some of his findings appear in the third volume of journals edited by Houston, *Arctic Artist: The Journal and*

Paintings of George Back, Midshipman with Franklin, 1819–1822 (Kingston: McGill-Queen's, 1994). MacLaren's impeccable scholarship, so generously and gladly shared, was a continuing pleasure.

The most insightful approach to northern animal personality (and a lovely book) is *Caribou and the Barren-lands* (Ottawa: Canadian Arctic Resources Committee, 1981) by scientist and photographer George Calef.

Scholarly research on the Dene is too voluminous to detail here. The best general study is *Drum Songs, Glimpses of Dene History* by Kerry Abel (Kingston: McGill-Queen's, 1993), but of course the *Handbook of North American Indians*, volume 6, *Subarctic,* edited by June Helm (Washington: Smithsonian Institute, 1981), proved indispensable. *An Interdisciplinary Investigation of Fort Enterprise,* Northwest Territories, 1970, (Edmonton: Boreal Institute for Northern Studies, 1973), edited by Timothy C. Losey, provided scientific analyses of the fort site.

It is a pleasure to thank the following persons who were helpful at particular times: Aritha van Herk, Michael Ondaatje, Robert Kroetsch, Margaret Atwood, Patricia Demers, Linda Woodbridge, Lynda Schultz, Marguerite Meyers, Maurice Legris, Tina Petersen, Erica Rothwell, Fred Wah, Katherine McLean, Helen Chen, Elizabeth Grieve, Lisa Wray, Astrid Blodgett. Also sincere thanks to The Alberta Foundation for the Literary Arts (Calgary) for a grant early in this project that gave me time to research and write; and to the Canada Council for travel assistance.

Last, I salute the intrepid members of The Land, Air and Water Expedition of 1988, Edmonton, Alberta, to Obstruction

Rapids, Northwest Territories. In established Arctic traveller fashion we raised a cairn on the highest point of Dogrib Rock, and in it placed the following narrow note to mark our passing:

Dan Dueck
Margaret MacLaren
I. S. MacLaren
Detmar Tschofen
Chris Wiebe
Rudy Wiebe
En route, tracing as canoe
will allow, Franklin's
route of October 1821:
Starvation Lake to
Fort Enterprize
19 vii 1988
A University of Alberta -
Canada Council
Research Project

And then, after contemplating again the endless round of the horizon vanishing into every distance around us, we added:

A Land Beyond Words

— Rudy Wiebe